MW00768496

EVIL ALIVE

Also by Andrew Hunkins

No Such Thing as Evil: Book 1 in the Circle of Six Series

EVIL ALIVE

BOOK 2 IN THE
CIRCLE OF SIX TRILOGY

ANDREW HUNKINS

— Beaver's Pond Press —
Saint Paul, Minnesota

Edited by Scott Alexander Jones and Wendy Weckwerth.

ISBN 13: 978-1-59298-649-1
LCCN: 2019906206
Printed in Canada
First Printing: 2021
25 24 23 22 21   5 4 3 2 1

 Beaver's Pond Press
939 Seventh Street West
Saint Paul, MN 55102

(952) 829-8818
www.BeaversPondPress.com

To order, call (800) 901-3480. Reseller discounts available.

www.AndrewHunkins.com

It seems to be one of the fundamental features of nature that fundamental physical laws are described in terms of a mathematical theory of great beauty and power, needing quite a high standard of mathematics for one to understand it. You may wonder: Why is nature constructed along these lines? One can only answer that our present knowledge seems to show that nature is so constructed. We simply have to accept it. One could perhaps describe the situation by saying that God is a mathematician of a very high order, and He used very advanced mathematics in constructing the universe.

—Paul Dirac,
Scientific American, May 1963

Certain wise men of old wrote in their sacred books that angels came down from heaven and joined themselves to the daughters of Cain and had children by them. This cannot be true. They were not angels. They dwelt on the mountain, high up, while they preserved their glory like angels, and were then called angels. But when they transgressed, these angels came down from heaven and mingled with the daughters of men, who bear them giants.

—*The Conflict of Adam and Eve with Satan, ca. AD 500*

CHAPTER 1

"**W**HEN DID YOU FIRST SEE THE DECEASED?"

"Why doesn't the FBI have its own office in Philly?" Chris asked Special Agent Frederick Harrison as he stole a glance around the interrogation room. "How come you use the police station?"

"Efficiency. Now answer my question."

Chris didn't answer right away. He tried to relax. But not *look* like he was trying to relax. Cameras? There had to be. He'd seen rooms like this in his favorite action vids, when the police interviewed some crusty criminal. And now he was in that same kind of situation—suspected of aiding and abetting a murder suspect. His friend Al Fuentes had killed the man who chased their friend Katie Leonard through their neighborhood park. Chris hoped the interrogation session was being recorded, because he knew he didn't look very crusty in his white T-shirt, denim shorts, and sneakers. The idea that he was a criminal was ridiculous.

"I never saw the deceased," Chris said. "You know that already."

The FBI was desperate to gather facts because forensic evidence was abnormally absent—both from the crime scene (physical) and from the public surveillance system (digital). Consequently, the FBI didn't have enough evidence to charge Al. Al and Katie wouldn't even be on the FBI's radar if it hadn't been for the sketchy descriptions from neighbors in the park who "saw something." Harrison was hell-bent on finding proof that Al killed the man.

"I only know what your parents said. You're eighteen now. You three can't hide behind your parents any longer."

"So that's it. When Al and Katie turn eighteen, you're going to haul them in here and interrogate them about the dead man in the park too?"

"Of course. And I'm going to get to the truth. I'll track down your link to the Robin Hood terrorists if it's the last thing I do."

"There's no link to track down. That man was trying to kill Katie. Al had no choice but to shoot the man in self-defense."

The man was trying to kill my mom too, Chris remembered. Harrison wanted the truth? The truth was that Chris and his friends didn't know much about the dead man either. It all started after Chris's mom had linked a group of men from Nevada to a series of disappearances of young women. When the men discovered the probing, they began a sequence of helter-skelter murders they called the six layers of death as a strategy to end his mom's prying and kill off anyone with knowledge of the group. When one of the men came to kill Chris's mom as the final death, Katie was able to draw the man away. That's when the man turned on Katie. If Al hadn't killed the man, it would've been Katie's body surrounded by yellow crime-scene tape in the park.

The group of men's freakish strategy had almost worked. The fear generated by the relentless murders nearly drained his mom's conscientious desire to help the young women. But instead of running and hiding, Chris and his friends went to Nevada to try to free the kidnapped women and confront the men, with the aim of ending their evil acts once and for all. In a building—part luxury resort and part industrial complex—located deep in the Nevada desert, Chris and his friends had found holding cells, but no women.

Chris said, "Who was the deceased?"

"I ask the questions here."

The look on Harrison's face made clear that the FBI didn't know the man's identity either. Chris wanted to find out what the FBI had learned about the man, if anything, but he also wanted to learn what the FBI *didn't know*, because that would reveal how little evidence they had to charge Al. Chris suspected the lack of forensic evidence was driving Harrison crazy. He decided it was time to use a little reverse psychology to prompt Harrison to disclose what else the FBI didn't know.

"We told you everything. Besides, you have all the data. You have all the evidence." He hoped that little zinger would push Harrison over the edge. In the year 2058, no crime could be committed without mounds of physical and digital evidence. Yet somehow the men had deleted footage from the park's public surveillance system. If vid footage did exist, it would clearly show Al had killed the man in self-defense. The group destroyed the footage along with every other trace identifying their slain member. Unfortunately for Chris and his friends, the missing evidence created a mystery the FBI was determined to solve. The teens had agreed not to share any information with the FBI, confident that the amount of remaining evidence was insufficient to charge Al. The FBI would eventually give up. Chris and his friends simply needed to wait out the silly investigation.

Harrison tilted his head and grinned. Unfortunately for Chris, Harrison didn't look like he was losing control. In fact, he looked downright cunning. Obviously, Harrison had spotted Chris's lame ploy. Chris almost laughed at himself for thinking he could outsmart a career FBI agent during questioning.

"Your girlfriend, Hope Avenir, she's still ignoring you, isn't she?" Harrison's grin lingered. "Yeah, that's right, sport. Two can play that game. Just remember, in a few months, she'll be eighteen too. Then I'll invoke Executive Order 13224."

"If that's supposed to be some kind of threat, I have no idea what you're talking about." Chris tried to sound confident, but Harrison had just stabbed Chris in his soft spot.

Harrison was good—amazing really. Because Chris's feelings for Hope were something he had shared with practically no one, not even Al and Katie. Hope was indeed ignoring Chris. He rationalized she had to ignore him in order to stay hidden. But Chris wanted to be with her in the worst way. Just knowing she was safe would be a relief.

How did Harrison know how deeply he cared for Hope? *Maybe Harrison didn't know.* Chris realized the look on his own face probably confirmed one of Harrison's suspicions: Chris cared for Hope. That knowledge gave Harrison leverage. *Damn it.* Chris had to be careful. But it was no use. Harrison had set off a flood of feelings, all rooted in a visceral need to protect Hope. Now, Chris felt as if *he* was the one who might lose control.

But Chris knew the real threats—especially to Hope—were the men from Nevada, not the FBI's investigation. Finding out more about the group of men was the most urgent task for him and his friends. The trip to Nevada had been a failure. They didn't find any women. No one was rescued. However—and unfortunately—they learned that the group of men were engrossed in something much more sinister than kidnapping. But what exactly? Chris had to find out.

Worse, the ultimate consequence of the failed rescue mission was that the group's zeal for retaliation had multiplied. It was only a matter of time before another man showed up on Chris's doorstep intent on murdering them all. Chris could only think of Hope. *Maybe the men from Nevada found her already. Is she alive? Safe?* Chris was desperate to know. Yes, the fact that Hope was ignoring his attempts to communicate was driving him crazy. Score one for Harrison.

Under normal circumstances, the FBI would be an obvious source of help. But the authorities couldn't be trusted. The group of men seemed to have access to every database in the world and were able to trick the authorities into acting in favor of the group's shadowy goals.

But Chris sensed Harrison's jab about Hope as his girlfriend was more than simply another volley in Harrison's "two can play at that" game. *Harrison doesn't care about me, or Al, or Katie, or even the dead guy in the park. He wants Hope. But why?* "She's not involved. Leave her out of it."

"Not involved? Ha." Harrison leaned back. The grin was gone. "The Avenir girl deleted the video footage of the fatal moment from the park's surveillance system. What she couldn't delete, she locked down so tight even I can't get at it. For example, where is Hope Avenir at this very moment? There's no trace. And that's impossible. Unless—" He leaned forward. "—Hope Avenir is a Robin Hood cyberterrorist. Executive Order 13224 gives me antiterrorism powers. Then you'll see your whole world unravel."

There it is. He practically admitted it. This investigation is just a way to locate Hope, arrest her, compel her to talk, charge her for cyberterrorism, and score a flesh-and-blood conviction against the Hoods. It made sense now. Every law enforcement entity of every government in the world was relentlessly searching for the Hoods, cyber thieves who relentlessly stole digital currency from the rich. If Harrison convicted Hope as a Hood, it would justify his entire existence as an FBI agent. He'd be famous. He could retire from the bureau, do the speaker circuit, write a book, and rise from the relative comfort of employment to the elite ranks of the independently wealthy.

Harrison was right about one thing: Hope was a master of cyberspace. As soon as Al had killed the man in the park, the group from Nevada had falsely generated an arrest order for Al. Al would've been immediately taken into custody if it hadn't been for Hope's cyber skills. Modern police procedure was entirely dependent on data. She had the authorities chasing their tails before the dead guy's body hit the ground.

But Hope hadn't deleted evidence of the incident itself. The men from Nevada did that. Unfortunately, if Chris explained how Hope was falsely accused, he'd also have to explain why the dead man had been after them in the first place. Then Harrison would have reason to hold Chris, his friends, and his family while he dug deeper. The FBI would fill their databases with log entries telling the men from Nevada exactly where Chris and his loved ones were being held—trapped in jail and completely vulnerable. The men would finally succeed in killing them once and for all. Chris, his family, and his friends would become just another pile of victims in a string of unsolved murders by killers capable of miraculously evaporating into a vacuum of forensic nothingness.

No, Chris and his friends needed time to find out who the men were and come up with a new plan to stop them. Hope Avenir might be the only person on the planet to keep Chris and his family hidden from the men in Nevada *and* out of the FBI's clutches. *If we keep our mouths shut, can Hope hide forever? Is the FBI even capable of penetrating her cyber defenses to learn her physical location?* Hope was always confident about her abilities. She'd explained many times how she was able to block the authorities from tracking her. Chris didn't understand a word of her technobabble. He was desperate to see her again, but not if it meant leading the FBI straight to her location. He assumed she was ignoring his comms because two-way communication would compromise her cyber shield. But the lack of response was unnerving.

This is a waste of time. I have to get out of here. Chris leaned forward too. "So as an FBI agent—correction, FBI *special* agent . . . ," Chris began, remembering Harrison's initial handshake. It was pinchy, like the bony-fingered shake of a germaphobe old lady. Harrison was pale and slightly hunched, but not in an old-man sort of way. He was a keyboard-jockey type of FBI agent. "Do they give you any martial arts training?"

"Mr. Lumière, your black belt certification is no threat to me." Harrison scrolled the data on his display. "Says here, you're six three, you weigh one eighty, with seven percent body fat. Impressive on paper, I'll give you that." He looked up. "But all I see in front of me is a privileged high-school senior who's more likely to be voted homecoming king than a gang leader. Karate? You expect me to believe your hands are lethal weapons? I bet your hands have popped more bra straps than rival gang members." He glanced down. "Judging by your yearbook portrait here, with your short brown hair and blue eyes, you won't get voted Most Likely to Assault a Federal Agent. No. I'd guess Most Likely to Get Laid." Harrison smirked. "Sorry. You don't scare me."

Chris ignored him. "In a street fight, do you know what it means when a guy brandishes a knife?" Chris paused for effect. "It means he's not going to use it. Threat only. A means to a different end. That guy doesn't want to hurt you. He wants something else: to rob you." Chris leaned closer. "But, if a guy keeps the knife hidden? That's the guy to worry about. That guy is going to cut you as soon as he's close enough. You'll never see it coming." Chris folded his arms on the table and leaned even closer to Harrison's face. "You broadcast your threats over a loudspeaker and write them on billboards in fluorescent graffiti. You got nothing on us. And I couldn't care less about your Executive Order 8675309."

"I'm warning you," said Harrison. "We're talking federal law here. Dire consequences."

"Oh no," Chris feigned. "Worse than the punishment for cutting off the mattress label?"

"You'll be singing a different tune when I'm through with you."

"To that point, are you done?"

The screech of his chair confirmed as much. Harrison escorted Chris back to the security checkpoint.

Outside, Chris let his eyes adjust to the sunshine. The morning was hotter than usual for late August. Lucky wasn't under the shade of the bench where Chris had left him. Looking around the lawn surrounding the station, he found his yellow Lab watching something through the shrubs. On the other side of the shrubs was a fenced lot where police vehicles were parked. Chris parted the bushes for a better look. "What is it, boy?" Nothing out of the ordinary that Chris could see.

Chris needed to get back home. The killers from Nevada would show up again at any time. With the help of Al and Katie, Chris needed to find out more about the group they were up against. But Chris felt overwhelmed, and he only wanted to be with Hope. *Why me?*

"Come on, pal."

Lucky followed reluctantly.

At the masstran stop, Chris pulled his percomm out of his pocket. No messages. He tapped to initiate a comm to Hope. No answer.

The driverless, computer-navigated, battery-powered masstran vehicle glided to the curb. Chris climbed aboard and found an open seat.

"Mommy, a dog!" The little girl reached for Lucky, but the mom caught her hand. "No, sweetie. It's not polite to pet a working dog."

"It's OK," said Chris, "he's not that kind of dog. Go on. His name's Lucky."

The girl began to stroke the ivory fur. And so did a dozen other passengers. Few unemployed people could afford a pet. Just like in his own neighborhood in the Philadelphia suburb of Wynnewood, every time Chris rode the masstran it turned into a petting zoo. Lucky couldn't have been happier.

Unemployed? Chris challenged his own assumption about the girl and her mom. Both were wearing denim shorts and a

T-shirt—the so-called Poger uniform—same as Chris. It's not an official uniform, just a plainness so universal that all personal differentiation faded to nothing. Poger was the derogatory term for a person of an unemployed family. But growing up, Chris's parents had always dressed him in shorts and a T-shirt, or the equivalent for winter: jeans and a sweatshirt. Chris's dad had a good job at Benjamin Franklin University. His mom didn't work now, but when Chris was young, she also worked at Ben-U.

Chris watched the dozen hands smooth down Lucky's fur. The little girl got too close to Lucky's muzzle, and he stole a kiss. She giggled.

Maybe these passengers were part of employed families but chose to wear the Poger uniform, like Chris. He reminded himself not to prejudge.

He checked his percomm again. Nothing. If Hope didn't want to be contacted, there was nothing he could do about it. Her skill at manipulating the global network didn't mean she was a cyberterrorist. But the FBI was unable to entertain any other conclusion. Chris wondered if Hope was even aware of his comm attempts, or if she'd blocked him completely.

The masstran people mover headed north along Ridge Avenue. It traveled three city blocks before pulling to the curb at the next stop. Two passengers got on: an old blind man—judging by the white cane—who had his free hand at the elbow of a guy about Chris's age. The masstran merged back into traffic.

Before they reached the next street, multiple percomm chimes went off—a crazy mixture of music clips backed by the buzz of vibration. Half a dozen passengers looked at their percomms. Chris did too, without thinking, but his percomm showed no message or notification.

One man got up, went to the exit, and pried the masstran's doors open.

"Warning. Door ajar," an automated voice intoned. The vehicle slowed, pulled over, and stopped. "Warning. Door ajar. Please allow the doors to close."

The man sat over the threshold while keeping his legs and feet pressed against one door and his back against the other. *What the heck?* He pulled a device from his pocket and tapped a button.

The omnipresent electronic hum of the vehicle died. Emergency lights came on. "Communication interruption. Equipment malfunction. Service delay. Please stand by." Warm, moist air rolled in.

Like a flash mob, six passengers—men and women—each donned a mask. The masks were all different styles and colors but generally looked like . . . *What was the vocabulary word Katie used?* . . . balaclava?

Lucky barked. Chris had never seen anything like this. He looked to the girl's mother. "What's going on?"

She refused to meet his eyes. "Stay close, dear." The girl looked anxious and pressed in under her mother's embrace.

The masked passengers dashed from the vehicle. Once the last of the group was out, the man holding the door followed. Chris watched as they ran to the corner and turned down the cross street. He could see a few other masked people heading in the same direction.

The lighting returned to normal. Air blasted from above, becoming frigid. The vehicle lurched forward.

"What was *that* all about?" Chris asked again.

Still the woman didn't answer.

"Come to the city much?" the blind man called.

"Grandpa, don't," said the guy with him.

Chris looked at the mother. *I won't get any answers from her.* He crossed to the rear of the vehicle and sat next to the blind man. "No. I'm from Wynnewood," said Chris.

"The burbs, huh?"

Chris nodded. Then, realizing his mistake, he hurried to verbalize his response. "Yes. Why did those people get out?"

"Call to action."

"Grandpa, no."

"I don't understand. Why were they wearing masks?"

An agitated Asian man across the aisle blurted, "Why do you think they call them Hoods?" He seemed to immediately regret his outburst.

Hoods? Chris had never actually seen one. He only knew about Robin Hood terrorists from news reports. Were Harrison's suspicions about Hope being a Hood justified, at least in a can't-rule-it-out kind of way? Surely Hope wasn't a Hood, but was it possible that real, live Hoods operated in the city? Growing up, it seemed like there was no reason to stray from home. His mom and dad traveled each weekday to Ben-U, of course. And because both parents were employed as professors, the family could afford a private transportation vehicle, a pertran. But everything Chris needed was within bike-ride distance. His family almost never traveled to the city. Now he felt sheltered. The world seemed much larger somehow, like he'd grown up on a desert island and was just now learning there's land beyond the horizon.

"Simpleton," said the grandfather. He let the word linger, testing to see if the Asian man had anything more to say.

Lucky leaned into the grandpa's leg and rested his heavy head in the man's lap—a blatant invitation.

"Oh my, who's this?" He pushed the cane toward his grandson and petted the dog with both hands.

"His name's Lucky. Mine's Chris."

"I had a dog like this once. Are you blind too?"

"No." Chris waited patiently but then couldn't resist. "So were they really Hoods?"

"Of course not." The grandpa gazed in the general direction of the Asian man before continuing. "They're educated people."

"Grandpa, please."

Ignoring his grandson, the blind man asked, "How old are you, boy?"

"Eighteen. Going into my senior year of high school."

"Then off to college?"

"Sure."

"Sure because . . ."

"Well . . . ," Chris thought for a moment. "Everybody goes."

"Because it's free, right? Tuition paid by the government?"

"The Mexican government," the Asian man corrected. His hostility seemed pent up but still under control.

"Yeah, it's free," continued Chris. "Education is the foundation of a healthy individual, a happy society, and a strong economy."

"You memorized that quite well. And what are you going to do when you graduate from college? What type of work do you think you'll do?"

"I don't know."

"Well then . . . you'll be educated too."

Educated, but with nothing to do? Is that the reason for so much unrest? The narrowness of his own life was shocking, like he'd been raised in a laboratory and just now escaped. "But why the masks?"

"Hoods," said the Asian man. He was gripping the edge of his seat and the edge of self-control. "They jam the connection to the cameras before putting on the hoods. Creates reasonable doubt. What they're too lazy to earn, they steal."

"Enough!" yelled the mother, holding her daughter tight. "That's, *enough*." The word landed like a gavel.

Chris sat back. He had more questions, but decided not to ask them.

IT WAS ALREADY SIX MINUTES PAST THE HOUR. FIRST LIEUTENANT HECTOR
Eladio was still missing two update reports. "Let's go, people. It's
past eleven hundred. They call it a hundred report for a reason.
You know the drill. Every hour, on the hour."

The fireteam readiness report—one of the two overdue
reports—finally popped on his screen, detailing the status of
Omega Force Fireteam Echo. All four marines were flying high
above the Eastern Seaboard, cruising far from Eladio and his
staff, who were monitoring the fireteam from their command
center located in the US Marine Corps base in Quantico,
Virginia. The status of all four Omega Force marines and their
supersonic scramjet was FMC (fully mission capable). The
Omega Force was one small piece of the US government's war
on cyberterrorism. All other war assets focused on monitoring network activity of the Robin Hood terrorists in the hope
of tracing the activity to some physical location, typically a
computer complex. Such a complex would contain people
with knowledge of the terrorist organization. Once located, the
Omega Force would perform the subsequent physical apprehension. But speed was imperative. If the reports indicated terrorist
activity, it was Eladio's job to get the Omega Force into the area
of operation—fast.

Eladio needed one more report: the civilian activity report.
He searched the many display screens on the walls of their command center and found the one with the scrolling list of cities,
cities where automated detection systems identified hostile
civilian behavior. The most recent were Chattanooga, Tampa,
Alpharetta, and, at the bottom of the list, Philadelphia.

Eladio was the human link between the *recommendation*
to deploy the Omega Force—as calculated by artificial intelligence—and the *actual order* to deploy. With so much civil unrest
across the country, it was difficult even for the AI to sift through

surveillance data to detect a link to Hood activity. Like a Cold War–era human operator in a concrete bunker next to a nuclear missile silo, Eladio was trained to make the decision to "insert the second key"—the first key having been inserted by the AI. In that analogy, deploying the Omega Force was akin to pressing the launch button. Eladio was the human circuit breaker between artificial intelligence and lethal force.

Eladio stood and walked to the man monitoring civilian activity. "What's the holdup, Jenson?"

The half dozen warrant officers under Eladio's command were practically kids; all were in their late twenties. Eladio himself was just thirty-three but felt like their father. He'd give his life for any of them. But sometimes he had to hound them for the simplest things, as if nagging about homework.

Chief Warrant Officer Tom Jenson said, "Sir, I can't clear the flag on Philly." Like Eladio, Jenson and the rest of the marines in the center wore the MCCUU (Marine Corps Combat Utility Uniform), with its distinctive digital MARPAT-2 (Marine Pattern, Mark 2) camouflage, consisting of tiny squares of tan, light green, and dark green. Jenson always rolled his sleeves up high. Sun's out, guns out, as the saying goes.

Eladio widened his stance, looking like a bulldog, with his broad chest and narrow waist. The dense black hair above the bronze skin of his face was buzzed in the ubiquitous flattop they all wore. The overall effect was that of stiff black bristles on a mahogany brush handle. At five feet ten inches, he wasn't tall, but not so short as to have a small-man complex. Eladio always kept his sleeves down, preferring a more professional look. His brown eyes scanned the data on Jenson's screen. "Show me the Hood involvement."

"That's just it, sir. No confirmed involvement."

"Why is it flagged?"

"AI heuristics."

Oh great. Normally, the AI system made a clear determination: either Hoods were involved or they weren't. But heuristics were a different story. Like voodoo magic, somehow, the AI could infer relationships by sifting through decades of data of the most obscure variety. If the source of a hurricane could be traced back to the flap of a butterfly's wing, then a strike by the Hoods could be traced back to the expenditure of a single subsidy credit, or so the social scientists believed.

Eladio asked, "HIP assessment?"

"HIP is at fifty-one percent, sir."

HIP was the acronym for Hood involvement potential. Fifty-one percent was a nasty value. Eladio hated heuristics. It was as if the AI knew the raw value was 50, so it fabricated a trumped-up 1 percent addition to justify its unjustifiable brain fart saying that Hoods were, in fact, involved.

"And the threat risk?"

"Elevated."

The threat risk was on a five-point scale, elevated being the middle point. Hood involvement alone didn't necessarily require a response. Even if HIP was at 100 percent, meaning Hoods were definitely involved, Eladio wouldn't necessarily send the fireteam. He would never deploy the Omega Force—referred to as Oscar Foxtrot by the marines—to interdict activity that represented a low threat. The benefit-to-cost ratio had to be high. "Show me the data sources for the heuristics."

"Working on it. Some appear to be purged. Others are LIMDIS. When I override the 'limited distribution' classification, I just get another LIMDIS link. It's an infinite stream, or a loop. I'm not sure." An indicator flashed on Jenson's screen. "Sir, threat risk has increased to high."

The AI is riding the yellow line, thought Eladio. Deployment of an Omega Force fireteam was extremely expensive, but any delay in reaction time would jeopardize the likelihood of actually catching Hoods. *I have to be sure.*

"Attention, everyone." They all looked up. "Priority task. We have an AI hit on Philly. Get me a satellite view. Put it on the big board. Launch a drone. I want it in position in ninety seconds. Correlate network transactions. Pull the logs from the public scanners and sniffers, half-a-klick radius. Send the logs to Dietrich. Morales, you and Kendall get me a list of possible targets." There was stunned silence. "OK, people, move!"

Heads dropped. Hands flew across input screens. Orders were barked through headsets.

"Come on, come on. What are we dealing with?"

"Runners. I have runners, sir."

"Get me a view," Eladio called out, pacing the now-frenzied room. "What's the scramjet's position?"

"Marlton, New Jersey. Practically on top of them. But heading south. Shall I send a course change?"

"Yes," Eladio said confidently, not betraying his inner doubt. *Hell to pay if I'm wrong.* He examined the images from the satellite feed. The view had too many buildings in the way. "Zoom. Show me a cross street." He stopped pacing. "Now, people. Move!" The image swelled, filling the screen, zeroing in on an intersection.

"Spring Garden and North Fifth, sir."

Eladio saw civilians sprinting between the buildings. "Switch to street cam. Enable tracking." The view snapped to show masked civilians running on both sides of Spring Garden. *Not as sharp as a drone view, but not bad.* Small rectangles flashed over the faces of bystanders. Eladio knew facial recognition was useless on the hooded runners, but the data was food for the voraciously hungry AI. You never know when today's bystander will become tomorrow's suspect. Larger rectangles flashed over the hooded figures dashing down the city sidewalks. Analysis of their body movements, known as gait recognition, easily identified the running civilians. "Come on, people. What's over there? Where are they headed? Talk to me, Morales."

Chief Warrant Officer Chico Morales hesitated. "Uh . . . a casino . . . uh . . ."

"The Delaware River," blurted Chief Warrant Officer Jon Kendall.

"River? Goddamn it. What's over there? Financial? Utility? Motorcade? Come on."

"Sir, Oscar Foxtrot course change complete. Scramjet inbound. Prep initiated. Landing zone auto-selection in progress. Deployable in twenty seconds."

"Do we have correlated network transactions?"

"Affirmative. Correlation to Homeland Security. Fresh. Only six minutes old."

"Who're the runners?"

"The usual activists. Bio data coming up now . . . nobody special. Hold on—"

"Quickly!"

"I have a DNA hit. The subject is on a watch list."

"Sir, Oscar Foxtrot is in the pipe. Prep complete. Selected LZ at one hundred percent confidence. Window to deploy is closing. If we miss this window, it'll be twelve minutes to bring her around for another pass."

"What watch list?"

"Uh . . . not military, not DHS. It's civilian . . . uh, medical in nature."

"DNA on a medical list? Really, Einstein? Come on, people. River? Infinite loops? Work it."

"Sir, threat risk is now at critical, repeat critical. HIP is at fifty-one percent."

"Holy shit," somebody breathed.

Eladio wiped the perspiration from his lip. "Where's that drone?"

"Still forty seconds out, sir. Oscar Foxtrot deployment window nearly closed."

Goddamn it.

Jenson turned toward him with an anguished look. "Sir, do you wish to deploy Oscar Foxtrot?"

The frenzied activity paused. A few men looked up. Dead silence. *Fuck.* "Yes," said Eladio. *Fuck.*

| | 0 | | 0 | | 0

"BYE, LUCKY," THE GIRL CALLED AS CHRIS EXITED THE MASSTRAN AT HIS STOP.

Crossing the park, he took the long way around to the place where Al killed the man who attacked Katie earlier that summer. There was no trace of the incident now. *Why is this happening? Why my life? Why me?*

Lucky sniffed along the bushes, then trotted to the grass and lifted his leg. Chris couldn't be sure, but he assumed the piss went right on the spot where the man had lain dead. The spot was just outside the entrance to their childhood hideout, a small clearing between the bushes that lined the park. Chris had spent many hours there with his two friends, Al and Katie, planning adventures together. *Fun times. All history now.* And then there was the night with Hope. They talked for hours under the moonlight. It was probably the only time the small enclosure served the literal purpose of its name: hideout.

At least Hope's dad was out of her life now. *Her dad? Does he know where she is?* Chris couldn't even think of actually talking to the man after what he did to Hope. That moonlit night, she'd confessed to Chris about the incest. Chris couldn't imagine all she'd experienced. Her mom wasn't spared the abuse either. Just days after school had let out for summer break, Hope's dad beat his wife so badly that it landed him in jail and sent Hope's mom to the hospital. That's when Hope came to stay with Chris and his family. That's when he finally had a chance to really get to know the girl down the street, the girl he'd had a crush on for as long as he could remember. It was also when the group of men smashed into their lives, literally. And wrecked everything. *Why me?* All he wanted was to be with Hope.

Chris dug into the pocket of his jean shorts and pulled out the chunk of homemade gum wrapped in wax paper. The bright blue color was a sharp contrast to the chocolate smell. Chris brushed lint from the folds of wax paper. The gum was flattened now, having been in his pocket for weeks. *Why me?* Chris threw the gum, sending it far into the bushes. It was a reminder of his unwanted responsibilities. He glanced at his percomm again. Nothing.

Continuing home, he reached the alley of his block. The corner house was Hope's—well, used to be. He'd tried all the ways he could think of to contact her. Hope's mom, Sue Avenir, wouldn't divulge any information about Hope's whereabouts or her condition. Hope wouldn't approve. And now both mom and daughter were gone. Moved? But to where? He had no way to find her, no way to reach her. And more than most, a cyberspace master like Hope Avenir knew how to avoid contact. If he was ever to see or hear from her again, it would be on her terms.

At the back door of his three-story prefabricated house, Chris leapt up the steps of the stoop but stopped short at the door. Lucky stopped too, looked up, then sat and waited.

The special button next to the door wasn't part of the prefab model. It was a retrofit by Chris's dad, who wasn't good at handyman stuff. But he was very good at computers. He knew how to bypass the seccomm (security and communication) system so Chris could open the doors of his own house. *Why me?* Chris heaved a sigh and pressed his thumb on the button so it could read his print. The door swished open.

The back hallway and the living room had the most damage from the two break-ins. The first happened when the man went after Katie. And the second happened when a different man went after Chris's mom and dad while he and his friends were in Nevada, on the failed mission to rescue the abducted women. The floor, walls, and living room window had replaceable modules, but most everything else was post-fab—fabricated using the 3-D printer in the garage. Every house had one. Chris liked using the 3-D printer, so repairing the house was one of his chores. He was nearly finished fabricating replacements but had procrastinated printing the chandelier. Chris entered the hallway under the electrical connector that dangled from the ceiling. Lucky went to the laundry room and started lapping water.

In the kitchen, the pubcomm display was logged in, but his mom wasn't there. The screen showed real estate listings. She was obsessed with the idea that selling their house was the way to escape the killers who were after them. She was equally obsessed with Bruce Cohen, Chris's karate instructor, who put the idea in her head. Bruce had told her about his ex-military friends who could hide people off the grid. She thought they should listen to Bruce because of his past military service with the Israel Defense Forces. She said it was because of Bruce that Chris, Al, Katie, Hope, and Bruce himself had survived the attempt to free the kidnapped girls held captive in Nevada by the group of killers. *That's probably true. But move? To a safe house? Not finish my senior year? Never see Al and Katie again? Never see Hope again? Why me?*

"Computer, locate occupants."

The seccomm system responded, "Laura Richards: indisposed. Benjamin Richards: basement level three."

Lucky came in and sprawled out on the cool kitchen floor.

Chris went to the refrigerator. He smeared safflower mayo into the pocket of a whole-wheat pita and then filled it with shredded chicken followed by three fingers' worth of fresh spinach. He'd taken only a bite when he heard the toilet flush.

"Hey, buddy. How did it go?" asked Laura.

"Fine."

He watched her sit down. Growing up, he'd always known Laura and Ben weren't his real mom and dad. They never tried to keep the adoption secret, following the death of his birth mother, Marian Lumière, also Laura's best friend at the time. Chris never thought about it much. But lately, he'd thought about it a lot. He'd grown so tall. And Laura was so tiny, about five three, nearly a foot shorter than Chris. And she always worried—especially about things Chris didn't think were important. When he was little, he never questioned her protectiveness. Lately, he wasn't so sure. He felt sheltered, smothered. The attempt to rescue the kidnapped girls from the men in Nevada turned his life upside down. It made him question everything he'd always believed, blindly so. What truths were Ben and Laura shielding him from? On purpose? Or was being overprotective just something parents inflicted on their children out of the goodness of their hearts?

Laura said, "Come on. What did the FBI say?"

"I don't want to talk about it." Chris walked out of the kitchen to the stairway. Lucky scrambled to follow.

"You have to," she called after him. "We all need to know. I need to know how much time we have to sell the house and move."

He went up to his bedroom on the third floor. He took another bite—a huge bite, nearly half the sandwich. A chunk of chicken fell to the carpet. Lucky eyed it, sat, and looked up. Chris nodded, and the dog snapped it up.

The bedroom was the standard configuration for a prefab: two twin beds, a dresser, a nightstand, and a desk. The window was situated above the nightstand between the two beds. Chris gestured for the window shade to be opened. The seccomm system complied. He looked out over the backyard. *So many memories.* He always slept on the bed on the right because if he lay on his stomach, he could see Hope's house.

He jammed the rest of the sandwich into his mouth and checked his percomm. Lucky, seeing no chance for another scrap, stepped into his dog bed, circled, and lay down. There was a message from his friend Al, saying he was on his way over. Chris wondered if Laura had contacted Al, figuring he would get the information out of Chris about the FBI questioning.

Chris sat on the bed. It might be one of the last times in his room. Three karate trophies adorned his dresser. His most recent ones, anyway. The rest were in a box in the basement. Next to the trophies was Lucky's first dog collar from when he was a puppy. And next to that was the laminated card for his K9 search-and-rescue certification. Finally, there was the class president pin. He'd been elected class president for his upcoming senior year of high school—and wouldn't even get to be there. *Why me?*

He considered his many fantasies about holding Hope while dancing during their senior prom. She would look amazing in a prom dress. Over the years, kids made fun of her because she always wore oversized clothes. Except for the hottest days of the summer, she wore the hood of her sweatshirt over her unruly brown hair. But Chris remembered the day she got back from shopping with Laura. Wow. Chris assumed Hope went to such lengths to hide her body and generally tried to be invisible because of the abuse. But she was never invisible to Chris. All he wanted was to be with Hope. But the events of the last several months had steered them apart. *Why me?*

Chapter 2

THE IRON BARS ACROSS THE WINDOWS OF THE FIRST FLOOR OF THE apartment complex reminded Hope of the women's shelter where she'd visited her mom half a dozen times, until the court finalized the divorce from her dad. Once the marital status had changed, like a guillotine, the government cut their housing subsidy. Apparently, a divorced woman and her seventeen-year-old daughter didn't qualify for an actual house, only an apartment. They were given two weeks to pick from available vacancies. The online listing hadn't included any pictures. *No wonder. Nothing temporary about these iron bars. So much for curb appeal.*

"It's OK, right?" Sue asked from behind, using her signature whisper, perfected over years of being intimidated by Hope's dad. Her mom's question wasn't about the apartment; it was about their situation. Sue wasn't seeking an opinion; she wanted reassurance.

In either direction, for as far as Hope could see, not a single vehicle was parked on the street. To the left were storefronts with residences above. And beyond that, more apartment complexes like hers. Some residents sat in the shade of their entryways. A group of kids played wallyball next to a small parking lot that was empty—empty except for broken asphalt and knee-high weeds. To the right was the rest of her complex, which ended at the corner, by the masstran stop. A freeway overpass stood beyond that.

Hope shifted the weight of her backpack higher on her shoulder. "Sure." She walked the concrete path to the main entrance. Her mom followed—never beside, always behind.

At the door, the seccomm vid display came to life. "New tenant?" asked the manager. His voice sounded like a crotchety neighbor. The salt-and-pepper stubble and bedhead completed the picture.

Hope nodded.

He glanced off screen. "Susan Avenir and Hope Avenir?"

"That's us," said Hope.

"All right. Come in, and I'll get you confirmed in the system."

The door swished open, revealing a small lobby. On the left, the manager was sitting in a booth behind thick glass. Ahead was the elevator. To the right was an alcove with a sign above that read TELEPHONE. The spot where a pay phone had once been attached was still visible on the wall. The rest of the alcove was lined with rows of small mailboxes. Postal delivery had ended before Hope was born, but she still knew what mailboxes looked like. Quite a few of the metal cubbies were missing doors. Others were open, but the doors were bent. Next to the alcove, a man on a bench held the leash of a dachshund curled at his feet. The dog was old and didn't stir when Hope and Sue entered.

"Over here." The manager's voice had come through a round speaker installed in the glass. A metal basket, built into the counter, allowed items to pass from one side to the other.

Hope walked over. On the floor behind the manager was a thin mattress, a cookstove, and a pile of clothes.

The manager gave Hope a thorough up and down with appreciation and then glanced to the old man on the bench and popped his eyebrows. Hope's extra-large shirt and baggy jeans usually helped to avoid this type of reaction, but not this time. Having developed early, she quickly learned she could stay home sick from school for ten days straight without triggering truancy. Once, she used all ten days during a much-feared two-week period when gym class was held poolside for swimming lessons. Other tactics didn't work quite as well. Once she tried overeating—which wasn't easy on rationed food credits—but unfortunately, the only parts that got bigger were the ones the boys especially liked. Girls would kill for her hourglass shape. It was Hope's curse.

"Susan Avenir and Hope Avenir?" the manager asked.

"You got a memory problem?" said Hope, surprised by her own self-confidence.

"Ooo. Hot *and* sassy," the manager called over her shoulder. He tapped his screen.

Hope eyed the thick glass. "I guess you can let the comments fly while you're all safe and cozy inside your little fort here." Again, she was surprised by her own combativeness. It was an alien feeling. Apparently she was the family leader now, filling the vacancy left by her dad. She'd never wanted anything to do with her father. She always modeled her mom's demeanor. Invisible. Stay out of his way. Avoid attention. Escape confrontation. Confrontation never ended well. *I'm half my father.* The realization frightened her. But only briefly. It was a strength. Instead of denying it, she could channel it. Own it. For good or for bad.

"Oh, you like it?" said the manager. "Part of the building's charm. Used to be a hotel before they converted it. A real palace." He pounded on the glass, showing its strength. "This is from a simpler time. Back when crime was a thing. Before our current state of societal bliss. Before our brilliant government leaders stomped out all unlawful behavior . . . and human spirit. Yes, back in the day, it was a fine establishment of capitalism. Rooms by the hour. Sheets extra." He smiled. "You'da done good here, darlin'."

His whole act wasn't just for Hope's benefit. She glanced back to the geezer on the bench with the toothless grin on his face.

"Now, about payment," the manager continued. "Poger or Loyd?"

"Fuck you," said Hope. Her newfound fluency with confrontation was almost comfortable now. She could model her dad's demeanor, when needed.

"Poger it is." He tapped at the screen. "OK. Subsidy payments applied. Credentials are in the seccomm. Network access enabled. All part of the deluxe package. Mexican pesos at work." He sat back. "Can I help you ladies with your bags?" Without waiting for an answer, he tapped the screen, and his vid resumed streaming. He reclined fully and put his feet up.

"Apartment two-one-seven," Sue whispered, her hand on Hope's arm with the subtlest of pressure toward the elevator.

Hope relented.

Toothless made a guttural noise as they waited for the elevator. He still had an amused look on his wrinkled face, under wild strands of thin white hair. His clothes looked like they'd come out of a dumpster, which would also explain the smell. His tongue sloshed back and forth along his gums, as if he had a poppy seed stuck between teeth he didn't have. "Want to pet my wiener?" he asked, massaging his crotch. He gave another grunt, followed by a pelvic thrust.

Finally, the elevator doors swished open. The building retrofits—security doors and seccomm system—were no doubt the minimum requirements to meet building code. As for the elevator, only the door had been upgraded. The rest of it was ancient, like a vintage VW Bug outfitted with computer navigation. Inside, Hope visualized the scene as if in a grainy black-and-white history vid in which a man with a little cap announces, "Ground floor. Women's apparel, sporting goods, home appliances. Going up."

The elevator lurched and groaned as it battled gravity. Half the carpet was missing. Strips of double-stick tape covered the bare parts of the floor. The strips were thoroughly coated with dirt and gravel and were no longer sticky. A clicking sound came from some unseen ventilation fan. The car shuttered and bobbed at the second floor until the doors opened. The hallway was well lit. But the carpet was completely worn through here too. At one spot, the textured ceiling had bubbled off around a huge brown water stain.

At door 217, the seccomm light turned green. The door swished open to reveal a short entryway that led to a main room. Linoleum floor throughout. The government movers had stacked their belongings in the corner. Each box had a florescent yellow tag that meant the moving fee was covered by the subsidy. Otherwise, the room was completely empty. To the left of the entryway was a small kitchen. To the right, a hallway, presumably leading to the two bedrooms, bathroom, and linen closet described in the online listing. "Home, sweet home," said Hope, letting her backpack slide off and drop to the floor.

"At least the windows don't have bars," said her mom.

Hope stepped to the window. *No drapes either.* The adjacent apartment building was just the width of the alley away. Only half of those windows were covered. Some had drapes; some had bed sheets pinned up in makeshift fashion. All the other apartments were completely exposed. Some looked lived in. Some vacant.

Hope's percomm vibrated. It was Chris again. She tapped to ignore.

"You should talk to him."

"Why?"

"He cares about you."

"He nearly got me killed." Hope massaged her left shoulder. Those freaks in Nevada had dislocated it, claiming her pain allowed them to know the future. She had no idea how her pain could have anything to do with the future. Those men were nut jobs as far as Hope was concerned. There was still pain in her shoulder, but it was healing well. She was thankful it wasn't her right shoulder because that's where she slung her backpack. She turned to face her mom.

Sue wouldn't meet her eyes. She would just stand there, motionless, waiting for a command.

Is this how it's going to be? The new apartment was a shit hole. But it was a new start. For both of them—without her dad.

Or would it be more of the same? Evidently her mother expected Hope to assume her dad's role in the family hierarchy—without discussion or open acknowledgement. Sue would do whatever Hope said at this very moment because he never let her think for herself. The twisted dysfunction would continue. Or it would stop here and now.

Hope shook her head and pocketed the percomm. "You don't understand."

"Chris cares. You don't find that often in this world. You should talk to him."

"Have *you* talked to his mom? You saved Laura's life, right? While we were in Nevada, that creep came to kill Laura. You hid Laura. And Ben. You saved their lives. She owes you. Lifelong friends now, huh? Have you even said a single word to her?"

Sue remained motionless.

Figured. Hope grabbed her backpack and went to the hall.

"Don't make the same mistake I did."

Hope stopped. Her mom's voice had a surprisingly desperate tone. After a moment, she heard the sounds of boxes being opened as her mom started to unpack. She let it be and continued down the hallway to the smaller bedroom.

More wall-to-wall linoleum. A closet. Not even a bed. *Just as well, no bed bugs.* She pulled the comm display from her backpack and wiped it clean before propping it up on the floor. Sitting cross-legged, she tapped at the input screen.

PrincessLIMDIS: Hey.
SalaciousFrog: You're late.
PrincessLIMDIS: Whatever.
SalaciousFrog: What's the situation?
PrincessLIMDIS: Better. 33% firewall penetration.
SalaciousFrog: Good. Notify me once you're through.

110 110 110

"VISITOR ARRIVING. QUANTITY ONE," ANNOUNCED THE SECCOMM SYSTEM OF Chris's house.

Standing up from his bed, Chris peered out his bedroom window and saw Al pull up on his little red bike.

His lifelong friend waved up to him. Al's two hundred pounds made the tires bulge, and he had to pedal with his heels, even with the seat at its highest possible setting. Chris and Katie had offered many times to help him get the money for a bigger bike. But Al always refused. Too proud. Chris noticed something strapped to the back of Al's bike.

With Lucky following, Chris cruised down the stairs.

Before reaching the back door, Laura called, "Where are you boys going?"

"I don't know," Chris said without slowing. He sprinted around to the garage, got his bike, and pushed it up the ramp from the garage and over to Al.

"Where?" Laura asked again from the door.

Al said, "I'll have him back before dinner, Mrs. Richards."

"What about the chandelier, young man?"

Chris rolled his head around and down. His shoulders slumped.

"I'll wait," said Al, unable to hold back the smirk.

Chris trudged back to the garage and down the ramp. The behemoth was situated in the corner of the garage, taking up nearly a third of the space on that level. The fabrication area inside the 3-D printer was large enough to hold a pertran. Huge glass doors allowed the operator to see what was being fabricated but kept the process safely enclosed. Almost everything in the house could be reproduced here.

At the printer's control panel, Chris pressed the button to initiate the precheck cycle. Large robotic arms extended and rotated as the computer calibrated the motion. Chris searched the database for chandelier specs in one of the three designs his mom liked and then verified there was enough raw material. He pressed start. The safety doors locked, and two mechanical arms came together at the center platform and began extruding material. The process would take many hours, maybe a day or longer. Exiting the garage, he noticed Laura had gone back into the house.

"What's all that for?" Chris asked Al. A sledgehammer and what looked like two metal pipes, each about three feet long, were strapped to Al's bike.

"I'll show you when we get there." Al kicked off and pedaled out of the driveway and into the alley. As black belts, both were in good shape, but Geraldo "Al" Fuentes was exceptional. When they were younger, Al had always been smaller and shorter than either Chris or Katie. But other than cocoa skin and the dense black hair he'd always worn in a buzz cut, Al had completely changed at puberty. He was still shorter than Chris, but only a tad, and he was huge by comparison. Two hundred thirty pounds of solid muscle. Even though his bike was too small, his powerful legs worked the pedals like a steam engine. He often pedaled standing up, for extra power. And he worked the gear-shift like a musical instrument. Chris had a hard time keeping up as Lucky galloped beside them.

"Get where?"

"You know Horseshoe Bend?"

"Of course. Why there?"

"They're doing some road repair."

"So?"

"You'll see."

| | 0 | | 0 | | 0

ELADIO'S OFFICE DOOR CLOSED BEHIND HIM. HE HAD THREE MINUTES BEFORE the conference with his commanding officer, Colonel Daniel B. Wesson. Wesson had ordered Captain Winchester Schofield, Eladio's direct superior, to be on as well. *Schofield better have my back this time.*

The notification chime sounded. "Your conference is about to begin. Would you like to join now?" asked the natural-sounding voice of Vixen, the command center's virtual assistant. Her full name was Vixen the Virtas. *Virtas* was the generic term for any AI system more advanced than the ubiquitous variety of sec-comm system found in nearly every home, business, and public area across the globe. Those basic systems were invoked with the bland keyword *computer*. In contrast, every virtas was given a name at the time of activation.

"No," answered Eladio. He needed time to think. "Has Captain Schofield joined?"

"Yes. Captain Schofield is waiting in the virtual lobby."

Eladio tapped out a message to Schofield on his percomm. "I followed procedure."

Schofield replied. "I know. It'll be fine."

Fine. Sure. Like last time? Major Nolan will be on the conference too, no doubt. Then Nolan will come up with some bullshit story like always. Schofield'll leave me hanging by the neck, yet again. Eladio sat down at his desk and took a deep breath. "Vixen, join me to the conference."

"Joined. You are in the virtual lobby."

It was only a few seconds before Colonel Wesson admitted them all to the vid conference. Colonel Wesson, Captain

Schofield, and Major Dick Nolan all appeared via vid stream, each in their own window on Eladio's screen.

"Well, gentlemen, we have ourselves a real situation here," said Colonel Wesson. "Let me get this straight. You deployed the Omega Force directly onto the lawn of the Philly police department's precinct building?"

"Yes, sir," said Eladio. "LZ confidence was one hundred percent."

Captain Schofield added, "Fortunately, the Omega Force team leader kept everything under control."

"Oh really?" Wesson challenged. "More than a hundred vid clips were uploaded to the network—and were then taken up by thirty-three hundred news agencies. You call that under control?"

In the third window, Major Nolan, who was in charge of cyberterrorism defense analytics, looked frustrated with the line of questioning. "Not news agencies," he corrected. "Most were one-man posts. Neighborhood community news sites and the like. Nothing organized. We estimate—"

"I don't care what you estimate, Major. Do you know what they're chanting in the streets? 'Enough is enough.' The battle cry of the civilian activists couldn't be more appropriate. Can you make our job any more difficult? You're just giving the activists justification to stage more protest marches."

"It'll blow over. We blocked most of the vid clips before they posted. And we're working with the comm providers to mop up the rest." Nolan smirked. "A few of the clips caught the marines' good sides." He waved dismissively. "We're spinning it as a public relations stunt. A few lucky Pogers are having their clips go viral."

"Bribed them with overnight stardom?"

"Yup. We picked the most pathetic people. They'll say anything we want."

"Where's the team now?"

Captain Schofield answered, "In a SWAT van, headed to the airport for extraction. Eladio followed procedure."

Wow. For once, Schofield has my back, thought Eladio.

"Yes, I can see that," said the colonel. "Well, that leads us back to you, Major. Explain."

"HIP eventually reached ninety-nine percent. Hood involvement was certain. Nothing to explain."

"And why did your AI determine the threat was critical?"

Nolan's AI was an order of magnitude more advanced than even Vixen. It didn't have a name that Eladio knew of. It never said anything, and you never spoke to it. It was a deaf, mute, weaponized brain.

"We've never seen this level of obfuscation," answered Nolan. "Incredibly sophisticated. We suspect our own systems have been compromised. And that the compromise happened years ago. A sleeper. Disinformation. Used to throw us off."

"There was a DNA hit," offered Eladio.

"Right," continued Nolan. "But we couldn't correlate the DNA to the threat for some reason. I have an asset on the way to pull the skin cells from the sniffer."

"Major, if our systems are compromised, that sniffer could be full of pixie dust for all we know. I'm missing the part about an actual threat—and why you're declaring this deployment of Oscar Foxtrot a success."

"What I mean is, discovering this type of compromise was worth the no-joy deployment."

"You gotta be shitting me." The colonel shook his head. "Enjoy your little discovery. But what am I supposed to say to the mayor? Tell her we'll give her more notice next time? So she won't miss her chance to get a selfie with a handsome Omega Force marine?"

| | 0 | | 0 | | 0

LEANING INTO THE TURN, AL TOOK THE LAST CURVE FAST. THE PAVEMENT WAS covered with sand and gravel from the construction work. He scraped one foot along the road in a controlled skid, then pedaled hard out of the turn. Chris kept clear of the gravel. Orange cones lined the street where workers had demolished the guardrail along Horseshoe Bend. They were in the process of building a new guardrail. The automated street-construction machine, resembling the bastard child of a Zamboni and a 3-D printer, sat motionless at the curb like a sleeping elephant.

Al skidded to a stop, hopped off his bike, and started unstrapping the hammer and poles.

Lucky sniffed along the line of thick brush separating the road from the drop off to the ravine below.

Chris parked his bike next to Al. "Talk. What are we doing here?"

"Why are you so cranky?" asked Al. "We live for summer break, right? Every day is an adventure. Carpe diem. This is what we do, migo. If Katie wasn't working on the warden's words, she'd be here too. And if she was here, she'd say it was top jazz. But just because she's busy, doesn't mean *we* can't have fun."

The warden was Chris's imaginary guardian angel, or so he'd always thought. Except, they'd discovered, it wasn't imaginary, and by the time he hit puberty, evidence of the warden became unavoidable. Ever since the failed attempt to rescue the kidnapped women from the Nevada compound, Chris had been asking, "Why me?" The answer to that question was the warden. Why the warden chose to take up residence in Chris Lumière, he didn't know. Being the warden's host was a duty he never asked for. Part of Chris wanted to ignore his troubles and just have fun with Al, like always. Yet, another part of him felt the tug of responsibility. It was one of many signs of growing up. So much was changing. So much of what he loved would be gone forever—his carefree childhood . . . and Hope. He could hardly bear the thought of never seeing Hope again. But it was a real possibility—especially if the group of men from Nevada attacked again. The warden had the answers. But the painstaking task of interpreting the warden's clues, like so many other tasks he didn't ask for, was one Chris didn't want to deal with.

In an effort to force himself to face his adult responsibilities, Chris argued with Al, knowing full well he should take his own advice. "Katie's figuring out what the warden is trying to tell us about the men in Nevada. She *wants* to figure it out. So do I. So do you."

"Sure," Al said sarcastically. "So why aren't you cooped up with her in her bedroom?"

Chris didn't say anything. Al had made his point. Katie was the smartest of the three, but that was just an excuse. The work was tedious, and neither Chris nor Al had the stomach for it.

"Relax," said Al. "You're gonna love this. Check it out. We're going to stretch a cable across the road and see what happens when drivers approach it."

This was another one of Al's crazy ideas. Chris had to admit: every summer for as long as he could remember, their days had been filled with adventures that Al had cooked up in his head. They had a blast. Katie too. Maybe Al was right. *Maybe I just need to relax.* "They won't even notice," Chris pointed out. "The autopilot does the driving."

"That's why we have to do it here. Construction sites have a beacon that sends a signal to every pertran that approaches. A warning goes off inside. Drivers need to hold the steering wheel to be ready to take manual control to protect the workers, or they get a ticket."

"But there aren't any workers."

"I know. I noticed they only work during the morning. They fill the machine with raw material, and it runs until empty. Then they do it again the next day, until the street is finished. But the important thing is that the beacon is on twenty-four seven." Al began pounding one of the heavy poles into the ground at a 45-degree angle away from the street.

Chris said, "We're going to string a cable across the road? What if a tran actually hits it?"

"No. You and I are going to pretend," he said. "Like this." Al demonstrated by gripping the air in front of himself, as if holding an invisible rope.

"That doesn't look very convincing. I don't think I'd stop."

"Right. That's where the stakes come in." Al demonstrated again, but this time he leaned his body back onto the pole. "See? It makes it look like the cable is real, because what else could be holding me up?" Al stood straight again. "Now, take the other pole across the street and pound it in. Oh, and take your bike too. You're gonna need it."

CHAPTER THREE

"I CAN'T RUN ANYMORE." CHELSEA LEANED OVER WITH HER HANDS ON her knees and gasped for air.

"You can. You must push yourself. Stopping just makes it worse." Chelsea's sister-in-law, Adrienne, waited at the top of the hill. "You made it yesterday."

"It's hotter today." Chelsea found the strength to stand straight. Never an athlete, she would never enjoy exercising the way Adrienne did. *Look at her, in her skintight running outfit. Slender. Toned. I used to look like that. And I will again.* Chelsea willed herself to make the last thirty meters up the hill.

"Next time, push yourself." Adrienne wasn't looking at her, but rather out across the horizon. The woman could run for kilometers on end. Chelsea had no hope of working up to that. She just needed to get back in shape—to have the appropriate image as the wife of Evangelos Venizelos, heir to the Venizelos Greek Shipping empire, and to resume her place as their son's mother.

Sweat streamed down from Chelsea's blonde hair, and her pale skin glistened with perspiration. Greece in August was unforgiving, nothing like foggy, gray England, where she grew up. For Adrienne, the run seemed less about fitness and more about stamina—a battle, something to be won or lost. Maybe *trial* was a better word. The hotter the crucible, the stronger the steel. Chelsea had no use for strength. But she did want the *look* of strength because looking fit was sexy.

Chelsea's hair was up in a pony like Adrienne's, but the similarity between the two women stopped there. Adrienne had the same coloring as Evan: dark, thick hair and olive skin. Adrienne hadn't broken a sweat. She coached Chelsea only because Evan asked her to. Chelsea wished he'd asked his other sister, Triana, who was younger and not so athletic. And, well, not so bitchy either.

"You must hydrate. I told you." Adrienne's Greek accent got heavy when she was annoyed. Her English sentences became short and pointed. She glanced at the wearable on her wrist and tapped it. A beep confirmed the beginning of her real workout. She dashed on.

"Cheers," called Chelsea, to Adrienne's back. Chelsea wiped the drops from her brow and walked down the hill in the direction of the Venizelos family's main house. She was a member of the Venizelos family, but the residence area of the main house was off-limits to her unless she was with Evan. Unescorted, she was only allowed to use the gym and the showers.

At the bottom of the hill, she reached the decorative fence where the dirt road and dry grass met the paved road and irrigated lawn. Walking farther, she reached the low brick wall with high black iron fence atop that surrounded the estate. Just one guard manned the side gate. Sitting in his little air-conditioned booth, he glanced up as Chelsea approached, but only momentarily. She longed for the days when she could snatch a man's attention. At thirty-six years old, she still had plenty of sizzle. Since returning from America a month ago, Chelsea had followed the new exercise routine. *It won't be long.*

She entered the athletic facility situated between the pool deck and main house. It was furnished like a luxury spa but devoid of people. Over the weeks, she hadn't seen a single soul. She grabbed a towel from the counter as she passed. There were always six towels. Not five. Not seven. Always six. The grounds' maintenance staff meticulously maintained the facility, but she never saw them. It was like a private health club in which she was the only member. She swung the towel around her neck and dabbed the sweat from her forehead.

In the women's changing room, she found the locker on the end that she'd adopted as her own. She opened it and hung the towel over the locker door. Then she undressed and tossed her workout shorts and top into the nearby basket intended for items to be laundered. She wanted an outfit like Adrienne's, the kind that showed off every curve. The material was so thin it looked painted on. Adrienne was a goddess.

At the long row of shower stalls, she entered the nearest one and tapped the wall panel for the desired temperature. Cool water sprayed from the showerhead over her body. She held her hand under the soap dispenser until it whirred and clicked. A dollop of gel coiled in her palm. She lathered and rinsed. She placed her hand under the shampoo dispenser and then worked the product into her hair.

She closed her eyes and leaned back, allowing the water to loosen the thick suds. With her eyes still closed, she listened to the sound of the water spraying into the bubbles as she turned her head from side to side and felt the needlelike streams as they reached her scalp. Water and foam splashed to the tile at her feet and trickled down the drain. The sound echoed against the porcelain walls of the vacant facility.

Stepping out of the stall, she took a large, soft, thick, luscious towel from the shelf, patted the beads of water, and wrapped the towel around her body—first under one arm, then the other—finishing with a tight fold over her breasts.

Careful not to slip, she walked back to the changing area as she dried the left side of her hair using the free corner of the towel.

That's odd. Where's the small towel I hung on the locker door?

She looked in the laundry basket. The small towel was now resting on top of her workout clothes in the hamper. She froze and listened.

No sound.

She looked around.

Nothing. No one.

Then, from the corner of her eye, she glimpsed a flicker from the hall, like something passed by.

She thought about calling out but reconsidered. *Maintenance staff?*

The shadow passed again.

She waited. Nearly a full minute passed with no sound or movement. She squeezed the towel against her body, keeping it snug under both arms, and tiptoed to the corner of the hallway.

"Chelsea?" came a voice from the hall. Chelsea would have jumped out of her skin, but the tone was caring and respectful. It was Georgios Gregory, the family's butler and chauffeur as well as the managing director of the estate.

Chelsea stepped out, staying close to the wall, holding the fold of the towel to her chest. When she first met Gregory seventeen years ago, his hair was the color of flecked charcoal. Now it was completely white, but still thick, without any hint of receding. He had to be pushing seventy, yet with limitless energy.

"Ah. Sorry to disturb you, madam. Evangelos sent me with a message. He asks that you join him in the family residence as soon as you're dressed."

"Why? What is it?"

Gregory gave her the look that said she knew better than to ask. She did. No harm. Gregory was one of the few sources of information about her son. Chelsea was allowed almost no involvement in their son's childhood, but things would be different now. He was becoming a man, an invincible man. She looked at Gregory pleadingly.

"Well," he relented, "I imagine there's been a development." A hint of a smile appeared when he saw Chelsea light up. "So hurry along."

Chelsea dressed quickly. It had been nearly a year since she'd seen her son—awake anyway. It was time for him to enter the world. Jewish culture has the bar mitzvah, Mexican culture has the quinceañera, and the British aristocracy had debutante season. All are coming-of-age celebrations. According to Evan, it was their son's time now. Yes, things would be different. Finally, she would get to live the glamorous, public life she was destined to live.

At the elevator, a guard waited to escort her up to the residence. She followed him through the halls. Evan was waiting outside the room with the double door, the same room where she'd been allowed to visit with their son before. Over the years, Chelsea had seen Evan almost as infrequently as her son. Evan always said she was like a fine wine, kept on the shelf until the perfect time.

"You look great," he said.

Shelf sitting had taken its toll, but Evan always knew the right thing to say. Soon she'd be back in shape. Evan was still in great shape himself. He had the classic good looks you'd expect of industry royalty—reminiscent of John F. Kennedy Jr. Yes, Evangelos Venizelos was the full package.

"You too." She wanted to hug him, or have him hug her. She longed for a kiss. How long had it been since they'd spent more than six minutes together? Years? He'd said it would be different when they could be together as a family. *Soon*, she thought. *Soon*. "Gregory said there's been a development. What is it?"

"For once, I don't know. I—"

The door opened. Chelsea squinted at the harsh artificial light.

"Please, come in," said an unfamiliar voice. American.

Chelsea's eyes adjusted. The voice came from a man next to the silver bedchamber where their son lay sleeping with the same blue light bathing his naked frame. Chelsea noticed the strange milky coating was now gone from his skin. He looked completely normal, as if truly sleeping instead of hibernating.

"Yes, join us," said a second voice. Unmistakable. Unforgettable. It was him. Aeron Skotino. His voice was so deep it seemed more animal than human. His appearance was nearly identical to the few times she'd seen him before. Dark suit, exquisitely tailored. Probably silk. The sheen was luxurious. White shirt. Red tie. Cocoa skin, not so different from Evan's. But Skotino's complexion looked weathered, ancient somehow. Maybe a reflection of knowledge, experience, and wisdom. Yet not a bit of gray in his black hair. They say the shoes make the man. His had to be actual leather, as in dead-animal leather— incredibly rare. Black, with a shine like a mirror. Chelsea grew up as a Poger, so all her clothes had been 3-D printed. If the fabrication of a garment involved an actual human being, only the rich could afford it. For as long as she could remember, Chelsea had been fascinated by apparel design. She'd always dreamed of wearing handcrafted clothes. And she'd done so for a time after she married Evan. She would again. *Soon*.

"This is Dr. Otto Betasten," said Skotino.

The doctor smiled. Mid to late forties maybe. But baldness could be deceiving. He might've been younger. He had a round face with bags under bright blue eyes. The man wasn't fat, so the bags had to be from eyestrain or something. He was average height, but the trunk of his body seemed long in comparison to his short legs. The long white lab coat he was wearing only highlighted the imbalance.

"Dr. Otto Betasten," he said as he stepped forward, a movement that reminded Chelsea of a penguin. He stopped with his toes outward like a duck and extended a hand to Evan. "You must be Evangelos." He shook Evan's hand the way Americans do sometimes—with his left hand coming up to grasp the forearm.

Evan nodded. "This is my wife, Chelsea."

She didn't offer her hand. Her gaze returned to the chamber.

"And, of course, you know who this is." The doctor stepped aside, allowing Chelsea an unobstructed view. "I'm taking over for Dr. Cornelius. But you should know I've been a part of the project from the start. I'm the chief technology officer for TerraMed Biotech." He paused, as if his pronouncement was backed by fanfare.

"One of the TerraHoldings subsidiaries," explained Evan when he noticed her blank look.

Chelsea shrugged. "American?"

"Yes," said Dr. Betasten. "I'm based in the United States, out of Rochester, Minnesota." Again, he delivered the information as if the whole world had paused in awe.

"Headquarters of the Mayo Clinic," explained Evan, "where the technology to end the healthcare crisis was developed."

Chelsea glared at Evan. For as long as she'd known him, he'd always blamed the Americans for the state of the British economy. "Don't you mean *Amexican* technology?" she asked, using the same word Evan used when he complained about how the Americans exported their creativity along with the rights to exploit the ideas. The Mexicans, in turn, developed and manufactured the innovations into products and then sold them to everyone in the world. Mexico was the current superpower, at least economically. *Why is Evan hiding his true opinions from this man?*

Evan glared back at her and was about to say something, but Dr. Betasten continued.

"In any case, we're monitoring your son's vital signs. He could wake up at any time."

So much fuss about him becoming a man. At seventeen, he still looked boyish. Very handsome, like Evan. They kept his head shaved, but there was the undeniable shadow of gorgeous hair, a shade lighter than Evan's but not quite brown. As an infant, the luster and natural waves gave him a godlike quality. She had seen him most often then. As he grew, they kept his hair in a crew cut. Incredibly masculine looking on a small boy. "Can he grow out his hair, once he's out?"

"Yes," the doctor replied. "In fact, we'll be preparing him to be a full member of society."

Skotino adjusted the knot of his necktie.

"Oh yes," the doctor continued. "Now is also the time to give him something very important. Something he's been missing his entire life."

Chelsea searched the blue eyes for an answer.

"A name," prompted Dr. Betasten.

A name. Yes. It had been so long, she nearly forgot.

"Do you remember, Chels?" Evan asked. "Do you remember why we had to wait before we could give him a name?"

She only remembered bits. Evan had been confused initially too, wanting to follow his family's Greek Orthodox traditions. "Baptism?"

"That's right," said Evan.

Skotino cleared his throat.

Dr. Betasten glanced toward him. "Not baptism precisely. A similar ritual when he receives his given name."

"They said at the time, he'll get his name once he's baptized," said Chelsea. "I remember now. I remember saying, 'Very well then. Let's baptize him.' Then they said, 'Baptism comes after birth.'" She looked at the doctor. "They were talking in circles."

"Not baptism . . . but, yes, following birth."

"Now *you're* talking in circles."

"Born again," offered Evan. He was trying to sound authoritative, but it came out as more of a question.

"Sort of. Well, actually, no," said Dr. Betasten.

"But he *was* born," Chelsea insisted. "He's seventeen."

"Well, in some ways, yes. In some ways, no. His awakening will be a kind of rebirth."

"The first birth didn't count?" she asked, louder now. "I carried him for nine months, and it means nothing?"

"Please, Chels, don't think of it that way," said Evan, "Remember how Mr. Skotino explained about the coating on his skin? He said it was like a cocoon."

"Yes, your son is about to emerge as a magnificent butterfly," said Dr. Betasten. "His life until now hasn't really been a life at all. It was a different kind of existence. He wasn't yet your son. That's why we limited your exposure. What would be the point? Yes? He's different now."

"But he looks the same." She couldn't resist. She stepped to the bedchamber and put her hand on the glass. Up close, she saw now that he wasn't completely naked. There was a strip of fabric at his waist, covering his genitals, like a loincloth. "He's the same."

"By outward appearances, yes, but—"

Skotino cleared his throat again.

"Never mind. In due time. What's important is that he'll have a name."

He looks the same.

Dr. Betasten stepped to her side and put his hand on her back. "Do you remember his skin?"

Yes. Oh, she remembered. Dense and hard. It seemed to be the reason for all their toil. His skin was like armor. Terrorists could *try* to hurt him, but he was invincible. Chelsea nodded. She also remembered the weight. The hardness of his flesh also made him heavy. Laying in front of her now, he looked like a lean, fit young man. Hard to believe he actually weighed six times more than normal. "His skin protects him."

"That's right," said Dr. Betasten. "So maybe a butterfly is the wrong analogy. Think of . . ."—he turned and whispered—"a beetle." He paused, his lips coming even closer to her ear. Still whispering, but with the cadence slowed, he said, "Yes, a beetle. Emerging from its pupa." The *p*'s popped in her ear, each with a breathy puff. "He'll be . . ." The doctor's hand drifted down her back, to a point just past her hip. "Magnificent."

Chelsea stepped toward her husband. "Evan and I will have to discuss it, to decide on a name."

"Actually, Chels," said Evan, "I've had longer to think about it. I—" He looked to Skotino and then back. "The name has already been decided."

She looked up and searched his face. She stepped away, away from all of them. Alone. Alone like the last seventeen years. *It should be different now*, she thought. *I'm his mother. It's supposed to be different now.* "How could you? Without me?"

Evan looked wounded. He seemed as powerless as she.

She wrapped her arms around herself. "Fine. What did you decide?"

"Not before." Skotino chopped off the discourse like a butcher removing fat. "Not before the ceremony." He had a way of speaking. It wasn't a statement as much as a commandment.

"Yes," added Dr. Betasten. "It's imperative you don't learn the name before the ceremony."

She threw out her arms. "Evan just said he already knows the name."

"And I just said it's imperative that *you* not learn the name." The doctor's blue eyes flared, piercing now.

Me? Everyone knows but me? Chelsea looked at Evan. She wanted him to act like her husband. *It's been so long. Maybe he forgot how. Maybe I forgot how to be his wife.* She stepped back, next to Evan. "When?" she asked. "When is the ceremony?"

Dr. Betasten looked to the bedchamber, and so did everyone else. "Soon."

CHAPTER 4

"**W**HY DO YOU GET TO BE IN THE SHADE?" CHRIS CALLED TO AL, FROM across the road at Horseshoe Bend.

"Because I'm smarter than you," Al yelled back.

Chris mimicked Al's posture: arms out in front, holding the imaginary cable. He kept his legs over the pole the way Al had instructed, to hide it from view of the approaching drivers. The pole wasn't long enough to support his whole body, so his back had started to ache. Chris had adjusted himself such that the belt loop of his jean shorts went over the end of the pole. His shorts were now kind of twisted up at the waist, but it took a lot of pressure off his back. He was half leaning, half hanging.

Lucky lay in the shade nearby. Apparently he was smarter than Chris too.

"Don't worry," called Al, "all that sweat on your face looks pretty convincing."

Two trans had already passed, but despite Al's theory about the in-cab warning, the drivers just touched the steering wheel without ever looking up.

"Boring," yelled Chris.

"Be patient. It's a virtue."

Educated, but with nothing to do? Is that what my life is going to be about? Am I going to spend my whole life as an accomplice to Al's pranks? Maybe the blind man was right. Maybe those Hoods were right. Maybe if you get an education but can't find work, you

eventually turn to violence. But the blind man said they weren't
Hoods. Maybe—

"Pay attention. Here comes another."

The pertran headed toward Horseshoe Bend at a perfectly computer-controlled speed. Even from the curb, Chris saw the man grab the steering wheel. The driver's head swiveled between Chris and Al as he tried to make sense of it. The tran crept to a stop about three feet from the imaginary cable. Al was grinning like a bear in honey. The man looked from curb to curb. Al waved in a neighborly way while keeping the other hand on the invisible cable.

The man got out of the tran, and no sooner after he'd taken a few steps did reality hit. With the tran's door open, Chris heard a baby crying. Chris saw now that there were three kids in the tran, each one in a child restraint bucket, one of them an infant, crying that kind of cry when the kid turns purple.

The driver looked pissed. "What the hell do you think you're doing?"

Al leaned off the pole. "Just having a little fun." He went for his bike.

"Who are you? Give me your name." The driver pulled out his percomm and started recording a vid of Al.

"Come on!" Al flipped his bike around toward the ravine and jumped on the seat almost before the bike hit the ground. He pedaled out of the construction area, down the embankment, and out of sight. Lucky raced toward Chris.

The man turned the camera on Chris. "Fun? Just ignore the cost to others, huh? You. Come here."

"We didn't mean any—"

Lucky barked.

No time for explanations. Chris lunged for his bike, but his legs slipped out from under him because his waist was held fast to the pole at the belt loop. He slid down the pole, getting a sideways wedgie.

The man stepped closer and held out his percomm. "Tell me your name."

Lucky got between Chris and the man but didn't bark.

Chris scrambled off the pole and jumped on his bike. The man dashed back to his tran. Chris tore off as fast as he could. The tran caught up to him immediately. Chris realized why Al had gone off road. He veered hard, popped his bike over the curb, and reversed direction. The man looked furious as he tried to turn the tran around. Chris raced back to the construction area and followed the path Al had taken, over the edge and down to the ravine. Al was waiting at the ravine's edge and started off as soon as he saw Chris. Chris and Lucky followed Al along the bank. Al steered his little bike masterfully between the larger rocks. Chris's bigger touring bike, with its thin tires, sunk into the damp sand and slipped on the gravel.

After about three hundred feet, the ravine's valley flattened. Al rode up the embankment and stopped. Chris pulled up next to him.

"Told you to have your bike close-by." Al laughed. He bounced the front tire of his bike on the ground to knock off the sand and mud. "What's the matter?"

"Really? Was it really that much fun?"

"What do you mean? Sure." Al's smile faded. "Come on, migo. You're all stressed again."

Chris didn't say anything. The whole thing seemed so childish. He *was* acting like a child, following Al around like he always did.

Al reached down and pulled the plastic water bottle from the bike frame, took several deep swigs, and then flipped it to Chris.

Chris took a few swallows while Lucky sat patiently. Then Chris squirted a stream, and Lucky chomped at it.

"He'd rather drink from the creek," said Al.

"I know." Chris tossed the water bottle back.

"What's wrong?"

"The creek water gives him *Giardia*."

"No, I mean *you*. What's up with you?"

Chris pulled out his percomm. No messages.

"Oh right," said Al. "Stop worrying. Hope will loosen up eventually."

"She hates me."

"Katie thinks she's running shotgun for us by locking down all the data. That means Hope cares. After experiencing those psychopaths in Nevada firsthand—or maybe I should say first shoulder—Hope's not going to leave you out in the open."

"Not funny. What part of her time with me do you think she finds attractive? It's not exactly what you'd call a sentimental journey. My mom discovering her students are being kidnapped? Me dragging Hope into the mess to help me rescue them— unsuccessfully, I might add—and Hope nearly becoming another captive? Yeah, I'll have her completely seduced in no time."

"See? During all that, she stood by you."

"Al, look at the facts. The leader of the evil group dislocated her shoulder. She's had enough. She hates me."

"Hope understands the long game. There's a reason all that happened. We have to find out. The warden is the key. You've known that since the day you were born."

"She hates me. And it's not over, migo. If what the warden said is true—and you know it is—it's just the beginning. Remember the first words from the warden? *Feral emergence?* Something cataclysmic is coming, something that has been building for years, maybe hundreds of years. Those killers in Nevada are part of it. The warden is here to stop the men from Nevada. Unlike us, he knows what their horrible scheme actually is, but he can't do anything in our world. Like he's half a dimension away, the warden needs me in order to have any effect. The warden picked me to be its human proxy. I ask myself why every day, migo. All I know is Hope wants nothing to do with the warden, the men from Nevada, or their apocalyptic plan. And by extension, she wants nothing to do with me. I've brought her nothing but a world of hurt."

I managed to haul someone who just escaped the control of an abusive father into a brand-new, hurtful life controlled by psychopaths. Chris shook his head. *Why me?*

"This too shall pass," said Al. "We stick to the plan. We finish what we started. With the warden's help, we stop the killers from Vegas. Everybody lives happily ever after." Breaking into song, he added, "Chris and Hope, sitting in a tree. K-I-S-S-I-N-G."

"We should be helping Katie decipher the warden's clues." Chris said the words out loud for himself as much as for Al.

"That's Katie's department."

"So you're just the entertainment committee?"

Al took another swig. "Yup."

I IO I IO I IO

LAURA'S DISPLAY SCREEN FLICKERED AND WENT DARK. THE HUM OF THE refrigerator faded and was replaced by birdsong coming from the open kitchen window. The seccomm panel on the wall was one of the few electrical devices in the house backed up by battery power. It displayed POWER FAULT in red letters.

"Ben, it happened again," she called out, mostly out of frustration, knowing he probably couldn't hear her from the basement lab three levels below.

She knew the cause. The 3-D printer blew a fuse. Again. Chris had been using it a lot lately to finish repairs on the house. Ben's computers used a lot of power too. There wasn't enough to go around. *What's taking Ben so long to flip the fuse?* The power interruption surely wrecked the chandelier in the printer. Every time it happened, whatever was being printed got wrecked. *Chris'll have to set it up again.*

What's taking so long? Lately, Ben had been working down in the lab past bedtime and then also getting up again in the middle of the night. *Did he fall asleep down there?* She went to the stairwell in the hall, past the lifeless elevator. The stairwell doors used old-fashioned doorknobs. Unlike the modern pocket doors around the house, the stairwell doors could be opened manually in the event of a power outage.

The glow from emergency lights illuminated the steps. She paused. The doorknob reminded her of the customizations they'd added to accommodate Chris. Chris was invisible to the scanners that triggered modern doors to open automatically. Ben had discovered it was because of a heavy metal called unbihexium in the warden. The warden didn't have a body in the conventional sense; he was an invisible cloud of molecules far apart from each other but bound by energy. Wherever Chris went, so did the warden. *Will the safe house have doorknobs?* The thought challenged her resolve to relocate. No one could be sure if it was even possible to hide from the strange group of men who were both kidnappers and murderers. *And only the warden knows what else.*

"I'm on it," came Ben's voice from below.

Down the steps, she met him at the fuse panel in the hallway outside the lab.

Click. The lights came back on, and he shut the fuse box. As if she wasn't even there, he headed back to the lab.

"Are we doing the right thing?" she asked.

He stopped and looked at her with a blank expression on his face.

It used to make her so angry. His mind seemed to always be a million miles away. Over the years, he'd helped her realize that she often processed a bunch of stuff in her own head and then expected him to pick up her train of thought. "Sorry. Can we talk?" she asked, keeping the edge out of her voice. They needed to work together. She didn't want to make him defensive.

He nodded and led her into the lab. Racks of computers with blinking lights lined one wall. The other walls had display screens. Workbenches and input consoles were strategically placed throughout the lab.

"Talk about what?" He sat down.

She stepped toward the Compton chamber—a booth against one wall with glass on three sides. This was where Ben had discovered the warden. The chamber was able to interpret brain activity, like a mind-reading machine. When they used it on Chris, the chamber found brain activity for two. Two people? Two entities? Two brains? All they knew at the time was that the chamber registered Chris and something else. Laura often thought how convenient it would be if Ben could read *her* mind, so she wouldn't have to explain the obvious all the time. On second thought, no.

She put her hand on the glass. "Are we leaving all this behind?"

"I don't see how we can take it with us."

"We don't need the chamber anymore, right? The warden can talk to us through the portable medical scanner."

"We don't need the chamber, true, but it's my computers that crunch the data. After the explosions at all three data centers, this is the only remaining computer system capable of the task."

Not only were the men from Nevada intent on wiping out her family, they were equally intent on wiping out any stored record of themselves. Ben had found a way to detect the whereabouts of the men. Almost immediately, all three data centers related to Ben's dark energy project had mysteriously burned. He'd built his set of servers over the years. The lab was like another family member to him, and she could hear the emotion in his voice.

He seemed to catch himself emoting. "Don't forget the galactose maltose. When Chris drinks malted milk, the sugars from milk and germinating grain—galactose and maltose—allow him to communicate with the warden." He smiled, apparently pleased with himself for looking at the bright side. She knew he was just trying to prove to her that he could walk away from his quantum-computing babies with no hard feelings. She wasn't convinced. Whenever emotion leaked into Ben's thinking, cracks appeared in his usually flawless logic.

"I haven't forgotten anything. You said Chris is able to connect with the warden, *but* the connection is limited to abstract concepts. You said we need the computer to translate the analytical concepts. You said the meaning of the warden's words become clear only when the abstract and the analytical concepts are interpreted together."

His smile faded.

"Ben, it's too much. Over the course of six weeks, a killer smashes into our home, our son learns to fly like a bird, he and his friends go to Nevada and end up battling the Omega Force, who were somehow convinced to protect a group of men that kidnapped and tortured young women—it's all too fantastic. It's all too sudden."

"It's not sudden," said Ben. "Remember when we took Chris home from the hospital as an infant? The warden was a part of him then. Puberty made the connection stronger, strong enough for the warden to tell us about the sugars in malted milk to improve the connection. Recent events have only made it *seem* sudden. The truth is, on the day Chris was born, our lives changed forever."

"Like my two students?"

"Exactly. How is it that you—a poli-sci professor at Ben-U at the time—are linked to the disappearances of young women over the course of nearly two decades? What are the odds two of them just happen to be your students? It's like fate, but on some kind of ballistic trajectory. Remember the day Chris was in a trance with the warden? You told me Chris kept uttering, 'For the chance of reality's path doth tip.' These events are culminating now for a reason, like we're all being drawn to an epicenter."

Laura said, "The warden knows."

"Yes. The warden has a purpose. We have to find out what it is *exactly*."

"Obviously," said Laura, thinking out loud, "we're in a much better position to learn the warden's plan if we stay in this house so we can use your computers. Staying here may be the only way."

Ben nodded in agreement.

"Well, that's only half the equation. We need Chris to interpret the abstract side, but he hasn't been drinking the malted milk. Not since they returned from Vegas."

"Maybe he's been chewing the gum. It's ingenious the way Katie was able to infuse it with malted milk powder."

"No, he isn't. I checked," said Laura. "Hope is all he thinks about."

"He has to drink it—while in the chamber or while we use the portable scanner—to get the analytical translation from the mind-reader program. If we decide to stay here." He looked at her. "I think we just decided." He smiled.

Laura nodded and smiled back. It was a relief. She'd discovered facing danger was less stressful than running from it.

"If we stay here," he continued, "we're sitting ducks. One of the men will come to try to kill us. They could come anytime. Let's hope the third time's not the charm. More than ever, we need the warden's help. And we need it now." Ben never got angry, but he was now.

He's really trying.

He asked, "What about the FBI? Are they as clueless as we hoped? Or do we have to worry about the authorities trying to catch us too?"

"Chris won't tell me what he learned during Harrison's questioning."

"Well, he'll have to. There's no telling how long it will take to crack the meaning of the warden's clues."

| 0 | 0 | 0

CHRIS WAS CONTENT JUST TO CONCENTRATE ON THE SPINNING BACK WHEEL OF Al's bike. Even Lucky seemed to be keeping closer to Al instead of his usual place, trotting behind Chris. Chris felt like his pedaling legs were attached to a different person, as if he was floating behind Al and Lucky like some kind of dogsled musher having an out-of-body experience.

Al dismounted by the water faucet in Katie's backyard. Like all the homes in their neighborhood, her house was a prefab with three stories above ground and three levels below. A ramp led to the garage on the first underground level. But there was never a pertran in Katie's garage. Nor Al's.

Al directed the hose water in Lucky's face, and his dog lapped it up. Then Al refilled his water bottle and redirected the stream back at Lucky again. Al raised the water bottle to Chris with a questioning look.

"No, I'm good."

Al snapped the bottle back into the clip on his bike frame. "She won't bite," he said, referring to Katie.

Chris wasn't so sure. He knew he should be more assertive, but he couldn't rally himself. Even Lucky seemed to sense it. It made Chris mad that Lucky was already at the back step of Katie's house instead of at his heel.

"Fine." Chris got off his bike.

Before going up to Katie's room, they swung by the family room to say hi to her older brother, Teeter. His real name was Peter, but Katie called him Teeter when she was little, and it stuck.

"What's happ'nin?" came the voice from the computer on Teeter's wheelchair. Once his ALS—a neurodegenerative disease he'd been diagnosed with years earlier—progressed to a certain point, Teeter wasn't able to speak anymore. He could spell out phrases into his synthesizer, but that took forever. "What's happ'nin?" was one of many phrases on a preset list he could choose from. The whole system was covered by the federal subsidy. And judging by the canned phrases straight out of the 1970s, it had to be the bargain model, or maybe a cruel joke by the designer.

Teeter was facing the window, which he often did when he tired of watching vids on the pubcomm. His head was permanently shifted to the right, held by a cushion. From behind, you could see the curve in his neck and spine. It looked painful. Teeter never complained.

Al touched Teeter's shoulder as he passed, and crouched in Teeter's view. "Oh, you know," answered Al. "The usual."

"Right on," said Teeter. The phrases were always the same, but he liked to vary the accent. Today it was Australian.

Chris fist-bumped Teeter's other shoulder and took a knee next to Al. Lucky sat next to Chris and waited.

"Up," commanded Teeter.

Lucky gently put his front paws on Teeter's lap and began sniffing around, licking here and there—drops from a recent liquid meal, no doubt. Ever since the ALS took such firm hold, they always checked in with Teeter when visiting Katie. And Lucky was a key part of the ritual. Teeter never said anything during this time with Lucky. But you could see the thrill in his eyes.

"Where's your sis?" asked Al.

Teeter didn't respond right away. Then his eyes rolled up for a moment, indicating Katie's bedroom.

"All right. Catch you later, Teeter." Al went for the elevator. Lucky hopped off and lay on the floor by the wheelchair.

Chris stood, and Teeter caught his eye. "Good luck," said Teeter.

Al laughed from the hall.

"Oh, thanks for the support," said Chris with a wry smirk. "Remember, you're the one who has to live with her." He dashed after Al, leaving Lucky behind to hang out with Teeter.

Taking the elevator was annoyingly slow, compared to the stairs, but that's what normal people did. It gave Chris's dread about talking to Katie time to build. She'd been researching the words and phrases they had gotten from the warden. They were clues toward learning how to stop the group of killers from Nevada. Deciphering the clues was the next and only option. Without more information, they were targets in the open. The killers would be back. Maybe weeks. Maybe days. Maybe hours. Chris had been giving Al a hard time about leaving the task to Katie, but he'd been procrastinating too. Katie was best suited for the work, but that was really just an excuse. The three of them had always done everything together. They supported each other completely. Chris knew, deep down, that the task of cracking the warden's clues should be no different.

Thinking about how they got the words from the warden reminded Chris of the time they'd brought Teeter over to his father's basement lab and put him in the Compton chamber. This was after his ALS got so bad he couldn't talk anymore. The chamber read Teeter's mind and converted what he was thinking onto the display—the same process used to record the warden's thoughts. For Teeter, the painstaking delay between utterances was gone, and no need for him to shorten his thoughts for brevity. They all joked and laughed together. It was incredible to get reacquainted with Teeter, to finally and fully see the young man he'd grown into. It was like reading a book with its final chapters ripped out, and then, years later, finding the missing pages and reading how things turned out for the story's hero. Chris remembered how the conversation that night had gradually shifted to be primarily between Teeter and Katie. That's when Ben suggested they leave Katie and Teeter alone for a while. The two were in the basement for hours. It was almost midnight before they came upstairs. Chris recalled Katie pushing Teeter's wheelchair into the kitchen, her eyes red and cheeks wet.

When Chris and Al reached her bedroom, Katie asked, "What did the FBI say?"

Al jumped up and back, imitating a high jumper using the Fosbury flop, onto Katie's bed and landed with his legs already crossed.

"Never mind that," said Chris. "What about the warden's words?"

"No, *you* never mind that. Tell us what the FBI said during the questioning. Now."

Fine. "They said they're going to keep interrogating me about the man Al killed in the park. When you guys turn eighteen, they'll haul you in too." Chris sat on the corner of the bed. "Hope too," he added. "They threatened to use some kind of antiterrorism law to go after her."

"That's bad."

"It doesn't matter. She's not a Hood."

"You don't know that."

Not this again. Chris wanted to charge at Katie and put her in a headlock until she took back the words. Katie was barely more than a hundred pounds. It seemed like it would be so easy to just put her in her place, so she'd never again accuse Hope of being a Hood. But Katie was the fastest of them all. Chris knew he couldn't get the jump on her—not without help from the warden, anyway. And she was pretty tall, about five eight, so she had good reach, and her legs seemed to hit you from nowhere.

Chris wanted to grab her brown hair by the pony and swing her around the room.

"Well, you don't," she repeated, driving the knife deeper.

Chris felt the anger boil inside. Clenching his teeth, he readied his next words. He really wanted to rip into her. Then he felt the vague presence of the warden. The warden became evident when Chris experienced pain. He realized that Katie's words had hurt him. Like physical pain but not. Chris thought about nothing but Hope. She was the most important thing in his life. How could Hope be more important than Al and Katie, his lifelong friends? Or his parents? Again, he felt the subtle company of the warden in his mind. He searched for the reason. *Hoods.* Katie had called Hope a Hood—a Robin Hood terrorist—just like Harrison had. *But it's only a name.*

The pain and anger seemed to fall away, like a drape snipped from its rod, falling to the floor, allowing clear sight through the window behind. *Hoods.* Why was it such a horrible name? Growing up, it was one of the worst names you could call someone. He'd heard a lot about the Hoods because his mom was a political science professor. Or had he? He realized he didn't know much about the Hoods. And, thinking back, Laura never actually said they were bad.

"I think I saw Hoods on the masstran coming back from the city," said Chris finally, the defensiveness gone now.

Al sat up. "Migo, no way."

"No, I'm serious."

"I know. I'm saying there's *no way*," said Al. "You never actually see a Hood, not in plain sight."

"But these people covered their faces and everything. One of the passengers even said they were Hoods."

"No, Al's right," said Katie. "Hoods are cyberterrorists. The people you saw were most likely protestors. They were probably going to some civil disobedience demonstration."

Al leaned back again and jammed a second pillow behind his head. "Some of them throw rocks and break stuff," he pointed out. "They find where the rich people are hiding and then harass the hell out of them."

"True," said Katie. "Some of them aren't so civil."

Chris thought about what the grandpa had said during the masstran ride earlier that day. He remembered what he'd said about young people receiving free education, only to then enter a world where no jobs were available. All that studying, and for what? Chris had to admit it would be frustrating. Certainly frustrating enough to protest. Maybe even enough to become violent. It started to make sense. Chris asked, "What are we going to do?"

"We have to know more about the group of men trying to kill us. The warden knows."

"No, I mean *us*," said Chris. "What are we going to do after high school? After college? What are we going to do for a living?"

"Don't go there, migo," said Al, agitated.

"Chris, you live in a bubble," said Katie.

Chris looked at her blankly.

"Your parents are both employed."

"My mom's not," objected Chris. "And after the explosion at the univ—"

"Not right now, no, but growing up, they both had jobs at Ben-U. Do you know how rare that is?"

"Other kids at school have employed parents."

"Not most. Some. And even then, only one parent," said Katie. "And the ones from unemployed families call you a Loyd."

"Sticks and stones . . . Besides, I can kick their asses, so who cares?"

"On top of that, you live in *this* neighborhood, with us Pogers." She let the word hang.

In elementary school, kids called each other Pogers and Loyds all the time. Chris knew they called him a Loyd because his parents were employed but he never understood why it mattered.

"To answer your question," said Al, "we're going to sit on our asses our entire lives while we collect the federal subsidy. Just like my old man." Then Al seemed to shake it off, to get off the subject, or maybe it was just his defeated acceptance. "I bet they have a cushy university job with your name on it."

Chris's thoughts went into rewind. All those years . . . Was he naively arrogant? Or cluelessly insensitive? Pompous? Entitled? *No*. He was sure there was never any kind of difference between the three of them. He would never—*could* never—humiliate them. Not on purpose at least. How many times over the years had he put his foot in his mouth? Apparently, he was too stupid and too oblivious to understand what life was like for his two friends. Apparently, you had to be smart and empathetic to be knowingly arrogant. Chris looked at the two of them. "I'm sorry."

"Nothing to be sorry about. Just stop thinking about yourself all the time," said Katie.

"That's just it. All I can think about is Hope. It pisses me off when you call her a Hood."

"Well, we don't know she's not," said Katie. Her repeated verdict landed like a second slap in the face.

Chris felt the rage return. He shifted his weight forward.

"Woah, woah, woah," said Al, vaulting off the bed and getting between them. "Let's just get back on task."

"Well, she could be," Katie said again. The girl was a warrior, freakin' relentless—one of her best weapons. It was one of the many things Chris liked about her. But it was no fun when she used it against him.

"Jeez, Katie. Drop it for now, OK?" said Al. "Listen you two, we need to know everything about the men after us. Let me refresh your memory. I'm talking about the men we confronted in that Nevada house of horrors. The men protected by the Omega Force. The men who are—at this very moment, no doubt—finding a way to kill us, in a way that won't backfire on them like the last two times. The warden knows. We need to dissect every bit of information the warden gave us. And then we need to get more words—as many as we can—from the warden before you and your parents move to the safe house."

Katie nodded. "Chris, I'm sorry too," she said. "One thing's for sure, Hope's saving our bacon right now with her information blackout."

"Ah. There, see? All better now," said Al. "Go on."

"OK. Let's start from the beginning. The men from Nevada who are after us know where you live, Chris, so it's only a matter of time. All we really know is that our attempt to try to rescue the kidnapped women has brought down their wrath on us. They'll show up again. It could be any moment. You need to move to the safe house and gamble that Hope will tip us off if she detects any sign of danger. And we have to count on her to prevent the authorities from arresting us. You need to do whatever she says to keep your digital breadcrumbs off the network. We need time to put the warden's information into a new plan. We need to find out who those men really are."

Chris couldn't bear the thought of reminding them that Hope wasn't even talking to him. "So, Katie, what did you learn about the warden's words?"

She didn't answer right away. She sat down. "I found some good things . . . and some bad things . . . and some things that scare the crap out of me."

"Start with the good things," said Al.

"Well, *Übermensch* is one of the words. It's a kind of superman. I think that word refers to you, Chris, because of the superpowers you get from the warden. I think it's a clue about how you fit into the warden's plan. I mean, that seems pretty obvious, right? Your enhanced abilities—resulting from the warden's control of the air pressure around your skin, to give you the ability to fly, strike with force, and protect you from external force—are definitely super. *Übermensch* is a German word. It was first used by this guy, Friedrich Nietzsche. Nietzsche had this entire philosophy about life. In his writing, he describes a world where people are dissatisfied with life—unhappy—and are always looking for a place beyond earth where it will be better. These people take no action to help themselves. Instead, they blame others for their unhappiness and want those at fault to be left behind on earth to be tormented, like in hell. As a result, the people have no ambition, no sense of purpose, no self-responsibility. They simply blame others for what they don't have. So, to fix the problem, the *Übermensch* tries to teach people to seize the day, to devote their time on earth to working, to making dreams come true, to making life on earth perfect for everyone. The warden must be referring to you, Chris."

Chris wasn't sure he agreed. He was hoping for something more specific. From that word, it felt like the warden wanted him to boil the ocean just for a cup of tea.

"What's the bad part?" asked Al.

"*Übermensch* is associated with the disbelief in God," she said. "You see, Christianity and most other religions have the concept of heaven—a perfect place many people believe you go after death. The *Übermensch* believes people take the idea too far, that time on earth is simply to be bided, with no real in-the-moment reflection about how we should live. Because the *Übermensch* views life as a waiting game, he tries to convince people to give up on the idea of heaven and instead take responsibility for their own happiness. Essentially: be present, be happy, make your own heaven on earth. Some people think the *Übermensch* concept is viewed as promoting the death of God."

"Well, who can know?" said Al.

"*Übermensch* is also associated with a radical form of self-improvement. Not in the floss-your-teeth-twice-a-day sense, but more in the Nazi-Aryan-race-takes-over-the-world sense. The philosophy promotes the improvement of the human body by breeding desirable traits over time using genetic selection. Ultimately, *Übermensch* comes to represent people—plural—becoming super. But the question is *how*. In the benevolent case, *Übermensch* helps everyone to help themselves. In the malevolent case, *Übermensch* helps only 'the chosen ones' to become super in order to dominate over others."

"Super," Al muttered. "I guess Hitler's SS doctors would've loved to get their hands on a bunch of wardens. It would've made the process of making super soldiers a lot easier."

"Uh-huh." Katie frowned.

Chris felt like his head would explode. He didn't understand anything she was saying and was afraid to admit it.

"All along I just assumed the warden was good," Al said, looking at Chris. "You've always said you thought the warden was good. Do you still?"

"I always assumed so, yes," said Chris. "Was that wrong?"

No one answered.

Al said, "Let's move on. Tell us the meaning of another word from the warden."

"*Parthanogenesis*. It's Latin. *Parthanos*, meaning *virgin*, and *genesis*, meaning *creation*." Katie paused.

"Uh-oh," said Al. "This one sounds like it's about Chris too."

Katie nodded. "All I can come up with is the fact that Chris was adopted. Chris, do you know who your biological parents were?"

"Yes. I mean, I was told about them. I kept their last name, Lumière. Marian Lumière was my biological—" Chris's percomm jingled. "Hey, Dad. . . . Yes. . . . OK. Now? . . . Fine, I'll be right there." Chris stood. "I gotta go home."

"Now?" said Al. "We just got started."

"Later," said Chris. He saw Katie was looking down. She looked wiped out. "Katie needs a break."

She looked up. "Hurry. I don't know what it all means." Her eyes closed. She shuddered.

I 10 I 10 I 10

"SIR, YOU HAVE A PRIORITY MESSAGE."

Eladio stepped to his own display console. The message was from Captain Schofield. *The shit finally hit the fan.* He went to the privacy of his office, off the command center floor.

"Vixen, connect me with Captain Schofield."

"Connecting. Conference in progress."

"Hector, thanks for joining."

First name? Oh boy.

Schofield announced, "You're on with Colonel Wesson."

"Take a seat, son. I want to see your face."

Eladio walked around his desk, sat down, and tapped to activate the vid cam. "Well, this can't be good."

"Nope," said the colonel. "I'll get right to it. Nolan wants your head."

I knew it. Schofield let the arrows fly right through, unobstructed. He's just going to sit there and let me hang. "This is bullshit. I didn't—"

"I know, son. We both do."

Schofield nodded but said nothing.

The colonel continued, "I convinced Nolan to keep you on. He agreed, with the condition that I have you reassigned."

"Oh great. What, so I can have a career peeling potatoes?"

"Sure, if that's what you want." On-screen, the colonel locked his steely gaze. The man was like your dad and your granddad all rolled into one. When he called you *son*, it was more than a figure of speech.

"No, sir," Eladio responded.

The colonel sat back. "We have an opportunity here. Before your reassignment, I'm going to put you on administrative leave."

"How long?"

"Three weeks."

"What am I supposed to do with myself for three weeks?"

"That's a good question," said Colonel Wesson. "Captain?"

Captain Schofield piped up. "Hector, do you know who Corporal Juan Rodriguez is?"

"Of course. Everybody knows. Nolan had him canned—" Eladio stopped himself. Rodriguez had been in Colonel Wesson's chain of command, but everyone knew the decision came from Nolan's organization: a toilet bowl filled with the remnants of the Central Intelligence Agency, National Security Agency, and National Reconnaissance Office, all swirling together, all casualties of the financial collapse triggered by the healthcare crisis. When you put a bunch of geniuses in a room and slash their funding, scary shit starts to happen. "Sorry, sir. I meant no disrespect."

"That's all right," said the colonel. "A fair assessment."

"What I should have said, sir, is that none of us believe you gave Rodriguez the boot. It wasn't your style. Nolan's fingerprints were all over it. Anyway, that's why I'm assuming I'm the scapegoat for Omega Force Fireteam Echo returning from Philly empty-handed."

"Forget Nolan. What have you heard about Rodriguez?"

"He botched the mission to capture the Hoods responsible for the murder of Dr. Cornelius—the same Hoods who wanted to finish the job by going after Dr. Cornelius's gestation and training facility in Nevada run by TerraMed Biotech, a civilian contractor."

"And?"

"And, if possible, capture the British MI8 agent, the traitorous woman who conspired with the Hoods to perform the actual hit on Dr. Cornelius—a kill that wasn't quick. It wasn't execution style, nothing out of the MI8 handbook. Dr. Cornelius was mutilated. He was meant to suffer."

Colonel Wesson reframed facts. "So Rodriguez had a chance to capture or kill the person or persons responsible for killing Dr. Cornelius, the man who oversaw the Omega project for both the US Marines and British military intelligence. Essentially, Rodriguez was blamed for missing the chance to avenge the brutal murder of the father of every Omega Force marine and every MI8 agent. Is that about right?"

"Yes, sir, that's my understanding."

"Piss you off?"

"Hell yes."

"Keep going."

"Hmm . . . I don't think I know anything more about Rodriguez."

"You're not alone. The data are all fucked-up. Just like our little fiasco in Philly. Eladio . . ." After a beat, the colonel leaned forward. "Hector, tell me what you know about the Omega Force marines themselves?"

"Genetically modified humans. They're exceptional. Not just physically but in every other aspect too. As an example, the four-member Omega Force fireteam is a special-ops unit led by a corporal. That's unheard of. The Omega Force marines come fresh out of training—or whatever you call it—fully battle hardened, as if they've got twenty years of frontline experience."

"Forget about the textbook definition. What do you *really* know about the men and women under your command?"

Eladio shrugged. "Nothing," he admitted.

The colonel sat back. "Well, that's going to change. Let's discuss your three-week vacation."

CHRIS SKIDDED TO A HALT, LEAVING A RUBBER MARK ON THE GARAGE FLOOR. Even as he lifted the bike into the storage rack suspended from the ceiling, he could see the warning lights on the 3-D printer. He immediately smelled the telltale acrid odor that signaled a production interruption. The system was fully automatic, except of course when your dad blows the fuse.

Chris pressed the button to open the fabrication chamber. On rollers, the huge doors took a moment to open wide enough for him to slip in. The chandelier was two-thirds complete, looking now like an octopus with eight amputations, or maybe one that tried to walk on the sun. He pulled the unfinished fixture from the assembly stage, dropped it into the trash hopper, closed the safety doors, created a new job list, added the self-cleaning cycle as task number one, searched the database for the chandelier design, created a new task, added it to the job list, and started the process.

Inside the house, both Ben and Laura were waiting for him.

"I'm on it," he said preemptively. He started to cross the kitchen to get to the hall and ultimately to his bedroom. He'd have to go right past them. He knew he wouldn't get far. He hadn't even taken a step when they started in on him.

"Chris, we need to hear about your session with Harrison," said Ben. His voice was uncharacteristically stern. *He must have practiced that sentence in his head all morning.*

"I told you, the FBI knows nothing about the group of men after us. The man Al killed in the park is still unidentified. It doesn't matter that Al killed the guy in self-defense. All they care about is catching Hoods. The FBI thinks Hope is a Hood. They're just trying to get to Hope. Harrison wants to be a hero. He's desperate to distinguish himself by scoring a win against the Hoods. He wants Hope."

"We can't let that happen," said Ben.

"How can you say that? So we're planning to move—just run away and hide?"

Ben looked at Laura. She shook her head, conveying "not now" to her husband.

"What's that about?" asked Chris. "What haven't you told me?"

"You have quite the nerve, young man," said Laura, "accusing us of not sharing information with you. You don't seem to have an appreciation for . . . for what happened to the people around you when we stood our ground against those killers, instead of running and hiding."

"One of those men dislocated Hope's shoulder. You don't think I appreciate *that*?"

"My point exactly," said Laura. "I mean *all* the people around you." She sat down and looked to the side. "Heinrich . . ."

Chris remembered the vid of his dad's friend, Heinrich Miller, tortured to death by the same unidentified man who smashed through the house after Katie, the same man with whom Katie and Al made a final stand against at the park, the same man the FBI now called "the deceased."

The incident in the park was so public. And, unfortunately, it created a digital trail leading to Hope. *She's good at blocking the authorities' network queries without any trace leading back to her. But the FBI knows it's Hope doing the blocking because all queries about Hope's physical whereabouts come back empty, which just doesn't happen in this day and age. Unless you're a Hood. The FBI is swarming, but not sure around what.*

"You're doing it again," said Laura. "You're thinking about Hope again." She looked at him. Her eyes welled up. "When the unidentified man tortured Heinrich . . ." She trembled and started over. "We can't forget about the six layers of death. In order for the men from Nevada to kill the warden, they have to force me to witness the death of my loved ones. Let me narrow it down for you. That's your father." She gestured to Ben. He stepped next to her and put his arm around her. "My *husband*." She was practically screaming. "Then the layers continue to me, Chris. You must finally witness *my* death." She began to cry. "And all you can think about is Hope. She's not your wife. She's not even a proper girlfriend. What's happened to your priorities? What's happened to you?" She broke from Ben's embrace and dashed from the kitchen.

"Mom—"

"Let her go," said Ben.

Chris let his shoulders slump. He leaned back against the kitchen counter. "I don't mean to minimize any of this. Not for Mom. Not for you. Not for anyone."

"I know," said Ben. "Try to see it from your mom's point of view. Remember, it wasn't just Heinrich. It started with his wife. Heinrich was forced to watch as they killed her. Then I had to watch Heinrich be tortured and murdered. I'm next, so they can make sure your mother watches. A prerecorded vid is sufficient, apparently. It started with Heinrich's wife. It will end with you, and therefore the warden. That's what the unidentified man said." Ben sat down. "Your mom believes she has a solution. If she 'runs away and hides,' as you say, she can't witness anyone's death. She breaks the layers. She can save the warden. She can save you."

"We can't believe anything the unidentified man said."

"We don't have a choice. There's too much at stake."

"You don't understand. Mom's not my real mother."

"I know that, but—"

"You don't understand. They're coming after the warden. Me. Not mom. Not you. Not any of you. You're all just in the way. They're coming for *me*!" Chris stormed out of the kitchen.

| | 0 | | 0 | | 0

SalaciousFrog: Your lover can't seem to stay out of trouble.
PrincessLIMDIS: He's not my lover.
SalaciousFrog: We're chewing up considerable resources to keep him cloaked. It's a big risk.
PrincessLIMDIS: I do what you ask. You do what I ask. Besides, you're no one to lecture me about risk.
SalaciousFrog: The feds retrieved the skin cells from the sniffer. Nothing we could do.
PrincessLIMDIS: I'll deal with it.
SalaciousFrog: I just don't understand your interest in Chris Lumière.
PrincessLIMDIS: None of your business.

Hope checked the time. Her cyber-infiltration work had taken nearly the whole day. *One more thing to get done today. But not online.*

PrincessLIMDIS: Adios.

After logging off, Hope stowed her display screen in her backpack.

In the apartment's living room, Sue was on her knees, taking clothes out of a moving box. Next to the hallway, her mom had stacked the items destined for the bedrooms. Clearly, she'd parked the items there instead of disturbing Hope. In their old house, Hope could work in the basement, out of everyone's way. In the new apartment, it was harder.

Sue turned from the box. "Hungry?"

Hope *was* hungry. "Nah."

Sue's eyes darted to the backpack. "Where are you going?"

Hope headed for the door. "I'll be back in a while."

"For dinner?"

"Sure."

Hope stepped from the elevator, into the lobby. Toothless was asleep on the bench. She walked up to the glass window of the booth. The manager was asleep too, with his feet up, practically in the same position from that morning. She could see the reflected light of the vid images dance across his face, but the sound was off.

Phwap, phwap, phwap. Hope turned to see the dachshund lying under the bench where Toothless slept. The dog didn't get up, hardly moving at all. It stayed lying on its side, but was watching her with the most adorable eyes. *Phwap, phwap, phwap* went the tail against the lobby floor. Hope stepped over and bent down. *Phwap, phwap.* She let the dog sniff her hand. The little wet nose twitched. *Phwap.* She scratched its head. The eyes became heavy, rolling in ecstasy. Hope was surprised the animal could even see; the eyes were so blue with cataracts. Maybe it could only hear her. She scratched a bit more and then left the three of them to sleep.

She managed to get into the masstran and the relief of its air conditioning before things got too out of hand. Her shirt, with tank top under that, sports bra under that, and regular bra under that, started to cling like wet tissue paper. Keeping her chest well concealed was a challenge. Layers helped, but the arrangement wasn't great for summer humidity. She needed to look presentable for the job interview.

There were only a few people on the masstran. They all seemed unremarkable, except for a couple at the other end. Hope couldn't take her eyes off them. A boy and a girl. Teens. Locked in a public display of affection. His tongue was inside her mouth. Her hand was deep in the roots of his hair. His arm was across her waist, with his hand cupping her butt. Her leg was over his crotch, practically dry humping him. Hope was drawn to the sight of the French kiss, mesmerized, trying to vicariously feel what the girl was feeling at that very moment.

Hope realized her own lips had parted. She closed her mouth, yanked her eyes away, and pulled out her percomm. *Swipe, tap, tap.* Chris Lumière. She stared at his picture. The digits underneath indicated thirty-three unread messages and three unanswered comms, all since midnight. She looked again at the picture, put two fingers on the screen and zoomed. Usually she zoomed to his eyes. This time, it was his lips.

It took about thirty minutes to reach her destination. She checked the list of companies outside the building and found where it listed Ferguson Logic Controllers, LLC. Hope knew about FLC long before she started job hunting. The company designed programmable logic controllers, the tiny chips that allowed the global network to have a physical presence in the non-cyber world. The chips were found in everything from the electric motors in modern pocket doors to the servos that aimed surveillance cameras. Logic controllers interpreted remote commands from the global network into instructions for motors and servos—catalysts for motion and force, allowing the global network to come to life and manipulate the physical world like muscles and tendons. To maintain global security, cyber protection was paramount, hence the encryption and decryption of the network commands. FLC was one of the few remaining design firms still in the United States. Of course, the manufacturing was done in Mexico, just like everything not 3-D printed. Hope knew this information firsthand because she cracked her first FLC logic controller at the tender age of ten.

"Can I help you?" came a young man's voice.

"I'm here to interview for the cipher specialist position."

"I'm sorry. The last interview ended at noon. You'll have to resubmit."

"Can you check again, please?"

"No, I can't. You'll need to resubmit."

"Please?"

"No. I already told you there's no—" Seconds passed. "That's odd. It's right here in the calendar. But I could swear . . ."

"So you'll let me in?"

There was no reply, just the metallic clap of the dead bolt followed by the swish of the door. Inside the office suite, a young man sat behind the reception desk, presumably the same man on the intercom. His forehead was wrinkled up behind a display screen. A woman was leaning over his shoulder.

"Hi. I'm Hope Avenir, here for the interview."

The two looked up, confused.

"Four o'clock, right? I'm not late, am I?"

The woman said, "There must be a misunderstanding. I know you weren't scheduled." She shook her head. "In any case, I don't have a copy of your CV. I need to review it before the interview. You'll have to reschedule."

"I sent my CV this morning," said Hope.

The young man pointed to the screen. "Here it is. Curriculum vitae. Hope Avenir."

"That's impossible." The woman cocked her head. Then, confusion switched to suspicion. Her eyes narrowed. "You realize I'm going to give you an IQ test?"

"Of course," said Hope.

"I bet." She turned to the man. "I've seen this before. Go to the network room and pull the cables."

"What?"

"You heard me. Pull us off the grid. I want an air gap. No copper between us and the rest of the world. No wireless. No information passes in or out of this office. Go now."

He disappeared into a back room.

She settled her gaze back on Hope. "Percomm on the desk."

Hope pulled out her percomm and put it on the desk, as instructed.

"We get your type in here every so often. Think you're pretty clever by hacking in, do you? Not one for following rules, huh? We'll see how smart you are. Before you can piss in the cup, you have to meet the requirements. But you won't be able to use any of your tricks. Come with me."

Hope followed the woman into the adjacent office.

"Sit there. Tap on the screen when you're ready to begin."

The woman worked patiently at her desk, glancing over occasionally. The test took thirty minutes.

"I'm finished," said Hope.

"How prophetic. I can't agree more." Smirking, the woman tapped her screen and scrolled through the results. *Scroll . . . scroll.* Then her face relaxed, eyebrows up. *Scroll.* Her mouth fell open. She swallowed and looked up.

"I don't think we've been properly introduced," said Hope.

| | 0 | | 0 | | 0

CLICK. LAURA OPENED HER EYES. THE SOUND OF THE BEDROOM'S VENTILATION fan faded to absolute silence. She sat up. The red POWER FAULT letters from the seccomm illuminated the otherwise black bedroom. She reached out with her left arm, groping for Ben, but found only sheet. *Not again. Why is he working in the middle of the night? Chris will have another half-baked chandelier for the trash.*

She crawled across Ben's side of the bed, reached the floor, and stepped into the hallway. The seccomm there too showed POWER FAULT, glowing with enough light for her to find the door to the stairwell. She proceeded down. And as she approached the bottom landing, she found the emergency floodlight blinking sporadically.

"Ben?" she called out. "It happened again."

Step-by-step, she descended to the last flight of stairs. The emergency light acted as a strobe, freezing her motion at unpredictable intervals.

"Ben?"

She crossed the hall to the fuse box and opened it. She realized she didn't know what to do. Ben had always reset it. In

,the flashes of light, she looked for the faulty fuse. The frequency of the blinking slowed. Darkness dominated over light. *They all look the same.* Entire seconds of darkness prevailed between snatches of light. She waited for each successive flash. Her eyes searched the panel during the instant. *There.* She waited for the next flash and then put her hand on the errant switch and pressed. It wouldn't go. She pressed harder. *Oh my god.* She pressed as hard as she could. Nothing. So she put one hand on the edge of the fuse box, put the entire palm of her other hand on the switch, and threw all her weight into it. The plastic corners of the switch pressed into her flesh. *Click.* She nearly fell over when the switch gave way.

But the lights didn't go on. The blinking stopped entirely. She was in total darkness except for the glow of the red POWER FAULT from the seccomm at the end of the hall. That's when she saw it: a giant number six painted sloppily on the door to Ben's lab.

"Ben!" she screamed.

No answer. She inched her way to the door, her hand on the wall as a guide, moving step-by-step. The red seccomm letters shined in her eyes, making the surrounding darkness even blacker. At the lab door, she smelled an odor, like iron. With her fingertips, she touched the paint. It was sticky but dried quickly as she rubbed her fingers together, rolling into chalky bits that fell away. The odor was strong now, almost palpable, like sucking on a penny. *Blood.* "Ben!"

"Six layers." The voice came from behind.

She wanted to turn but was held as if by a spell. She shut her eyes. "Ben!" she screamed again.

"Open your eyes," commanded the voice.

"No!"

"You must witness the final layer of death."

"No, never!"

A hand touched her shoulder. She screamed.

"Open your eyes. Wake up," said Ben.

She sat up in bed.

"You all right?" The hand on her shoulder reached across and around her.

She buried her face and cried.

He held her tight. "Another nightmare?"

She trembled.

"We can't live like this," he said.

Chapter 5

VICTOR TYVOLD, EXECUTIVE ASSISTANT TO AERON SKOTINO OF
TerraHoldings, LLC, waited at the entrance to the data-
storage complex under Yucca Mountain in Nevada. Tyvold
unfolded the auxiliary screen of his percomm. The thin
transparent sheet shimmered with millions of multicolored
pixels showing information transmitted from his central
command center, also located in the complex deep within.
Able to select views from any security camera in or around the
facility, he now watched the one monitoring a black pertran
transporting the leader of the Circle of Six, Aeron Skotino. He
watched security personnel inspect the vehicle. After it departed
the gate, inbound toward the complex, the viewpoint changed
every few seconds along the progression of tracking cameras.

A thundering boom shattered the silence of the cathedral-like
entrance tunnel as the gigantic outer door began to rise, revealing an indigo blanket over the Nevada desert. An enormous
concrete wedge blocking all vehicular traffic hydraulically lowered its facing side, sinking into the driveway. Behind that, six
iron posts, each a foot in diameter, also retracted into the road.
There was now an unobstructed path from the outside. Tyvold
watched across the horizon for the pertran to appear.

He refolded the screen and slipped it back into the breast
pocket of his suit coat. His extensive work during the preced-
ing weeks to re-create the headquarters of the Circle of Six
inside the mountain complex, called the megaron, had kept

him in shirtsleeves. Tyvold normally displayed a more polished image. Yet he was the hands-on type. So he'd forgone his usual suit coat and rolled up his sleeves, literally. At times he'd been indistinguishable from the construction personnel. During the weeks-long project, he'd felt out of his skin. But the hard work was finally over. Now, wearing a suit of sleek gray, with its exquisite lines accentuating his tall, thin frame, he felt normal again.

The first visible sign of the approaching vehicle was a dust cloud under the stars. Then a black dot appeared at the cloud's base, growing larger. The luxury pertran slowed as it entered, passed a series of loading dock doors, and stopped next to Tyvold. Another boom thundered across the space as the outer door lowered. The concrete barrier reappeared, flanked by the posts rising from the road. The barriers locked in place, and the door touched bottom with a resounding thud. The pertran door didn't open until the echo had faded and silence had returned.

Aeron Skotino stepped from the vehicle.

"Host of my god's brother, welcome," said Tyvold.

Skotino said nothing initially. He took a moment to survey the area—visually taking it in, with a rare appreciative expression.

Each of the two men hosted a god, true. And the two gods were brothers, also true. But Victor Tyvold and Aeron Skotino were not related in any way. The only thing they had in common was black hair. Where Skotino's skin was bronze, looking generally Mediterranean in appearance, Tyvold was white—as in white-Anglo-Saxon white. Neither man was fat, but Skotino's build was thick, especially at the chest. Tyvold was long limbed, but not so much as to appear a weakling. Both men dressed finely. But Skotino's suit was classic and conservative, whereas Tyvold's was fitted and fashion forward, complementing his lean build.

Skotino said, "Our new megaron." His voice rumbled across the walls.

For millennia, it had been the practice for Tyvold to report to Skotino regarding the Circle's top priorities each and every time the Circle's leader returned to the megaron. The location and physical structure of the megaron rarely changed over the centuries—only when the technology of the mortals progressed sufficiently to allow an upgrade.

"Yes," said Tyvold. "Construction of our new base of operations is nearly complete. It's unfortunate that the warden forced us to abandon the other megaron."

This was the first time the construction of a new megaron was involuntary. After the warden's teenage host and his friends invaded the previous megaron, its location was no longer secret. The Circle of Six had no choice but to abandon the location and erase any evidence it ever existed.

Skotino continued to admire the facility. "Formidable."

"Yes, the entrance here certainly is. But moving operations to this place adds risk. All our eggs are in one basket. Or shall I say, all our ova are in one womb. In any case, we've expanded the tunnel network to accommodate my command center as well as the sanctuary for the Circle of Six."

"Oubliette?"

The oubliette was always the first topic in the status report to Skotino. The dungeon complex of six holding cells was critical because it held the abducted young women—the pharmakoi—whom the members of the Circle of Six used to see the future. For millennia, the group had monitored the future, looking for any clue signaling the inevitable advance in mortal evolution—a spontaneous genetic alignment in human development that would create the first male fetus with the potential to become Skotino's servant.

"The whole place is an oubliette," said Tyvold. The feature that made an oubliette unique, compared to any given jail or prison, was that it had one, and only one, way in or out—great for trapping prisoners but potentially a nasty place to find yourself if someone's trying to get you from outside. Indeed, the entire fortress under the mountain had one and only one point of passage: the enormous door Skotino had just passed through. Tyvold didn't like it. Yes, it was defensible, but they could also become trapped.

Skotino gave him a you-know-what-I-mean look.

"Yes, we have six holding cells for our pharmakoi. And we even have some storage space for bodies, in case there's any complication with the dumping site."

Fear and pain experienced by the pharmakoi allowed the Circle of Six to glimpse the future. Some women lasted several weeks. Some less. Consequently, another complication of the new location was that it was even farther from the subterranean lake the group used to dump the bodies of the young women after they expired.

"Unbihexium?" asked Skotino.

Unbihexium was always second on Skotino's list. The heavy metal didn't exist on earth. Mortal technology had recently advanced sufficiently to construct an apparatus capable of creating the necessary conditions under which unbihexium would materialize, seemingly from thin air. Unbihexium was the missing ingredient to trigger the biological transformation of a human mortal possessing the rare genetic alignment. The Circle of Six had managed to detect and capture the mother of the first male fetus with the genetic alignment, administer the unbihexium to the boy for seventeen years, and protect him during his hibernation through puberty, to ultimately morph into Skotino's servant.

"Unbihexium harvesting is on schedule."

"The Six?" The status of each member of the Circle of Six was always next on Skotino's list.

"Rick Anderson is overseeing the unbihexium harvesting, as well as his regular duties as CEO of TerraStore."

The mountain complex had always been Anderson's domain. As far as the public was aware, TerraStore Information Storage was a successful data-storage business, a high-tech darling of the quantum-computing age. The mountain was earthquake proof and impervious to a direct nuclear strike. The location was certainly a safe place for the Circle of Six's one and only unbihexium harvesting laboratory. Unfortunately, after Tyvold had been forced to rebuild the headquarters and oubliette inside the fortress under the mountain, he had to deal with Anderson on a regular basis. Both were type A personalities.

Tyvold continued, "Mark Spire is with Ken Barrister, acquiring a new pharmakos."

Spire and Barrister's job was to abduct fresh young women (pharmakoi) to replace those who expired.

Skotino's eyebrow raised at the mention of Barrister's name.

"Don't worry. Barrister's getting used to being a member of the Circle of Six."

"The Bear," Skotino said sarcastically, rolling his eyes.

Ken "the Bear" Barrister was a replacement host and therefore a new member of the Circle of Six. Somehow, the warden and his mortal friends had managed to kill the previous host, Erik "Big Vega" Mathers. The loss of a member of the Circle of Six was unthinkable. Unfortunately, the gods' foresight into their own futures was unreliable. Vega had been a tank of a man. And his god had selected Ken Barrister, a man with a similar physique. Barrister even had a preference for nicknames, just like Vega. And Barrister was stupid, just like Vega. Barrister was having an unusually hard time adapting to life as a member of the Circle of Six.

"I know. I know," said Tyvold. The other members of the Circle of Six were tired of Barrister insisting on being called the Bear. Tyvold shook his head and continued his report. "Anyway, Dr. Betasten is back in Greece, where you left him. And here I am."

Tyvold never reported the location or status of the last member of the Circle of Six. Tyvold never knew the location. So there was no point in mentioning him. That last member completed the Circle of Six. With Skotino leading the entire group, there were seven men in total. Seven gods in total. Six plus one. Skotino the one—one over six, once one over twelve.

Skotino nodded, still admiring.

"Is the boy awake yet?" asked Tyvold.

"Man," corrected Skotino, bringing his focus back to Tyvold and the business at hand. "No."

"Still in hibernation?"

"My servant is unborn."

Tyvold nodded. "I won't ask you when your servant will complete his transformation. I know we haven't had a glimpse into the future for a long time."

"When will Spire return with a fresh pharmakos? So we may have clarity. To commune with our gods. To behold the future."

"Soon. By morning."

| 0 | 0 | 0

"JESUS, MOM. LEAVE ME ALONE."

"Unlock this door right now, Veronica. Or I'm going to have Jim break it down."

"If your fuckhead boyfriend sets one foot in my bedroom, I'll charge his ass with attempted rape."

"You're messaging with that man again. Don't deny it."

"Leave me alone."

"It's not safe."

"Your just jealous. He's more man than your Jim."

Veronica2058: Ugh! My mom won't go away. But my bedroom door's locked. She'll leave after a while.

UrsaVonTrapp: Good, I don't want anything to ruin our

chance to finally meet in person.

Veronica2058: OMG, I've thought of nothing else. The anticipation is killing me.

UrsaVonTrapp: I feel your pain. Let's review the plan.

Veronica2058: OK. I wait until 1:00 a.m. Then I sneak out my window. You'll be waiting in your pertran.

110 110 110

"YOU KNOW, I'VE MESSAGED OVER A THOUSAND CHICKS," SAID KEN BARRISTER. He looked in the rearview mirror to check Mark Spire's reaction. Spire's onyx-black skin with his whisper-thin black Afro and black clothing made him nearly impossible to see sitting in the rear of the pertran. The visible part of him looked like the shadow of a black cat on a moonless night. Spire said nothing. A man of few words, Barrister had learned.

"I picked the username UrsaVonTrapp," said Barrister. "Get it?"

No response.

"Cuz we've set a trap. Get it? You know von Trapp, right? *The Sound of Music?* Chicks really dig that older dude, singin' and all. And *ursa* is like a foreign word for *bear*, and—"

"It's Latin, dumbass. Just shut up."

Barrister was trying really hard to fit in. He'd noticed the members of the Circle of Six seemed to get off on foreign words. *Backfired this time.* Barrister looked at the time—12:56 a.m. Not much longer. "*Pharmakoi*—the word you use for the girls we nab—it's Latin too, right?"

"Greek."

"What's the big fascination with all the foreign words?"

"History," said Spire. "Pharmakoi are the catalyst in a ritual between a god and its mortal host."

"What do you mean by *catalyst?*"

"Human sacrifice. But not death. Pain. Fear. Anticatharsis. Anagnorisis."

Whatever. Pain and fear experienced by a human captive allowed the members of the Circle of Six, in a process they called clarity, to see the future. *Or control the future?* Barrister wasn't sure. The whole thing had been very confusing. He wanted to ask Spire more questions, especially about the god who now possessed him. But it wasn't the time.

"Here she comes," said Barrister, looking at the side mirror. The young woman came bouncing down the sidewalk under the glow of streetlights. "Wow, she's a real spinner." He glanced at Spire. "You know, you can't trust the pics they send you. Once I thought I was meeting a runway model. But she ended up being a cow. She acted like nothing—"

"Just shut up," said Spire. "Remember. Practice using the guilt trip. No need to use force. She'll do whatever you ask."

Guilt trip. Of all the things Barrister was supposed to learn, the guilt-trip technique was one he could do with ease. How do you make someone act against their own values, beliefs, and inclinations? Guilt. Powerful shit. And the weapon of choice for the Circle of Six.

110 110 110

VERONICA SPOTTED THE PERTRAN RIGHT WHERE HE SAID IT WOULD BE. SHE glanced back to make sure no one was following. *This is so exciting!* She reached the last tree between her and the vehicle. Using her percomm's camera, she checked her hair, adjusting the left side by dabbing with her fingers. Then she pursed her lips and wiped a speck of lipstick from the crease of her mouth. She'd considered lip gloss initially but didn't want to get him too excited. The lipstick made her lips the focal point of her round, heart-shaped face, drawing attention away from her wide-set eyes, which she considered her least attractive feature. The choice of lip color was always complicated by her curly red hair. Boys either loved redheads or put them at the bottom of their list, no in-between.

She dashed to the passenger's side and hopped in. *Wow.* He looked just like the pics he'd sent. Huge, strapping chest and thick arms with muscles bulging out from his short-sleeved shirt. Brown hair. And his face had that all-American boyish look. *Jock-pot!* "I can't believe we're finally together," she said. "Don't forget, I need to be back in an hour."

"I can't believe we're finally together either."

His words matched the response she expected, but his tone implied an impending consequence, like lighting a fuse. She had a feeling like she was riding up the first hill of a roller coaster, with the clattering sound fading to the rear as she approached the top, feeling the anticipation of that first free fall.

He said, "I'm glad you're away from your mom."

She swallowed. "Just for an hour."

"You're twenty-four years old," he said. "You're still living off your mom."

Now his tone hung in the air somehow, suspended, as if sitting in the first car of the roller coaster train inching over the first drop.

He said, "Your mother is a prisoner because of you."

Her vision began to tunnel, closing in on his eyes. She heard the throb of blood coursing past her own eardrums. The street and houses, visible through the window behind him, seemed to stretch away into the distance.

"No, I . . ." The roller coaster plummeted. *Oh god, it's true. I've done nothing with my life. I don't even look for a job. I'm a parasite. Mom's only with Jim because of his money. I made her dependent. He takes advantage of her. And she lets him. Just to support me. How could I be so selfish?* Filled with shame, she longed for a way to extricate herself from the situation, to not be the problem.

"You can come with me," he said.

"What?"

"Jim has your mother locked in chains. You're the key to setting her free. Let's be together. I'll take care of you."

That's it. I'll have my own life. I won't be a burden to her anymore. Her vision returned to normal. The stabbing feeling of guilt was replaced by a deep yearning to be independent.

"Yes," she said.

"Your mom won't understand right away. She'll try to find you."

Veronica pulled out her percomm and handed it to him.

He crushed it like it was a soda cracker.

Chapter ΣΤ'

CHRIS GROANED AS LUCKY'S TOENAILS PRESSED INTO HIS SKIN. HE squinted from the morning sun shining into his bedroom. He kept his eyes closed. The fog of sleep returned. Then a wet nose sniffed under his chin and ear. "You're not allowed on my bed," Chris grumbled. He rolled over, too relaxed to command Lucky to get off. Annoyance returned: Lucky was really pushing it.

Chris covered his head. Lucky's nails and rough pads continued to scrape against his skin. It seemed deliberate. Chris was about to shove him to the floor when the simultaneously familiar and alien sensation registered. *A smell.* The pain on his skin had triggered the connection to the warden, which in turn opened a connection to Lucky. *A smell,* he thought again. *Of what?* Chris calmed his mind, allowing the warden to fuse with his thoughts, helping him to explore the sensation, making the sensation more vivid while also tapping into Lucky's scent memory. *Master Cohen!*

Chris jumped from the bed with Lucky right behind him. He made his way down the steps but stopped when he heard voices coming from the kitchen. His karate instructor, Bruce Cohen, was talking to his mom and dad. Chris was only wearing boxers, so he dashed back upstairs.

Did his mom finally sell the house? Is Bruce here to arrange for transportation to the safe house? Chris sat on his bed, put on shorts, and then grabbed a T-shirt. "Thanks, pal." He patted Lucky on the head.

"It's all settled then," said Ben, as Chris entered the kitchen.

Bruce was leaning against the counter. Seeing Chris, he stood straight and extended his hand. It was a formality, but also a subtle reminder of the training Chris had received over the years. Respect. Bruce Cohen—or Master Cohen, as Chris had addressed him at the karate studio—taught Chris, Al, Katie, and all his other students about respect and etiquette. He taught Chris to have a strong handshake, to look the person in the eye, and to have a voice that was loud and proud. Chris did just that. "Hey, Bruce." At six feet, Bruce was about three inches shorter than Chris, but he was stockier and quite powerful looking. His years in the Israeli special forces had chiseled him into a human weapon.

"What's all settled?" asked Chris after the handshake.

"Your parents convinced me not to put you all in the program."

The program. A way to hide off the grid from the group of men from Nevada.

The rescue mission to Nevada to find the kidnapped girls had been a disaster but could've been much worse. Without Bruce, they never would've survived the confrontation with the Omega Force.

Between the attempt to rescue the abducted young women, killing one of the kidnappers in the park, and battling the Omega Force, Chris and his friends had become targets of three groups: the men in Nevada, the FBI, and the US military. The men from Nevada were after Chris and his friends as revenge for exposing their kidnapping ring. After Al killed one of the men in the park, the FBI started their relentless investigation. And when Chris and his friends tried to find the kidnapped women, they inadvertently clashed with the US military's counterterrorism unit, the Omega Force. Without Bruce's experience and weapons, the rescue mission would have turned into a suicide mission.

Bruce had arranged for a witness protection program of sorts. It seemed the only option. But Chris never wanted to hide. He was relieved to hear his parents had given up on the idea. He could go to his regular school for his senior year. He could hang out with Al and Katie. He could find Hope. And he could try to talk to her, to apologize.

"I didn't have a say in that decision in the first place," Chris reminded them. He surprised himself with the immaturity of the statement. But he was feeling raw. Still, he never wanted to be treated like a child, so it frustrated him when he caught himself acting like one.

"Chris, the problem is you're not sharing information," said Laura. "After I walked out of the kitchen yesterday, you said the men in Nevada are *not* trying to kill me. Trust me, young man, I can assure you, after those two men broke into this house, I'm certain they were trying to kill me. You have information you haven't shared."

"No. I'm saying we don't know *what* information to believe. Why should I share something that could be wrong? Or worse, a trick? We shouldn't make decisions on that information."

"Enough with the logic games," said Ben. "Tell us what happened in Vegas. The facts. Don't interpret. Just say it. You need to trust that we can be just as circumspect as you."

Chris's shoulders slumped.

Laura prompted, "You said the situation is different because I'm not your birth mother."

Chris wasn't standing straight now, wasn't looking anyone in the eye, and his voice wasn't loud or proud. "The man who grabbed Hope seemed to be the one in charge. Before I could find where he'd taken her, he had time to hurt her by dislocating her shoulder. I could feel the waves of pain and fear from her. My connection to the warden became intense, like with the malted milk, but in sort of an inverse way. I don't know how to explain it. But I was able to understand things I hadn't before, like I was seeing a different side of the warden, hidden until then. It became clear to me that the man—along with each of the other men we encountered in Vegas—also have some kind of warden or alien surrounding them. Hope's pain and fear let the man connect with his warden-like alien to learn things about me."

"Like what?"

"He explained the six layers of death—the ritual that could send the warden away forever. Each victim must witness the death of a loved one before they themselves are murdered. The final layer—or final act in the ritual—was that I, as the warden's host, needed to witness the death of my mother. While Hope was in pain, he learned that I was adopted."

"I see," said Ben. "The ritual won't work because your birth mother is already dead. That's great news. It means the warden can't be killed."

Chris sat down at the kitchen table. Lucky followed and buried his head between Chris's legs. Chris scratched his neck and ears.

"There's more?"

Chris nodded. "The man also said that it's all part of the warden's master plan. He said it was the warden who killed my birth mother. He said the warden made her experience horrible agony on purpose. He said the warden used her pain to take control of me. He said the warden kept her alive long enough for the paramedics to whisk me away. He said the warden murdered my birth mother to ensure its own invulnerability. He said the warden is using me, and will sacrifice any of us for its own purposes." Chris looked at them. "He said, he said, he said. We can't trust anything he said. So that's the 'information.' Happy? Well, here's the worst part. After I heard what the leader said—even though I don't trust it—I started to question my trust in the warden. Think about it. All the work we're doing to get the warden's words and interpret them? What if it's all part of a deception to make me do the warden's bidding?"

Chris wondered if any part of his life was founded in truth. *Why me?*

| |0 | |0 | |0

"SIR, YOU DIDN'T HAVE TO COME DOWN HERE YOURSELF."

"I'll decide what I need to do, Lieutenant," said Major Nolan.

Inside the huge, hastily erected inflatable dome located on the grounds of the Philadelphia Transit Authority, the disassembled masstran rested at one end. Dozens of parts were spread out, all equidistant from one another, and all with a small card listing a description and evidence number. Floodlights illuminated the entire scene. Several cameras atop tripods targeted specific parts. Six mechanics wearing plastic suits stood by, apparently happy for a break from the mind-numbing work.

"Walk me through it," said Nolan.

The young lieutenant stepped across the naked drivetrain, toward a set of bus seats. "Your Caucasian male, John Doe, sat here. Then held those rails over there." He pointed. "Then also sat in these seats here."

"Who was on the bus with him?"

"The civilian runners. We know that for sure."

"Who else?"

The lieutenant's expression showed frustration. "Half the city, Major. It's a bus."

Nolan let the crack go. *He's right. This is fruitless.* The evidence was in the worst possible place to isolate DNA: public transportation. *A Poger cattle car.* Nolan stepped across the parts, then looked left. He pulled out his percomm. "What's the progress on the DNA from the skin cells of our John Doe?"

"Negative, sir," said the voice over the comm. "The LIMDIS can't be bypassed."

"I assigned our best coders and signal analysts, and you have nothing?"

"It's as if our own systems are fighting us. I've never seen anything like it."

Nolan took another step in the maze of parts. "Keep looking. I want that DNA correlated." He ended the comm. Then he smirked.

"What are you thinking, sir?" asked the lieutenant.

"An infamous criminal in the 1900s, John Dillinger, tried to minimize his evidence trail by burning off his fingerprints with acid. Don't ask me why he didn't simply wear gloves. Anyway, the procedure was more or less successful at permanently removing his fingerprints. Unfortunately for Dillinger, the resulting surface wasn't completely smooth and it left a signature of its own. In the end, the authorities could just as easily determine that the not-a-fingerprint fingerprint was evidence of John Dillinger." Nolan turned to the lieutenant. "We know we have a hit whenever we get the LIMDIS result. When that happens, we can catch John Doe. I want to be notified immediately when any scanner or sniffer detects DNA from a subject whose identity is protected by LIMDIS."

| IO | IO | IO

SKOTINO'S FINGERTIPS CARESSED THE CHEESE GRATER HANGING ON THE pegboard of the holding cell deep within the oubliette of the Circle of Six's Yucca Mountain facility. Tyvold had done a beautiful job of preparing each of the six rooms for their pharmakoi. This new oubliette was a near-perfect replica of the deep dungeon in their previous headquarters.

The cheese grater was one of the few tools that generated fear in the minds of their captives even before it touched flesh. It seemed that every female mortal had cut herself with one during her lifetime. That was also true of the razor blade, but it was such a crude instrument of obvious danger. The cheese grater, on the other hand, was deceptively treacherous. An elegant tool to conjure fear. Skotino only needed to dangle the cheese grater above a pharmakos's skin to generate a fear response nearly capable of triggering clarity—the connection to his god, allowing a glimpse into the future.

Skotino's percomm vibrated, piercing the nostalgia. "Speak."

"Dr. Betasten is on his way to see you," said Tyvold.

"I ordered him to stay at the Venizelos estate to monitor the rebirth of my servant."

"He claims he must commune with his god."

Damn the warden. One complication after another as a result of his meddling. Skotino reminded himself not to underestimate the warden. *If the son of my own god has forced Dr. Betasten to seek communion, then it's probably best to heed.* "Where is he now?"

"Arrived by scramjet and is already through the front gate. He's in a cart, speeding your way. He'll be there in a few minutes."

Skotino ended the comm and exited the holding cell. He walked to the end of the corridor to the access point—the one and only way in or out of the oubliette. Just inside the access door was Tyvold's secondary security station, a backup for the primary station located in the facility above. Monitors lined the walls, giving Tyvold, or any member of the Six, eyes on the entire area and complete control of the facility's systems.

Skotino watched the image on the display as the outer door to the oubliette's access corridor opened and Dr. Betasten waddled inside. The door closed behind him. Before opening the inner door, Skotino tapped the intercom button. "You should have told me you were coming."

"Host of my god's father, I hear and obey, but . . ."

"But what?"

"Where is Barrister?"

"He left an hour ago. Why?"

"What future events did he reveal during his clarity communion?"

Nothing, thought Skotino. He'd assumed the Circle of Six simply needed to continue clarity sessions until the gods foretold the future. However, Dr. Betasten's implication was unmistakable. *Is Barrister's struggle to reach clarity simply a result of his stupidity? Or is there another reason? Again, best to heed the will of the gods.* Skotino tapped the button to open the inner door.

Dr. Betasten appeared in the security substation's doorway.

"Veronica," said Skotino. "Room six."

Dr. Betasten's eyes drifted closed. He licked his lips. He rubbed his left hand against his side and tilted his head back slightly. His hand rubbed harder, as if trying to scrape indelible ink from his palm. The rubbing continued, harder still, and at the point it seemed his lab coat would ignite from the sheer friction, his eyes snapped open. His lips shaped the words of the familiar and ancient hymn. Skotino could easily follow along even though Dr. Betasten's lips carried no sound.

Hear me, son of the god who ruled over twelve, now over six

Hide the before, peer to beyond, our fate unfix

Humanity's false beauty, infected with the disease of mortality

For thee, I wield the threat of pain, now and unto eternity

Open my eyes and reveal future's grip

For the chance of reality's path doth tip

Dr. Betasten proceeded down the corridor, pounding his left hand on the wall as he went and yelling his name. "Betasten." *Bang.* "Betasten." *Bang.* He repeated the act five full times. Facing the door to room number six, he pounded on the door a final time and yelled, "Betasten is here." A scream came from within. He turned the knob and stepped inside.

"Brilliance personified," Skotino said with veneration. He watched the events unfold on the display monitoring room six. The waves of fear from Veronica reached even to where he sat, intensifying artfully, like a symphony building toward a grand crescendo.

"LOOK, I KNOW WE GOT OFF TO A BAD START," SAID NANCY HERNANDEZ IN THE FLC office. "The work you did on the security protocols of our logic controllers in only a few days is amazing. I hope you can forgive my initial reaction."

"No apology necessary," said Hope. "It's completely understandable. It's my own fault, after circumventing your hiring process. I took a risk."

"But without prior work experience, you never would've made the first round." Nancy smiled.

Hope nodded.

"Well, go home. You put in a solid day's work. Get a good night's sleep. I'll see you tomorrow."

It had been only days, yet the ride home on the masstran was becoming routine. Hope kept to herself, pleased the other passengers did the same.

Checking her percomm, she registered that the attempts from Chris were getting fewer and farther between. Staying on top of his movements was more challenging while at her new job. She had her AI bots handling the predictable stuff, but if he got himself in a real jam, her reaction time would be crucial. Working on something other than FLC's logic controllers was difficult to hide. She asked SalaciousFrog and her other online friends for help, but there were certain techniques she didn't want even them to know. Once Nancy became comfortable with her work and trusted her, she could work from home, or anywhere. There was no reason to physically be at the office. It would be easier, then, to juggle priorities without drawing attention.

Along the walk from the masstran stop to her apartment complex, she took a short detour, stopping at the corner store for a few items.

Phwap, phwap, phwap. The little dog was awake when she entered the lobby.

"She's back," called Toothless.

There was a creak and crash from inside the booth. After picking up his chair, the manager appeared at the window above the counter.

Phwap, phwap.

Hope walked over, bent down, and petted the dachshund under the bench, scratching behind the ears and getting the same reaction as before.

"I told you you'd like petting my wiener."

Indeed. She was at crotch level. She kept her cool. She just stared up at Toothless. His disgusting grin faded. The creepy-old-man act gave way, revealing an actual person. Toothless sat up a little straighter and looked repentant.

"What's your wiener's name?" asked Hope, still petting. Then she added, "If you say Johnson, it won't be funny."

"Ha!" The manager's laugh was involuntary.

Still kneeling, Hope looked back at the manager. He tried to hide his appreciation of her sense of humor and returned to his crude scowl. Sort of. But, like a *Phantom of the Opera* mask coming loose, the scowl didn't really fit anymore, and he struggled to keep it on his face.

"Tinkerbell," answered Toothless. "She's old. Like me."

Hope pulled out the small pouch of dog treats she'd purchased from the store. "OK to give her one?"

Toothless nodded.

Hope took out a treat and brought it to Tinkerbell's mouth.

Laying on her side, she sniffed it but didn't take it. *Phwap, phwap.*

"She'll eat it eventually," said Toothless. "Just leave it. I think she'd just rather be pet right now."

Hope petted the dog's short brown fur until her knees started to ache. She stood up, pulled the package of beef jerky from her bag, and tossed it at the glass barrier of the booth. It hit the glass just above the retractable basket and fell into the tray.

The manager's expression brightened. His mask was gone completely now. Suddenly he looked very innocent, as if a small boy was hiding inside. He looked expectantly at Hope.

"Go on," she said.

The manager pulled the handle and opened the tray from his side of the glass.

"No jerky for me?" asked Toothless.

Both Hope and the manager slanted a look at Toothless.

"I'll give you a piece, and you can suck on it," said the manager, genuinely wanting to share with his friend.

"Yeah," said Hope, "now that I pet your wiener, you can suck his jerky."

Both men laughed.

Inside the apartment, Sue was waiting. Hope went straight to the bedroom.

Only a few minutes passed before Sue poked her head in. "I picked up your school supplies."

Hope didn't say anything. She crossed her legs in front of her display.

"Won't you tell me where you've been going off to for so long?"

Without glancing up, she said, "I'm not going back to school. I got a job."

I I 0   I I 0   I I 0

"*SEÑOR HECTOR ELADIO, SÍ, TENGO LA RESERVA AQUÍ,*" SAID THE HOTEL DESK clerk. "*¿Y eso es por tres noches?*"

"*Sí,*" replied Eladio.

"Ah, a US citizen, I see here. Welcome to Mexico. Please, present your passport."

Eladio placed his percomm on the desk's surface at the designated spot.

"Thank you. One moment, please, while I finalize authentication to your room."

The hotel was lavish by American standards but middle-of-the-road for Mexico. Tijuana had some of the most luxurious spots in the world, enjoyed by Mexicans as well as American Hillites from San Diego and other parts of the United States. Eladio would've preferred to be closer to the nightclub—the one that intelligence reports indicated Juan Rodriguez frequented—but this hotel was all he could afford. Still, the task should be easy. He had three weeks to find Rodriguez, make contact, and learn the details of the former Omega Force team leader's last mission. Rodriguez may be the only person with information leading to the true source of Major Nolan's data breach. Unfortunately, if Rodriguez never showed up to the nightclub, Eladio's so-called vacation would drain his life savings before the three weeks were up.

"There you are, *señor*. Room three-thirty-three. Elevators to your right. Enjoy your stay. Do you need help with your luggage?"

"*No, gracias.*" Eladio picked up his duffle bag and plastic case.

Room 333 was high enough to provide a decent view of the main drag. Eladio popped the clips on the plastic case and opened the lid to reveal his recon gear, each item nestled in protective foam. He pulled out the digital binoculars and stepped to the window. "Computer, open drape. Open blind."

The drapes of the window he faced parted mechanically, just as the liquid crystals in the glass faded from opaque to transparent. He raised the binoculars and peered as far down the street as possible, into the rough part of Tijuana. The club was deep in the old section of the city.

Around midnight, the city's nightlife finally settled down. Most of the storefront lights were dark, and few people walked the streets. He took a circuitous route to his destination, making sure he wasn't followed. Even before he reached the club, he could hear the music and raucous crowd inside. *This party's still rockin'.* Step one of Eladio's plan was to set up a surveillance network around the club. Software would identify Rodriguez by face or gait. When Rodriguez went to the club, so would Eladio.

From a distance, Eladio watched the establishment empty over the course of three hours. Groups and couples came out laughing, hooting, and giggling. The women made an immediate impression on Eladio. *Chola girls*, he thought. His apartment, on the Marine base in Virginia, had a high percentage of first-generation Latinos. Being Latino himself, he hadn't realized how Americanized his life had become by comparison. The Latinas back home were nothing like these girls. *Wow.* He literally had to adjust his fly. *This is where the beautiful people live.* He allowed himself a brief fantasy of having a girl like one of these on his arm. *Gorgeous.*

The club quieted until the only activity was from the rear of the building as the bar staff finished dishwashing. The sound of splashing water and clinking glass was interrupted occasionally when the rear door opened in a yawn of light as the trash was hauled to the back dumpster. Shortly after three o'clock, the activity finally faded to dead calm.

Eladio jumped the back fence, found a spot for the first microcam, and positioned it to cover the back door. He placed several more around the building, giving him complete coverage, with a special concentration on the entrance. With his percomm, he checked the satellite connection to the devices. Over the following days, all Eladio had to do was watch and wait. Like a spider, he would race to this very spot the moment Rodriguez stepped into his web.

CHAPTER 7

"COMMUNICATION FOR CHRIS LUMIÈRE," SAID THE FEMALE VOICE OF THE Richardses' seccomm system.

Chris pressed another rep with the dumbbells and ignored the announcement. Yet he was curious because he'd never heard the announcement sound like that before. He was working out in the extra bedroom, and he'd left his percomm in his own room. So it made sense for the computer to notify him. But it usually said "comm" instead of "communication." *Odd. Since when did the seccomm system get so formal?*

"Communication for Chris Lumière."

"Take a message," said Chris, starting another set.

"Unable to comply. Federal law requires receipt of communication in person. Communication for Chris Lumière."

What the? Chris put the dumbbells down. "All right, all right." He stepped to the seccomm and saw it was from the FBI. *What do they want now?* He tapped the screen.

It was Agent Harrison via vidcomm. "Morning, sport."

"What do you want?"

"You. Down here. Today. Eleven o'clock."

"I was already there this week."

"You prefer ten?" asked Harrison, with a twinkle in his eye.

"No, I can make it by eleven. But tell me why."

"You'll find out when you get here," Harrison said. "Actually, it doesn't really matter, does it?" He grinned.

102   ANDREW HUNKINS

"So you're just going to wreck my life until I say what you want to hear?"

Harrison shrugged. "Sounds good to me. Anyway, if you're not here at eleven I'll have you picked up. And I'll warn you now, the cost is billed to the citizen. By the way, I should also mention that the fees are a pretty nice source of revenue for us. Very profitable. Trust me, you don't want to see the bill." The comm ended.

Oh, for crying out loud. Chris picked up his water bottle from the weight bench but stopped before leaving the room. He recalled the time Hope stayed with them, at the beginning of the summer. *This was her room.* She cried out one night, during a nightmare—no doubt caused by everything leading up to the day the police arrested her dad for domestic abuse and Hope came to live with them while things got sorted out. She'd stood at this very spot. He'd comforted her. She'd wanted more. Now he wished he hadn't held back. *Harrison'll go after her as soon as she's eighteen. Her network skills are amazing, but can she stop them from just picking her up? She's untouchable in cyberspace but powerless in the physical world.*

"Where are you going?" asked Laura, coming out from the kitchen after hearing him in the back hall.

Chris explained while he finished getting ready to leave with Lucky. "It seems I have no choice but to go downtown to see Harrison again."

"But you need to meet with Katie and Al for more work on the warden's words. Look, I thought a lot about what you said: that the men from Nevada aren't going to kill me now that they know I'm not your birth mother. But I want you to understand. Losing you is worse than anything those men could do to me. Your dad and I will do everything we can to help interpret the warden's words. He's getting the mind-reader program ready for a scan this afternoon so we can talk to the warden. We need to find out who those men from Nevada are, what they're up to, and how to stop them."

"I know," said Chris. "I'll let Katie and Al know I'll be late."

"You should've told your dad you were working on the words when he called you at Katie's house to come home and restart the chandelier."

"It wouldn't have made a difference. You both were so focused on the FBI interview."

"OK. I understand now that the FBI is secondary to learning how the warden can help us."

"I know. Unfortunately, it'll have to wait."

"Chris, if we're staying in this house, we have to have a new plan."

"I know, Mom. Like I said, I have no choice."

"And you still haven't put up the chandelier."

"I know. Holy cow."

"But—"

"Mom. Jeez. Just leave me alone, would you? Come on, Lucky."

Chris made his way to the end of the neighborhood, toward the masstran stop on the other side of the park. He tried to feel like he was in control of his life, even though recent events proved otherwise. He hadn't even made it out of the park when Lucky bolted for a squirrel. *Not you too?* "Hey. Lucky! Heel!"

Lucky raced toward the tree as the squirrel leapt onto the trunk and scrambled to the opposite side. But instead of circling under the squirrel, Lucky went right past the tree and vanished into the woods along the park's edge. The squirrel spiraled up the trunk, keeping to the opposite side from Lucky, away from the threat, as squirrels tend to do.

"Lucky!" called Chris. He waited.

Lucky came barreling back with something in his mouth. He dropped it at Chris's feet. It was the piece of gum—the special gum Katie made with malted milk powder to let Chris access enhanced abilities from the warden. The wax paper was wet and covered with dirt and leaf particles.

"I should never have doubted you. You've got my back, don't you?"

Lucky jumped to Chris's side and sat at his heel. The squirrel was upside down now, limbs splayed and tail twitching as he taunted Lucky for another go.

Chris wiped the gum off as best as he could and put it in his pocket. "All right, let's go."

110 110 110

"PUPPY? WHAT DO WE NEED A PUPPY FOR?" ASKED BARRISTER, IN THE pertran outside the animal shelter.

"A *female* puppy," corrected Spire. "A meeting of the Circle of Six requires an expiation."

"You and your fancy words. I have no idea what that means."

"A sacrifice. You must understand, after communing with your god."

"I haven't been able to."

Spire gave him a disgusted look.

"That feeling you call *clarity*? I'm not able to reach it," said Barrister sheepishly.

"It requires pain and fear."

"I know. It's not working for me."

"Host of my god's brother, you're an idiot."

"Nobody teaches me anything. Like this puppy thing. Why do we need to sacrifice a puppy?"

Spire rolled his eyes. "Skotino is host of the god of gods, ruler over six, once one over twelve."

"We're the six, right? Then who are the other six to make twelve?"

"If you shut up, I'll tell you." Spire shook his head. "The other six are female. Skotino's god—the god of gods—locked them away."

Barrister started to utter *Where?*, but the look on Spire's face said *Shut up*.

"Mortals call the place Tartaros. It's as much a force as it is a place," said Spire. "Any meeting of the Circle of Six draws out the female gods. The power to release them comes from a source mortals call Hecate—often depicted in triplicate, always associated with dogs. To keep the females locked in Tartaros, a sacrifice is made—a damnation against Hecate."

Barrister just looked blankly.

"Look, English isn't the best language to explain this stuff. Older mortal languages are better. But like I said, you're an idiot. Now, recite the plan."

"We go inside and ask to look at the puppies," said Barrister. "While I distract the manager, you snatch a female pup. Meanwhile Tyvold will make sure nothing is recorded on their seccomm."

| | 0 | | 0 | | 0

"HEY, KID, CONTROL YOUR DOG."

Lucky barked again.

"Sorry," said Chris to the passengers crowded on the masstran. Chris had only been aboard for a minute when the barking started.

Lucky barked again.

"Don't worry, I'll get him to stop." Chris crouched down. "Hey, what is it with you?"

Lucky nosed around Chris's pocket—the one with the gum.

Chris pulled out the morsel. It was dry now but still caked with grime. "You want me to chew it?"

Lucky wagged his tail.

Chris tried to peel back the wax paper. The bright-blue gum was completely fused to it. He couldn't unwrap it without gouging into the gum. The edge where the paper seemed somewhat loose looked like it had mold growing under it. It felt slimy. "Ick. No way."

Lucky barked in Chris's face.

"Hey, do I need to come over there and throw you off?"

"Sorry. Sorry. Won't happen again." Chris looked at Lucky. "You better be right." Chris brought the gum to his nose. He could faintly smell the chocolate flavor, but that was nothing compared to the musty odor. He closed his eyes and put the gum in his mouth, paper and all. The sand crunched under his teeth. Slime oozed out and it tasted like the bottom of a lawn mower. But, after only seconds, Chris was not alone. The feeling was like being lost in a forest for days and finally hearing the call of distant rescuers. Or like sitting on a chair in an empty room and feeling the residual warmth from the person who had sat there only moments before. Time seemed to stop. Then the connection to Lucky hit hard. *Hope!* Chris shot bolt upright, barely missing the chin of the person next to him. *Hope's scent is on this bus. She's been on this very bus, this very route.*

Lucky turned and sniffed down the aisle, weaving between passengers, zigzagging from one section of seats to the next. Chris closed his eyes. His sense of time seemed to blur with his sense of smell. No, it was *Lucky's* sense of time. Lucky knew how long it had been since Hope was on the bus. Chris had heard about research explaining how dogs could tell time. For example, to know when their owners would return home from work simply by the decay of the owner's scent. Lucky knew, as did Chris now, when Hope was last on the masstran, almost to the minute.

Chris opened his eyes and flipped through the bus schedule on his percomm. She was here the day before, at 5:33 p.m., at a time when the bus would've been on a route out of the city, bound for the burbs.

Lucky returned, nuzzling his head against Chris's thigh. Chris rubbed his dog behind the ears. "Nice work, pal. We found her." Chris had an even more powerful thought. He could sense that she'd ridden the bus at the same time over the prior three days. The chance was good that she'd be on again that evening. *I can meet her. Tonight. I'll wait in the city after meeting with Harrison and then ride the route home. She'll get on. We'll be together. I can apologize.*

Reaching his stop by the Philly police station, he and Lucky got out. He walked the few blocks to the corner by the police station. Chris noticed a section of grass bending from a breeze. Oddly, he couldn't feel any breeze himself. The blowing air seemed to be coming from an unusual pillar or box contraption next to a fire hydrant. It looked like a municipal electrical box, but instead of being painted green, it was black, much narrower, and had vents along the sides. When Chris stepped closer, the breeze got stronger. Chris realized the breeze was coming toward him—away from the box. Stranger still, the breeze seemed to start near where Chris stood, not from the box. Text on the side of the pillar said, DO NOT TOUCH. FEDERAL LAW PROHIBITS TAMPERING WITH, DISABLING, OR DESTROYING THIS DEVICE. VIOLATORS WILL BE PROSECUTED. He stepped away, and the wind subsided.

Chris searched his mind for an explanation from the warden. He sensed relevance but wasn't able to learn what was going on. Just in case, he snapped a picture of the box with his percomm. Something to investigate later.

Like last time, outside the police station entrance, FBI Special Agent Harrison was waiting for him. Harrison ushered Chris through the security scanner while Lucky waited outside.

"Your father gave me some bullshit story about why the scanners don't work on you," said Harrison after sitting down in the interrogation room. "He said it was a medical condition."

"That's right."

"Bullshit. It's your girlfriend. Hope Avenir. She's manipulating our systems. She's a Hood."

THE CIRCULAR SANCTUARY INSIDE THE YUCCA MOUNTAIN FACILITY WAS ALSO
a near-perfect replica of the one in the abandoned desert
compound. *Tyvold did an excellent job*, thought Skotino. With
the ceremonial gathering of the Circle of Six in progress,
Skotino said, "We begin."

"We begin," chanted the six men around Skotino.

"We begin for the purpose of restoring the earth to that of
the beginning time. Yes, the beginning time, the glorious time
before humans infested beautiful terra. A time when mortals
worshiped their gods. A humbler time. My servant shall cull the
human herds, yet spare a small population of worshipers. Yes, a
population managed by my servant, as a shepherd manages a
flock. The gods will again have free selection of young rams as
hosts. The hosts will again have free selection of young ewes in
which to reach clarity, to commune, to glimpse the future. Yes,
by the hand of my servant, we will return to the time of Eden.
For the gods."

"For the gods," the group intoned.

Skotino turned to Dr. Betasten. "Host of my god's son, tell
us the future revealed during communion with your god."

Dr. Betasten sat across from Skotino. The canine sacrifice was
in the crate between them, placed in the very center of the room.
The light from six candles, one behind each member of the
Circle of Six, cast flickering shadows across the face of each man.

"Host of my god's father, in six days' time, fecund terra will
become the rebirth place of your servant. The required preparations are clear to me now."

"Tell us," said Skotino as he raised his arms up from his sides.

"First, we must prepare contact lenses so your servant's eyes
will appear normal. Second, because his teeth will fall out immediately after rebirth, we must prepare dentures so he will appear
to have teeth.

"We've known since the time of his human birth that his cloaca is located at the anterior orifice as opposed to the posterior orifice—meaning his tongue performs the reproductive function of a penis. But I've now learned that his cloaca has matured while in hibernation. When fully engorged, the phallus is significantly longer than an erect human penis—or tongue for that matter. Further, the mature cloaca is prehensile, similar to the end of an elephant's trunk. In any case, this all leads to the third preparation: padding must be affixed at the groin area so he'll appear to have genitalia in the normal place for a human male.

"Fourth, the naming ceremony must be held in the ocean, not fresh water, in order to populate his cloaca with polychaete worms that will live symbiotically within the organ.

"Fifth, his body will begin to eliminate excess unbihexium from his bloodstream. We must collect his urine in order to reuse the unbihexium, but also to avoid leaving behind a trail of evidence. The residual unbihexium, if detected, could be used to trace him. We must prepare a special catheter and filtration system.

"As the sixth and final preparation, we must train him to be cognizant of his weight. For example, getting in or out of a pertran. The vehicle's suspension will betray him. No mortal should be allowed to witness discrepancies that point to his extraordinary weight. It defies explanation."

"And what of the required details for the naming ceremony?" asked Skotino.

"Host of my god's father, the details of the ritual were not revealed to me."

Skotino turned to Barrister and glared. *The Bear.* Skotino couldn't deny the thought that the Circle of Six must be missing information, crucial information that Barrister's god would normally foretell through clarity communions. Skotino had no explanation why Barrister was not able to commune with his god. *The Circle of Six must proceed with the information we have. Nothing must interfere with the rebirth of the servant.*

| |0 | |0 | |0

AGAIN, LUCKY WASN'T WHERE CHRIS HAD LEFT HIM. HE FOUND HIS DOG AT THE same spot as before, around the side of the police station, watching the rear parking lot through the fence, black nose twitching. Instead of hauling Lucky away, he let his dog scan and sniff. Chris wished he had the connection to Lucky now, but the gum had lost its power halfway through the three hours with Harrison. In fact, the thought that he would see Hope again in only a few more hours was the only thing that kept him sane during Harrison's incessant questioning.

Chris commed Katie to let her and Al know he'd have to postpone meeting them, which meant putting off the work on interpreting the warden's words.

"What do you mean?" she demanded. Chris heard her talking to Al in the background. "He's not coming at all now," she said.

He heard Al's voice. "What? Give it here." There was a tussling sound.

"Chris," came Katie's voice eventually. He guessed she'd retained or regained possession of her percomm.

"I'll explain later."

"What do you have to do *now*? Harrison's unexpected meeting was delay enough. If it's so critical, we'll come help you."

"No, it's not like that."

"It better be like that. What could be more important? Look, Chris, we need to dissect the words from the warden. You can't expect Al and me to make any real progress without you."

"I know, Katie." There was barely enough time to travel home and back. He'd have to end the exploration of the warden's words almost before it got started. He didn't want to explain why meeting Hope was more important than the warden's words. Even if he could put his feelings into words, Katie wouldn't understand. She's so analytical, she'd accuse him of being ridiculous.

"But you didn't answer my question," said Katie. "What could be more important? Tell us. Why the change of plans? Is it something the FBI said?"

"Never mind. I gotta go." He ended the comm and looked at the masstran schedule. He needed to be at the bus stop by five minutes after five. Three hours to kill before his chance to see Hope.

Chris stepped away from the fence. "Finished?" Lucky turned and followed.

On the sidewalk in front of the police station, Chris looked around. *What am I going to do with myself for three hours?* The day wasn't super hot, but they both could've used a drink of water. There was a public water fountain across the street on the next block. Once Chris had crossed the street, he passed another of the strange pillars by the curb. This time, however, there wasn't a breeze.

Chris slurped water and then unfolded the portable dog bowl he carried and filled it. Lucky started lapping even before it touched concrete. As Chris stood up, he was unexpectedly bowled over by a girl about his age. They both went down on the pavement. Her percomm hit the ground and skidded to rest. She got to her feet and sprinted off. Chris saw she was wearing a hood similar to the ones worn by the people who ran from the masstran. He grabbed her percomm and raised it up. "Hey, you dropped this," he called. She didn't look back.

The percomm vibrated. Chris brought it down to look at the screen. Just then an elderly woman came out of the store as two masked boys raced past. One of them couldn't fully avoid her. She was knocked to the ground and her grocery sack spilled. A cantaloupe and three apples rolled across the sidewalk.

The boy turned, but instead of helping the lady, he saw the percomm in Chris's hand and prompted, "You coming?" The girl's percomm showed a countdown: *22 . . . 21 . . .*

"I lost my hood," Chris said impulsively, not sure where the words came from.

"Oh dear lord. Police! Someone call the police!" the woman squawked, still facedown on the pavement.

The hooded boy snatched the grocery sack from the ground, pulled out a switchblade, and made two rough holes.

"What's going on here," said the store owner from the doorway. "Hey, you." He whipped out a retractable baton. *Snap.* He waved the now fully extended weapon. Lucky barked.

The hooded boy tossed the sack at Chris's feet and ran.

The owner's fierce gaze zeroed in on Chris. "Come here, you."

Chris evaded the man's reach, grabbed the makeshift mask, and dashed away as he put it over his head, with Lucky right behind.

110 110 110

"SIR, YOU WANTED TO BE NOTIFIED IF WE DETECTED ANY ID THAT'S BLOCKED BY LIMDIS?"

"Yes," said Nolan over the comm. "What do you have?"

"Skin cells captured by a sniffer. Philadelphia. Nearly at the same location as before."

"Have you escalated to Omega Force Command?"

"No. I was about to, but contacted you first."

"Very good. No need to bother them. I'll take it from here."

110 110 110

CHRIS FOLLOWED THE TWO HOODED BOYS AS THEY RACED ALONG THE CITY sidewalk. They caught up to the girl and then they all ran together. They banked around a corner as several more sprinting youths merged with them. About halfway down one of the blocks, the group stopped at a point outside a garage door. The percomm in Chris's hand vibrated. *3 . . . 2 . . .*

Another hooded person came around the opposite corner with a burlap sack and emptied a load of bricks at their feet.

"There it is now," one of them yelled, pointing to a black pertran approaching. The garage door began to rise. The hooded people grabbed bricks and threw them at the vehicle as it swerved toward the open garage door. No damage was done that Chris could tell—the bricks just bounced off. Pedestrians ducked into storefronts. One screamed.

The luxury pertran raced into the garage and screeched to a halt. The garage door began to close. The hooded girl attached a padlock to the rails of the garage door. The closing door hit the blockage, moaned, and began to go back up. More bricks smashed across the tran's back window, still doing no discernable damage.

Chris heard the growing sound of sirens in the distance. The group fled the scene. Chris hesitated.

"Follow me! Now!" called the girl. Chris caught up. They dashed across streets until finally reaching an alley, where they vanished behind a door hidden between two dumpsters.

"What the hell is that supposed to be?" asked the girl, after closing the door once everyone was through. Over the metal door, a blue light glowed.

Chris realized she was asking about the bag on his head, and he took it off.

"First time?" she asked. Under her own mask, she had long brown hair on the right side, but it was shaved to a fine stubble on the other, shaved high above the ear, nearly to the top of her head. Her face was pretty, despite the rough image. "Four Nine Six," she said.

"Huh?"

"Don't use your real name," she warned. "What number did they assign you?

"Uh. Right. Seven Eight Six," said Chris, with a wild-ass guess.

"Wow, I had no idea they were up that far. You *are* green."
She looked at Lucky sniffing around. "Who's that?"

"Uh. Seven Eight Six and a Half."

Her rough image practically disappeared, the way she lit up.
Her smile was amazing. "Cute," she said, and then flushed, "I
meant the dog. I mean, I meant the comment." She looked away.

"Here, you dropped this," said Chris.

"Thanks." She took the percomm from his hand. "Come on
in." She led him down a dim hallway. Chris heard the sounds
of a group up ahead. He followed her until they reached a large
meeting room. Inside, there were about thirty people of vary-
ing ages, but most of them were young—late teens or twenties.
The place looked like a church basement. There was even an
old-fashioned coffee urn.

So as to not disturb the meeting, she whispered, "Welcome
to Cell Number Fourteen. Welcome to our safe house. *Mi casa
es su casa.*"

At the podium, in front of rows of folding chairs, stood one
of the boys from the street—judging by his clothes. Without his
hood, Chris could tell he was fairly young, just a few years older
than himself, with short black hair sticking up and full of sweat
after being under the hood. "That was sloppy. Next time, try to
go around people instead of through them."

"Here," she whispered, and led Chris to two empty chairs.
Lucky lay down at his feet.

The guy at the podium continued, "That's it for us. Cell
Number Fourteen's work is done for today. Cell Number Fifteen
has one more strike to complete tonight. Now, I have assign-
ments for tomorrow."

Chapter 8

THE GUY AT THE PODIUM TALKED FOR ANOTHER TWENTY MINUTES, AND then people seemed to break off into groups.

Chris looked at the time. Three thirty. "Well, I really should be going."

"What do you mean?" said the girl.

Chris looked at her blankly. He knew this was one of those points when his next words would either give him away or save him. His mind raced. They weren't treating him like a prisoner exactly. What could be the reason to have to stay? He still had time to catch the masstran Hope would ride, but he needed to figure this out. "Well, my dog needs to go. Outside. You know. Pee and poop?"

"That's not happening." She looked at him very closely now and wasn't smiling. "Did you read any of the instructions they sent you?"

Chris shrugged.

"Look around. This whole place is one giant Faraday cage. Check out the walls."

Chris did. It looked like everything was sprayed with a hardened foam, like fire retardant he'd seen coating roof beams of large rooms, like gymnasiums or auditoriums.

"The metal particles in the foam form a mesh. The flooring is metal too. It's all connected. When I shut the outside door, no signals can get in or out. It's the blackout period. To make sure no one traces us."

What? Chris hoped his inner feelings didn't give him away. *I need to get out of here.*

She tightened her gaze. "You *did* run the geolocation spoofer on your percomm when you got the encrypted broadcast, didn't you?"

"Of course," said Chris. He tried to look innocent but had no idea what she was talking about.

She glanced at Lucky. "Look, I'll show you to the bathroom. Well, it's more of a latrine, actually. Sealed plumbing. Maybe you can get your dog to squat on a paper towel or something, I don't know. I don't care. But don't even think about opening that door to the outside."

He followed her to the hallway. She seemed guarded but still helpful. She waited in the hall.

Inside the makeshift bathroom, the toilet was just a porta potty. Lucky went to drink from it but there was no water, just that nasty blue liquid. "Here, pal." The sink had an old-fashioned water-closet system. You had to pull a chain, and then the water drained into a bucket underneath. "Sorry, pal, I lost your bowl back there." Chris drank, leaning into the stream, then filled his cupped hand for Lucky. Between pulls of the chain, he tried to think. *No windows. How am I going to get out of here?*

Lucky finished drinking and started sniffing around.

"What are we gonna do, pal?"

Lucky sniffed a little more and then sprawled out on the tile floor.

"No, no. We can't stay in the bathroom. Let's go."

Outside, the girl's expression was still skeptical. "Everything come out all right?" she asked.

"Look, I admit I sort of skimmed over the instructions. How long is the blackout?"

"No way to tell. Central command is monitoring the authorities and they'll release us once they're sure we weren't traced."

She pointed down the hallway to the door. "That blue light is the only thing connected to the outside. When it turns off, we can leave."

| | 0 | | 0 | | 0

BARRISTER WAS GIVEN THE UNPLEASANT JOB OF REMOVING THE PUPPY'S carcass from the crate, putting it in a plastic bag, and then putting it in the freezer. He wasn't sure which part was the worst: pulling the spikes out of the poor dog's body, or knowing the carcass was saved and frozen so it could be fed to a different puppy prior to the next meeting of the Circle of Six. Barrister was cleaning the blood from the crate when Skotino spoke from behind.

"Host of my god's son."

Barrister couldn't get over how incredibly deep Skotino's voice was. It had a penetrating quality. Barrister turned to face him.

Skotino stepped forward. He stared for a moment, then adjusted his red silk tie as he grunted.

Barrister waited.

"Your communions are ineffective."

"I'll practice," said Barrister.

"Concentrate on creating fear. It's the *emotion* that triggers clarity. Pain is simply a means to an end. The pain must be inflicted to the left side."

Barrister wrinkled his forehead.

"*Her* left side, you moron." Skotino shook his head. "Sinistra-spherical pain." He grunted again. "You will understand eventually. But, my god knows, that could be a long time with your thick skull."

| | 0 | | 0 | | 0

THE BLUE LIGHT WAS STILL ON OVER THE DOOR OF CELL NUMBER FOURTEEN'S
safe house. Chris learned each group of protestors was called a
cell, and each cell was designated a number, not unlike the group
members themselves. Chris glanced at his percomm: quarter to
five. *It's too late. No way to get to Hope in time. I missed my chance
to see her. And I managed to waste a whole day I should have been
working on the warden's words. I'll never forgive myself if another
one of those men from Nevada got to Mom or Dad or Katie or Al
while I was just sitting in here.*

Chris was sitting on the floor in the hallway, with Lucky next
to him. The girl, Four Nine Six, sat on the floor across from him.
Her head was tilted back and her eyes were closed. He wasn't
sure if she was sleeping. Probably not.

Maybe, just maybe, if he got out in the next few minutes, he
could make it to the bus stop to catch the masstran that would
bring him to Hope. But only if he didn't waste time getting his
bearings once outside. He tried to recall the route. *How am I
going to explain this to Al and Katie? What if—*

Wink. The blue light went out.

Chris scrambled up and ran for the door.

"Hey, wait," the girl called. "I—"

Chris dashed outside, with Lucky right behind. He skidded
to a halt in the middle of the alley and looked both ways. Lucky
raced to the right without hesitation. Chris followed, trusting.
He ran as fast as he could and wished again that he'd brought
more pieces of gum. His sprint to the bus stop reminded him
of growing up with Al and Katie. They ran everywhere they'd
ever gone. Al and Katie were always by his side. *I shouldn't shut
them out.*

Lucky turned a corner and arrived exactly on the street of the
bus stop. *No!* The masstran was already three blocks away. Chris
ran. But it was no use. *I missed it.* He slowed to a stop and put
his hands on his hips to catch his breath.

Lucky barked. Chris looked up. Ahead, the vehicle drifted awkwardly out of its lane, ripping a side mirror off a parked pertran before bouncing against the curb. Hooded youths dashed from the open door of the lifeless bus.

Thank goodness for Cell Number Fifteen. "Come on, pal. This is our chance."

"Service delay. Please stand by." Chris was sweating like crazy but managed to reach it in time. "Service delay. Please sta—" The vehicle came alive, reanimated, like a vid stream resuming from pause, or like flipping the switch on C-3PO's neck, his android eyes blinking awake. The autonomous masstran merged back into traffic.

| 10 | 10 | 10

FROM THE FERGUSON LOGIC CONTROLLERS OFFICE, HOPE MADE SURE THE Department of Defense's database queries on Chris's DNA were blocked with the "limited distribution" classification. She couldn't prevent the sniffers from capturing his skin cells, but she could keep the authorities from resolving his identity. Her AI bots automatically blocked the DOD's attempts and then erased all traces of themselves.

Next, she checked her bank account. Her first paycheck had arrived. Over the years, she'd considered manipulating the financial system to get whatever she wanted. Maybe even a nicer place to live. She knew she was good at cyber infiltration, but commerce was the institution most protected against cyberterrorism. Being a rogue hacker was one thing, but being targeted as a Hood was another. The authorities spared nothing to keep the Robin Hood terrorists' tentacles from siphoning away the world's financial deposits. Every government in the world was after the Hoods. Messing around with her bank account was too risky, even for her. She had the technical ability—the task was child's play—but to do it properly required uninterrupted attention. She didn't have that luxury, not even with her perfectly programmed bot network watching 24-7 without a blink. No, she wouldn't do anything to involve her mom in anything illegal. She needed a legit source of income, and the new job was perfect. Everything was working out well. All she needed to do now was focus on getting the heat off Chris, so things could go back to normal. She flipped to his picture on her percomm.

"Who's that?" asked Nancy. Her boss had walked up from behind.

Click. The picture vanished. Hope put the device away.

"Sorry, I didn't mean to pry. I couldn't help but notice," said Nancy. "He's handsome."

"No, no. I was just looking at some old pics before I left for the day." She zipped up her backpack and made for the door.

"See you tomorrow," Nancy called.

Hope had to wait longer than usual at the bus stop. There must have been a service delay or something. She found a seat and thumbed through her messages. *Not a single comm from Chris today. Did he finally give up?*

Fur brushed up against her leg. Lucky planted his head in her lap with conviction.

"Lucky!" She scratched his head. His tail wagged furiously. Realization hit. *Oh my god. That can only mean—* She looked down the rows of seats.

Oh my god. Chris was standing at the back of the vehicle, holding a handrail. He must have grown even taller over the weeks since she'd seen him last. And those blue eyes were on her now. He must've been watching her from the moment she got on, like a missile locked on target. Curiously, he didn't seem surprised to see her.

She felt the urge to get off. She fought the feeling. She felt forced to look away and resisted that too. A blink was all she could manage.

Lucky pressed his head deeper into her lap because she'd stopped scratching. She obliged but kept her eyes on Chris. He came toward her, alternating his grip on the rails as he approached. The exhilaration finally overwhelmed her, and she looked away.

Stopping next to her, his scent wafted past. It was one of the most stimulating sensations she'd ever experienced, almost erotic. How could his body odor be the most intoxicating cologne she'd ever sensed? He'd obviously been sweating. The air around him was moist, hot. Below his denim shorts, the skin of his tanned legs shimmered.

He sat down next to her. His musky perfume washed over her again, bringing goose bumps.

"I didn't say you could sit here," she said.

"You know what? I'm done being timid. I'm done asking you if whatever I do is OK. I regret holding back when you stayed at my house. I'm going to do what my heart tells me to do, and you'll have to tell me *no* if you don't like it."

The kiss came fast and awkward. He managed to tilt his head. The kiss was soft. Then it was over. He searched her face for permission. She let her eyes give her approval—she fixed her gaze on his lips, to let him know it was OK. He came in for another. Slower this time.

She opened her mouth and let her tongue search for his. Startled, he started to pull away. She gripped his damp T-shirt and pulled him back. He relaxed. His lips became hungry, but his tongue remained shy. He slid his hand behind her head, parting her hair into thick cords. He exhaled through his nose. He'd been holding his breath. He pulled away, taking air urgently. She put her hand to his cheek as a guide. He came in again. Now it was *his* tongue that was the aggressive one. But the kiss was just as soft.

"Ouch!" Lucky's head had cracked Hope in the jaw, pushing the two apart.

She touched her tender chin as Lucky climbed up on her lap. "Hey!" He was way too big, and there wasn't enough room. Incredibly, the back legs hopped up too. "Oh jeez." Lucky's body pressed her against the seat. She was forced to turn her head to avoid suffocating under a wall of fur.

Chris was holding his mouth.

She could barely talk with the fur in her face. "Did I bite your tongue?"

"I think so," Chris mumbled. He dropped his hand and seemed to test his tongue against his teeth. "It's OK. Not much blood."

"I'm so sorry."

"Get down, you big oaf." Chris grabbed his dog by the collar and pulled him to the floor. "He's the one who should be sorry. How's your jaw?"

"His head must be made of rock," she said, rubbing her chin.

"I'm sorry."

"It wasn't your fault."

"Wasn't it?" There was an implied meaning in his voice.

She finished rubbing her chin. "You don't mean my jaw, do you?"

"Hope, I'm so sorry. I said it so many times. It *was* my fault. All of it. I dragged you to Vegas. My mom's abducted students weren't your problem."

"I wanted to help. You know that. Besides, someone had to jam communications. Even Bruce knew I was the only one qualified."

"I let you out of my sight for one second. That man—the leader of those men—he came out of nowhere. Dislocated your shoulder. Not as a result of a struggle but *on purpose*. Like, with emotionless precision. Like a doctor. Or some kind of antidoctor. It must have been unbelievably painful. You were so angry. You had every right to be. That's why you wouldn't let me visit you in the hospital."

She took a deep breath. "There was too much data to cover up. It was a challenge. Do you know how many more details go into the file if you dislocate your shoulder? No one gets a dislocated shoulder just by walking around. I altered my medical record to show I broke a finger so it wouldn't show up on so many lists. Do you have any idea how many law enforcement agencies were involved in that Vegas incident? Do you know how hard they were looking for someone to show up at a hospital with an unexplained injury? Anyone with half a brain cell would connect the dots. I'm a dot. You're a dot. The less contact we have, the better."

"We left our DNA all over that place in the Nevada desert."

"That's just it. Whoever those men are, they don't want to be identified by the authorities either. Their data, along with ours, was wiped clean even before I hacked in. There's no doubt those rooms held the missing girls. It's a shame we couldn't find even one." She shook her head. "You said the rooms were empty?"

"Yeah. I had to go room by room to find you. I sensed you even before I reached the room where the leader of the men held you. If there were other women close by, I would have sensed them too. And yet, the odors were fresh. The memory alone makes me sick."

"Maybe they had time to move the women? I hope our unexpected visit didn't mean a worse fate for them." She frowned. "Anyway, someone got to the physical-evidence locker too. Forensically, it's like the whole Vegas rescue attempt never happened."

"I know one FBI agent who's convinced something happened."

"Well, once you're in that Israeli protection program, you'll be safe from the FBI."

"I'm not going."

"What?"

"Good news, right? We have time to investigate the words from the warden. He's trying to tell us how to stop the men in Nevada from hurting any more women. We can stop them for good. Then things can go back to normal. We can be together," said Chris. "We can go to school together."

"Look, it doesn't work like that," she said. "Do you have any idea the size of the rattlesnake nest you kicked?"

"But you can fix that, you—"

Hope stood. "Apparently you don't." She looked at the few passengers in the masstran, worried she might've drawn their attention, but all heads remained down, distracted by percomms.

Chris stood up too. Keeping his voice down, he said, "OK. I admit it. I don't. But those men are never going to stop coming after me. I have to stop them. Or rather, I have to help the warden stop them. Then you and I can be together."

"Listen to yourself. You have no idea what you're up against. You have no idea what I have to do to keep you hidden. The simple act of walking around makes you show up on the network as if you're made of white phosphorus. You think because you don't show up on scanners that you're invisible. Again, *proof* you have no idea how close the authorities are to locking you up. If you're behind bars, your quixotic warden plan is pointless."

"You don't understand. Once we—"

"And now you're going to keep at it? Just go right back and kick the nest again?" Grabbing her backpack, she said, "Maybe you should hold a press conference." She walked to the exit, fuming.

He followed. "I have to stop those men. I have to help the warden. It's the only way for things to return to normal. So we can be together."

The masstran slowed for the next stop. She turned to him. "Wake up from your daydream. No one can protect you if you keep after them. This is no fairy tale. We can't live happily ever after." From the look on his face, those last words had a devastating effect. It was another moment when she could recognize her father within herself. *Verbal abuse—we've both got a talent for it.* She hated herself for that.

"The kiss meant nothing?" His voice let her know how truly wounded he was.

She didn't crack. "You were born a prince. Now you're a frog. You're safer as a frog. You're welcome."

She got out as soon as the doors opened.

"Please. Hope, listen—" He was halfway down the steps when she turned.

"Don't even think about following me. We're done. You hear me? You said all I had to do was give you the word. Well, here it is. *No.*"

The doors closed between them. The vehicle glided away.

CHAPTER 9

FROM HIS TIJUANA HOTEL ROOM, ELADIO CHECKED THE FEEDS FROM THE microcams he'd planted around the entertainment establishment located in the old section of the city about a mile away. He checked the facial- and gait-recognition software that processed each stream. It was only a matter of time—Eladio gambled—before Rodriguez showed up at the club and was identified. Eladio would then make contact and convince Rodriguez to help him find out what was really going on with the Omega Force. Rodriguez might be the only person on the planet able to slip into Nolan's domain. And through his bullshit.

Eladio reviewed, for the third time, the information from Rodriguez's dossier, including the man's psych evaluations and service record. The latter was complete up to his Nevada mission, at which point it became heavily redacted. Eladio scrolled to the picture. Underneath, it said CORPORAL (OTH) JUAN RODRIGUEZ. He'd received an other-than-honorable separation from the Marine Corps. Anyone officially attached to Omega Force Command or Britain's MI8 knew the real reason. Scapegoat. Somebody else screwed up. But it was Rodriguez who got the big green one up the ass. *The guy has a perfect record for years, and then things go suddenly off the rails? No way.* As Colonel Wesson had ordered, Eladio was learning about Juan Rodriguez. On paper at least. Before Eladio could meet the ex-marine in person, he first needed to find him.

Shortly after midnight, Eladio noticed one of the microcams had fallen. Unfortunately, he now had a perfect view of the parking lot's asphalt surface. Maybe it got jostled? Maybe an animal bumped it?

Well, it's pretty late. If Rodriguez hasn't shown up by now, he probably won't, not tonight anyway. The best course of action was to fix the camera now so it would be ready for the next night. This time, Eladio brought the binoculars along. He wanted a closer look at the chola girls. Since seeing them the night before, his imagination had become steamier than hotel porn.

Approaching the nightclub, Eladio found a spot in the adjacent lot, up on top of a shed. As was the case each night before, the place was lively. On his belly, he focused the binoculars, peering over the bushes dividing the lots. Sure enough, it looked like a microcam had come loose. He'd have to fix it once everything settled down.

The music was incredible, even outside and at that distance. From the promotional signs outside the club, the performance was a live band called The Ex-Boyfriends. Eladio realized he'd never experienced live music before, only studio recorded or livestreamed. As a teenager, he'd known Loyds who claimed to have gone to a concert. Initially, he'd dismissed the whole idea of live music as urban legend. But later, he learned concerts were a real thing. If you paid enough money, crews would re-create an entire studio, complete with giant speakers, mixing boards, and a dedicated network to connect it all. Some had computer-controlled laser light shows, smoke, and pyrotechnics. The performers might even change outfits multiple times during the concert. *If you paid enough money.*

Eladio scanned the parking lot. Groups of people were outside smoking. He had trouble getting over the sight. Smoking had become nearly nonexistent worldwide. Not because it was declared illegal, which it was, but because the health scanners could tell instantly. It had taken decades for the associated health costs to subside, but the US economy was now less burdened and gradually improving. *Hopefully*, thought Eladio. With so much government propaganda, it wasn't easy to know what to believe. Anyway, this old part of Tijuana was certainly where the privileged Mexicans came to party. *These people can have and do whatever they want.*

Eladio zoomed in on a group of three girls. *Gorgeous.* He watched as one woman brought the tip of a handheld electronic hookah pipe to her lips. She held it with long lacquered fingernails, each exquisitely decorated—bejeweled. Her makeup was a masterpiece. Her lips were expertly painted, with the edges a slightly darker shade, accentuating the fullness. Eladio zoomed in tighter, captivated, envious of the hookah pipe as she sucked.

Click. Eladio felt the barrel of the gun behind his ear.

"OK, migo. Nice and easy now. You move, I blow your fuckin' head off."

110 110 110

BY THREE IN THE MORNING, HOPE WASN'T SURE IF SHE'D GET A CHANCE TO sleep. Chris had created a mushroom cloud of data. She'd been working for hours, through the night, to try to contain it. The DOD had finally analyzed Chris's DNA from the skin cells they captured using the sniffers along the sidewalks in the city. She was able to hinder their progress but nothing more. The human body sheds thirty thousand skin cells every hour. A sniffer only needed one.

She'd blocked the FBI's access to any data that would allow them to bring charges. Chris would just have to endure the process until it worked itself out. The FBI's budget was limited. Without turning up enough evidence, they'd eventually shut down their investigation. Chris just needed to wait them out.

LUCKY SAT PATIENTLY ON THE FLOOR OF BEN'S LAB AS CHRIS, SITTING CROSS-
legged in front of his dog, attached the tube to Lucky's collar. "I
never want to be without the galactose maltose again," Chris
explained.

Al raised an eyebrow and cocked his head. "Now he looks
like one of those big dogs with a whiskey barrel under the neck.
You know, a Saint Bernard?"

"Never mind him, Lucky. You look dashing," said Katie.
"Ready?" she asked Chris.

"Yup."

Katie tossed him one of the pieces of blue chewing gum from
the pile on the table in Ben's lab. Ben and Laura watched too.
Lucky tried to get a sniff of the gum as Chris loaded it into the
cylindrical tube the size of a pill bottle and pressed the cap closed.
Snap. "There," said Chris. "It's hardly noticeable." Now, if Chris
ran out of gum, he'd have a backup in the makeshift stash.

"What will the other dogs say?" asked Al.

"Can you be serious?" said Katie. "We have work to do."

"No, I can't," said Al. "Sorry for the racial slur, Lucky. I'll
never call you a Saint Bernard again."

"Speaking of serious," said Laura, "what happened yesterday,
Chris? Why are you suddenly so available to work on the warden's words and sit for mind-reader scans for new words?"

Chris scratched Lucky behind the ears and got to his feet.
"Long story." Chris wasn't sure if it was because he finally got to
see Hope—as disappointing as it was—or being with the group
of protestors, but he felt more able to face his responsibilities.
Still, he wasn't prepared to elaborate on either incident.

"We have all day," said Laura.

"No, we don't," said Chris evasively. "I think Harrison is
going to haul me down every day. Make my life miserable until I
give in. I'll probably get the call any minute."

"I've got the mind-reader program prepped," said Ben.

Al said, "Before we do that, let's hear what Katie found out about the rest of the warden's words we already have. I'm all for getting new words, but we have a backlog as it is. Maybe the new words are dependent on understanding the words we already have. Let's not get ahead of ourselves."

Katie nodded. "Well, I'm not finished researching them all yet." She whipped out her percomm to view her notes. "Let's see. I told you about *Übermensch* and *parthenogenesis*. And of course, we know about two other words already, *galactic* and *malt*, which turned out to be *galactose maltose*." She looked up. "That's just a reminder that some of the other words could be garbled up too."

"Whatever," said Al. "What's the next one?"

"*Frashokereti* is roughly equivalent to judgment day. Good survives, and evil is wiped out. The idea is to return the world back to a state similar to the time of creation. Like the time of Adam and Eve, but not necessarily when everything was new. The diversity of nature and humanity endures, meaning men wear pants instead of fig leaves, and cows roam instead of dinosaurs. On frashokereti judgment day, ancestors of the good people are reborn. Then the good people and their reincarnated relatives drink something called parahaoma, which makes the people immortal. Essentially, it reverses the effect of the bite of Adam's apple. Like a do-over on original sin. The good people and their ancestors live forever. The evil people die a natural death and never return. Only good remains. It all ends in sort of a happily-ever-after thing. Heaven on earth."

"What's so bad about that?" asked Al.

"Well, this same doctrine shows up in devil worship too. In other words, good and evil are flipped."

"Meaning all the good people are wiped out? And only evil people remain?"

"Yup. And if all this comes to pass, they live forever. Hell on earth." Like before, Katie seemed unusually drained and defeated.

"OK, what's the next one?" asked Al.

Chris said, "Come on, Al. Let's give Katie a break."

"I agree," said Ben. "Let's use the scanner and the mind-reader program for a while. We need to know what the warden thinks about all this."

"I just don't see what's so hard about it," said Al.

"It's creepy, Al," said Katie angrily. "I dare you to pull up a definition of one of those words late at night and research it when no one's around. You won't believe where it leads you. It chills me to the bone."

"Yeah, but they're just words. I—"

Katie turned and walked out of the lab.

"I—"

"Let her go, Al," said Laura.

Al started to speak, but Chris stopped him. "Katie says you have the emotional sensitivity of a brick. She's right. Just let it go."

"What's wrong, Ben?" asked Laura.

Chris could see his dad seemed suddenly worried.

"Remember all the years we spent trying to figure out what was special about Chris? About his condition? All the years we didn't know about the warden? Then the breakthrough. Remember? The warden said something like *emergency*, or *emergence*, or *urgent emergence*." Ben paused. "The warden has been trying to warn us all along. Something bad is going to happen."

||0 ||0 ||0

"LEAVE US," SAID RICK ANDERSON, CEO OF TERRASTORE INFORMATION STORAGE.
The dozen scientists and technicians in Pete Rasmussen's staff walked out of the control room of the unbihexium harvesting lab deep under Yucca Mountain. He watched them as

they bunched up at the door, like somebody had yelled "fire" in a theater. Pete longed to leave with them. One of his scientists, unable to get around those in front of her, glanced back to Pete. He knew that look.

Once the door was closed, Pete didn't even turn to face Anderson. What was the point? Another chewing out? Something was always wrong. There was never enough unbihexium. Anderson would never be happy. *What's it going to be* this *time?*

The seconds ticked away. Finally, curiosity got the best of him and he looked over. Anderson was peering out the observation window, which spanned the entire side of the control room, down to the enormous vat of liquid formaldehyde used in the miraculous harvesting of unbihexium—unbihexium 310 to be exact, a stable isotope. The chemical reaction was nothing short of modern alchemy. No one knew why the reaction created unbihexium. It was a case of applied science being far ahead of theoretical science.

Anderson still hadn't said anything. Pete wasn't sure what to do. This had never happened before.

"In a Catholic church," Anderson said, finally, "did you know that the sacristy sink doesn't lead to the sewer, but rather drains to the earth directly under the house of worship?" Anderson spun, locking eyes with Pete.

Pete could only shake his head, unable to fathom where this question would lead.

Anderson continued, "In the event the consecrated body or blood of Christ should accidently fall to the floor, all—including the water used to clean the spot—is returned to the earth."

Pete had no idea what this had to do with anything or what to say. He was never told what the unbihexium was used for. Did Anderson expect him to make sense of this explanation?

Anderson turned back to the window. "The filter you use in

the tank here to separate out the unbihexium—I need you to adapt the design . . . to extract unbihexium from a fluid other than formaldehyde."

"Filter it from what?" asked Pete.

"Urine," said Anderson, turning back to face him. "We can't have consecrated material going to the sewer, now, can we?"

||0 ||0 ||0

EVERYONE IN BEN'S LAB WATCHED AS CHRIS UNWRAPPED A PIECE OF GUM and popped it into his mouth. From the first chew, Chris felt the presence of the warden swell inside him. It felt like days and weeks of stress across his back and neck were suddenly relieved, as if someone had pressed that one spot—that spot just over the shoulder blade that makes a tingling sensation ride up the spine, to the back of the skull. Chris's mind raced independently of passing time. Or maybe time was no longer passing. Yet somehow, he was aware of time's splintered future. Each blink of time solidified one of an infinite number of future paths, which in turn spawned a completely different set of infinite futures. One's choice of action, in the tiniest instant, determined the chance of reality. That selection locked in place a single path leading to an infinite number of new paths, like pictures of fractals where the lines seem to continuously branch forever. Chris lingered on the concept of multiple infinities. Infinity infinities, each completely different. "Antikythera mechanism," said Chris involuntarily.

"Wait, I'm not ready," said Ben. "The software is just coming online now."

Chris turned to face Ben, Laura, Al, and Lucky—everyone except Katie, who still hadn't returned after walking out on Al. "Sorry," said Chris. "That phrase just popped out."

"Let me write that one down," said Ben. "OK. The mind-reader program is running now. I have the portable scanner picking up the cognitive activity of the warden. The warden's thoughts will appear on the screen of the scanner. You may begin."

"What should we ask first?" asked Al.

"Who are the men coming after us?" Laura prompted.

6 + 1 appeared on the screen.

"It says six plus one. We've seen that before," said Ben. "It equals seven, obviously. I don't know what else to make of it."

"Seven isn't right," said Chris, trance-like, helping to interpret.

Then the screen filled with a string of numbers endlessly repeated: *123456 123456 123456 123456 . . .*

"The numbers one through six, over and over again," said Ben. "A circle," said Chris.

The flow of numbers stopped. The text *CIRCLE OF SIX* appeared.

Without looking at the screen, Chris said, "Circle of Six."

"That's right," said Ben. "The group of men from Nevada are called the Circle of Six?"

"Yes," said Chris.

"What's the plus one?" asked Al.

The memory of the confrontation in Vegas flashed across Chris's mind. The one who grabbed Hope. The one who dislocated her shoulder. The one who inflicted pain to reveal the warden's plans. *For the chance of reality's path doth tip.* The one with the voice—a voice so deep that everything seemed to vibrate, like standing in a forest of tuning forks, all moaning in sepulchral resonance. *He's the one.* Chris had to close his eyes at the memory. "One over six," Chris chanted, "once one over twelve." Chris opened his eyes. "The guy who hurt Hope. He's the leader of the Circle of Six. He's the plus one."

Chris's percomm jingled, followed by "Communication for Chris Lumière." The seccomm's oddly formal notification confirmed Chris's summons back to the FBI office downtown.

"This time," said Al, "we're coming with you."

WHEN THE HOOD WAS YANKED OFF HIS HEAD, ELADIO CRIED OUT, SURPRISING himself. He couldn't help it. How much time had passed? Hours certainly. Into the morning? They'd put a hood over his head and zip tied his wrists and ankles. They'd tossed him, like a sack of potatoes, into a vehicle. He'd memorized the route: left out of the alley, straight for almost a minute, left again, and, thirty seconds later, two quick rights. The location had to be fairly close, still in Tijuana for sure. They had dragged him through three doorways, down six flights of stairs, into some kind of room. Judging by the echo, it was small. Smelled like garbage. Damp. Cool. They stripped him naked. From the brief contact with the floor, it felt like concrete, cold and gritty. They hung him up by his wrists with a heavy chain secured from above. They shackled his ankles with another heavy chain anchored from below. Legs dangled, unable to kick. Hours had passed.

Now, with the hood finally removed, he blinked and tried to focus. It was dark. The only light came from a dim source behind him. The appearance of the room wasn't far from what he'd imagined. Four concrete walls. Maybe twelve feet on each side.

Facing him was a figure. A man. Standing. His face was partially obscured by Eladio's own shadow. Filled with some kind of Stockholm syndrome, Eladio almost begged for help. But his marine training kicked in. Who was his captor? Male. Latino. Maybe late twenties. Something about his hair and beard seemed unusual, as if it had recently grown out, as if the man had worn his hair short and had been clean-shaven just a few weeks before. He was a big man and looked extremely fit, formidable.

Over the man's shoulder, Eladio saw the exit: a tunnel extending into darkness.

"Who are you?" asked Eladio.

The man didn't say anything but merely raised an eyebrow and cocked his head slightly. Even without words, the implication was clear: Eladio was in no position to ask questions.

"I'm Ignacio Mendez," said Eladio, using the name on the fake credentials he carried on his person, which surely they had found. "I'm a US citizen. Here on business. I demand you release me."

Then, almost silently, three other men emerged from the darkness of the tunnel. Eladio recognized the one in front immediately as Corporal OTH Juan Rodriguez. *Oh shit.*

The four men stood in front of Eladio. One handed Rodriguez a duffle. Rodriguez unzipped the bag and upended it. With a clatter, Eladio's surveillance cams spilled out onto the floor. *Shit.*

Standing before him were the four members of the infamous Omega Force fireteam that botched the opportunity to capture or kill the rogue agent who murdered Dr. Brandon Cornelius, the scientist credited with inventing the techniques that made the Omega Force marines superhuman. Dr. Cornelius was revered as the father to them all. Rodriguez, as fireteam leader, had been in charge of the failed mission.

These four men knew Eladio was *not* Ignacio Mendez.

I I0 I I0 I I0

"SEE? I TOLD YOU. HARRISON IS JUST TRYING TO WASTE TIME AND MAKE MY LIFE miserable," said Chris, stepping off the masstran after the return trip from downtown.

At midafternoon, the park near his home was alive with kids and parents. Chris let two stroller-pushing women pass by and then he and Lucky caught up to Al and Katie, heading across the park. "By the way, when I was inside with Harrison, did Lucky spend any time prowling around the side of the police station? Like over by the fence surrounding the back parking lot?"

"Yeah," said Al. "Katie and I waited for you under a tree. We could see him from where we sat. Eventually he came and lay down with us. Why?"

"I'm not sure. Every time we go, he's obsessed with something in the parking lot on the other side of the fence."

"The FBI is the least of our problems," said Katie. "We have to figure out how the warden can protect us from the Circle of Six."

"The warden wants to stop them," said Chris. "And by extension, *I'm* supposed to stop them." The trio passed the swing sets and the horseshoe pits. Chris continued, "I want to feel excited about school starting. I want our senior year to be a blast. But all that seems surreal now, like someone else's life. I'm being pushed into a future I didn't choose, into responsibility I never accepted."

"Boo-hoo," said Al. "Let's just get back to your house and pick up where we left off."

They reached the edge of the park. "When we get to your house," continued Al, "I know we need to work on the warden's words." Al glanced over to Katie, to see if she was still mad at him. She didn't react. "But I'm hungry."

"My mom keeps hassling me about the chandelier," said Chris. "I'll put it up while you guys find something to eat at my house."

"Is the chandelier finished?" asked Katie.

Chris pulled out his percomm. "I'll check the status of the printer." *Tap, tap.* "That's weird. I can't connect." Chris stopped walking.

Katie watched over his shoulder. "Let me see that." She took it from him. "Something's wrong." She pulled out her own percomm. *Swipe, tap, tap, tap.* "Your house is off the network."

Chris looked at Katie, then to Al. "Come on!"

They ran the few streets to Chris's block and down the alley. Katie got to the house first but stopped as soon as she reached the driveway. Chris sped past her and slowed to a stop as soon as he saw it too. The garage door had been ripped away. The back door was smashed in. Yellow crime-scene tape was strewn about the house, especially across the gaping holes.

"Oh my god," said Katie.

"The Circle of Six," breathed Chris, barely able to process the sight. "We said all along they could return at any moment."

Al stepped past both of them and turned to face them. "We don't know that."

Chris put his hands on his forehead. "Mom! Dad!" He started to bolt for the door, but Al got in his way. "What are you doing? Let me go!"

"Look, Chris! Look," said Al. "Does the Circle of Six use yellow tape? Think about it."

"Well, I know they *crash through doors and windows*," said Chris, fighting. "The police probably came and found my mom and dad *dead*, and the *police* put up the tape." He tried to push past again.

"Al's right," said Katie, putting her hand on Chris's shoulder. "We can't jump to conclusions."

"Think about it," said Al. "It could be a trick."

"What do you mean?"

"It's a criminal offense to cross the tape and contaminate the scene," said Al. "Maybe all this is set up for you to do something stupid, so they can legitimately arrest you."

"That's ridiculous," said Chris.

"Maybe," said Katie, "but Al's right. It's called Locard's exchange principle. And Harrison would like nothing more than to lock you up for a couple years." She added, "But the home invaders weren't a random group of thieves. Such crimes haven't been possible for decades, not with the advent of DNA analysis, public vid surveillance, and the ubiquitous seccomm systems. It has to be the authorities, or—" Katie seemed to regret her own line of argument.

"Or what?!"

She continued in a defeated voice. "Or a group able to manipulate the global network without the authorities knowing."

"See!" said Chris. "The Circle of Six!"

"We have to be sure," said Katie. "We have to check."

"Let Lucky go," said Al.

Chris stopped fighting and tried to calm himself. "OK." He backed up a step. "That's a pretty good idea, actually." He pulled out a piece of gum.

From the first chew, he could see, hear, and smell from Lucky's perspective. As if knowing the language of dogs, Chris could express his desire for where Lucky should go. Lucky responded dutifully and approached the back door. With his eyes open but not looking at anything in particular, Chris concentrated on the vision in his mind's eye. Lucky leapt up the back stoop and peered inside.

"Oh no," blurted Chris.

"What?"

"There's a spent tear-gas canister in the hallway. I can smell it too."

"Your parents probably thought it was the Circle of Six trying to get in," said Al. "The changes that Hope made to the sec-comm system probably blocked even the federal override."

"Yeah," said Katie. "I bet that only further convinced the feds that we're all Hoods."

"They probably used a battering ram to get in," said Al.

"Lucky can't open the doors or use the elevator to check the other floors, but there's a strong scent of strangers in the hallway." Lucky emerged from the house, sniffing the ground. He stopped at the driveway. "They took my mom and dad. Their scent is fresh, and the trail vanishes at the driveway, like they were loaded into a vehicle."

CHAPTER 10

"IT'S BARRISTER," SAID TYVOLD, ENTERING SKOTINO'S OFFICE UNDER Yucca Mountain.

"The Bear?" asked Skotino sarcastically.

"We have a problem," said Tyvold.

"Put it on the list."

"I'm serious."

Skotino didn't take anything Victor Tyvold said lightly. As host to his god's brother, Tyvold had seniority over the other members of the Circle. Skotino—ruler over six, once one over twelve—relied on Tyvold as his left-hand man, his executive officer, his proxy.

Skotino sat at his desk and motioned for Tyvold to take the seat across from him.

"We know Barrister is struggling to reach clarity," continued Tyvold. "So I watched the recording from his last communion attempt. He's reluctant to inflict pain. And he's clueless about creating fear."

"He's stupid. He'll learn. Eventually."

"No, there's more. At one point, he was leaning over his pharmakos. I couldn't figure out what he was doing. I enhanced the audio," said Tyvold. "Turns out, he was apologizing to her—apologizing for hurting her. He told her he had no choice."

"What are you saying?"

"I'm saying Barrister is not a sinistral host to your god's son, but rather a dextral host. Barrister's god isn't left-aligned, but rather right-aligned."

How could that be? wondered Skotino. The only possibility was from the influence of the female gods, his god's daughters. But Skotino had banished the six females to Tartaros, just like Saoshyant, the warden, known to the Circle of Six.

Skotino asked, "You're suggesting Barrister flipped from left to right because of one of my god's daughters?"

"It's the only explanation. I suspect that not only did Saoshyant escape but that he found a way to free at least one of your god's daughters from Tartaros."

Skotino couldn't deny the logic. Over the countless years, he'd admonished himself repeatedly to never underestimate the warden. Was the new megaron a distraction? Not only were the sanctuary and the oubliette exquisite reconstructions, but Tyvold had re-created Skotino's office too. The last office had windows all around. Skotino had insisted on maintaining his ability to see any threat long before it got close to the megaron. Of course, Skotino's new office was subterranean, under Yucca Mountain. Tyvold's solution? The new office had floor-to-ceiling display screens along its entire circumference. The screens displayed a live feed from an array of vid cams positioned on top of the mountain. Skotino had a 360-degree view of the area surrounding the megaron. The images were so crisp it was nearly impossible to tell his office walls weren't glass and that the office wasn't atop the mountain. Ingeniously, a simple hand gesture would zoom in. Skotino could see the twitch of a jackrabbit's whiskers six miles out, if so desired. Or—now more importantly—if Saoshyant, the warden, came for another visit. Skotino thought he'd taken every precaution. But had the precautions themselves distracted them? The timing of the warden's interference was truly inspired.

For millennia, the Circle of Six had prepared for this delicate point in time, the time when the mortals' technology had advanced sufficiently to construct the unbihexium harvesting lab. The Circle waited decades more until, finally, the gods foresaw the conception of the first fetus to possess the unique genetic alignment enabling a mutation of the human form—a mutation into Skotino's servant. Unfortunately, the first fetus was female. The fallen member of the Circle, Erik "Big Vega" Mathers, eliminated the mother along with the fetus. The Circle of Six waited years more until the gods detected the next fetus with the rare genetic alignment. Again, a female. Again, mother and fetus were eliminated—this time by Mark Spire. Still more years passed, waiting, until the gods led the Circle of Six to the first male fetus: the son of Chelsea Venizelos.

But the waiting didn't end. Years of tedium had only just begun. First, as divined by the gods, the Circle of Six had orchestrated in vitro infusions of unbihexium into Chelsea's unborn child. After Chelsea's son's birth, as the boy grew, the gods ordered ever larger quantities of unbihexium. The harvesting process barely kept up with the demand. When the boy neared puberty, he slept more and more hours of the night, until finally he remained asleep entirely. He'd entered a form of hibernation—the start of the crucial transformation into Skotino's servant.

The waiting and painstaking preparations had continued, even over the recent weeks, as Chelsea's son slept, becoming the servant. The unbihexium was triggering a physical transformation, as foreseen by the gods.

Now, in only days, Chelsea's son would be reborn, to become Skotino's servant and the enforcer of Skotino's plan to return the earth to a world the mortals would describe as Eden, at least its physical characteristics. But Skotino's plan was in jeopardy—years, decades, centuries, and millennia of effort were now teetering on the edge of irrelevance. *Goddamn the warden!*

"Wait," objected Skotino, "when the host of a left-aligned god is killed, the god seeks a fully grown host. When the host of a right-aligned god is killed, the god seeks a virgin woman, and the host grows from her egg. Since Vega's god found and possessed Barrister as a fully grown man, his god must be left-aligned. Sinistral, not dextral."

"True," agreed Tyvold. "Under ordinary circumstances, yes. But the females wield the power of Hecate, a power we don't fully understand. The circumstances are extraordinary. Somehow, Barrister's god flipped *after* taking residence."

"Impossible."

"Don't talk to me about impossibility," said Tyvold. "Saoshyant escaped from Tartaros, and you have no idea how. It *must* be an evocation of Hecate unforeseen by our gods. It's the only explanation."

But Skotino was flawlessly consistent about the ritual to guarantee his god's six daughters remained trapped in Tartaros. He made the required sacrifice at each and every meeting of the Six. The canine sacrifice kept Hecate at bay. *Canine?* Skotino remembered the confrontation with the warden's host, Chris Lumière, while holding the girlfriend at gunpoint. Realization hit. "The yellow Labrador," said Skotino. He looked up. "The dog."

"Yes, the dog," confirmed Tyvold. "Saoshyant has created some type of affinity with the dog."

"Canine grok human. Human grok canine."

"Indeed."

"Consequently," said Skotino, extending the line of thinking, "the warden was able to free one of my god's daughters, which caused Barrister's god to flip from left to right."

"Yes. Something happened after Vega's god possessed Ken Barrister," said Tyvold. "But that's not all. We can't assume only one female is free."

"So if another one of the Circle of Six is killed, that god will also flip."

"And end up hosted by a single cell in the womb of a virgin," said Tyvold. "One by one, left to right. Eventually, we return to the old ways. Your god will once again be ruler over twelve—six males, six females, all right-aligned, even you."

"And so, the exponential human infestation of terra continues unchecked."

"Yes," said Tyvold. "It will inevitably expand off-planet. The virus of humanity will surely spread to the children of Sol. The solar system will be irreversibly defiled, starting with terra."

"But for now, Barrister is unenlightened?"

"Yes," said Tyvold. "He may remain unenlightened indefinitely, or—"

Skotino pounded his fist and stood up. "Or any one of the dextral religions they preach on this godforsaken planet could enlighten him."

Tyvold added, "Or even one of the quasi religions, such as the Free Zone, the Jedi, or the Hillites. But more likely, he'll experience pain or distress at some point during his lifetime, causing him to feel fear deep within his soul. He'll be receptive to help, and his soul will prepare to receive it. He'll pray to a greater power for the pain and suffering to end. At his lowest point, at his time of greatest need, when his pain and fear become unbearable, he'll accept his god. For the chance of reality's path doth tip."

"Ask and you shall receive," murmured Skotino.

"Exactly. That first connection will be weak. He won't yet know how to quiet his mind to fully receive his god. But if he has a strong dextral clarity event—if he becomes enlightened, aware of his god, and learns to trust it, to unconditionally release control of his mortal life, to allow his god to guide him, to show him the path—he'll become a threat. Barrister, the host of your god's son, is formidable. Stupid, but formidable. Once enlightened, he becomes . . . well, our enemy."

Skotino raised his arms, curling his fingers into fists. "The warden's stench is surrounding me, choking me. How could I let this happen? Stopping the warden must be our top priority." Skotino forced himself back to composure. He smiled. "My servant will have the pleasure."

"We still have five more days until he's reborn. And we'll need time to prepare him."

Skotino nodded. "We need to glimpse the future. We need more pharmakoi. Can Barrister do *that* at least?"

"Yes, his compassion for women makes him an effective lure. And he's 'fucking sexy,' to quote one of the women he's been messaging. But since he'll never reach sinistral clarity, he can't help us interpret the future."

"It's a risk to keep him around. A risk we'll have to manage. Inform the others. Tell Dr. Betasten to investigate your flip theory. And make sure Spire keeps an eye on Barrister. If Barrister shows any signs of enlightenment, we'll have no choice but to eliminate the Bear ourselves."

||0 ||0 ||0

"NEXT ON THE AGENDA," SAID COLONEL WESSON VIA VIDCOMM, "IS THE STATE OF our compromised systems."

From his office at the Quantico base, Major Nolan watched his display. The colonel glanced down at his briefing notes.

"Says here," continued Colonel Wesson, "that Major Nolan has a lead. And—get this—he *personally* is the link to that lead. I can't wait to hear this."

On his display, Nolan watched Wesson and Schofield smirk. But he wouldn't let those jugheads get under his skin. "That's right. This terrorist cell has been active for a long time. Approximately six years ago, I received a request to investigate evidence of first contact."

"Little green men?" interrupted the colonel.

The look on their faces made Nolan steam. *Relax*, he coached himself. "Yes. It's one of the many responsibilities of my command."

"Why am I not surprised?" The colonel shook his head. "Sorry, Major, I didn't mean to imply that your contribution to the defense of the United States of America is anything less than vital."

"Let him explain," said Schofield, always the referee.

"Thank you," said Nolan. "Yes. We finally got the analysis of our John Doe's DNA. We had to search using manual queries, but we finally found a match to an adolescent male who happens to be the same person described in a report submitted to me six years ago. The report was from a civilian, Benjamin Richards, claiming his son was possessed by an alien presence. If the lead was simply a report in a database, I wouldn't trust it because our systems are compromised. But, I actually spoke to Benjamin Richards six years ago, so I know it's factual. I suspect Richards's assertion about the alien presence was an attempt to infiltrate our information systems."

"Like some kind of old-school phishing attack?"

"Right. Naturally, I didn't fall for the ruse. But at this point, we have to assume he found another way in."

"Your next move?"

"This afternoon, I had the family picked up. Incredibly, the house was locked down. We couldn't even override the seccomm. We had to break in. We arrested a married couple. The man is confirmed to be Benjamin Richards, the one who submitted the report to me six years ago. And, surprise, surprise, he's a software expert. Better yet, when we ran his wife through the system, we found all kinds of dirt on her too, like lint on corduroy. Laura Richards has been under investigation for years, has a fondness for protest propaganda, and was even fired from her job as a political science professor due to suspected involvement with a string of abductions of young women, several of whom were her students. The abductions remain unsolved. Probably a human trafficking scheme to fund their operations."

"You said *family*. What about the adolescent male described in the original report?"

"He wasn't there. When we tried to hunt him down, guess what we ran up against?"

"LIMDIS?"

"Yes, sir. We figured we'd just watch the public vid net for the kid to come home. Nada. No way to get a feed from any cam in the vicinity. The surveillance system is completely blocked. A perfect example of HIP at one hundred percent."

"Now what?" asked Colonel Wesson.

"An old-fashioned stakeout." Nolan shook his head. "You have no idea what a fiasco that's become. It's as if I was speaking a foreign language. Apparently, *stakeout* has fallen out of law enforcement's vocabulary. I'm moving heaven and earth to get actual bodies assigned. It'll take time."

"While you were smashing your way into the house, why didn't you just leave a 'don't come back' sign on the front door?"

"I know, I know. Still, at least it's a lead. I'm flying out to Philly to interrogate Benjamin and Laura Richards myself. I'll have the son in custody in no time."

| | O | | | O | | | O |

"YOU LOOK AWFUL," SAID NANCY VIA VIDCOMM.

"I know," said Hope, from her bedroom. "Must be a stomach bug. I was up all night. I need to take the day off."

Nancy frowned. "Well, technically you're still in your three-month probation period. You don't have sick-day benefits."

"I can work from home," said Hope.

"That wasn't our agreement. We agreed you'd have to earn the right."

"Look, my insides are water. I'll never make it to the elevator, much less the masstran. I . . ." She let her voice trail off and did her best to look overwhelmed and exhausted. She didn't have time for this right now. Even as her boss watched her over the vidcomm, Hope kept an eye on the flood of activity surrounding Chris. Streams of data scrolled up her screen. She made sure her AI programs—reacting faster than any human could—blocked all attempts to track him. She was one step ahead of the authorities, but she couldn't believe what was happening.

"OK. Just this once."

"Thanks." Hope resisted the urge to end the comm too abruptly, feeling the seconds tick by, making sure she paused the appropriate amount of time to match the social expectations of the situation, hiding her true intent.

"OK, then. Take care of yourself. I'll see you here tomorrow."

"Thanks again." Hope smiled and limply tapped to disconnect. *Finally! Free for the moment.* She got back to monitoring. *The feds break into Chris's house? Take Ben and Laura? I didn't see that coming.*

Her percomm vibrated. *It's him.* Countless times she'd ignored him, but now she stared at his picture. His eyes. His lips. She accepted the comm.

She heard both Al and Katie's voices come over the speaker. "She picked up!"

"Hope?" It was Chris's voice. "Is it really you?" The screen flashed, showing he added a vid stream. Chris's face filled her display, with Al and Katie crammed in behind.

Nancy's "you look awful" echoed in Hope's head. She glanced to the reflection of herself in the glare of her display screen. She pulled the strands of hair away from her face. *No use. It doesn't matter.* She tapped to reciprocate with her own vid stream.

"I was worried you'd blocked all my comms," said Chris. "You won't believe what happened."

"I know what happened," said Hope.

"I'm at Katie's house. And—"

"I know where you are."

"We need your help."

"No shit." She had to be tough. It was for his own good.

Their smiles faded. Al and Katie exchanged concerned expressions. Chris stayed focused on Hope. "If you know what happened, are you sure it was the FBI? We're worried the Circle of Six got in."

"Who are the Circle of Six?"

"That's what the warden calls the men in Nevada, the ones trying kill us. We have—"

"Will you knock it off with the warden crap? You have bigger problems. It wasn't the FBI who took Ben and Laura. It was the DOD."

"I'm afraid to ask what difference that makes."

Hope was about to explode on him when Katie jumped in. "The FBI is investigating the guy Al killed in the park. The DOD is trying to figure out what happened to the Omega Force unit we confronted while trying to free the abducted women held by the men in Nevada."

"That's right," said Hope, regaining her patience. "The FBI has nothing on you. No case. It won't be long before they exceed their measly budget and give up." Hope continued, "But those Omega Force marines were directly involved in our Nevada rescue attempt. True, your Circle of Six assholes erased all the evidence, but those marines know what they saw. They're starting to piece it together. The DOD is coming for you."

"How much time do I have?"

"I jammed the neighborhood cams. They're bringing in plainclothes officers to watch your house. But the locals have no budget for that. Right now, I'm interfering with their financial transfers and their communications. It'll probably be tomorrow before they can get anyone out there. You should go now—I mean right now—and get what you need out of the house. If you stay away from the house, away from the public vid net, and away from the sniffers, I can keep you hidden."

"Sniffers?" asked Chris.

"Yeah. Automated detectors that capture skin cells shed by pedestrians. They have scanners everywhere, of course, but you don't show up on those."

Hope watched Chris tap at his percomm. "Does a sniffer look like this?" he asked.

Hope saw the notification of the incoming image. She tapped to accept. "Yup. That's one. Depending on wind direction, the detection range is significant." She tapped the command to extract the geo-stamp information from the file's metadata. "Yup. This one is located right by the police station downtown. You were there yesterday morning."

"We have to get the gum machine out of the basement lab," said Chris.

"Forget that. Don't you understand? The DOD is coming for you. Just grab some clothes and then lay low for a few weeks."

"No, the warden knows about the sniffers. When I was using the gum while I was in the city, I could feel the air get pushed away from the sniffer. The warden can help."

She'd had enough. "If you *never go into the city*, the sniffers don't matter."

"We have to get my mom and dad out before they're interrogated."

"That already happened. It's too late," said Hope, aware of the uncertainty in her voice.

Chris's eyes narrowed. "You know that's not true, don't you? You know they haven't been interrogated yet."

Hope nodded. She wouldn't lie.

"You have to help me get my parents out."

"I can't."

"You can."

"I can barely keep ahead of this. And all you do is run around, crop-dusting your DNA, your percomm signal, and your geo-tagged, time-stamped, lens-imperfection-fingerprinted tourist photos all over the fucking network. You have no idea how hard it is. I can't keep it up."

"I'm sorry," said Chris.

"News flash: sorry doesn't help. If you want to help, find a hole and stay there." Hope disconnected.

CHAPTER 11

PRESSING ANOTHER REP ON THE LEG-LIFT MACHINE, CHELSEA HELD THE pump at the top of the movement. Her thigh muscles were showing beautiful lines. She was surprised how quickly her body was responding to the exercise program. *Maybe I wasn't as out of shape as I thought.* She eased her legs down until the weight stack hit bottom. *Clink.*

The exercise equipment was clustered at one end of the ground level of the Venizelos estate's main house. The entire area was a giant solarium with glass walls six meters high and glass overhead. The other end of the solarium housed the indoor pool and other amenities of a luxury spa, Chelsea had learned, having never known such services even existed before meeting Evangelos. The solarium extended out at the rear of the house, toward the outdoor pool, which was nestled in the middle of fairy-tale landscaping, under spectacular, towering palm trees.

Today was another hot, sunny day in Greece, but the air-conditioned space was comfortable. The intensity of the sunshine made everything dazzle as if set ablaze by stage lighting. The chrome surfaces of the equipment sparkled like tiny disco-ball mirrors. Chelsea was pretty sure she was the only person who used the equipment, because the weight machine settings never changed between workouts.

She pressed out six more reps. The last was a strain, and she couldn't get the full extension. *Clank.* The weight came down hard. She flipped over, onto her stomach, and did leg curls to strengthen her hamstrings, then finished with calves. Yes, the bombshell curves were coming back.

Hands on hips, she inspected herself in the mirror. She turned to the side and decided she had more work to do around the middle. *Won't be long. I'll be in prime shape for the naming ceremony. I need to talk to Evan about new clothes. Oh, and I can't forget about hair and makeup. I wonder if paparazzi will be at the ceremony? Will there be a limousine? A red carpet cordoned off with felt ropes? I must remember to ask Evan if there will be a rehearsal.*

She stepped closer to the mirror, touched her temple, and guided her fingertips down across her cheek and chin. *One thing's for sure: spending years indoors does wonders for the skin.* She'd always looked young for her age, and now that fact was even more apparent. She backed up a bit and assessed the whole package. *Adrienne has real competition.*

She tossed the towel over her shoulder and crossed to the front of the exercise area, zigzagging between the various machines, toward the entrance to the shower room. As soon as she turned the corner, she saw a man she didn't recognize behind the desk. "Oh, hello."

"Madam, I'm here to escort you to the residence area."

"For what?"

"Dr. Betasten requests your presence."

Another development? Maybe my son is awake! "Of course. I'll just clean up quickly. I'll be back, straightaway." She stepped toward the showers.

The man stood up from behind the desk. "You can't go in there." She could see now he was a guard, not a member of the housekeeping staff.

"Excuse me?"

"You heard me."

What? "On whose authority?"

"House orders."

"My husband owns this house."

"Alexander Venizelos owns this house."

"Exactly. My husband's grandfather." Chelsea took another step toward the showers.

The guard blocked her path. "Come with me."

The sweat was already starting to dry. She was filthy. *I don't want my son to see me like this, not after so long.* "I demand that you comm Gregory immediately. He'll straighten this out."

"You can either walk under your own volition, or I'll toss you over my shoulder."

The guard escorted her to the same room where she'd seen her son before with Mr. Skotino and Dr. Betasten. This time, however, only Dr. Betasten was present. As before, her son was inside the chamber under the blue light, unmoving, asleep. *Unborn*, she thought. *At least he won't see me like this.* She could smell her own odor wafting up from her cleavage.

Dr. Betasten had the same goofy grin. His hands were clasped above his short legs, which stuck out from under his lab coat.

"Come," invited Dr. Betasten.

Chelsea didn't move. She continued to look about the room. All manner of equipment was behind him. It looked like medical equipment, but there were many displays showing information, presumably the status of the chamber and her son. Then, off to the side, she saw a gurney. "What's that for?" she asked.

"When was the last time you had a physical examination?"

"I don't remember," she said. "But I'm sure you already know."

"I do," he said. "You're a very smart woman, Chelsea." He licked his lips. "And beautiful too." Her eyes darted to his. "And," he added quickly, "you want to look your very best for the ceremony, of course. An evaluation of your health is wise, no? We don't have much time. The ceremony is less than a week away now."

"How do you know?"

"Never mind. Please, come, sit on the examination table."

Chelsea didn't move.

"Do I need to bring the guard back in?" His blue eyes sparkled over his grin.

She crossed the room. Using the small stool, she hopped up on the table and was startled to see that he was already right next to her. *Waddle or not, he can move quickly when he wants to.*

"How have you been feeling?" he asked. His words sounded reflexive, and his gaze danced about her body.

"Fine."

"Getting enough sleep?" he asked robotically, his eyes flitting around, as if taking inventory.

She didn't bother to answer, he seemed so disinterested.

He put his hand on her arm. "I see you've been working out." He squeezed gently, testing the firmness of the muscles. "Extend your arm, please. Tense the tricep for me."

She did as instructed. The odor from her moist armpit drifted up. She wanted to turn away but kept an eye on his every move.

"Very nice," he said, pressing gently.

"Shouldn't you be wearing gloves or something?" she asked.

His piercing blue eyes met hers. "Oh, we're practically family, yes?" He released her arm, turned away, and stepped to the counter. "Now, I just need a sample." He turned back, holding a cotton swab on a stick. "Extend your arm again, please." He put the cotton tip to her armpit and rolled it in the stink. "Thank you." He turned back to the counter.

She couldn't see what he was doing. Then he abruptly tossed the swab into the rubbish bin and turned back to face her. He licked his lips again. "Magnificent," he said. Then he stepped close to her—uncomfortably close. "Chelsea, I have some bad news to share with you." He put his hand on her arm, as if to comfort her, but she could sense he was still caressing the muscles. "You are not to shower or bathe in any way until further notice."

"What?" Chelsea pulled her arm free and jumped off the table.

"Until the ceremony," he added quickly.

"Why?"

The blue eyes flashed. "Do you know what your median sulcus is?"

Who the fuck cares? she thought. "No, but I can tell you where you can shove it."

"It's the crease down the center of your tongue." He opened his mouth and pointed.

"I'll be bathing as usual, thank you. You can close your mouth now."

Ignoring her, he continued, "It's formed in the womb from two distal buds. One on the right and one on the left. They swell as they grow. And, at the sixth week of pregnancy, the two sides meet. The line is where the two halves join."

Chelsea shrugged.

"Your son is different. You could say the two halves never joined."

"No, I nursed him. There's nothing wrong with his tongue."

"I don't mean in such a way that you could tell."

"What does that have to do with my hygiene regimen?"

"Part of the naming ceremony involves his tongue. A union."

"You're not making any sense."

"Never mind. Forget it. For now, be comforted by the knowledge that your role in the naming ceremony—after having abstained from bathing—will celebrate the union between mother and son in the context of his rebirth. You, Chelsea, will complete his path to manhood. Just as Catholics sacrifice luxuries during Lent, or as Muslims fast during Ramadan, you must prepare for the naming ceremony by abstention. You must endure temptation. You must deny your ego. Asceticism, Chelsea. You must abstain from the sensual pleasure of bathing."

"YO. SUP, HOMIES?"

"Hey, Teeter," said Chris, as the trio entered Katie's kitchen. "Hey, Mrs. Leonard."

Katie's mom, Marcy, was connecting the jumbo syringe to Teeter's feeding tube. "Hey, kids." Her tone was polite, but Chris could tell her attention wasn't focused on them as she concentrated on her task.

"I'll put this in my room," said Katie, holding the gum machine they'd retrieved from Ben's lab.

"Wait, give me two for tonight," said Chris.

Katie handed him two pieces of gum and headed for the elevator. Al put the portable scanner on the kitchen counter.

Teeter's motorized chair and voice synthesizer were covered by the federal subsidy, but no in-home care. Lucky went to Teeter and sat. Lucky knew better than to jump up during Teeter's dinner. Chris picked up the water bowl the Leonards always had out for Lucky, filled it, and put it back in its corner of the kitchen. Lucky didn't flinch. Teeter kept his eyes on him.

Chris knew Mrs. Leonard appreciated the distraction. Sometimes Teeter was frustrated, and Lucky was able to sort of reset his attitude—or maybe strengthen Teeter's resolve to face the many challenges in his life.

Katie returned to the kitchen. "Mom, is it OK if we have a sleepover tonight?"

This was the start of Al's crazy scheme. They wouldn't tell anyone Chris's parents had been arrested by the authorities. Of course, it was only a matter of time before neighbors gossiped about the busted-down doors of his house and word got out. Despite Hope's insistence that Chris lie low, he was determined to get his parents out of jail, and then, with the warden's help, figure out what the Circle of Six were up to and come up with a way to stop them. For the moment, Chris just needed a place to sleep.

"Sleepover?" asked Mrs. Leonard, glancing back.

Her surprise was understandable. They hadn't had a sleepover in years. At their ages, it was borderline scandalous. Chris was ready with a convincing argument, leveraging his ability to convince others.

"OK," she agreed, standing straight. Chris was surprised how easy it was to get her permission. But then she added, "I could use your help with his respirator tonight." Clearly Mrs. Leonard had bigger worries than the appropriate age for a sleepover.

Katie glanced at Al. Helping with Teeter's routine would affect the timing of the next step in Al's plan.

"Of course," said Chris, not waiting for consensus.

Mrs. Leonard gave a relieved smile. She leaned over Teeter's chest again.

Chris thought about the years he helped at the animal shelter. He remembered how difficult it was for them to find volunteers. The shelter manager was grateful that Chris was so good at persuading people to volunteer.

Both Marcy Leonard and her husband, Dean, had been unemployed for as long as he could remember. So they certainly had the time to care for Teeter. But everyone needs a break. He thought about all the unemployed people in the country. *Why don't unemployed people volunteer more?* The thought made Chris feel guilty that maybe he should've volunteered for a worthier cause than the animal shelter.

Al put the bag of dog food in the corner by the bowl.

"Planning ahead, huh?" asked Mrs. Leonard.

"Yup. You know me, Mrs. L. Thanks for letting us stay."

Al had always called Katie's mom "Mrs. L." One time, Chris used it at home when talking about Katie's mom. It earned him a reprimand. Laura said it wasn't respectful. Chris did as he was told, but he didn't think Al was being disrespectful with the nickname.

Katie grabbed the scanner from the counter. Leaving Lucky behind, the trio turned for the hallway. "Keep on truckin'," said Teeter, as they left the kitchen.

In the privacy of Katie's room, Chris said, "Of all your crazy schemes, Al, this has to be the craziest."

"Nah. Nothing crazy about it. Since we can't break in to the police station, I got us an invitation," said Al. "Harrison went for it."

"He couldn't pass it up," admitted Katie. "Chris telling him we wanted to turn ourselves in—all three of us, even late at night—was too good to ignore. But what do we do once we're inside the police station?"

"We have to trust the warden," said Al. "That's why we need to wait until after dark, so the police station empties out, in case Chris has to do something extraordinary. The fewer witnesses, the better."

"We have no idea where in the building Laura and Ben are being held," said Katie. "Lucky can track them, but Harrison never lets Lucky go inside the building. We can't use the medical scanner because it's not designed to scan through walls. What do we do if the station is filled with police officers and FBI agents all night? Maybe Ben and Laura aren't even there. Maybe—"

"OK," said Al, "we get it."

"I'm just saying I think they're safer in jail. With the Circle of Six after us, jail is a safer place. Like in Monopoly. You know, toward the end of the game, when all the properties are built up? It's safer in jail."

"We already discussed this," said Chris. "The Circle of Six controls the authorities. Don't forget what happened immediately after Al killed the guy in the park at the start of the summer. Remember what Hope said? She said the Circle of Six changed the police orders, to arrest Al for murder. They manipulated Al's classification, from 'victim' to 'suspect.' That means

160   ANDREW HUNKINS

the Circle of Six could change the DOD's orders and have my parents in the electric chair by sundown. Jail is not safe."

Katie slumped.

"Besides," Chris continued, "the DOD is likely to get the truth out of my mom and dad without any trouble. No waterboarding required, not even drops on the forehead. My parents will start babbling as soon as the interrogator turns on the bright light. The authorities won't believe the parts about the warden and the incredible things he helps me do, but the rest of it—like Hope hacking into the communications of the police, FBI, and DOD—will only jack up the FBI's determination to find Hope, arrest her, and claim a win against the Hoods. Being a minor won't protect Hope then. And if they get to Hope, they get to me. And if they get to me, they get to the warden. And if . . ." Chris's voice trailed off.

"What is it?" asked Katie.

"One of the warden's words is ringing in my head right now."

"Which one?"

Chris looked up. "*Genocide.*"

"We all know what that means," she said.

"Oh, please, queen of all-knowingness," said Al, "grant us this one request. For we are simple folk and know not of these worldly matters."

She rolled her eyes. "Fine." She recited, from her percomm, "The systematic killing of all people from a national, ethnic, or religious group."

"Like that guy Nietzsche said: systematic killing of all the good people." Chris looked at both of them. "If that's the Circle of Six's goal, how on earth could they pull it off?"

| |0 | |0 | |0

THE GUARD ESCORTED CHELSEA TO ALEXANDER'S GRAND STUDY IN THE MAIN house. Chelsea was determined to convince Evan to let her bathe. She simply couldn't bear to live like a refugee any longer. But Evan had refused to accept her comms. That afternoon, she'd worked herself into a froth. It was evening by the time Evan finally sent for her. Over the years, Evan had had the estate all to himself because his grandfather spent increasingly more time on his yacht.

"Handlers? Since when do you have handlers?" Behind her, the guard closed the study's enormous double door.

"Settle down, Chels. I've always had handlers."

"And their job is to keep me from talking to you?"

"I was in a meeting," said Evan. He looked so stately, standing now by the cocktail service. Evangelos Venizelos had the same ability to command a room as his grandfather. Chelsea could see the resemblance in the line of Venizelos men. Captains of industry. Both Evan and Alexander had the look. She only saw pics of Evan's late father, but he had it too. There was no question in her mind that the family expected her son to follow in the same footsteps—and to *live* to do so. From the moment Alexander had learned of Chelsea's pregnancy, he'd devoted the vast power of the Venizelos empire to guaranteeing his great-grandson would survive any attack by the Hoods and not share the same fate as his son. Nothing could harm Chelsea's son, not even the blast of the car bomb that killed Evan's father.

"I'm talking about *after* the meeting," she said. "Your handlers refused to put me through to you."

"I'm always reachable in an emergency."

"It *is* an emergency."

"Your wardrobe for the naming ceremony is not an emergency."

"It's not about my wardrobe. It's—" Chelsea glared at him. Evan was being evasive and he knew it. *Work, work, work? Hardly. I'm not fooled. Evan has been spending his time on more than Venizelos Greek Shipping business.* Chelsea considered the last sixteen years. She'd been held in seclusion while their son grew up. She'd had lots of time on her hands but nothing to do. Evan had had time too, but she had no idea what he was *really* doing all those years. Considering that Evan already knew their son's given name, it was obvious now he was an insider. Now, more than ever, Chelsea felt like an outsider.

She crossed her arms. "You said it would be different now."

Evan took the last sip of Jameson from the tumbler. Coaxing the last drop, the ice crashed against his teeth. "Actually, I said it would be different once our son wakes."

"*Reborn*," she corrected sarcastically. "Can't you hear how fucked-up that sounds?"

Evan refilled the tumbler but skipped the ice. "Many religions have the concept," he continued. "You know—born-again Christian?"

"That's a figure of speech. Our son was encased in some kind of second womb."

"So which is more fucked-up?" asked Evan. "A person who claims to be reborn as a figure of speech, or someone who is truly reborn?"

"Listen to yourself. Not bathing until the ceremony? That's fucked-up."

"It's for our son. I swore a promise to my grandfather—about his *great-grandson*, I remind you—that I would comply with any request that led to the protection of our son. You don't understand—"

"No, *you* don't understand. You're blind to what's happening. You're blind to how they treat me. I deserve an explanation. But you don't even see a problem. I demand to see Alexander."

"Pappous is on his yacht," said Evan, using Alexander's family nickname. "It's late. I'm not going to ask him to come here. I'll see if he's available tomorrow."

"No. Tonight. Now. We go to see him right now."

Evan took a sip. She was surprised he was even entertaining the idea. She wanted an end to the shower moratorium, yes, but she assumed an appeal directly to Alexander was out of the question. Her demand to see Alexander was just a way to force Evan's hand, to poke holes in his excuses so he'd give his permission.

Evan tipped back the rest of the whiskey and set the tumbler down hard. "OK. I'll send word we're coming. Let's go."

Oh boy. Evan had called her bluff. *What am I going to say to Alexander?*

Together, they walked to the helipad. It was a warm night, typical of Greece, with millions of stars in the purple darkness. Six concrete slabs were surrounded by floodlights. Each slab was occupied by a quadcopter—a pilotless four-propeller aircraft. Three of the craft were passenger models with room for six people. The other three were cargo transports.

After they climbed in, Chelsea watched Evan enter the destination into the controls. The quadcopter came to life. With all four rotors spinning, they lifted off in seconds. The ride out to sea took only a few minutes. Ahead, the lights on the *Balkan Beauty* came into view. Chelsea had visited the luxury yacht only a few times during the nearly two decades since arriving in Greece, but each visit was a thrill. Only the rich and powerful had yachts. It was a confirmation that she was rich and powerful. Or at least rich. Well, rich by marriage. Maybe not so powerful.

Their quadcopter gently descended, swung around, and touched down on the *H* of the yacht's helipad.

Chelsea followed Evan into the main cabin. Unlike her previous visits to see Alexander, the yacht was bustling with people. She recognized several to be guards who patrolled the estate.

"What's going on?" asked Chelsea.

"This is all for our son," he said defiantly. "This is all preparation for the naming ceremony."

On the yacht? Chelsea hadn't even considered the location for the ceremony. She had assumed it would be at the estate, in a ballroom or something. "Here? But where will all the guests sit?"

"No guests, Chelsea," said Evan, matter-of-factly.

What? All the talk about things being different now, that she could finally take her rightful place as her son's mother, meant what? She remembered her wedding day. Unbelievably decadent. A fairy tale come true. That's what it should be like now. *Will things actually be normal after the ceremony?*

Outside the door to Alexander's stateroom, the guard stepped aside. *Swish.* The door opened. But instead of Alexander, they were greeted by a robot.

"Please, come in." The sound of the robot's voice wasn't robotic at all. It sounded very human, as if it came from a human operator just out of view.

"Welcome. My name is Holliday. I'm Alexander's personal medical assistant."

Chelsea had heard of PMAs but had never actually seen one. Only Hillites could afford them, she believed. Evan never said his grandfather was a Hillite. But then again, he never denied it either.

Gleaming white with stainless-steel trim, Holliday only scarcely resembled a person. It had a cylinder for a head, atop a rectangular torso between two arms. The orientation of its bent legs made it look like it was kneeling. It had wheels on its knees and toes.

Chelsea whispered, "Japanese?"

"Originally," said Evan. "But now they're manufactured in Mexico. Japanexican," he said derisively. "You don't have to whisper. You can't hurt its feelings. Besides, it can hear you no matter how softly you speak."

"I'm not whispering to protect its feelings," said Chelsea. "Your grandfather is sleeping. We should come back another time." She wasn't prepared to confront Alexander. Evan had sensed it, no doubt. He was going to make her face the consequences of skirting his authority by appealing to his grandfather. Seeing Alexander now, she regretted the intrusion.

"It's quite all right," said Holliday. "Alexander is expecting you. He's been looking forward to it. He simply drifted off. I'll rouse him for you." The PMA pivoted on its knee-toe wheels and glided to the bedside.

"Come back another time?" Evan said to Chelsea, his voice prickly, "It's an *emergency*, right?"

Alexander's health had clearly declined. The few times she'd seen him over the years, he'd generally looked the same, but now he appeared especially old and frail. The bed, though plush and well appointed, was a hospital bed. And his stateroom looked more like a hospital room than a luxury suite.

Holliday announced, "Your family is here." The back of the bed began to rise. Holliday's legs straightened to make it taller. It adjusted Alexander's pillow.

Alexander's eyes opened—slightly at first, and then wide when he recognized them. He coughed, patted his chest, and made a gesture. In the blink of an eye, Holliday extended its arm. The PMA's hand, which looked like a Swiss Army knife, rotated such that a tube appeared about a centimeter away from Alexander's lips. He drank, and coughed again. "Yes, please come in," said Alexander with his signature smile and warmth. He took another sip. "Now you see why I named him after the infamous gunfighter Doc Holliday. Fastest draw in the West." Sufficiently sated, Alexander raised a hand. Holliday backed away. "How is the beautiful couple?" He offered both hands. Evan and Chelsea each took one.

"She is beautiful, I'll give her that," said Evan, raising an eyebrow. "But we're having a row. She's upset about the preconditions for the naming ceremony."

Alexander looked wounded.

Chelsea said, "It's not that. It's just that I . . ."

Alexander squeezed her hand. "Tell me."

"I don't know. It's just so unconventional."

"What, exactly?"

Evan said, "She's not to shower or bathe before the ceremony. A simple request."

"Are we asking too much of you, dear?"

"No," she said. "I mean, it's weird, that's all. I mean, honestly, who does that? What's the reason? No one will explain it to me."

Alexander cleared his throat again. "When Evangelos was born, I had the tip of his penis cut off."

"What?"

Evan chuckled.

"Oh, you mean circumcision," said Chelsea.

"Yes, just the foreskin. Nonetheless, seems rather barbaric, wouldn't you say?"

"But circumcision is conventional."

"Conventional in your humble opinion," Alexander clarified. "Do you know why it's done?"

"Not exactly," she admitted.

"We should remember that not all cultures practice circumcision. On the other hand, did you know that some cultures—up until recent history—circumcised females too?"

"No," said Chelsea.

"Maybe you should look it up," said Evan.

"Dear Chelsea," continued Alexander, "a broad variety of rituals are practiced across cultures and history. Only a tiny fraction of those seem conventional to you because they are part of your own experience, your own culture."

"But—"

"Another example: Do you know why many cultures fast? Times of the year when worshipers refrain from eating?" He didn't wait for her answer. "This is an overly simplistic way to put it, but essentially, as a reminder of their devotion to God."

"But—"

"Chelsea, dear. Each day between now and the ceremony, what are you going to think about?"

"How disgustingly rank I am."

"Always thinking about yourself," said Evan.

"Indeed," said Alexander. "It's natural. It's human. And what will be your next thought?"

"Our son?"

"Precisely. Consider this: throughout history, how often did the average person have the opportunity to bathe?"

Chelsea shrugged. She didn't like where this was going.

"Rarely," he answered for her. "About as frequently as the average person had a day with enough to eat, which is to say almost never. The fact that you take a shower every day, sometimes multiple times a day, could be considered—what was your word?—*weird*?"

"But—"

"Please. Chelsea. My dear, Chelsea. Do this for me. Do it for Evangelos. Do it for your son. Every time you feel the desire to bathe, think of your son, my great-grandson. Think about the importance of him becoming a man—his coming-of-age."

110 110 110

AFTER DINNER, THEY HELPED MRS. LEONARD CLEAR TEETER'S LUNGS. AL WAS especially helpful because it was so easy for him to manipulate Teeter's body—as if handling a rag doll, yet with the gentlest of touch. Chris knew how much Mrs. Leonard appreciated their help but he was surprised at how quiet Katie had become. As Al cared for her brother, she watched with an odd expression of serenity.

Once Teeter was squared away, they fed Katie's mom a lie about playing flashlight tag and then headed out to the masstran stop. During the ride downtown, Al seemed deep in thought, probably still working out details of their plan.

By the time they reached their stop, the masstran had few passengers. Most of them had gotten off at stops along the way.

Night had fallen completely, and the streetlights illuminated only vacant shops and sparsely populated sidewalks.

"Ready?" asked Chris, after the masstran glided away.

Al and Katie nodded.

Chris popped the gum into his mouth. The connection to the warden—the ephemeral, virtual corpus callosum—snapped open. Like in the poem "Footprints in the Sand," the invisible owner of the footprints became overt, palpable. Chris's tenth muse was now perceptible. His mind's pervasive selfness evaporated and was replaced with an extraordinary sense of togetherness.

The police station was just a couple blocks away. "Let me show you how the warden keeps my skin cells from being captured by the sniffer," said Chris. "There's one of the black pillars near the corner."

With Lucky at Chris's heel, the trio walked the sidewalk.

"Why are people looking at us?" asked Katie.

The streets were mostly empty, but it did seem that the few pedestrians out and about were gawking at them.

"That's creepy," agreed Al.

"I don't know," said Chris. "Maybe—"

"Hey, Seven Eight Six," a voice called.

Chris walked back to a narrow gap between two storefronts.

It was the girl—the girl from the group of youths, one of the hooded protestors. "What the hell do you think you're doing out in the open?" she asked. She was thirty feet back, hardly visible in the darkness.

"Who's that?" asked Al.

"What do you mean?" called Chris.

"The curfew, you idiot."

"Oh my god," said Katie. "How could I forget? The city has a curfew. We never go to the city, especially not after dark. I totally forgot."

"Nice one," said Al.

"Hey, it's your brilliant plan, Napoleon. You—"

"You and your idiot friends need to shut up and get back on the bus. You're tripping all kinds of alerts. I'm surprised the police aren't here already."

"It's OK," said Chris. "We're going to the police station anyway."

"Going to report us, huh? The hell you are." She pulled out her percomm.

"Why are you even talking to her?" said Al. "Harrison is going to be waiting for us outside the station. We don't have time for this."

Still holding the percomm, she said, "This is your last warning. Leave now. Or Cell Number Fourteen will make you leave."

"It's not what you think," Chris called. "You don't understand. I'm sorry. I have to go."

Al pulled him away.

"Who was that?" asked Katie. "What was that all about?"

They reached the corner of the block with the police station, with its grand lawn out front. "I'll tell you later," said Chris. The entrance was still a hundred yards away, but Chris could clearly see Special Agent Harrison waiting outside the security doors.

As they approached the steps and concrete walkway leading to the station entrance, a group of hooded youths marched toward them from the opposite street corner.

"Oh no," said Chris.

"Who are they?" asked Al.

"Don't do it," called a young man at the front of the group. Thanks to Lucky's amazing canine hearing and voice recall, Chris knew it was the same young man who led the protestors of Cell Number Fourteen.

"What's going on?" Harrison called from the entrance.

"Holy cow, Chris. This isn't good," said Katie.

"You need to get out of here," said Chris to the leader of the group, who was now standing directly across from the trio.

"That's my line."

"No, you don't understand."

"I understand that I never should have trusted you. I can't let you compromise our team."

"I'm not. That's not what this is about. I—"

"Mr. Lumière, explain yourself," Harrison called.

"Chris, Katie's right," said Al. "This is a freaking Waterloo."

The girl came up from behind, also wearing a hood. "If we run now, we still have a chance to get away." She pulled out an odd-looking bag. "Put your percomms in here."

"Enough," said Harrison. Chris watched as Harrison raised his arm and made circles in the air with his index finger. All heads turned as, up the street, a huge black panel van screeched around the corner and accelerated toward them with blue and red lights flashing. Chris could see now it was a SWAT van.

"Holy shit," said the leader.

"Do as she says," said Chris to Katie and Al. "Put your percomms in the bag. Now!" Chris put his in the bag too.

"We can't outrun them now," said the girl, panicking.

"They want me," said Chris. "They'll come after me."

A sound in the distance started to build. A black helicopter marked with the letters FBI roared overhead from behind the station. Its powerful spotlight nearly blinded them. The SWAT van careened to a stop. The back doors flew open, and troops in tactical gear jumped out.

"Now," yelled Chris. "Run."

The members of Cell Number Fourteen, along with Katie and Al, bolted away from the nexus of converging forces.

Lucky charged the advancing soldiers and barked, giving Chris the precious seconds he needed. The soldiers aimed their weapons, but hesitated, unsure if they should shoot the dog. The soldiers kept their distance and skirted around, keeping an eye on the barking obstacle.

In a whoosh of air, Chris rocketed up at the helicopter. *Tshhhhh.* The floodlight went dark. Glass rained onto the street. Chris darted through the air and smashed the helicopter's exhaust pipe, shutting it. Smoke began to chug from the engine as the helicopter lost power, choking on its own exhaust.

Lucky raced away from the soldiers, in the opposite direction his friends had fled.

Whump, whump, whump. The helicopter began to auto-rotate down to the lawn, its rotor looking like a winged maple seed in slow motion.

Chris landed near Lucky and faced the soldiers. "You looking for me?" Chris called.

The soldiers gave chase.

CHAPTER 12

"**H**OW DID YOU ESCAPE FROM THE FEDS?" ASKED THE LEADER OF CELL Number Fourteen.

Chris, Al, and Katie sat on the step under the blue light shining above the sealed door of the group's safe house.

"I didn't have to escape," said Chris. "I was never caught."

"I mean, how did you get away without them catching you?"

"I can't tell you that."

"And how did you and the dog get here even before we did?"

"I can't tell you that either."

The leader stepped away, back into the huddle, and resumed his group's private debate regarding the trio's fate.

Al whispered to Chris, "You said the blue light might stay on until morning?"

Chris nodded. "They told me this is a special room that blocks all electromagnetic energy."

"Same with the bag," said Katie. "It blocks our percomm signals so the authorities can't use it to find us or this location."

"Well, I think our plan is screwed," said Al. "I don't see any way to rescue your parents tonight if we can't get out of here."

"I think our plan is screwed anyway," said Katie, leaning toward her friends so the group wouldn't overhear. "After that fubar situation, the police station is going to be protected like Fort Knox."

"By the way," said Al, "how *did* you get here before us?"

"I picked up Lucky, and we flew," said Chris. "You were right about coming at night. But if anyone saw us flying, Hope will skin me alive."

Unlike his first collision with Cell Number Fourteen, when Chris was invited into the belly of the safe house, this time, he and his friends weren't allowed to go any farther than just inside the door.

"She's pretty," said Katie.

"Who?" asked Chris.

"You know who. The girl, silly. The one they call Four Nine Six."

"Pretty?" said Al. "She's not pretty, she's smokin' hot. You got yourself some urban candy there, migo."

Katie gave Al a punch on the arm.

Four Nine Six was standing with the group in deep discussion. But her gaze was on Chris. Al was right. She wore a skintight Lycra crop top above painted-on jean shorts. No butt cheek hanging out, but it was close. He saw a hint of a smile appear on her face, letting him know his up-and-down glance hadn't gone unnoticed. He looked away.

"What are they saying now?" asked Al.

The gum was still working, so Chris could hear their conversation by channeling Lucky's more sensitive hearing. "They know I lied to them before, about being part of their group. Actually, I never really lied. I just didn't object when they assumed I was a new member. But they believed me just now when I told them we were going to the police station for our own reasons, not trying to report them. They wish none of this had happened. They're discussing how to get rid of us without any trace back to them."

"If Al and I don't get our percomms back," said Katie, "we won't be able to spin another alibi. My mom will start to worry. If our parents try to talk to each other, and can't reach yours, everything's going to unravel."

Chris nodded. And then said, "Uh-oh."

"What?"

"One of them is insisting we're Hillites," said Chris. Chris listened for a moment. "Phew. None of them seem to think that's too likely." Then he asked, "Say, what *is* a Hillite anyway?"

"A super-rich person," said Al.

"Yeah," said Katie. "But it's more than that. They have such extreme power and influence in the world that they believe laws don't apply to them. They can do anything they want. They bribe politicians to pass laws in their favor."

"Like what?"

"Like not paying taxes, getting exclusive access to trade markets, and operating factories with unsafe labor practices."

"That's bad, huh?" Chris wished he'd paid more attention in school. Even though his mom was a political science professor, he never understood why any of it mattered in the context of his own life.

"The world blames the Hillites for all the problems with the global economy. Hillites comprise less than one-tenth of one percent of the population but control thirty percent of the wealth. The Hoods are the only ones able to fight the Hillites because they have an edge in cyber technology."

"But the Hoods are terrorists," said Chris.

"Well, the Hillites control the government, and therefore law enforcement. So the establishment uses the term *terrorist* to keep public opinion against the Hoods. And to justify the use of force, even military force."

"Like the Omega Force?"

Katie looked at him. "Not the Hollywood variety."

"Sure, of course not," said Chris.

"We experienced the real Omega Force for ourselves. They're serious." She had that superior look on her face. "You don't actually believe all that glam slam you see in those vid flix, do you?"

"No. No way. Not me."

She slanted a disbelieving glance at him. "Anyway, vilifying them as Robin Hood terrorists doesn't really work because everybody hates the Hillites and roots for the Hoods."

Chris never rooted for the Hoods; he always rooted for the Omega Force. "So is the Omega Force good or bad?"

"Jeez, Chris, you can be so naive sometimes," said Al. "Katie's talking about real life. Nothing is purely one or the other. When are you going to grow up?"

It was just a glancing jab, but Chris was surprised how badly it stung. He *was* growing up, but it felt like one foot was on the boat while the other was still on the dock. On one hand, he wanted to run around with Al and Katie all day having endless adventures, watch Hope from afar, and fantasize about what it would be like to date her—and just ignore the growing presence of the warden inside him. But he felt compelled to make his life actually matter, to help others when he could. He wanted to embrace the warden, take on real-life challenges as a man, and achieve some level of greatness, if only on a personal scale. But most of all, he wanted a *real* relationship with Hope. Without her, everything else seemed pointless.

"It's a matter of perspective," said Katie, taking Chris's question about good and bad seriously. "The Omega Force is supposed to be good. But *mature adults*"—she eyed Chris— "know the Omega Force is a conventional weapon of war. The Hoods aren't a stand-up army. Their battles aren't fought in the middle of a field with one line of redcoats on one side and Colonial soldiers on the other, separated by musket smoke. To complicate matters, the Omega Force is an instrument of government authority. If the government is corrupt . . ."

Chris gave up trying to understand and just let her babble on. Besides, he really needed to concentrate on the group's deliberation. Cell Number Fourteen just kept arguing.

| | 0 | | 0 | | 0

THE DOOR TO ELADIO'S APARTMENT SWISHED OPEN. "SIR, PLEASE COME IN."

Colonel Wesson stepped inside and followed Eladio into the living room.

Eladio turned. "So, an actual in-person visit, huh? To see the damage for yourself?"

"How are you feeling, son?"

The searing memory of Tijuana replayed in Eladio's mind. Initially, he'd tried yelling for help. The loud echoes of his own voice, bouncing off the concrete walls surrounding him, were the only response. He nursed the fantasy that someone would hear him. He struggled and tested the chains. The clash was loud too. Surely someone would hear. The pain in his shoulders had become unbearable. Huffing and puffing, he'd thrashed, fueled by the fiction that he could loosen the chain from above or break it from below. With each yell, his hot breath filled the hood he still wore. He twisted himself, which created a metal-on-metal screech from the chain links. For hours—accompanied by an orchestra of clanging shackles—he cried an aria composed by Jacob Marley. The excruciating pain in his shoulders only continued to worsen.

Because his captors hadn't removed the zip tie at his wrists, the plastic strap was pinned under the metal cuffs. The plastic edges of the zip tie ripped into his skin. All his flailing made it worse. Blood trickled down his arm. He finally stopped thrashing. Exhausted, he had no choice but to simply hang. The pendulum motion of his body finally slowed. The constant melodic creak of the chain, like an abandoned porch swing, eventually subsided as he came to rest. Silence.

That's when he heard it. Breathing. Someone had been in the room with him the entire time.

"Hello?" Eladio had been shocked by the desperation in his own voice. "Who are you?" he'd demanded, reaching deep inside for some level of authority. No response.

Then Eladio felt something brush against his foot. A spark of a plan flashed in his mind: knee his captor. His legs were bound, so he couldn't really kick the person. But he'd show them he still had fight. He'd prove his defiance. Unfortunately, his body refused to respond. As if on strike, his body was on a different program. It had a different goal: self-preservation. Its priority was avoiding any sudden movement, avoiding any more pain. His body ignored any order for movement.

The something brushed against his foot again. Eladio tested it with his toes. It felt like the end of a broom handle, maybe an inch in diameter, rounded at the top. It was just high enough for him to put the ball of his foot on it, taking the weight off his arms. A godsend. "Thank you," he blurted. The words escaped his body defiantly, without permission from his brain.

His shoulders stung as he bobbed, struggling to equalize his weight. New pain came quickly with all his weight concentrated on one spot on the bottom of his foot. He switched feet. With all his fine motor ability long gone, he overcompensated, moving with big, jerky movements, flailing clumsily, like walking on a balance beam for the first time, but handcuffed. His arms screamed with each bob and twist. He had no choice but to relieve the pain in his arms and shoulders by transferring his weight onto the post below. When the pain on one foot became too much, he switched back and searched for a fresh spot on the other foot to endure the pressure. Before long, all the fresh spots were gone. Like being burned at the stake, he strained to keep his toes away from the searing pain.

That's when he realized the sick brilliance of it all. The post under his feet was part of the ordeal. The pain constantly shifted from wrists to shoulders, to toes, to the balls of his feet, and back again.

The ordeal had continued until the hood was finally yanked from his head.

The memory, even now, in the safety of his apartment back in Virginia, was so strong he had to blink to make sure it wasn't real. Eladio glanced down to his right arm in the sling. "I have a bunch of strained ligaments in my joints. My right shoulder's the worst. The cortisone shots help. I have treatments scheduled. Doc says I'll make a full recovery in no time."

"That was intentional," said Wesson.

"You're damn right it was intentional. If they wanted to kill me, they would've done it in the first second."

Wesson nodded. "You have to go back to Tijuana."

"Hell no."

"The torture session was just a warning."

"No shit. Message received."

Wesson folded his arms.

"No, sir. Not me." Eladio shook his head. "Count me out."

"What we need here is some old-fashioned creativity."

"I followed procedure," said Eladio.

"Tactical surveillance of a civilian, right?"

"That's right," said Eladio defensively. The colonel's words hung in the air. *Civilian?* Rodriguez and his crew were the furthest thing from civilians, despite their official classification. Eladio continued his defense. "Even if I treated them as hostiles, protocol still dictates that I surveil my target before taking action. They were on top of me before I even made contact. The result would have been the same."

"That's true."

Anger welled up inside. "You knew this would happen. You knew they would see me coming."

"Think it through, son."

Eladio didn't want to think it through. He wanted to tell Wesson to go to hell. During the torture session, Eladio had held it together. Even after they released him, and he'd arranged for transport home, he held it together. He held it together as the corpsman treated his injuries. He held it together as he boarded the military transport home. But that was all he could muster. Once the aircraft got into the air, once he was alone, once it was quiet, he bawled like a baby. The shaking was convulsive, unstoppable. He wept and trembled the entire way home.

"You sent me on purpose," said Eladio, red in the face now, "knowing full well Rodriguez would see me coming. You knew I wouldn't make contact on my terms."

"I sent you there to truly understand the Omega Force, the men and women of the United States Marine Corps under your direction."

"Well, hallelujah. Mission accomplished. After having been introduced, I want nothing to do with them. And they made it plainly clear that they want nothing to do with me."

Wesson unfolded his arms and scratched the stubble on his chin. "You said a minute ago that you followed procedure."

Eladio nodded, still fuming.

"Well, Rodriguez and his team also followed procedure . . . on that fateful day in the Nevada desert that earned them each a dishonorable discharge."

"Other than honorable," Eladio corrected.

"Nothin' honorable about OTH. So, I'm sure it's as good as dishonorable in Rodriguez's book. My point is, following procedure doesn't seem to be working too well." Wesson put his fists on his hips. "Eladio, you're a marine. I know you won't let me down."

"I'm not going through that again."

"I don't expect you to."

"Then, what?"

"Figure it out, First Lieutenant. Figure it out." Wesson turned for the door. As he strode away, he said, "Report progress when you have it." The door swished closed behind him.

| | 0 | | 0 | | 0

"MISS? MISS?"

Hope opened her eyes. She was still on the masstran.

"I couldn't help but notice that you usually get off at this stop." From her commutes, Hope recognized the woman who'd awakened her. "I didn't want you to miss it."

Hope realized everyone on the bus was looking at her.

"Service delay," said the masstran's synthesized voice. "Please complete passenger transfer and allow service to resume."

The woman made a gesture in the air, as if pulling an invisible cord. *Ding.* The sound confirmed the bus would wait another fifteen seconds.

"Thanks." Hope rubbed her face and went for the exit.

"Here," called the woman, "don't forget this." She handed Hope her backpack.

"Oh gosh. Thanks again." Hope stepped off. The vehicle glided away. *I can't keep this up.* She glanced at her percomm and verified that all her programs were still working to keep Chris, Al, and Katie hidden—and to make sure their communications were secure. But the list of parties trying to track her friends was growing faster than she could have imagined. *I really hate you right now.*

Inside the Ferguson office, Hope caught up on her regular work, until she was interrupted.

> *SalaciousFrog: Your boy is becoming a real pain in the neck.*
> *PrincessLIMDIS: Trust me, I know. And quit calling him that.*
> *SalaciousFrog: I have a job for you, but I'm not sure you can handle it.*
> *PrincessLIMDIS: As if. What's the job?*
> *SalaciousFrog: We found 30K blockchain credits in encrypted storage.*
> *PrincessLIMDIS: No problem.*
> *SalaciousFrog: I don't mean technically. How are you going to manage it with all your other, shall I say, interests?*
> *PrincessLIMDIS: Let me worry about that.*
> *SalaciousFrog: I wish I could.*

| | O | | | O | | | O | |

THE BLUE LIGHT OVER THE DOOR WENT OUT.

"We have your word?" asked the leader of Cell Number Fourteen.

"Yes," agreed Chris. Katie and Al nodded. "We'll never come back here. We're not going to report you to the authorities. And we won't do anything stupid, like violate the curfew."

Four Nine Six stepped forward with the bag containing their percomms. Handing them back, she said, "We installed a spoofer program. It's running now. When you get home, you can turn it off."

"In exchange for your promise," emphasized the leader, "that we won't ever see you again."

Four Nine Six held her gaze on Chris.

The door closed behind Chris, Al, Katie, and Lucky. The morning air was cool in the shaded alley, but the sun was coming up brightly.

"I'm starving," said Al.

"Never mind that," said Katie. "We need to get home. Our parents are probably freaking." The trio hustled out of the alley and headed for the masstran stop. "I want to check for messages, but I'm afraid to. I don't know what the spoofer program does. I don't want to do anything that would disclose our location."

"Better wait until we get home," said Chris.

CHAPTER 13

"I'M DONE WITH THIS," SAID LAURA, WHO SAT IN AN INTERROGATION room at the Philadelphia police station. "I wanted to help, but this is ridiculous."

"You admit to associating with known protest groups," said Harrison, standing next to the locked door. "You indoctrinated your son into terrorism. You're responsible for him becoming a Hood."

"We've told you everything. He's not a Hood."

Whenever Chris talked to Laura about Special Agent Harrison, he'd always said Harrison was just trying to harass him into a confession. Now Harrison was harassing Laura and Ben the same way. Maybe Chris was right, that Harrison's only real power was nagging.

"Before last night," said Harrison, "I might've agreed with you."

"Oh sure. Because everyone knows the usual meeting place for Hoods is on the police station's front lawn," said Laura. "Listen to yourself."

"A military helicopter shot out of the sky? Evading a SWAT team? *You* should listen to me. I can't decide if you two are Hoods, too—or just stupid, blind, uninformed, and incredibly bad parents."

That hurt. Harrison actually made her second-guess herself. Not that Chris was a Hood, certainly not. But how much of the danger he now faced was her fault? *My students. Abducted. Kidnapped. Disappeared. I had to try to rescue them, at least. But did I have to endanger my own child in the process?* The warning flags throughout the years flashed through her mind. First the prenatal scanner didn't work on Marian. Then the discovery that all scanners—of any type, even the ones that open doors—didn't work on Chris. *No. It's the warden*, she reminded herself. *Everything leads back to the warden. Chris never would've insisted on going to Nevada to rescue the young women if it hadn't been for the warden. Somehow the warden's influence over our lives is connected to the abductions of my students.*

"What now?" asked Ben.

"When I complete my report, antiterrorism powers will be approved. Then I'll hold you, your son, and his friends indefinitely. No requirement for formal charges. Once I have Hope Avenir, you'll all face a grand jury."

Laura looked at Ben. He was dealing with the strain better than she. The home invasion was initially terrifying. But they quickly realized it was the FBI rather than the group of killers. As shown in historical footage of drug busts from the twentieth century, the FBI agents had smashed down the doors, screaming, "Down! Down! Everybody down!" Even though she and Ben hadn't been in the hallway when the tear-gas grenade went off, Laura could hardly breathe when they handcuffed her, facedown, on the kitchen floor.

Before Harrison could continue his interrogation-room rant, the door swished open. Harrison seemed surprised and jumped, almost to attention. "Major Nolan. I, I wasn't expecting you for another hour."

A man in a military uniform stepped in, flanked by another military officer. Laura remembered the name Nolan. Ben had contacted him years ago, asking for help to learn more about the warden. Nolan hadn't done anything to help. As she recalled, he was kind of a jerk about it too. At the time, they'd dismissed Nolan's lack of response as any normal person's reaction to the claim that their son had an alien attached to him.

"Who's this?" Nolan asked dismissively, speaking to the other officer, but referring to Harrison.

Before Harrison could introduce himself, the other officer said, "Harrison, Frederick M. FBI. Special agent. Philadelphia branch."

"This is my investigation," said Harrison. "I'm in charge."

"You're part of the problem," said Nolan, waving his hand as if to clear an offensive odor.

The other officer grabbed Harrison, dragged him to the door, and tossed him out. The door swished closed.

"We told them everything," said Laura. "I'm not a Hood. I—"

"Shut up," said Nolan. Ignoring Laura, he leaned over the table to stare directly at Ben. But Ben, who despised conflict, was looking down.

Holding hands under the table, Laura felt Ben tighten his grip. She looked between Ben and Nolan. Ben refused to look up.

Finally, Nolan said, "Do you know who I am?"

Laura started to answer, but Nolan raised his open hand into her face.

"Answer me," said Nolan to Ben.

Ben nodded.

| | O | | | O | | | O | | |

WITH GRIM FACES, CHRIS AND AL LOOKED AT THE SIGHT IN FRONT OF THEM. AS with his own house, the doors to Katie's prefab had been smashed in. Katie wept with her face in her hands, unable to look at the scene herself. The trio had called out to her family and searched frantically. But Katie's mom, dad, and brother were nowhere to be found.

"I'll be back," said Al. He bolted out of the house. Chris thought of sending Lucky to investigate Al's house, but he knew Al would need to see it for himself.

Minutes ticked by. Katie's crying gradually eased. Stepping over the pieces of broken doorframe, she retrieved a tissue from the bathroom and blew her nose. With her back to the wall she slid down to sitting. She hugged her shins and put her head between her knees. "I can't believe it," she mumbled.

"We can't be here," said Chris.

She lifted her head. The anguish on her face made him look away. "I don't care anymore, Chris. It's not worth it."

"We have to get the gum machine out of your bedroom."

"I think Hope's right. What are we doing? This has all gone too far."

Chris said nothing.

After a few minutes, Al came back into the house, breathing heavily. "My house too," he said. "The FBI is still there. I wasn't able to get close, but my mom and dad are long gone. They looked like they were wrapping up." He caught his breath. "We can't stay here."

Chris looked back to Katie but didn't say anything.

"Maybe Hope sent them on a wild-goose chase, or maybe we got lucky this time, I don't know, but the FBI is going to be watching our houses," Al said. "We have to go."

Al finally registered Katie's state of despair. He knelt next to her. "Come on." After a moment, he put his arm around her and pulled her up. No sooner was she standing than she wrapped her arms around his neck, buried her head in his chest, and cried. "It's going to be OK," he said. "We have to stick together. We'll get through this. Our families are OK. You'll see. I won't let anything happen to them. Or you."

She pulled away and wiped her nose on his T-shirt. Then she held both his cheeks and kissed him on the lips.

Al turned to Chris. "You didn't see that."

"See what?" said Chris. "I'll get the gum machine. We gotta go." He left Al and Katie in the hallway to finish whatever they had started.

BEN SAID, "YOU'RE THE PERSON I CONTACTED, YEARS AGO, FOR HELP WITH MY son."

Nolan stood straight. "You said at the time that your son was possessed by an alien presence."

"That's right," said Ben.

"I reviewed the surveillance footage from last night," said Nolan. "We have countless cameras in the area. Unfortunately, nearly all of them were blocked. Except for one. We recovered the vid from our helicopter. It's pretty blurry. After the search-light was destroyed, the images are almost impossible to make out. Somehow, your son managed to bring the helicopter down in a matter of seconds." Nolan looked at Ben. "Are you saying he was able to do that because of the alien presence?"

"That's right," said Ben. "Exactly as I told you six years ago."

"Or is it more likely that you're all part of a Hood terrorist cell?"

Ben didn't answer.

"I suppose the alien just happens to be an expert in com-munications, is able to infiltrate our systems, and block our surveillance equipment?"

Laura said, "No, that's Hope doing that. She—"

Ben squeezed her hand.

Nolan raised his eyebrows. The other officer angled a tab-let-sized percomm so Nolan could see. *Tap, tap, swipe, swipe, swipe.* Nolan shook his head and returned his attention to Ben. "A seventeen-year-old?"

"Special Agent Harrison is convinced," said Ben.

"Harrison didn't do his homework; he doesn't know *you're* the computer expert."

"Software, actually."

"Better yet."

"And astrophysics."

"So that makes you an expert on little green men?"

"Yup."

"I don't buy it."

"Apparently not much has changed in six years," said Ben. "Are we free to go?"

"On the contrary," said Nolan. "Mr. and Mrs. Professor, prepare to be schooled. The FBI needs antiterrorism powers to deal with you in any serious way. I have no such restriction." He turned to the officer. "Move them to the infirmary and have them prepped for truth serum." He turned back. "Benjamin Richards, Laura Richards, I declare you enemies of the state. From this point forward, you will be treated as such."

|10 |10 |10

ON THE MONITOR, PETE RASMUSSEN WATCHED THE BIG MAN HOP OUT OF THE cart at the corridor leading to the control room of the unbihexium harvesting lab of TerraStore's Yucca Mountain complex.

Pete turned to the six scientists in the control room. "Ready?" They all looked pretty nervous, but each nodded. "OK. Anderson's new assistant is almost here. Game faces, people. Here we go." Pete stepped to the control room door and opened it.

The man striding down the corridor looked like he'd just left a photo shoot for a men's fitness magazine. The expanse of his torso and shoulders filled the corridor's width. Half bull, half news anchor, the man cruised right up the few steps to the door.

Pete said, "Good morning."

Unlike Anderson, the man actually replied, "Morning." He may have even smiled. "So, this is it, huh?" he asked, after stepping to the middle of the control room and taking a look around.

The scientists all had the same look of tentative curiosity as Pete.

Pete couldn't remember a time when Anderson hadn't come himself to spew fire and brimstone on Pete's laboratory team. At first, Pete had assumed the worst. Like, maybe this new assistant was some kind of enforcer. But Anderson explained he wanted Pete to introduce his assistant to the unbihexium harvesting process. Pete wanted to tell Anderson he didn't have time. *In my dreams.* In his macho fantasies, Pete might push back on Anderson, but never in reality.

"Yes. This is the control room. I'm Pete Rasmussen, project director. And you are . . ."

"Oh, sorry. I'm Ken Barrister. But you can call me the Bear," he said, grinning. Then, incredibly, he went to each of the scientists, shook their hands, and introduced himself.

What the heck?

As Barrister glad-handed his way down the line, the first scientist looked at Pete with a quizzical expression. Pete just shrugged. When Barrister got to the first of the two women, he seemed to linger. When he reached the second woman, he said his hello and added, "Nice shoes, by the way."

Huh? Pete looked for himself. *Come to think of it, they* are *nice shoes.* Pete hadn't ever noticed. When not wearing hazmat suits, they all wore lab coats. Shoes were one article of clothing not covered up. *Is he flirting?* Pete wasn't sure if it was the shock of this unexpected behavior or Barrister's raw charisma, but his team appeared to be genuinely captivated, especially the women.

"So what do we do first?" Barrister asked.

Pete was having trouble processing the whole interaction. Barrister was acting like a grade schooler out on a field trip for career day.

"Well, I guess I can give you a tour of the tank of formaldehyde where we harvest the unbihexium. We use a filter system to—"

"Hey, Pete," Barrister interrupted. "I can call you Pete, right? Look, I'm not into all the foreign words, OK? Can I just get the short version?"

What foreign words? Pete wondered. "Of course. Well, it's pretty simple, I guess. Approximately every seventy-two hours, we shock the tank of formald— Uh, the tank full of . . . uh . . . special liquid. I mean, we shock it with electricity. Then we filter out the . . ." Pete tried to think of a simpler word for the heavy metal, but couldn't come up with anything. "Unbihexium."

"This unbihexium stuff, it's pretty important, huh?"

"Yes, it doesn't occur naturally on earth, so this is the only known method to gather it."

"Uh-huh. And what do we do with it?"

"Actually," said Pete, "I don't know."

| | 0 | | 0 | | 0

"IF YOU CAN'T FIND THE WARDEN, I CAN'T SEND MY SERVANT," SAID SKOTINO.

"I didn't say I *can't* find the warden," said Tyvold, "I said I can't find him *now*."

"*Can't?*" asked Skotino. "This is a first."

"You don't understand how this works. To find the warden, I have to get through the cyber defenses protecting him. When I do that, I'll expose myself. It's the sixth law of information dynamics formulated by Nicholas Leonard in 2036 and proven by Sadi Carnot in 2046," explained Tyvold. "You can defend without exposing the defender, but you can't attack without exposing the attacker."

"What exactly are you saying?"

"I'm saying I have to wait until your servant is completely ready and poised to take action before I access the warden's location. The moment I breach the defenses to learn the identity and location of the warden's defender, our own location and identity will be revealed. We'll have little time, minutes or less, before the defenses shut me out again. In addition to your servant eliminating the warden, all parties to whom our location and identity are revealed must also be eliminated. Every trace."

"No way to keep us hidden?"

"None. It's the observer effect. Schrödinger's cat. You can't observe a system without affecting it. The observation can always be traced. Quantum firewalls act like black-body mirrors. Once the last one is defeated, there's nothing left to absorb the attack. The attacker will finally get a ping. But unavoidably, the defender will have a clear line of sight to the attacker. Like playing hide-and-seek, if I can see your eyes, then by the laws of physics, you can see mine."

"Four days until my servant is reborn. A long time to wait."

"Dr. Betasten says it's critical that the naming ceremony is performed as soon as he wakes—at the same moment actually. So we have to wait until the ceremony is over to even begin the preparations necessary for him to act on your behalf, to enforce your will, to find and destroy the cyber defenses protecting the warden, and, without delay, destroy the warden's host along with any other mortals who may have learned of our existence."

"What is the status of the preparations for the naming ceremony?"

"Going well. Your idea to use the moon pool of the *Balkan Beauty* for easy access to ocean water is pure genius. The chamber at the bottom of the yacht can be sealed such that the scuba hatch can be opened without flooding the chamber and sinking the ship. The chamber is luxuriously appointed, designed for the wealthy to dive in comfort. Apparently, Alexander enjoyed diving when he was younger. Anyway, we're converting the chamber into a sanctuary worthy of the naming ceremony. The scuba hatch will allow us to sanctify the boy in seawater, as directed by the gods."

"Any concerns?"

"Your servant's buoyancy is very different. Because he's six times heavier than an average mortal, he'll sink like a rock. He's strong enough to tread water, but he'll use considerable force to do so. Let's just say there'd be a lot of splashing. In any case, we need a way to lower him into the water and then haul him back up. Don't worry, I've got it all worked out."

ㅣ0 ㅣ0 ㅣ0

"DO YOU KNOW WHY THERE'S NO DOUBT MASTER COHEN WILL AGREE TO HELP us?" asked Al, lying next to Chris and Katie in the hidden clearing behind some bushes by the park. This place had served as their most trusted hideout.

The sound of Al's voice jerked Chris awake. He'd dozed off apparently. With three teenagers and a dog, the hideout was wall-to-wall bodies. The gum machine and the scanner were their only possessions. No food. No clothes. Thank goodness it was a mild night.

Chris concentrated, defogging his sleepy brain. He stated the obvious. "*Of course* Bruce will agree to help us. What kind of silly question is that?"

"I know. I'm asking you *why*."

"Because he cares about us?" said Katie. She was still awake and sharp as ever.

"What I mean is, who would believe the DOD is holding our parents?"

Katie said, "Bruce was in Vegas with us when we confronted the Omega Force. He saw those Circle of Six whack jobs for himself. He knows what they're capable of."

Both Katie and Chris presented straightforward arguments. But Chris could tell from Al's style of questioning that he already knew the answers. It was Al's way of sharing his thought process, and of leading them to independently arrive at the same conclusion.

"No," said Al. "Before that. Remember?"

Katie said, "Chris convinced Bruce to go to Vegas and help us find the abducted women."

"Exactly," said Al. "And Father Arnold. And Hope too. Remember? Remember when we played the stock market game and Chris could convince everyone that we could predict the stock market?"

"That's true," said Katie. "Hope said she sensed it when she was near Chris. He can make her fears and doubts go away just by being near."

"Right. And remember when Chris went to the K9 search-and-rescue training simulation, and the building collapsed on him? Laura was a basket case while he was away from her. Once Chris was back home, she relaxed. I know any mother would be anxious if their son was hurt and far from home—and, naturally, that anxiety would subside once their child returned safely home—but his effect on people is more than that."

"Yes," agreed Katie. "Even Chris's doctor accommodates his differences, even though he can't explain their origin. What're you getting at?"

"The effect has to be from the warden. Chris is able to convince people no matter how crazy it might sound. He gets them to help."

"I think you're right," said Chris, fully awake now. "All the years I helped with the animal shelter, the manager there always commented about how I could attract volunteers. I never thought too much about it," he said. "But back to Katie's question—what are you getting at?"

"Why can't we convince Harrison to release our parents and help us?"

"No way." Chris expected Katie to laugh in Al's face too, but she didn't. "Katie? That's crazy talk, isn't it?"

It was a few moments before she answered. "No, I think it's brilliant."

Chris forced himself to try out the possibility. "No. Harrison never believes anything I say."

"Were you *trying* to convince him?" asked Al.

Chris thought about that. "No, I guess you're right. I didn't care if he believed me or not."

"So, you have to try," said Al.

"There's no guarantee," said Chris. "What if we walk into the police station, and I can't convince him? He'll lock us up. We'd be finished. Besides, they probably have a sniper positioned on the roof to take me out if I even get close. That's not conducive to any kind of conversation, let alone a sales pitch."

"I agree," said Al. "Harrison needs to come to us. Alone. So we can have him all to ourselves, without any pressure."

"How?"

"Good question." Chris heard dry leaves rustle as Al crossed his arms behind his head as a pillow. "Let me think about that."

It usually took Al a while to concoct his plans. It could sometimes be days—not that they had days to spare. Chris forced himself to relax. He was nearly asleep again when Katie spoke.

"Chris?" she whispered.

"Yeah?"

"What's it like to fly?"

"Awesome."

"Oh come on. Describe it."

"I can't describe the feeling," said Chris. "Look, I'll take you sometime, so you can feel it yourself. OK?"

"That would be jazz. Really. But, just . . . just describe what it *looks like* when you're flying."

Chris organized his thoughts. "Have you seen those vids where the guy has a camera on his helmet and he's doing some kind of sport, like skateboarding or motocross? And the camera is on the end of a stick attached to his helmet, so his face is in the shot the whole time?"

"Yeah. A selfie vid."

"Right. And have you ever noticed that while the guy's body and the background are wildly moving all over the place, his head is anchored in the frame and doesn't move at all because the camera is attached to the helmet?"

"Yeah."

"OK. Hold that image. Now, do you remember those history vids we watched in school, of Apollo rocket launches back in the nineteen hundreds? The shot is from the top of the rocket, looking down the side. There's steam pouring out of the rocket—"

"It's moisture. Frozen by liquid oxygen."

"Right. Frozen moisture. I knew that. Anyway, the rocket blasts off, right? You see the huge cloud of flame below. The gantry falls away. The rocket starts going up. Chunks of frost fall away, and the picture really starts to shake from all the power. Then the rocket rolls, making the whole world rotate in the vid. And after only a few seconds, everything in the background gets really small. Remember? You start to notice the pattern of farmland, neatly divided into squares. And all the while, the side of the rocket is anchored in the frame because the camera is attached to it—like the skateboarder's face. That's what flying looks like."

Chris waited for Katie's response. He thought she might've fallen asleep. Al was breathing rhythmically, but not quite snoring.

Finally, she said, "Thanks." Another minute passed, and she said, "Good night, Chris."

"Good night, Katie."

CHAPTER 14

"**G**ET UP, YOU NEANDERTHALS." KATIE WAS MOVING UNUSUALLY FAST and rough.

"No," Al said, groggily.

Chris's eyes were uncomfortably dry, and so too was his mouth. He tried to muster up enough saliva to speak.

"It's starting to rain. Move. Now. We need to run for it."

Lucky was up and stepping over them.

Chris had to pee in the worst way. He was finally able to crack open his eyes after many attempts. It was morning, but he wasn't exactly sure how early. "It is not raining," said Chris, after choking down the cotton. That's when he felt the drop. It was a big fat drop, like the kind that comes just before a heavy storm. With his eyes fully open now, he could see the drops had hit Katie first because the canopy of branches over the hideout was thinner in the center. Most were hitting the leaves overhead, but some were getting through. *Fwap . . . fwap . . . fwap, fwap.*

"Argh." Al put a forearm over his face.

The sound of the rain became a roar. Chris and Al both sat up. Katie rolled forward and threw her body over the bag containing the gum machine and the scanner. The bag was nylon but not waterproof. A flash of lightning lit up everything, easily penetrating the branches. Seconds later, *BOOM*. The thunder-crack was one of the loudest Chris had ever heard. The rain was coming down in sheets now. The four of them were already drenched. Water streamed off of Chris's hair and down his face.

Lucky didn't seem to mind. A shake worked its way from his shoulders to his butt, sprinkling them with a warm mist of wet-dog smell. Katie and Al seemed to arrive at the same conclusion as Chris: nowhere to go.

Over the deafening *chchchchch* sound of the deluge, Al said, "Well, this is just splendid."

Katie, still shielding the bag, said, "Now what do we do, Napoleon?"

"We execute our plan," said Al.

"Which is?" asked Katie, yelling over the noise.

"Harrison comes to us."

"How?"

"*We* kidnap *him*," said Al, with his signature grin.

110 110 110

TYVOLD WATCHED AS THE QUADCOPTER CAME TO REST ON THE DECK OF THE *Balkan Beauty*. He waited until Skotino hopped out.

"This way." Tyvold led Skotino off the helipad, into the ship's interior, and down the elevator, to the lowest level of the ship—well below the waterline. The door leading to the moon pool was already open. "Leave us." Half a dozen workers wearing Venizelos estate maintenance uniforms stopped what they were doing and filed out. Each man kept his head down as he passed.

"This is it," said Tyvold, once they were alone.

Skotino stepped into the space. There was considerably more room now that storage closets designed for bulky diving gear had been removed. The room measured about six meters on each side. On the floor, positioned dead center, was the hatch to the sea. The room could be sealed and pressurized, allowing the hatch to be opened without sinking the ship.

Skotino looked at the mechanical apparatus hanging directly above the center hatch. "Winch?"

"Yes. We can raise your servant out of the water without any effort on his part. He weighs nine hundred pounds, but the winch is rated for one ton, so it should be fine."

"What new information has Dr. Betasten learned during his most recent clarity communion with his god?" asked Skotino.

"We know that polychaete worms will take residence in your servant's tongue. But Dr. Betasten has now learned why the hibernation state has killed all the bacteria in the boy's body. It's a lock-and-key mechanism similar to the zona pellucida that protects a human egg just prior to fertilization, ensuring that only one sperm of the correct species is able to enter. Even though your servant's milky cocoon is no longer visible, there is still an antibiotic film protecting him.

"Dr. Betasten learned that your servant must repopulate his microbial biome from two sources. The first is the ocean." Tyvold looked at the hatch. "From the time he awakes until he enters the sea, the film will keep bacteria from contaminating his internal biome, all except a very specific type—ocean bacteria presenting the proper protein signature."

"And the other source?" asked Skotino.

"His mother's vagina," said Tyvold.

Skotino simply nodded.

"That's why the gods instructed us to prevent Chelsea from bathing before the ceremony. A strong concentration will ensure transference of the bacteria."

"She will not submit."

"No," said Tyvold. "Initially we planned to keep her compliant by drugging her. But we've learned she must experience fear and terror to prepare the site of penetration."

"Estrus lordosis oedipus," said Skotino.

"Exactly. Genital vasodilation followed by an increase in vaginal lubrication. The response will be involuntary, driven by her emotional reaction. It's critical that her Bartholin's glands are activated.

Our main concern is the time after the ceremony, because the memory of the ordeal will negatively affect her relationship with your servant and likely the rest of us, including Evangelos. She's likely to refuse any new demands we place on her."

"Even the guilt trip would be useless," said Skotino.

"Yes. Guilt requires fear of loss. Chelsea has a deep desire to maintain her motherly image in her son's view. The ceremony will destroy that image. She'd have nothing more to lose. Guilt would have no effect. For this reason, we'll drug her in such a way that she'll have no memory of the ordeal, but she'll remain conscious throughout the ceremony and will experience her full range of emotions."

"Still, she won't agree to the precondition on the day of the ceremony. She'll expect to shower that day."

"Yes. We'll use the guilt trip to convince her to wait—voluntarily—until the ceremony is over. The drug will block her memory of what will happen"—Tyvold held out his arms, as if at the edge of the Grand Canyon—"right here."

| | 0 | | 0 | | 0

"I ASSUME YOU'RE FINALLY CONVINCED WE'RE TELLING THE TRUTH," SAID BEN, facing the image of Major Nolan on the wall display of their holding cell in the Philly police station. "The truth serum you injected us with prior to questioning must have worked."

"On the contrary, I confirmed your responsibility for the bombings at Benjamin Franklin University, the UK research park, and the satellite uplink station in Australia," said Nolan.

"I didn't blow up Ben-U's data center. Why would I blow up the equipment I need for my own work?"

"Why indeed? But you did blow it up. You admitted it."

"I did not."

"Under the influence of the truth serum, you were asked if your previous actions led to the explosion. And you said yes."

"That's not the same thing. I didn't do it."

"Of course not. I've uncovered a broad conspiracy. You didn't physically plant the bomb. But we'll find out who did. We'll have your entire terrorist cell rounded up in no time. We already have the Leonards and the Fuenteses—"

"What?!" said Laura.

"That's right. One of them probably planted the bomb. We'll know very soon."

"This has gone too far," said Laura. "The families of Chris's friends had nothing to do with any of this."

"I now have unlimited authority. I've started the extradition process for Rajiv Gupta."

"Raj is my colleague and friend," said Ben. "He had nothing to do with this."

"Hardly. The bombs were incendiary. Under truth serum, you admitted the halon fire-retardant system had been disabled. We analyzed the communications between you and Gupta. Surprise, surprise, we got a hit on the word *halon*. We confirmed he has the necessary permissions to override the halon system."

"You're twisting the truth. That's not—"

"Enough. It's over. Once I have Chris Lumière and the rest of your three-family terrorist cell, you'll all be executed." The display went dark.

"Ben, you have to stop them."

"How?"

"It's our son, you have to!"

"He's fine. The warden is with him," said Ben. "We talked about this. You've been away from Chris for a while. Your anxiety is returning and it's getting to you."

"Is that so? Well, your *spectrum* is returning, and it's getting to *you*," said Laura. "Even at this very moment you can't look me in the eye. A few more days and you'll be full-on autistic."

"I've never been full—"

"I know that! Stop analyzing everything! *Do something!*" She turned away and crossed her arms. She knew better than to expect him to try to comfort her.

I I0 I I0 I I0

WITH LUCKY IN TOW, THE TRIO ARRIVED AT THE ALLEY OUTSIDE CELL NUMBER Fourteen's safe house. Chris asked Al, "Have you figured out what I'm supposed to say? We're breaking our promise. We agreed to never contact them."

"We don't have a choice," said Al. "We need their help. After the bus ride, my clothes are dry, but my underwear is still wet, and my crotch is chafing. I'm not excited to sleep outside again. And I'm starving."

"Quit complaining," said Katie. "We don't even know if we managed to avoid the cameras, the scanners, and the skin-cell sniffers on the main streets. Those detectors are more concentrated in the city. We have to trust that Hope is still hiding our digital trail, and that the spoofer program on our percomms is preventing our location from being revealed."

"What's next? Just knock on the door?" asked Chris.

"Yup," said Al. "You know me. I like the direct approach."

Al stepped into the narrow space between the two dumpsters and rapped on the shadowed door. Nothing. He knocked again. Still nothing.

"What now, Napoleon?" asked Katie.

"Enough with the Napoleon cracks. You're being so negative. How about helping for a change? I prefer MacArthur. Or, simply General would be fine."

"Yes, sir, General Simpleton, sir."

"Seriously. Now what?" asked Chris.

"Well, let's think," said Al. "They all pass through this door, right? Let's have Lucky trace their scent to where they live." To Chris, Al said, "I suggest the urban candy." He winked.

"Disgusting," said Katie.

"It rained this morning," said Chris. "The scent will be hard to pick up."

"It's already ten o'clock. I'll never make it to lunchtime without food," said Al. "Either you're eating the gum, or I am."

"We've got nothing to lose," said Katie. From the nylon bag slung over Al's shoulder, she pulled out a piece of gum and handed it to Chris.

In a matter of seconds, Lucky was zigzagging across the alley with his nose to the ground. He disappeared around a corner.

"Where's he going?" asked Al.

"Relax," said Chris, staring at nothing in particular, concentrating on the connection to Lucky. "It's not as easy as it looks."

"It looks impossible, migo. Jeez."

Lucky reappeared, sniffed, retraced himself, and rounded a different corner."

"He's got it," said Chris. "Let's go."

110 110 110

SUE WAS SITTING AT THEIR NEW APARTMENT'S TINY KITCHEN TABLE. "GOOD morning."

"Morning," said Hope. She'd actually gotten up very early that morning to stay on top of events surrounding Chris. She put a slice of whole-grain bread into the toaster, dropped a tea bag into a cup, and filled it with hot water from the dispenser. When the toast was ready, she sat across from her mom at the table.

"Do you want something with that? I'll make it for you."

"No, I was up earlier and ate then."

"What did you have?" asked Sue.

Hope didn't answer. She munched on the dry toast.

"School starts next week," said Sue. A minute passed with no response from Hope. "Won't you reconsider?"

"No." She sipped her tea.

All their belongings were fully unpacked now. Sue had done all the work. She'd even taken the things from the old house that didn't fit in the apartment to the recycling depot and gotten some money in exchange. Pennies on the dollar, but it was something.

"Have you talked to Chris?"

"Yes."

Sue's face lit up like never before.

Why is she so obsessed with him? What's the big deal? Hope decided to go the limit. "He kissed me."

The series of expressions on her mom's face was unbelievable. She looked shocked, pleased, doubtful, pleased again, and then her face returned to her usual neutral, as if she was consciously beating down all the emotions. The whole episode looked like a game of whack-a-feeling.

"Happy now?"

Sue opened her mouth but said nothing.

Hope gulped the last of the tea, put away her dishes, and grabbed her backpack.

"Have a good day," Sue said, fleetingly.

When the elevator door opened to the lobby, Hope noticed Toothless and Tinkerbell weren't there.

"Hey, little lady," the manager called from his booth. "Everything OK? I didn't see you yesterday."

At the glass partition, Hope asked, "Maybe you were sleeping?"

"No," said the manager confidently.

"I'm fine. Thanks." She glanced to the bench. "Where are your friends?"

Just then, the outside door swished open, and Toothless shuffled in with Tinkerbell on a leash.

"Potty break," said the manager.

"Feeling better, dear?" Toothless sat heavily on the bench. Tinkerbell was making a beeline for Hope. The dog seemed a bit younger now. Maybe the exercise allowed her old bones to loosen up. Toothless simply dropped the leash. It dragged behind the little brown dachshund trotting to Hope. "Your mom said you weren't feeling well."

Hope bent down to pet Tinkerbell. "I'm fine." She scooped her up, held her, and continued to stroke. "How are *you* guys?" The question seemed to pop from nowhere, involuntarily, as if a small talk program in her brain had started of its own accord. She walked to the bench and set Tinkerbell down underneath.

"Fine and dandy," said Toothless.

Hope went to leave.

"You take care now," said the manager.

Hope tried to decide if he was saying that because he wanted more jerky or had genuinely dropped the creepy act. He sounded sincere, almost fatherly.

After the uneventful ride to the Ferguson office, Hope got to work.

PrincessLIMDIS: Status?
SalaciousFrog: Your surveillance program targeting the bank has completed. Systematic vulnerability testing in progress.
PrincessLIMDIS: Good.
SalaciousFrog: Your boy is using a spoofer now.
PrincessLIMDIS: I know.
SalaciousFrog: Pretty soon he'll be able to hide all by himself.
PrincessLIMDIS: Very funny.
SalaciousFrog: You're going to tell him it's junk, right?
PrincessLIMDIS: It blocks the police.
SalaciousFrog: Not the feds. And not even the police if they get motivated.
PrincessLIMDIS: I know. Let me worry about that.

CLINK. CLINK. CLINK. CLINK. BARRISTER COULD HEAR THE WEIGHT STACK BUT couldn't see who was working out. *The exercise facilities of this Greek migo's mansion are incredible. Actually, this entire place is incredible. Greece is incredible. Even the scramjet ride was incredible. These Circle of Six characters travel halfway around the world in the time it takes most people to commute to work.* Barrister reminded himself that *he* was one of these Circle of Six characters.

Clink. Clink. Clink. Barrister weaved his way through the equipment, following the sound as he went. *Wow. A hot blonde.* She was on the leg press and seemed to be really squeezing them out.

Barrister got closer. He watched from behind as her pony bobbed and swayed with the beat of each press. She had nice definition in her quads, he noticed, as her legs extended. The cadence slowed. She grunted softly as she strained for another rep. Her legs trembled near the top of the movement. *CLANK.* She eased off the machine, unsteady on vanquished legs. She screamed.

"Oh, sorry," said Barrister, "I didn't mean to scare you."

She had her hand over her mouth, body frozen, and seemed to be deciding if what he'd said was true. Then the hand came down. "Well, you bloody well did."

Sexy English accent. Really hot. Thirtysomething. Fuckin' nubile. "Sorry. Really. I'm Ken Barrister." He stepped forward to shake her hand, and she immediately backed away. The fear in her eyes was unmistakable. He put his arm down and kept his distance. "You can call me the Bear," he offered. She was still tense. "That's what my friends call me."

Finally, she seemed to relax a fraction. And, just as quickly, seemed embarrassed. She grabbed her towel and put it over her chest, defensively, trying to make it look like she was dabbing at sweat. She brushed the strands of hair from her face in vain. Keeping her eyes on him, she made a wide circle while maintaining her distance, always facing him. "I'll leave you to it."

"I didn't mean to interrupt your workout."

She kept moving. "No trouble. I was finished."

"I could spot you."

"Maybe some other time." She was practically walking backward now, toward the exit. She turned and strode away.

"Wait. What's *your* name?" He used his seductive voice. No woman could resist it. *That's right, baby. The Bear is interested in you. Now's your chance.*

She stopped dead in her tracks.

That's right. Works every time. Nice little ass on her.

She spun. The look on her face told him she was not enchanted. "My name is Mrs. Evangelos Venizelos."

Chelsea, recalled Barrister. *It's her. The mother of the kid in the glowing chamber. The naming ceremony thing. The whole reason the Circle of Six said I had to come to Greece. Oops.*

"That can't be," said Barrister, his mojo unbroken. "The same woman I met only weeks ago in Nevada?"

"Of course," she snapped.

"You've changed." He just let the words hang. He could actually see the effect, like solvent eating away rust. The flattery, only implied, had seeped under her defensiveness. "You were a ghost of a woman then. And now look." He smiled appreciatively.

"My husband owns—" She stopped herself. She looked less confident, more vulnerable. Then rallied, "I own this house." She rephrased it again, "This is *my* house."

Barrister nodded.

She turned and marched out. Her legs moved like pistons, giving her ass a cute little jiggle. *Wow. Catch ya later, MILF.*

| | 0 | | 0 | | 0

IT WAS WELL PAST NOON WHEN THEY ARRIVED AT THE STREET WHERE FOUR Nine Six lived. Chris didn't see any pertrans parked on the street. He was no expert on Philadelphia, but even he could tell this was a pretty rough part of town. The street was full of potholes, with dry weeds growing out of its many cracks. Broken glass, gravel, and unidentifiable junk littered the curbs. Kids ran and played right in the middle of the street. At the far end, a stickball game was in progress. Shouldn't they be in school? He realized he'd lost track of the days. He looked at his percomm. Tuesday, September 1, 2058. Holy cow. August is over. School's about to start. The thought of him returning to school—and normalcy—seemed like someone else's life.

Chris didn't say it out loud, but he was hungry too. The plan was to eat-and-run—incredibly rude to Four Nine Six, Chris knew, but it would take time to further decipher the warden's words, learn the Nevada group's evil plan, and find a way to stop them. The trio needed food, but there was no time to spare. It was too risky to use food credits via their percomms. They didn't need Hope to tell them how monumentally stupid that would be.

Across the street, a small mob had formed around Lucky. A few kids were brave enough to pet him.

Chris, Al, and Katie crossed the street to rescue Lucky from all the affection.

"Is this your dog?" asked one raven-haired young girl of elementary school age.

"Yup," said Chris.

"What's his name?"

"Lucky."

The rows of homes weren't the prefab kind—not the kind that he, Al, and Katie lived in. *These houses have to be two hundred years old.* Each was two stories high with a porch on ground level. On almost every porch, folks were sitting in the shade. Some were older people—fanning themselves against the late-summer heat as well as the humidity fueled by the storm earlier that morning—but most were able-bodied adults. It was a weekday afternoon, and none of them were working.

"Lucky," repeated the girl, with approval. "Why is his name Lucky?"

"Because of the amazing things he can do. People say, 'It must be luck.'"

"What kind of amazing things?"

"Like finding people. He can find anyone."

"Is he a puppy?"

"No."

"How old is he?"

"Seven."

Her face lit up. "Me too. What kind—"

"OK, OK. Enough questions," said Four Nine Six. She'd come out of her house. "Run along now. All of you." Most of the kids raced away, but not the girl with all the questions. "You too, Juanita."

Defiantly, Juanita continued to pet Lucky and gave Four Nine Six a mischievous gaze. "Is he your boyfriend?"

"No."

"Him?" She indicated Al.

"No. Now beat it."

"Why not?"

Four Nine Six took a step forward.

Juanita ran off, giggling.

"Thanks," said Chris.

"Sure. Death by Juanita's curiosity is a horrible way to go." Four Nine Six's expression turned serious. "You shouldn't be here."

"We need your help."

"Not happening."

"Just hear us out." Chris was aware of his ability to influence people. The sugars in the gum sharpened his empathy with others. He knew he could convince others to help him. It worked best when his need was genuine, sincere, and benevolent. "Please. Just hear us out."

"Fine. Come inside. You've created enough of a circus."

The house was well kept but was showing its age. It seemed pleasantly comfortable to Chris. He wasn't sure how to ask for food. Again, he was ashamed at how unaware he could be. Even though the gum was wearing off, he sensed his power to convince her. The meta message from the warden was vague but perceptible: stopping the Circle of Six wasn't just personal— their evil plan affected everyone. Everyone gained from stopping them. Including Melissa. Melissa Monaco was Four Nine Six's real name, Chris learned, after being invited inside. She'd given up on all the secrecy of Cell Number Fourteen.

"You have quite the nerve," she said. "First, you break your promise. And then you want me to feed you? Do you think I have credits to spare?"

"I can pay you," said Chris.

Her voice turned icy. "Because you're a Loyd. Thanks for shoving that in my face."

"*I'm* not," blurted Al.

"Me either," said Katie.

"You're all from the burbs." She glared at them. "Practically the same thing."

"The protest group you're with," said Chris, "you're taking action to bring change?"

"That's right," she said.

"You're not just sitting around taking the government handout."

"Exactly," she said. The anger started to subside. "Enough is enough."

Chris looked to Al and Katie.

"Oh my god. You don't even know what that means." Melissa looked at Al and Katie too. "None of you." She was louder now. "Have you even heard it before?"

"Of course," said Chris. "It's a chant." His shoulders slumped. "But I admit, I have no idea what it means."

She stood up from the couch, took a few steps, then sat back down. "In one sense," she said, in a calmer voice now, "it refers to the Hillites, who hoard all the wealth. A huge proportion. I don't know exactly how much—"

"Thirty percent," offered Katie.

"Right. Thirty percent. OK." She seemed to notice Katie for the first time. "Anyway, all that wealth is held by a fraction of the population. I mean, really, how much wealth does a person need? Why take more than what is *enough*? Enough is enough. Get it?"

Chris nodded.

"In another sense, it refers to the government's overspending. Everything they do is over-the-top, except for the things that will help us Pogers. Like last week, when the Omega Force blasted out of the sky, right on top of the police precinct building."

"Seriously?" asked Chris, trying to contain his excitement. "That actually happened? The real Omega Force? Here?"

"Yes. You live under a rock? It was all over the pubcomm." She shook her head. "The government's spending is outrageous. Unbelievable. It turns out, the entire Omega Force stunt was for publicity. Can you believe it? What a freaking waste."

"Enough is enough," said Chris.

She nodded. "And the most obvious meaning is that we are all fed up. A tipping point, when the never-ending abandonment pushes you from a state of passive misery into one of corrective action. Enough is enough."

"Sorry to get you all riled up," said Chris.

"It's not you. It's constant. Like a vibration that never ends. You can't relax. You can't sleep. You can't enjoy life. No passion. No purpose," she said. "Do you know why the population of the United States is shrinking? Because the birthrate continues to drop—at a record decline. Why? Because we live in a world that's unfit for posterity. What mother would want to raise a child in this hell?"

"Hell on earth," mumbled Katie.

Melissa nodded. "Everybody gets free healthcare. Everybody gets free education. Everybody gets free shelter. Because crime is nonexistent, everybody has security. But our society is dead. It died from the inside out. There's nothing to live for." She let the words hang. Finally, she said, "Yup, we even have free food. Come on. Let's eat."

CHAPTER 15

MELISSA'S FAMILY TURNED OUT TO BE SUPER NICE. THEY INVITED THE trio to stay for dinner. Chris offered to pay, but the family refused. He was still unsure if it was insulting to offer to pay. It just seemed wrong not to. He didn't push the issue after they said no, and that seemed to be the right balance. Someday he'd find a way to repay them, not necessarily with credits.

Despite Al's constant objectification of Melissa as *urban candy*, she had wicked kitchen skills. She was smart and street savvy—and cute, no question about it—but watching her in domestic mode made her that much more attractive. Melissa could surely do anything she set her mind to.

In fact, things were going *so* smoothly, Chris dreaded the moment he'd have to explain to Melissa why they needed to leave. The trio needed privacy to work on the warden's words. Even before they could deal with the Circle of Six, they needed to strategize how to get Harrison to release their parents. It made Chris wonder how Hope was doing.

To keep his thoughts in the present—and because it was the polite thing to do—Chris offered to help prepare dinner. Melissa turned to him with an amused smile. She finished drying her hands and set the towel down on the counter. Keeping her eyes on him, she stepped to where he was sitting, put her hand on the back of the chair, looked at him, and leaned down ever so slightly, still smiling. "No," she said politely, as if she'd just been presented with a huge platter of pastries and confections, only to decline.

Chris was suddenly tongue-tied. His body felt like it had been hijacked. He blushed, and there was nothing he could do about it.

She released him from her gaze. "Thanks for the offer though," she said just as sweetly, turned, and got back to work.

Al caught Chris's eye and gave him the hubba-hubba-urban-candy smirk. Oddly, Katie's mouth was open. She was looking between Chris and Melissa, as if trying to work out a puzzle, like she was in chemistry class and noticed the periodic table for the first time.

"But we'd love it if you all stayed in the kitchen while we fix dinner," said Melissa. "Getting to know you better will make the time go faster." The kitchen was small, but everyone managed to fit. Katie rated a chair, and so did Chris. Al was on the floor with Lucky.

The meal was spectacular. And not simply because they were starving. The entrée was baked chicken. Roasted potato wedges and green beans that had been sautéed in garlic rounded out the menu. The chicken skin was crispy and perfectly seasoned, the kind where you want a little bit of it with each bite. The bird was incredibly juicy, even the white meat.

"The trick is to bake it breast-side down for the first half," said Melissa. "Then flip it. The skin turns golden brown, but the meat stays moist." She leaned over to check Chris's cut portion. "See? Just a whisper of pink. Perfect, right?"

To Al's delight, he got his own bird and raved through the entire meal. Melissa's mom enjoyed watching him devour his food. "Trust me, I know exactly how much a young man your size can eat." It turned out, Melissa's older brother was in the military. "The way to a man's heart is through his stomach."

Again, Katie was off in her own world. She appeared to be taking mental notes.

"LET ME GET THIS STRAIGHT. *YOU* GET TO RETURN TO THE US? BUT *I* HAVE TO stay here? What gives?" Barrister asked Spire. They stood outside the front entrance of the estate's main house.

Spire said nothing. He remained focused on his percomm as he waited for transport.

"It's because I can't reach clarity, isn't it?"

Without looking up, Spire blinked, his eyes staying closed longer than necessary, as if enduring pain. Barrister was amazed at how much the guy could communicate without saying a word.

As the black limousine approached, Barrister reminded himself that staying at the Venizelos estate wasn't so bad. In fact, it was pretty incredible. The Greek mansion looked like something out of a vacation fantasy. He watched the luxury pertran cross acres of lawn surrounding the curving parkway between manicured shrubs. The parkway split at a circular drive around an island of flowers. The half of the circle nearest the house went under a magnificent structure Spire had called a porte cochere. To Barrister, it just looked like a two-story roof attached to the house on one end and held up by two enormous columns on the other. The limo stopped at the circle's apex, where white marble steps flowed elegantly from the formal entry doors down to the drive's edge. The steps alone covered an area equivalent to an Olympic-sized swimming pool.

Before getting in the tran, Spire turned. "Go see Dr. Betasten. Don't do anything stupid." The windows of the pertran weren't tinted, but it looked as if Spire disappeared inside. Blackness into darkness; shadow into shade.

"*Don't do anything stupid,*" Barrister scoffed as the vehicle glided away.

The mansion's towering double door had modern hinge mechanisms. But Barrister had learned the sensors didn't work on any member of the Circle of Six. He tapped the panel on the wall outside, and the doors opened. Back inside, he heard the sound of the door locking behind him. While not loud, the click echoed across the enormous entry area set between matching curved staircases. With hardwood walls all around and polished granite below, there was nothing to absorb the sound.

He crossed the space and followed the route he'd memorized, arriving at the room where Dr. Betasten worked on the boy in the tube.

"Hey, Doc," said Barrister.

"I'll be with you in a moment," said Dr. Betasten. "Wait there."

Barrister did. The room looked like a medical clinic, but makeshift. Partitions on rollers lined the walls, but the ceiling was quite high, and it was easy to see the dark wood behind. The ceiling, with its intricate wooden coving, was visible and entirely inconsistent with a medical laboratory.

"OK, hop up on the table."

Again, Barrister did as he was told.

"Have you been feeling all right?"

"Of course."

"Such confidence," said Dr. Betasten. "You obviously take good care of yourself. Eat right? Exercise?"

"Sure, Doc. You don't get guns like these from sittin' around eatin' donuts." Barrister popped a bicep pose for good measure.

"No, certainly not." Dr. Betasten put his hands on the muscle. Squeezed. "Great definition." His hands continued to explore the arm. "Nice vascularity."

"Yeah, you should see when I get my pump. Wanna see? I could bang out a few dozen push-ups."

"No, that won't be necessary." Dr. Betasten's probing fingers migrated across the Bear's shoulders, pressing at spots. Then one hand came around to the front. "Abs?"

Barrister sat straighter and tightened his torso.

Dr. Betasten's hands confirmed the bands of muscle through the shirt's fabric. Then the probing drifted north, to his pecs. Dr. Betasten cupped and squeezed one, as if Barrister was a woman. Against the pressure of the doctor's palm, involuntarily, the nipple stiffened.

"Want I should turn my head and cough for ya, Doc?"

"No. Thank you." Dr. Betasten's hand glided an inch to the left, allowing his fingertips to linger on the hard nipple.

"If you bat for the other team, you might be impressed. You seem to like things stiff and hard."

Dr. Betasten's hands flew off and down to his sides. He stepped back. His face flared with anger. "You think this is funny?"

"Nothin' funny about bein' gay, Doc. I'm not too proud. Been a while since I cleaned the pipes. A blow job would be all right by me."

"You don't seem to be taking any of this very seriously."

"You mean you playing pin-the-tail-on-the-donkey with my body? It's like you're blindfolded but can see with your hands. Migo, it's a bit creepy, is all."

"This is about you, not me. It's about your inability to reach clarity."

"That's what I'm talking about. You don't seem to understand how to treat women, but you look like you're gettin' a hard-on just touching me. And you got a naked boy in your iron-lung contraption over there. You could teach Michael Jackson a thing or two."

"Let's get to the bottom of this. Tell me *exactly* what happened when you became the host of my god's brother."

"It was a business meeting. I was pissed. I'd been promised a promotion, and I was skipped over."

"You weren't just pissed, you were enraged."

"That's right. Really mad."

"Use your fucking vocabulary, you imbecile. You were more than mad. You were *jealous*."

"Yup."

"An invidious position beyond imagination. You were incensed with jealousy."

"OK, sure."

"And then it happened."

"Yeah." Barrister definitely remembered. "It felt like someone started dragging a razor across my scalp. I didn't know what was happening."

"And then you wanted revenge."

"Yes."

"You wanted to inflict pain and fear!"

"Yes. I stormed out of the room. All I could think about was payback."

"Yes, *revenge*. And how did you get that?"

"I didn't."

This seemed to really surprise Dr. Betasten. "Why not? What changed?"

"I don't know. I cooled off, I guess."

Dr. Betasten slapped him across the face. "Think."

"Hey." His wimpy little slap didn't hurt much. But still.

"*Think*, you moron. What changed? When did the rage subside?"

"Hit me again and I'll twist you up like a pretzel."

"Retrace your steps, damn it. What happened after you left the room?"

"Well, I—" He paused. "Oh, I remember now. When I got to the elevator, there was this babe I'd seen earlier that morning. She smiled and said 'hi' to me. Doc, you gotta see this gal. Cute as a button. I said 'hi' back and—"

"You can shut up now." All the animation was gone from Dr. Betasten's face. He looked down and shook his head.

"What? What did I say?"

"Just shut up."

INSIDE CELL NUMBER FOURTEEN'S SAFE HOUSE, CHRIS ASKED THE PROTEST group's leader for permission to stay in the safe house overnight. Melissa's family had been so generous, the trio didn't want to overstay their welcome. And the safe house would be more private and closer to downtown, where they planned to kidnap Special Agent Harrison. But getting permission to use the safe house was a long shot.

When they first arrived at the safe house, Chris, Al, and Katie had learned that the group's leader had another name: Mersenne Prime. Mersenne wasn't his real name either, but it was shorter than One Two Seven. Chris was thankful, too, because all the numbers were getting confusing. The moderation of protocol, Chris had hoped, was also a sign that Mersenne was warming up to them and felt comfortable with fewer layers of anonymity. But the task of convincing Mersenne had seemed impossible from the moment dinner concluded at Melissa's house. When Melissa commed Mersenne to ask him if the trio could use the safe house overnight, he'd initially refused. But Melissa sold it enough to negotiate a chance to plead the trio's case in person. That meant Melissa would go to the safe house too, which made Chris happy because he didn't want to eat-and-run.

Even during the walk from her house, Melissa had shared that she estimated there was zero chance the trio would get permission to stay in the safe house overnight. She also admitted she was glad the trio hadn't asked to stay at her family's house. She didn't want her family involved. Melissa's responses signaled that dealing with Cell Number Fourteen was worth the effort. Before they left for the safe house, Melissa made sure the spoofer program was running on their percomms and taught Katie how the program worked. She also explained how to avoid the street cams and scanners, especially during curfew hours. Katie was pleased to discover they'd been doing it right. Mostly.

Just inside the door of the safe house, Chris told Mersenne that they were being accused of murder, that it was in fact self-defense, that the police and the FBI were convinced they were Hoods, that each of their homes had been raided, and that their families were being held. Al explained his scheme to kidnap the FBI agent, how they planned to convince Harrison of the truth, gain his trust, and ask him for his help with freeing their families.

Mersenne was a brick wall—completely devoid of compassion, like a poker player watching a National Geographic documentary in which a pack of hyenas is devouring an adorable little lion cub.

Chris concentrated on appealing to Mersenne's empathy. He remembered an iconic photograph from the middle of the previous century. It showed a counterculture teenager putting a flower into the barrel of a rifle held by a national guardsman. The gesture was a peaceful demonstration against authority. Chris tried to channel the feeling from that photograph. He told Mersenne that the trio had *no choice* but to act—otherwise countless other innocent people would be arrested in the absence of probable cause. Chris's plea had all the right ingredients. At some point, he touched a nerve. Mersenne let on that getting tossed in jail was not such an unusual occurrence within the community. He said the protestors believed the recently passed laws against civil disobedience to be fundamentally in conflict with the First Amendment.

Reluctantly, Mersenne agreed to let them stay overnight. But he made it clear they wouldn't be left alone; three of the cell members would stay too.

"I'll stay," Melissa volunteered, with a glance to Chris.

Mersenne said he would stay also and "voluntold" another member—a guy with the pseudonym Sedenion Cayley-Dickson—to do the same.

Melissa led Chris, Al, and Katie to a storage closet to retrieve a bunch of sponge mats. Apparently, the group had to sleep in the safe house fairly regularly. The overhead lights winked out row by row as Mersenne and Sedenion shut everything down for the night.

"I need to take Lucky out for one last piss and dump," said Chris.

"I'll go with you," said Melissa.

It was a nice evening with a clear sky after the morning's storm, and a bit cooler too. The summer was winding down.

Lucky did his business, and after the poop bag went into the dumpster, the job was done. Melissa didn't seem eager to go back inside the safe house. She sat down on the ground against the wall opposite the safe house door. The nonverbal invitation was obvious. Chris sat next to her. Lucky sat next to Chris, waiting to be pet. His nose twitched, and his ears remained perked up and alert. Light illuminated both ends of the alley but not in the middle, where they sat. The group probably disabled the lights around the safe house entrance.

"What's it like," Melissa asked, "growing up in the burbs?"

"Prefabs instead of regular houses," said Chris. "But not much different from your neighborhood."

"Everybody has a pertran?"

"No, not everybody."

"Does *your* family have a pertran?"

"Yes," said Chris, "because I'm a Loyd, remember?"

"Sorry about that."

After a while, Chris asked, "Do you hate it when people call you a Poger?"

"Yeah."

"What does *Poger* actually mean?" asked Chris. "I know *Loyd* comes from *employed*. But where does *Poger* come from?"

"I'm not sure. I heard it was originally from an old Canadian word, *pogey*, that means unemployment subsidy. Other people say it's a Scottish word for workhouse."

"What's a workhouse?"

"I don't know. Seems backwards, right? Pogers *want* to work. If you could go to a house to get work, wouldn't that solve everything?"

More minutes passed. Chris asked finally, "What do you want your protest demonstrations to achieve?"

"For the Hillites to stop hoarding their money so the economy can support more jobs."

"Why do the Hillites hoard their money?"

"They claim the Hoods wouldn't stop stealing from them even if they did share their wealth."

"*Would* the Hoods stop stealing?"

"Of course. Why would they have to continue stealing?"

"I don't know. I don't know how any of it works."

"Well, it doesn't work. That's the problem."

Just sitting next to her would have been perfect if it wasn't for the stench of rotting garbage. Eventually, she said, "Time to go in."

Inside the safe house it was pitch-black. Melissa used the light from her percomm to guide their way. A couple clusters of bodies lined the hallway. Chris could make out Al and Katie. They lay together, but not close to Mersenne or Sedenion. Someone had the bright idea to put the two unoccupied mats side by side, but also some distance away from the others. Melissa wasted no time claiming hers.

Chris joined her. Lucky lay at his feet. Chris could hear Al and Katie whispering but couldn't make out their words.

Minutes ticked by. Chris felt like he might fall asleep. But then he heard giggles intertwined in Al and Katie's whispers. He sensed Melissa roll to her side, facing him, with her head on her elbow. "You awake?" she whispered.

"No." He thought she would ask him a question, but she didn't. He could feel her gentle breath on his neck. It was sweet. Not like toothpaste. More like honeysuckle. He recalled a particular summer day, pulling the flower from its stem and touching the tiny drop of nectar to the tip of his tongue. He expected her to eventually roll back, but she didn't.

"Kiss me," she said.

"I—no."

"Please? Just kiss me."

"I can't."

"You don't want to?"

"I'm not going to answer that question; that's not the point."

"There's someone else?"

"Yes."

"Well, that's a little unfair."

"How do you figure?"

"You know what I mean. You. With your eyes. Watching me. Watching me watching you. Don't deny it."

"Sorry. Yes, it's unfair. Nothing intentional. I meant no harm. In Al's words, you're smokin' hot. I won't deny that either."

"I just assumed, since Al and Katie are together, that you were available."

"Al and Katie aren't together," said Chris.

"Could've fooled me."

Their giggling is annoying. She's right.

Finally, Melissa said, "Can I kiss you?"

"What? How is that any different?"

"That way, you can tell your girlfriend you never kissed another girl. And you'd be telling the truth."

"No. Not happening."

"I don't mean on the lips. Just a good-night kiss. On the cheek."

"You're being ridiculous."

"No. There's something about you, Chris Seven Eight Six."

"No."

"Please?"

"You're not going to drop it, are you?"

"No."

"Fine. Make it quick."

She leaned in. "That wasn't part of the deal," she whispered. Her face was inches from his—so close he had to turn his head away. Her hand came alongside his cheek and turned his head back.

"Hey."

"Shhhhh."

He felt her sweet breath pass across his lips. *Honeysuckle.* She was leaning closer now. Her face over his. Nose to nose. Lips almost touching. He felt her eyelash flutter on his nose.

"Hey," he said again.

"Relax. That was just a butterfly kiss. Before the real thing."

He said, "That wasn't part of the deal either."

"No, it wasn't. My turn to be unfair. Now, just relax. OK. Here goes. Are you ready?" She gently tilted his head away, giving her clear access to his cheek. Starting at his chin, the tip of her nose glided up his cheek, almost to his ear. For a kiss on the cheek, it was very full. Her lips were warm and moist. He couldn't help but imagine what a kiss on the mouth would be like. Just before she pulled away, her tongue darted inside his ear.

Tickled, his shoulder came up, and he rubbed his ear.

"That's right. Wipe off the cooties."

"Satisfied?" he asked.

"Dangerous question. I could ask you the same thing," she said. "But the answer is yes." She sighed. "See? It wasn't so bad after all now was it?"

"How does the phrase go? Enough is enough?"

"Whatever." She rolled over with finality. "Good night, Chris."

"Good night, Melissa."

Chris tried to push all his thoughts out of his mind. After a while, Al and Katie's giggles changed to whispers in desperate tones. Then he heard Katie sobbing. He wanted to call to them, to ask if she was all right. But the truth was, none of them were all right.

CHAPTER 16

NOT LONG AFTER MIDNIGHT, THE SOON-TO-BE SERVANT'S EYES QUIVERED. The activity was detected by the hibernation chamber sensors and logged, but it wasn't significant enough to trigger an alert to Dr. Betasten. The eye flutter was captured by no fewer than six cameras monitoring his body, a body illuminated by the ever-present blue sterilization light. Dr. Betasten wouldn't examine the recorded event until morning.

Anyone who might analyze the vid would see the color of the soon-to-be servant's eyes as well as the shape of his pupils. Neither the yellow color nor the rectangular shape were unique among the fauna thriving on the planet called Earth. But they were certainly unlike any human's eyes.

For him, the term *human* was technically inaccurate. He was a different species, following the definition of *species* that hinged on the ability to interbreed. An odd concept, considering the fact that no opposite sex of his species existed, he was told. The Circle of Six had made sure of that through a painstaking process of fetal selection. There was no female of his kind. And there never would be, he was told.

The knowledge that he was a different species from *Homo sapiens* had initially created a feeling of inferiority. But it was later explained that he was a progression of the *Homo* genus. Over time, superiority replaced inferiority.

At first, he considered the odds of being *the one* representing the next step in human evolution. Nothing Aeron Skotino did was left to chance. *For the chance of reality's path doth tip.* Without the Circle of Six's manipulation, a being like him wouldn't have appeared on earth for another six thousand years.

His training taught him that he was born with a remarkable genetic variation absent from the humans around him. His genetic alignment enabled the second of such abrupt accelerations in human advancement. The first shift, named the Upper Paleolithic Revolution, occurred fifty thousand years ago. Mortal scientists had determined that a dramatic change occurred almost overnight, in evolutionary terms. Humans advanced beyond all other hominids in a relative blink of an eye. Mortal scientists didn't understand what had caused the sudden advancement. But the Circle of Six knew. The Upper Paleolithic Revolution was the result of the first genetic alignment, allowing humankind to express unconditional love. The earth's human population had since grown unchecked—ending the golden age of the gods, causing millennia of chaos and struggle, and culminating in a great battle between the gods. The battle occurred prior to the time of recorded human history, but verbal accounts were passed down through generations, and the battle was named Titanomachy. When the battle ended, the Circle of Six—victorious, but sapped—vowed to restore the earth to its original state of glory, the golden age.

In a rare moment of mortal clarity, the human sage Calchas had a glimpse into the future. His prophecy was shockingly accurate:

> *From the lofty trees falling groundward were many*
> *beautiful leaves shed; earthward the fruit would fall*
> *as Boreas blew furiously by the dark one's decree.*
> *The sea would swell, and everything trembled at this,*
> *mortal strength would wither, the fruit would dwindle,*

in the spring season, when in the hills, the dark one bears
six children from within earth's nook, nirvana revived.

Without intervention by the Circle of Six, the second genetic alignment would have brought no consequence because the gene configuration would have remained dormant. The dominant genes would spread down through generations completely unexpressed. Eventually, after thousands of years, all humans would possess the second genetic alignment. But during the propagation, humans would remain unchanged because the human body needs a catalyst to physically evolve: unbihexium, also known to the Circle of Six as homa.

Forged in massive stars of the galaxy, dust of unbihexium, the element with atomic number 126, would eventually settle to Earth as a stable monofluoride, also known to the Circle of Six as parahaoma. The unbihexium salt would trigger a fork in human evolution. He, Skotino's soon-to-be servant, was the first of that fork, he was told.

Homo habilis had been crowded to extinction by *Homo erectus*, who had been crowded to extinction by the Neanderthals, who had been crowded to extinction by *Homo sapiens*, modern-day humans. Skotino's plan was to decimate the human population and thereby protect the earth from inexorable defilement. He, Skotino's soon-to-be servant, the one and only *Homo sinistralis,* would cull the herds of *Homo sapiens* to a level similar to that of the golden age. The Earth would recover from the blight of humanity. The task of reducing the human population was left to him, the servant, he was told.

Presently under the sapphire glow, alone in the darkness of the makeshift laboratory of the Venizelos main house, his transformation approached completion. These remaining hours were the last moments of his first life's twilight with the dawn of his rebirth (*fajr sinistral*) becoming oh so near.

"LET'S GO, MIGO. RISE AND SHINE."

Chris could feel Al's hand on his shoulder, but he couldn't see anything because it was still pitch-black inside Cell Number Fourteen's safe house. Chris heard the jingle of Lucky's collar as his dog shook. Down the hall, in the main area of the safe house, banks of lights came on. "I'll make coffee," yelled Sedenion from somewhere.

Chris sat up. "What time is it?"

"Five," said Al, standing up. Katie was next to him. "Harrison seems like an early riser. We need to get over there. We can't afford to miss him. We need to learn his commute."

Melissa sat up too. "I'm coming with you."

The three friends exchanged looks.

"What? One kiss and I'm dirt?"

"You kissed her?" Al's expression turned infantile. "Migo, you animal."

Chris fumed. "I did not. Drop it." To Melissa, he said, "That's not the problem."

"What is the problem?" she asked.

Katie shrugged. "You might as well tell her everything."

"Tell me what?"

"Make it quick," said Al. "I'll take Lucky outside to do his business."

Chris explained to Melissa about his invisible friend, the warden, who had been a part of him since birth. There was nothing quick about the explanation. He described the special gifts he possessed when assisted by the warden, about how he could fly, and how he could see, smell, and hear through Lucky. He explained that the abilities were only possible when he had a connection to the warden. The gum had special sugars that connected him to the warden, but it was temporary. The sugars encapsulated inside Katie's special gum lasted an hour at best.

Even as Chris explained his incredible story to Melissa, he could sense his ability to convince her, even without the gum. Whenever his goals were honorable, the truth became credible. In fact, people who heard the bizarre story not only believed it but were also motivated to help.

"After I chew the gum, and while I have the connection to Lucky, I'll be able to trace Harrison's scent back to his mode of transportation. At that point, we can pick a suitable spot to kidnap him and convince him to release our families." Chris stood up. "Now you know my secret. If you come with us, you might see me do some unexpected things, things you'll have a hard time believing."

"Why do any of us have to go to the police station?" asked Melissa. "If distance doesn't matter, Lucky can watch Harrison's movements by himself."

"Chris is the only one who can see what Lucky sees," said Katie. "We need to pick a place where we can nab Harrison without other people around. Al's very good at strategy. He'll come up with a plan, but he needs to see the area for himself. Chris's description won't cut it. Come on. We need to get to the police station before Harrison."

| 10 | 10 | 10

HOLY SHIT, THOUGHT CHIEF WARRANT OFFICER JENSON. HIS OMEGA FORCE Command Center console flashed with alerts. HIP was at 99 percent, and the threat risk was high.

Jenson heard Morales yell, "I got activity."

"Same here," said Jenson. "Where's Captain Schofield?"

"In his office," said Morales. "Again."

"Call him out here." Jenson's hands flew across the input screen as he organized the rush of information.

"He's not answering," said Morales.

"I don't care if you have to drag him out!"

Morales sprinted to the back of the command center. Jenson heard him bang on the door.

Finally Schofield came to stand over Jenson's shoulder. "All right, all right. What's all the fuss?"

"Sir, we got a hit. Likely a data center."

"Source?"

"AI heuristics."

"Not again," said Schofield.

"Sir, it's legit. A Hood data center. We have to get Oscar Foxtrot on location, ASAP, and catch as many support personnel as possible."

"Confirmed. It's a data center," yelled Morales. "But they're on to us. New firewall resources in play. We're blocked again. But we got the data center's location. San Antonio, Texas."

"Sir, shall I order a course change for Fireteam Echo?" Jenson waited for a reply but didn't get one. He turned. "Sir?"

Schofield's forehead wrinkled. "What if it's another red herring?"

"Sir, HIP is at ninety-nine percent. Oscar Foxtrot is thirteen minutes out. Shall I redirect?"

"How can we be sure?" Schofield looked over to Morales. "Run it again. Double-check."

"Sir," said Morales, disbelief all over his face, "the firewall is back up. We can't. The Hoods made a mistake, or we got lucky, or I don't know, but . . . but they're on to us. They're purging data as we speak, guaranteed. Our only chance is to apprehend the staff before they escape the building."

"But it could be another error," said Schofield thoughtfully.

Jenson looked at Morales, who mouthed *Oh my god.* Jenson rolled his eyes in agreement. While Schofield was paralyzed in thought, Jenson discreetly tapped out an urgent message to Colonel Wesson.

"JUST GET OVER THERE," SAID COLONEL WESSON. "SCHOFIELD DOESN'T KNOW what the hell he's doing. He's got a real situation."

"I'm on administrative leave, remember?" said Eladio, from his James Norman Mattis Military Housing apartment at Marine Corps Base Quantico, affectionately called "the Kennel" by its residents.

"I know. I'll deal with Nolan," said Wesson. "Look, this is the biggest break we've had in a long time. We can't afford to screw it up. No time. Go."

The trip would only take a few minutes, but Eladio would have to hustle. He left his apartment and headed for the moving-sidewalk system. Eladio jumped on the system of moving rubber belts, hopping left as he weaved through the streams of other pedestrians on the crowded moving-sidewalk system. Each belt to his left moved faster than the one to his right. Leaning forward against the rush of air, he zipped across the base. Nearing his stop at the Omega Force Command Center, Eladio danced right, slowing his progress at each successive belt until he jumped off completely.

After clearing security, Eladio headed for the control room for Fireteam Echo, one of the two Omega Force fireteams on station twenty-four hours a day, operating as a quick-reaction force. Each fireteam of four marines cruised aboard a military scramjet that was constantly patrolling the US. Echo Team covered the East while its sister fireteam, Whiskey, covered the West. At supersonic speed, the Omega Force fireteams could be deployed within minutes to anywhere in the US, with the goal of stopping or capturing Robin Hood terrorists.

When the door swished open, Eladio knew from the faces of his team—*ex-team*, he reminded himself—that things were pretty fucked-up.

"What are *you* doing here?" asked Schofield.

"Colonel Wesson sent me."

"I'm in command here."

"Uh-huh." Eladio moved toward Jenson's console.

"You can't just—"

"Comm him yourself," said Eladio. Peering over Jenson's shoulder, he saw relief on the warrant officer's face. "What do we have?"

"HIP at ninety-nine percent," said Jenson. "Risk is high. Target is a data center. San Antonio."

"How old?"

"Eight minutes."

"Oscar Foxtrot?"

"Inbound. Five minutes to deployment window."

"I didn't order that," said Schofield.

"You did the right thing, Jenson," said Eladio.

"Sir, our drone is entering the area of operation," said Kendall. "Putting it on the big board." The main display snapped to a bird's-eye view of an office complex consisting of generic concrete buildings surrounded by neat landscaping. In the morning Texas sun, lampposts cast long shadows across the parking lot. "Correction, make that three drones." Two more images appeared, each a view from a circling drone. "Data center personnel are fleeing the building." The images showed people running from every exit. It looked like a chicken coop with a fox inside. "Suspects acquiring transport." The view showed the escapees piling into pertrans.

"I got hits on facial recognition," called Morales. "Pertran IDs too. Correlating. Satellite tracking on each vehicle. Route prediction in progress. I won't lose them. Jackpot."

"Good. Delay apprehension. Let 'em run. Tap all communications. Track contacts and destinations."

"Yes, sir. All communications tapped. We'll follow every comm. And we'll follow every comm from that comm. We should reach Kevin Bacon in no time."

"Instruct local law enforcement to prepare for residential raids."

"Aye, aye, sir."

"Nice work," said Eladio. "We can sift through the little fish later. For now, let's concentrate on the big fish while they're still inside the data center—the ones who know exactly what to erase. What's Echo Team's status?"

"One minute to deployment. LZ confirmed. Confidence at one hundred percent. There's a nice area of lawn out front."

"Put me through to Number One," ordered Eladio, referring to the leader of the fireteam. Each marine had a call sign designation from one to four.

The display image switched to the cabin of the scramjet. All four marines were in their insertion tubes. Each was wearing self-contained battle armor, suits of high-tech armor any ten-year-old boy would recognize from the popular Omega Force vids. "Looks like a cream puff, Lance Corporal."

"Aye, aye, sir," said Number One. "We'll get 'er done."

"I've never seen this many fish in the net."

"Understood, sir."

The image started to shake, and the marines got jostled around. He heard the female voice of the scramjet's virtas pilot say, "Insertion cycle activated. Combat release in fifteen seconds." The scramjet was now plummeting out of the sky, its powerful engines slowing the craft out of supersonic flight, about to deposit the four marines right on target.

"Good luck," said Eladio. "Command out." He stood straight. "Well, it's up to them now."

Turning and looking up to Eladio, Jenson said, "Thanks." But his broad smile faded when he caught Schofield's eye. Jenson turned back to his console.

"You better be right about this," warned Schofield.

"That's true," said Eladio. "Well, congratulations, Captain. Even if only one of those trails leads us to a point of Hood command and control, it'll be a turning point in the cyber war. It'll look great on your record."

Schofield's expression softened.

Eladio turned and addressed the room. "Captain Schofield and I will be in his office. Let us know once you've received Number One's sitrep." Eladio turned to Schofield. "After you, Captain."

| 1 0   1 1 0   1 1 0

"ARE YOU KIDDING ME?" ASKED AL. "ANYONE CAN JUST WALK UP AND BUY A pretzel?"

"Of course," said Melissa.

The friends were positioned between two buildings. The stakeout of Harrison's morning commute had begun. The four could see the entrance to the Philly police station. They could also see the street vendor selling soft pretzels from his cart.

Melissa continued, "By law, they're made with whole grain, but my mom told me that when she was a girl, they were made with white flour. But I still think they're great."

From the instant they arrived, Al had been hypnotized by the pretzel man, who was old and bald, with a bushy white mustache. And he was pretty fat, too, which was an increasingly unusual sight after so many years since the end of the healthcare crisis. The end of the crisis coincided with the invention and subsequent global deployment of medical scanners. Food credits were then allocated to citizens based on scan results. The pretzel man was surely obese, and he certainly didn't make enough money to be considered a Loyd. Chris suspected the pretzel man must be consuming a fair amount of his own inventory.

Chris tried to ignore their conversation. He was directing Lucky to the rear of the police station. The search for Harrison was on. Once spotted, Lucky would follow the agent's scent back along the path of his commute. Al would then analyze the route and select a location to nab Harrison when he left work that day.

Not knowing from which direction Harrison would arrive for work, Chris somehow had to monitor all directions at once. But he allowed himself a glimpse with his own eyes, to watch the source of Al's fixation. Chris watched as a pedestrian touched her percomm to the pretzel man's cart. The pretzel man opened the top. A wisp of steam escaped. With tongs, he pulled out a pretzel in the shape of a narrow number eight, slid it into wax paper, and handed it to her.

"Golden brown. Lightly crusted with coarse salt. They're really soft and warm too," teased Melissa.

Chris just had to sneak a peek at Al and the priceless expression on his face.

"Ha," said Katie. "That didn't take long. Melissa knows exactly what buttons to press on you." She high-fived Melissa. "Nice one, miga."

"Oh great," said Al. "Not only am I starving, but I'm surrounded by—"

Glassy-eyed, with the connection to Lucky, Chris said, "What the heck?" He shuddered.

"What? What happened?" asked Al.

"Lucky just made a break for the parking lot. I couldn't stop him," said Chris. "Remember when I told you he's been obsessed with something back there? Now I know why. He picked up the scent of one of the Omega Force soldiers."

"So?" said Melissa. "I told you they were here. I saw it on the news. It was a publicity stunt. Of course their scent is here."

"No, it has to be one of the marines we battled in Nevada when we tried to rescue the abducted young women."

"Again, so what?"

"That's right," said Katie. "It has to be the marine that was out front because the one in back got blown up. And Lucky was never near the two inside."

"But that's just it," said Chris. "The scent *is* from the marine who was blown up. The man must have survived. Not only that,

234   ANDREW HUNKINS

the scent Lucky's picking up is only a few days old, more recent than the publicity stunt."

"What does it mean?" asked Katie.

"I don't know," said Chris. "Keep your eyes peeled."

They had to wait another twenty minutes before Lucky spotted Special Agent Harrison. The scrawny man approached from the south, along the sidewalk, and went in the back entrance of the police station.

"OK, he's inside," said Chris.

"Now what?" asked Melissa.

"I'll have Lucky backtrack Harrison's scent. Once we find his pertran, or bus stop, or whatever, we'll pick a place to lay our trap. When he leaves for the day, we'll grab him and convince him to release our families."

| 0 | 0 | 0

"WHAT ARE THOSE?" ASKED BEN, SITTING NEXT TO LAURA ON THE COT OF THE holding cell inside the Philadelphia police station. Harrison had just tossed them each an orange coverall.

"Your traveling clothes," said Harrison.

"Traveling?" asked Laura. "Where?"

Harrison glanced at his percomm. "Major Nolan will be on-screen in a moment to explain." He tilted his head to the display on the wall. "In any case, you're not staying here."

"Happy now?" asked Ben.

Laura noticed her husband was looking straight at Harrison. She knew eye contact was difficult for Ben, especially in situations of conflict. Ben was rarely in touch with his own emotions, much less anyone else's. *He's really trying.*

"Actually, I *am* happy," said Harrison. "Or I will be once you're out of my hair."

Laura tried to gauge Harrison's attitude. From the start, he'd been consistently antagonistic. But once the Department of Defense took over, headed by Major Nolan, Harrison had seemed neutered.

The tiny yellow light at the corner of the display screen turned green. Nolan's face appeared. "Well, I hope you enjoyed your life in Philly."

"What are you talking about?" asked Laura. "Where are we going?"

"I can't tell you. And I'm not just being vague when I say that. I actually don't know. The best word to describe it would be *nowhere*." Nolan asked, "Are you familiar with the Guantánamo Act?"

When Ben saw her reaction, he put his hand on her shoulder.

Nolan noticed too. "Ah, yes. I forgot. You were a political science professor. What a convenient cover for a soldier of terror."

Ben said, "I've heard of Guantánamo Bay in Cuba. And I've heard of the infamous prison there. But I've never heard of the Guantánamo Act."

Nolan raised an eyebrow, inviting Laura to enlighten her husband.

Even though her wits were frazzled, the task gave her a sense of confidence, like when she was in front of her students. "Early in the century, the detention prison at Guantánamo Bay created a political nightmare for the US government. It was supposed to be a legal bubble within international law, giving the US complete freedom to treat terrorists in any manner they wished, ostensibly with the goal of extracting information that would uncover future terrorist plots. Regardless, it was a political and military boat anchor, as well as a target for human rights advocates."

Laura's voice became somber. "The Guantánamo Act was passed to create a place that actually delivered on the promise of its namesake prison. No one from the outside knows where this new prison is located. It may not even be a single place. Or it may be mobile, relocated from time to time." She looked at Nolan. "*Nowhere* is a fitting name."

"Most eloquently stated," said Nolan. "Unfortunately, you forgot the most important aspect. Can you guess? It's one of the reasons its location has never been divulged." Before she could answer, he said, "No, wait. Let's see if *Professor* Benjamin Richards is as smart as he thinks he is. Let's see if *he* can figure it out."

Ben looked to Laura and back again. "Because no one has ever returned?"

"Excellent. You live up to your credentials. You've done your propeller-headed brethren proud. Yes, it's a one-way trip." To Laura, he said, "Fortunately, you'll have plenty of time to tell your hubby all about the rumored details."

She didn't follow.

"Come now. Think. How about the individual camps within the original prison? For example . . ." He grinned. "Camp No?"

Laura looked down and nodded.

"Yes," said Nolan menacingly. "It's the only feature of the original Guantánamo Bay prison scheme that actually produced results." To Ben, Nolan said, "You're a computer wizard. You'll figure it out eventually—I mean, why Camp No continually accepts new prisoners but, curiously, never fills up. Habeas corpses, I like to call them. Anyway, get your blaze orange on. You'll be on your way before sundown."

The tiny green light on the display turned back to yellow.

Laura watched Harrison leave. As the door swished closed behind him, she remembered what he'd said about wanting them out of his hair. Maybe Harrison was simply in over his head and thankful to finally be done with the DOD. But now she worried it was because Harrison didn't agree with Nolan's decision about their fate. *Maybe Harrison has a conscience.*

"I suppose now you're going to scream at me," said Ben. "To *do* something."

"I'm OK. Sorry about before. No, I thought you handled that really well."

He had a skeptical look.

Ben's right. What's different about me? Long before she met Ben, she had always been a worrier. And because she always saw the world half-empty, she even worried she might end up an old maid. But, as the saying goes: opposites attract. Ben never worried about anything. In fact, he was usually unaware of what others around him were feeling. His behavior lacked any evidence of empathy. Sometimes, she felt like he didn't care about anything, not even her. When she became frantic, she could be incredibly cruel and call him autistic. Everyone's on the spectrum, but Ben's core nature was close to clinical.

Together, they were an unlikely pair to expect a successful marriage, like one plus one equaled one-half. Her constant worrying became nagging. Her needs bordered on irrational. As a result, he focused more and more on his work, retreating into the world between his ears. A vicious cycle. Eventually, they had reached a cold equilibrium. A minimum of peace via maximum independence.

That all changed when Chris entered their lives. Ben became empathetic. She could handle the stress of everyday life, but even then, Laura still panicked easily whenever Chris was away for any significant period. At those times Ben, too, would drift back to his old ways, becoming lost in his own thoughts and unable to take action on basic, everyday tasks. But just now, she was able to muster confidence from somewhere inside, without Chris being near. *What's different? How did I do it?* It was almost as if Chris *was* nearby.

| |0 | |0 | |0

PrincessLIMDIS: Earth to Frog. Come in, Frog.

In the Ferguson office, Hope waited for a reply from her online friend and mentor. She hadn't heard from SalaciousFrog the entire morning. She tried to remember if there was ever a time he hadn't responded right away. Now that she thought about it, *that* fact was a bit odd. Although, she was well aware of entire subcultures that ate and slept with their percomms. *Nature call? Shower?*

She reconsidered the notion that SalaciousFrog was a man. She recalled the few times they'd had audio-only comms. It was a male voice but sounded electronically altered. She assumed he'd altered his voice to protect his identity. That would be consistent with everything about SalaciousFrog.

"Are you finished with the code review?" called Nancy from her office. Hope heard her boss get up from her desk. She stepped around the corner where Hope sat at a table in the hallway. "I'd like to get the code burned into firmware by the end of the week."

"Yes," said Hope. "I found three vulnerabilities. I documented the attack vectors for each. The third one was particularly nasty because it had three subvectors of its own. Anyway, I sent everything back to the dev team. They should have it recoded by the end of the day. A burn by the end of the week should be no problem."

"Excellent." With a smile, her boss disappeared back to her office.

"Say, Nancy?"

After Nancy's head popped back around the corner, Hope continued, "I was wondering—about your commitment to consider allowing me to work from home *before* my three-month probationary period ends. I know I've only been working here a couple weeks. But, well, things are going pretty good, don't you think?"

Nancy stepped fully around the corner, crossing her arms as she leaned against the doorframe. She smiled even more broadly. "Yes, I do."

"So I was wondering—"

"Yes, yes. You've earned it. For Christ's sake, if anyone has earned the right to work wherever they want, you have." She put her hand on Hope's shoulder. "I've resisted blowing sunshine up your ass because I wanted to retain some semblance of a negotiating position. But it's no use. I'm thrilled to have you. You'll be getting a thirty percent raise. As of now, you can work from anywhere you like. You don't have to come into the office." Somewhat more seriously, she said, "I *do* want you to check in once in a while, though. In person. Maybe once a month?"

"Sure," said Hope, "And thank you. You won't regret it."

"Not a chance."

Once Nancy was back in her office, Hope reached out to SalaciousFrog again.

PrincessLIMDIS: Switching to tin can and string . . . you there?

Still nothing.

In the past, she'd thought about tracing SalaciousFrog's comms. She knew if he ever found out, he'd be furious. *The trick would be to do it without him knowing.* It was the kind of work she did for him all the time, in exchange for teaching her. But over the years, he'd had less and less to teach her. In fact, they both acknowledged that she had superior skills. Not all the time, just frequently.

SalaciousFrog's real advantage was that he knew about the security protocols the network service providers would change even before they changed them. He'd never told her how he knew, but he was always right. Hacking skills are just one advantage—at her level of expertise, the real differentiating factor was information. Information was everything. That's why hacking took so long. First all the information had to be gathered. Then a plan created to anticipate all the possible contingencies. Zero tolerance for error. Measure three times, cut once. SalaciousFrog always had the information advantage. Was it even possible for her to hide her activity from him? She had to try. She realized now that her expectation that SalaciousFrog be consistently online wasn't just beyond unrealistic, it was downright foolhardy. She really knew nothing about him. *I can't fully trust anyone.*

Decision made, she started to devise a way to move information that even SalaciousFrog could never detect. It would have to be more than a new encryption scheme; it would have to be an entirely unique way to transport data—an entirely new way to communicate.

| 10 | 10 | 10

"STATUS," ORDERED SKOTINO, STRIDING WITH TYVOLD INTO THE IMPROVISED laboratory inside the Venizelos estate, which functioned as the medical support center for his soon-to-be servant.

Dr. Betasten looked up as the two men entered. "On schedule. Your servant experienced eye flutters last night. And I witnessed it myself again today. His vital signs show he's beginning the process of emerging from his hibernation, just as the gods foretold."

Skotino stepped toward the chamber. "You won't have much time, doctor."

To Dr. Betasten, Tyvold qualified, "Once I break through the cyber defenses of the individual blocking our searches for the warden's location, we'll have precious little time. Minutes will count."

"I know." Dr. Betasten gave Tyvold an expression that made it clear he understood and didn't need to be told more than once. "The servant will be ready."

Tyvold nodded.

Skotino said nothing.

"I still think you should let Spire have another crack at the warden's host," suggested Dr. Betasten.

Skotino shook his head. "Spire failed twice already."

"And don't forget Vega," said Tyvold. "Think about it. After Vega was killed, his god ended up picking the Bear—who's definitely formidable, but stupid—for a new host. Spire is formidable *and* smart. Can you imagine if Spire were to be killed and flipped from left to right? We can't afford the risk. It's all playing into the warden's hand. For the chance of reality's path doth tip."

"Precisely," said Skotino.

"The warden is leaving nothing to chance," said Tyvold. "Nor can we. If Spire is killed, who knows who'd take his place."

"How many goddesses are free?" asked Dr. Betasten.

The word *goddess* sent a chill across the room. Dr. Betasten sensed it, stepped away, and turned his attention back to his equipment, letting the two senior members of the Circle of Six work it out on their own.

Skotino had ordered Tyvold to accompany him to Dr. Betasten's lab so together they could assess the preparations for the naming ceremony. However, even Skotino was surprised at the glaring holes in their plan. He should've consulted Tyvold, host of his god's brother, sooner.

"Unknown," said Skotino in response to Dr. Betasten's comment, but now speaking to Tyvold only.

Tyvold continued the train of thought. "And if the gods don't know, no number of tortured pharmakoi will make it clear. We can't take the risk. No member of the Circle of Six should directly challenge the warden." Tyvold's analysis was always exacting. "When we tried turning the mortals against him, even their feeble military was unable to apprehend Saoshyant's host, Chris Lumière."

"Saoshyant chose his host well," said Skotino.

Tyvold stepped closer, shoulder to shoulder with Skotino, who was peering into the chamber protecting his soon-to-be servant. Tyvold asked, in a low voice, "When Chris Lumière found you, did you know the risk then? Did you know the consequences if he killed you?"

Skotino shook his head.

"I can't imagine what we would do if *you* were drawn to a dextral host."

Skotino put his hand on the glass of the chamber. "At the time, my only thought was to send the warden back to Tartaros."

"So our plan, as it stands now: Once your servant eliminates whoever is protecting Chris Lumière in cyberspace, we'll track him down and kill him. Then the warden will once again be drawn to a virgin mother. The cycle repeats."

"It will buy us at least fifteen years—the time it takes for the host to reach puberty and become a legitimate threat once more," Skotino confirmed.

"And again, we'll have to find the mother and perform the six layers of death. The warden may again find a way to murder the mother without her son present, just as he did with Marian Lumière."

"It's the only way to return the warden to Tartaros forever."

"True. Certainly the only way we know of." Tyvold paused. "What if we kill the virgin mother while the warden's host is in vitro? If eliminated just before birth, that would buy us nearly nine months threat-free."

"Interesting," said Skotino.

"If we repeat the process, the warden would be without a developed host indefinitely."

Skotino turned and locked eyes with Tyvold. "Even the gods won't know who the next virgin mother will be. How do you suggest we locate his host fetus?"

"Let me think about that," said Tyvold. "Once your servant kills Chris Lumière, we'll have nine months to search."

PrincessLIMDIS: You there?

SalaciousFrog: Sure. What's up?

PrincessLIMDIS: What do you mean, what's up? I've been trying to reach you all day.

SalaciousFrog: Sure. What's up?

```
Received: from server SATMS1733.telsat115 ([5361:6C61
:6369:6F75:7346:726F:6720:6973:2041:7274:6966:6963:6
961:6C49]) by PHLMS0359.satcomm ([5072:696E:6365:737
3:4C49:4D44:4953:2069:7320:486F:7065:4176:656E:6972])
Content-Type: application/pcm-sec; name="percommmail";
Content-Transfer-Encoding: binary-secure; Message-ID:
<53616E20416E746F6E696F2C2054582044617461204365
6E74657220446F776E> Accept-Language: en-US; Content-
Language: en-US; Message-Body: "Sure. What's up?"
```

SalaciousFrog: Sure. What's up?

SalaciousFrog: Sure. What's up?

SalaciousFrog: Sure. What's up?

What the hell? Hope wondered.

PrincessLIMDIS: I think there's something wrong with our comm link.

SalaciousFrog: Could be. We lost a data center. Significant computing resources went offline without warning.

PrincessLIMDIS: What does that have to do with anything? Comm traffic puts negligible load on the system.

SalaciousFrog: Yeah, but security protocols were triggered as a safety measure.

PrincessLIMDIS: What protocols?

SalaciousFrog: Sure. What's up?

Hope had never seen this type of behavior from SalaciousFrog. She didn't know how to express her concern—and she didn't have time. Chris was downtown again, against her wishes, and broadcasting his DNA. Her Ferguson work was piling up. And SalaciousFrog's odd behavior meant she needed to devote even more time to finishing her new way to transmit data without SalaciousFrog being able to detect it.

PrincessLIMDIS: Never mind. Later.

| | 0 | | 0 | | 0

"UGH," SAID AL. "THIS ISN'T GONNA BE EASY."

On the sidewalk next to Al, Katie, and Melissa, Chris watched the continuous flow of people in and out of the train station. Jefferson Station wasn't as big as the Thirtieth Street Station, but nearly so.

After wolfing down three soft pretzels, Al was in a better mood to concentrate on their plan to nab Harrison. Lucky had traced the FBI agent's scent along his morning commute. Unfortunately, it didn't lead to a pertran or a masstran stop. It led to Jefferson Station.

"There's a shopping mall in there too," said Melissa in a defeated tone.

"Unfortunately, you can reach the station from multiple sides of the building," said Katie. "The fastest exit from the eastbound platform may not be the fastest entrance to the westbound platform. Harrison's evening path could be completely different from his morning path. We could miss him completely when he leaves for the day."

"Well then, we'll have to pick a spot closer to the police station," said Al. "Hopefully, a spot with a lot less people."

The four friends and Lucky worked their way back along the route Harrison had used that morning, toward the police precinct building.

"So, General Simpleton," asked Katie, "what's your plan once we find a good ambush spot?"

"We need to lure Harrison away from any onlookers, to a place where we can talk privately."

"Will talking be enough?" she asked. "Chris is very convincing, but still."

"If we can get Harrison to a back alley, Chris can demonstrate his abilities from the warden," said Al. "You know, fly around or something. Make our story undeniable. Obviously, there's a risk of being seen, but we have to try."

After much scrutiny, Al selected a spot to grab Harrison that was closer to the police headquarters than the train station, with its multiple entrance points that made Harrison's exact course hard to predict. Together, the friends decided on a plan: Chris and Al would come up from behind Harrison and take him by the arms. Al would shove a couple fingers in the agent's ribs and say he had a gun and to come quietly. Once they reached the alley and were out of view of others and the public surveillance system, they could explain everything to Harrison. The only thing left to do was lie in wait while Lucky watched for Harrison to leave work.

│ │0 │ │0 │ │0

KNOCK, KNOCK.

"Come in," Chelsea called.

Evan stepped into her bedroom.

She looked away.

"Not even a hello?" He sat on the bed, next to her. "Come on, Chels. It's going to be fine, you'll see."

"I stink. And my hair is greasy." She sighed. "I hope your grandfather is satisfied. I'm reminded constantly of our son and the naming ceremony tomorrow. Only one more day. It will be such a relief to shower."

"Remember, not until our son is awake."

"How will I know?"

"I'll comm you. I've arranged to have a livestream, so you can see for yourself on the pubcomm." Evan motioned to the display screen on the wall of her bedroom.

For anyone else, a pubcomm was a portal to all the information of the world, past or present. But ever since the birth of their son, Chelsea had been forbidden to access the public network—no contact with the outside world. She remembered all the social networks she used to visit. She loved to learn about fashion and apparel design. She loved to follow celebrities. In fact, she was a celebrity herself—a minor celebrity perhaps—when she married Evangelos Venizelos, one of the most eligible bachelors in London. *That was such a long time ago.*

"What will I wear tomorrow?"

"Let me show you." Even pulled out his percomm and tapped. "Here. I know it's not what you were hoping for."

The image on Evan's percomm showed a simple ivory shift, sleeveless, with a high collar. Fortunately, it had some curves. Darts at the breast, to support her ample bosom without the material draping below. The hem fell just above the knee. It looked like a classic little black dress, but ivory and very plain. *Cute.*

She'd worked so hard on getting back in shape. Her waistline was now as slim and firm as it had ever been. She was pleased the dress would let her hard work be seen. A simple design but, she had to admit, quite flattering. Evan always said she'd look great in a burlap sack. *He was right.*

For seventeen years she'd been living in what the family called "the old house." It was the oldest of the Venizelos homes, constructed over the centuries, that were still standing. Even though it was small compared to the main house, which was the size of a luxury resort, the old house was still a mansion by anyone's standards.

Her anticipation of the naming ceremony couldn't have been greater. Everything would change. She'd live at the main house with Evan and their son. She'd use the pubcomm. She'd go to concerts. Evan would bring her along to fancy events. It was a rebirth for their son but, almost more so, it was a rebirth for her as well.

CHAPTER 17

"ANKLE CHAINS?" LAURA ASKED INSIDE THE HOLDING CELL.

"Yes. Handcuffs and ankle chains." Harrison was flanked by two other agents.

"Do we look like we're capable of escaping?" asked Ben.

"Doesn't matter. Rules are rules."

The two agents put the shackles on Ben and Laura. There was even a chain around the waist that connected to the wrists and ankles. "Well now," said Harrison, "you have to admit, it's the only way to accessorize an orange jumpsuit. Let's go."

Ben and Laura shuffled, behind Harrison, to the main security door of the holding area. Once through, they followed corridors until arriving at a loading dock at the rear of the police station. Several uniformed police officers were waiting. One of the loading dock doors that faced the rear parking lot was open. A small bus stood waiting. It was unmarked, and all the windows had been replaced with metal plating.

"We're riding in that?" asked Ben.

"Nothing but the best, my friends," said Harrison. "Make yourselves comfortable. I'll be back with your traveling companions."

"Who?" asked Laura.

"The Leonards and the Fuenteses, of course."

"Oh dear," breathed Laura as Harrison and the two agents headed off. "I completely forgot about Al and Katie's parents."

Only a few minutes passed. When she saw them, Laura cried out, "Oh my god!" She ran, but almost fell because her stride, constrained by the ankle chains, was limited to a shuffle.

Ben couldn't believe what he was seeing. Emerging from the corridor, behind Harrison, was Katie's family. First came her parents, Marcy and Dean. But the most shocking sight was Katie's brother, Teeter, on a stretcher carried by the two agents. It was the basic kind of stretcher—poles with fabric between, like vintage World War I.

Laura hugged Marcy and Dean but immediately went to Teeter's side. "Where's his wheelchair?"

The two agents kept moving even as Laura tried to keep up alongside. Reaching the edge of the loading dock, they set Teeter down. "I said, where's his chair?"

Harrison ignored her. He disappeared again down the corridor.

"They sold it," said Marcy, huddled with Dean over Teeter.

Laura sat on the polished concrete floor next to Teeter. "What? Why?"

"'A confiscated asset,' they called it," said Dean. "They're going to sell all our belongings. Thank god they let us keep his feeding kit and respirator." He put his hand on a small case he was carrying. He looked over to Ben.

Ben realized he should say hello. Hugging made him uncomfortable, but he joined the huddle. While kneeling, Dean offered his hand. Ben was relieved that a handshake was the extent of the physical contact.

Teeter was in a fetal position. Looking like a Halloween paper skeleton that had fallen from the wall, his delicate limbs were arranged by the whims of gravity. The pronounced curve in his spine created an alarming image, with his neck and head at an unnatural angle.

"Are you in pain, dear?" asked Laura.

Teeter blinked twice, indicating no.

"Don't listen to him," said Marcy. "He is in pain." She put her hand on Laura's arm. "Do you know where Katie is?"

"No, we just—"

"Well now, the chain gang's all ready to go," said Harrison. "Load 'em up, boys."

Carlita and Luis Fuentes, wearing orange coveralls and chains, hobbled along behind Harrison.

Without waiting for Ben or Laura to say hello, the two uniformed officers broke up the huddle, lifted Teeter, and marched down the concrete ramp to the waiting bus.

"Move," said Harrison.

A third man stepped from behind the rear of the bus. He was a bald black man wearing sunglasses, and Ben saw FBI printed in bold white letters on the man's dark-blue T-shirt. The shirt was probably an extra-large, but it was nearly skintight across his chest and thick arms. With a pistol holstered at his side, the imposing figure opened the rear door of the bus, reached inside, and pulled out what looked like a stack of black cloth bags. Without an ounce of fat on his frame, the movements of his hands created ripples across his forearms. He took one of the bags and put the rest of the stack under his arm. Ben could see now that they were hoods. As Teeter was carried to the rear of the bus, the FBI man shoved one over his head.

"Oh my god," said Marcy. "There is no cause for that. Stop. You can't treat my son—" Marcy's plea was cut off as a hood went over her head.

"I can, and I will," called Harrison from the loading dock. "Pray I don't put chains on him too."

| | 0 | | 0 | | 0

"A BUS!" CRIED CHRIS. FROM THE LOCATION THEY HAD SELECTED TO WAIT FOR Harrison, Chris couldn't believe what he was seeing from Lucky's vantage point in his mind's eye. The shock of the scene made it difficult to focus. He concentrated on the connection to Lucky as his dog watched the police station a few blocks away. "They're getting ready to load my mom and dad into a bus."

"What? If they leave, we could lose them forever," said Al.

"Harrison will know, right?" said Chris, unable to keep the doubt from creeping into his voice.

"There's no guarantee," said Katie.

"What do we do?" asked Melissa.

"Let's get over there and watch for ourselves," said Chris.

The four youths raced across the streets of Philadelphia to a spot across from the back of the police station. They found a vantage point with good cover between two buildings. Chris saw it wasn't just Ben and Laura—all three families were being loaded.

"Chris, what are you waiting for?" asked Katie in desperation. "Fly over there and save them."

"It's too dangerous," said Chris.

"Dangerous?" Katie was incredulous.

"I can't explain how I know," said Chris. "If I try now, we'll lose our only chance to truly rescue them."

"Are you nuts? You have to go," Katie screamed. Al held her back. The intensity of Katie's voice echoed off the brick walls on either side.

"You need to chill, miga," said Melissa.

A pedestrian stopped on the sidewalk and peered into the darkness between the buildings, looking for the source of the sound, then continued on.

"Do it," Katie yelled, ignoring Melissa. Tears streamed down her face. "Fly over there. Toss every one of those cops in the dumpster. You're so fast, you can dodge the bullets. *I've seen you do it! Do it now!*" Katie was hysterical.

Chris shook his head. He took the gum from his mouth and whipped it into the air.

"Katie," said Al, trying to calm her, "it'll make things worse."

"Worse? Open your eyes, damn it. Did you see Teeter? My god, Chris, look at your *own* family." Katie stepped around Al and yanked the nylon bag from his shoulder. She shoved it in Chris's face. "Take another piece. Here."

Chris turned his head and backed up.

Like a mother forcing her child to swallow cough medicine, she kept pushing.

In a flash, Chris snatched the bag from her hand and smashed it against the brick. It was hard to tell if the crunch was from the gum machine, the portable scanner, or both.

"No!" She looked across the street to the scene in the parking lot. "There's no time, you—" Katie never finished the sentence. The short bus pulled out onto the street. Reenergized, she said, "You can still do it. Fly after them. I've seen you do that too." She scrambled for the bag, picked it up, and was about to shove it in his face again when Al stepped between them. This time, she let Al hold her. She went limp and cried in his arms.

Chris was stone-faced and flushed. He was stunned and furious at the same time. The presence of the warden was overwhelming. Time had slowed, and he began to feel nauseous, similar to the time he confronted the leader of the Circle of Six. Chris pressed his eyes shut. He tried to push the warden away, create distance, reach for independence. *Why me?*

From an open window three stories up, a woman called down, "Is everything OK down there? Is someone hurt?"

"We can't debate this here," said Melissa.

Katie's head snapped with a seething look, ready to make Melissa shut up for good.

"She's right," said Al. "We need to regroup. We can't be impulsive."

"The safe house," said Melissa. She backed deeper into the shadow between the buildings. "Come on."

Al, with his arm around Katie, followed.

Chris didn't move.

Melissa went to him.

"Don't even think about touching me."

Melissa held up her hands and kept her distance.

"Come on, migo," Al called.

"Please?" asked Melissa.

Chris took a deep breath and followed.

|10 |10 |10

CHRIS SAT ALONE ON THE FLOOR OF THE SAFE HOUSE. THEY WERE TALKING about him in the third person, as if he wasn't even there.

The gum machine looked like a Lego set poured from a cement mixer. Katie sat cross-legged in front of the mess. Al had given her the task of assessing the condition of everything in the bag. So she'd have something to do. So she wouldn't try to rip Chris's head off. The portable scanner didn't look broken, but Katie said it was.

"Could he really?" asked Melissa, talking to Al on the other side of the room. She kept one eye on Chris, as if he was a rabid dog. "Could he really have flown to catch the bus?"

"Sure," said Al. "But in broad daylight? Stupid idea, right?"

"Well, maybe that's what we need. You know, for the whole thing to go public?"

"The military, the FBI, and the police all have the same agenda. They want to catch Hoods. They're convinced we're Hoods. No one will help us."

"And now we're screwed," seethed Katie, looking up from the pile of parts. Every drop of venom was still in her voice.

"Don't start," said Al.

She ignored him. Staring at Chris, she said, "You could have saved them. It's all your—"

Chris cut her off. "It's the warden's fault."

"No. The warden can save them. It's you who won't. The warden helps *everyone*."

"No, you're wrong," said Chris. "The warden isn't the answer; he's the cause. None of this would have happened if it wasn't for the warden."

"But it did happen. We can't change the past. You have to—"

"No!" Chris screamed back, standing to face her. "I never asked for the warden or the abilities he gave me."

Thirty feet away, Katie stood and retorted, "All of us *normal* people start out life with big dreams. But then we grow up. Then we realize dreams are just Forrest Gump chocolates. Life's a lottery—and normal people are the losers. Reality's just a low blow that hits you right in the prospects. Our lives are a Poger sandwich that we have to choke down every day. We try to make the best of it, but it's nothing but a sweet-lemon po' boy. But not you, mister. Your whole life is everyone's dream. With a pertran in the garage and food credits to spare, you dine on Loyd caviar. Oh, but that's not all. On top of that, you're born with superpowers. What was your biological father's name again? Jor-El? *Everyone* wants what you have. You're *living the dream*, Chris Lumière, and you're so incredibly selfish that I have to stand here and explain it to you—"

"It's not *my* dream, Katie. If I could give the warden to you I would. I—" It was too much. Chris started to cry. He was an eighteen-year-old boy—no, a man, a grown man—and he just let it out.

Katie's expression didn't soften.

"Do you know how horrible I feel? If I thought, for a second, I could save our families by using my powers, I would. You have to know that's true." He took a convulsive breath and regained a bit of self-control. "You're right about me being selfish." He wiped away the tears, sniffed back his runny nose, and took another deep breath. "For my entire life, I've only wanted one thing."

Engrossed, Melissa asked quietly, "What?"

"Hope," said Al.

Melissa considered this. "Hope is good, right?"

"No, Hope is the name of our friend," explained Al.
"*Girlfriend* might be too strong, but he's right. Ever since we've known Chris, he's . . ." Al struggled for the right phrase.

"I love her," said Chris.

"Jesus, expand your fucking horizon, migo," said Katie. "You can love more than one person. My family. Your *own* family."

"You're missing the point. I've felt this way my entire life. I've had the warden my entire life. The point is, it's not *my* life." Chris remembered what the Circle of Six leader had called him: a vessel, a slave, a tool. "Somewhere deep down, I know the reason I love Hope is *because* of the warden. See? Even the *one thing* I've been drawn to my entire life is nothing more than another twist in the warden's plot. I love Hope like it's a disease. Why is that? The warden controls *everything*. Maybe the warden loves Hope, not me."

"That's not true," said Katie.

"You don't know that. The warden chose my parents. I'm supposed to love who the warden picks. Everything in my life has been manipulated by the warden. The warden is the cause of all of this chaos and heartbreak. You say I have gifts? No. I'm the warden's slave. Do you know what it's like to realize your whole life is founded on falsehood? On deception?"

"Us too?" asked Al.

"That's right," agreed Katie, compassion back in her voice. "The three of us. We love each other. Was that the warden's doing?"

"Who knows?"

"Well, as it turns out, I have a say in the matter. I love you, Chris Lumière, with or without the warden," Katie said.

"A minute ago, you wanted to kick my head in."

"You can't be mad at someone you don't care about. Besides, I still want to kick your head in. Maybe some sense will make it through."

A fresh flood of tears nearly squirted from his face. After a shudder, he pulled it together. He knew it was true: his lifelong friendship with Katie and Al wasn't built on deception. It was something firm to stand on. Something on which to build a new perspective. No matter how big his mistakes, they still loved him. No matter how clueless and disrespectful he was about their economic differences, they still loved him.

"And, of course, your mom and dad love you—with or without the warden."

"No," said Chris, "I have an effect on people. I can convince them."

Al piped up. "Convince? Yes. To follow? Yes. To make people hear and believe the truth? Yes. But force them to love you? No. Migo, when I said I wanted you to convince Harrison, I didn't mean for you to romance him."

Everyone laughed. Leave it to Al to break the tension with humor. Chris wiped his eyes. "All these years . . . loving Hope like a sickness. Do you have any idea what it's like to go that long without seeing the person you love? Hope is so angry at me. In her eyes, I can't do anything right. Do you know how far out of her league I am? She's a genius, and I'm an idiot. I'm nothing but a burden. She hates me."

"That's not true."

Again, Katie was shattering the doubt that had always haunted Chris. He'd never been fully able to accept the warden. The Circle of Six leader said so many things that made him doubt himself and the people he loved. Now Katie was focusing her brilliant logic on the single person his entire life had revolved around.

Instinctively, he pushed back, like sparring in karate class, to challenge her, to force her to bring her A game. "You have no idea."

"I do," said Katie. "Girl to girl. Woman to woman. I know." In a flat tone, she said, "Love hasn't come easy for her. You might say she grew up in hell."

"She has love in her life," Chris argued. "Her mom loves her."

"Sue had no chance to model motherly love—you know that—because of the same hell." Katie sat down cross-legged again. "When I begged you to save my family today, you said it was the wrong thing to do but you couldn't explain how you knew that. Well, it's my turn. I'll tell you this, but I can't explain how I know it's true: Hope sees you as her savior. You're the one capable of pulling her out of the hell she's experienced her entire life. She loves you."

Chris couldn't deny it. It rang true. "She loves me," said Chris, almost to himself. It wasn't a statement, more like a new outfit he was trying on for size. The last of the shadows were gone. From foundation to pinnacle, his life was now fully illuminated, free of the shadows of doubt. "And *I* love *her*."

"No," said Katie, "it's more than that. You love her *unconditionally*."

At that moment, Chris's head felt like it was on fire. He fell to his knees as his vision tunneled to black.

I IO I IO I IO

THE BLACK LIMO CARRYING PETE RASMUSSEN EXITED THE FREEWAY TOWARD McCarran International Airport. Under the clear night sky, the autopilot ignored the passenger terminal and instead headed for the service road leading to the enormous pubtran maintenance facility. Giant elevators lifted vehicles into the towering matrix of stalls. The fully automated complex recharged and repaired the fleet of computer-piloted taxis hailable from LAS and greater Las Vegas.

What an odd place to meet Anderson, thought Pete. Able to service more than sixty thousand pubtrans, the sixteen-story structure looked like a parking ramp large enough to serve six sports stadiums.

As his limo sped through a series of surrounding security gates, each gate's crossing arm raised in succession with perfectly controlled timing—a motion reminiscent of the legs of synchronized swimmers, rising and falling above the water's surface with perfect timing.

Pete saw another black limo—identical to his own—parked and waiting on the ground floor of the structure. Like marching ants, pubtrans streamed in and out of the facility, each moving at a computer-regulated speed calibrated for maximum efficiency and safety, yet also with only inches between.

Pete felt smothered, as if swarmed by a pre-Columbian megaherd of bison being corralled by a team of invisible AI cattle dogs.

His boss, Rick Anderson, stepped out even before Pete's vehicle came to a stop alongside. Holding the black case, Pete got out and crossed the few feet to where Anderson waited. Though Anderson always wore a business suit, his silver crew cut appeared more military than corporate. Pete didn't know if Anderson had ever served, but military service seemed like a natural career launch for the CEO of TerraStore Information Storage, responsible for municipal, state, federal, defense, and international contracts.

"You're cutting it close." Anderson was practically yelling to overcome the cacophony of noise around them. Sixty feet away, a dozen robotic arms rotated around the chassis of a pubtran on a hydraulic lift. Torrents of sparks showered the ground while the robots effected repairs. Pete realized the meeting place was no accident. Since the facility was fully automated, there were no public surveillance systems. There wouldn't be a human being within miles. And even if there were, a passerby would never notice two vehicles amid so many others. "Walk me through it," said Anderson.

Pete set the case on the hood of Anderson's limo, unsnapped the latches, opened the lid, and turned the case to reveal its contents. Pete tried to relax. "Here's the catheter." He pointed to a thin plastic tube leading to a small yellow canister with another tube coming out the opposite end. "It connects to the filter, here." Demonstrating, he hefted one of the fist-sized canisters and unscrewed it. "Inside is the filter cartridge. I'm giving you a supply of six cartridges. After each urination, you replace the cartridge. Return the used one to me, and I'll extract the unbihexium. I'll send you a fresh cartridge as a replacement."

Anderson inspected the parts. "It will filter *all* the unbihexium?"

"Every atom."

Anderson nodded.

Pete reassembled the parts and returned the device to its nest inside the case.

Who or what is pissing unbihexium? The thought was unimaginable. But obviously, some human or animal had consumed the unbihexium. *Why? For what purpose would Anderson have to—*

"How's Tina?"

As if Anderson knew his thoughts had strayed to the impermissible, the question about his six-year-old daughter yanked him back in line.

"She's fine."

"Her dance recital was tonight. You missed it."

"I got the filter done."

"Lucky for Tina."

| | O | | | O | | | O | |

"THIS SITUATION IS GETTING WORSE BY THE MINUTE," SAID MERSENNE IN THE middle of a rant. Chris had regained consciousness and was sitting up on the floor of the safe house. "I'll have to disband the cell."

"How are you feeling, Chris?" Al, Katie, Melissa, and even Lucky were crouched over him.

"You don't *have* to disband the cell," said Sedenion, arguing with Mersenne.

Chris rubbed the back of his head. The knot growing there was tender. "I think I'm OK. What happened?"

"Oh, sure, we'll just have paramedics pull up," said Mersenne sarcastically. "Once the authorities know about our safe house, I'll be *forced* to disband the cell."

"Look, he's fine," said Sedenion. "I'll get him some water."

"What's going on?" asked Chris.

"I'll tell you what's going on," said Mersenne, directing his hysteria at Chris. "You crumpled to the floor and bonked your head. Are you diabetic or something? Then you started babbling something about a Nephilim emergency."

"I think it was 'Nephilim emergence,'" corrected Katie.

"Whatever. And your friend here," said Mersenne, indicating Katie, "pulls out her percomm and starts comming paramedics."

"I was looking up *Nephilim*."

Chris could see the blue indicator light above the safe house door. He knew Mersenne had turned on the system that blocked all communications in or out of the safe house.

"He took our percomms," said Katie.

"We should have told them the rules," said Melissa to Mersenne.

"*We*? I've been trying to avoid these clowns ever since we ran into them. It's you who keeps attracting them. Him, specifically." Mersenne indicated Chris. "Why don't you just get a hotel room?"

"That's enough," said Melissa.

"Hardly. They promised to never contact us again. They broke that promise. We can't trust them. We can't risk it. When that light turns off, they're outta here. Permanently. And *you*, Four Nine Six, can go right along with them."

CHAPTER 18

CHELSEA COULDN'T BELIEVE WHAT A BEAUTIFUL, PERFECT DAY IT WAS FOR the naming ceremony. She sensed a special energy around the estate. The walls of the old house weren't soundproof, and the place bustled with the sounds of doors opening and closing while the staff hurried about. It was like birdsong signaling spring. Like when Snow White arrives at the cottage of the seven little people, and the woodland creatures "whistle while they work" to tidy up. Chelsea felt like Cinderella herself, watching as everything around her became enchanted. Miracle by miracle, the magic would build until reaching its finale: the transformation of her dress. A fairy godmother could make it happen with a flick of her wand. Chelsea had waited seventeen years.

The pubcomm chimed. It was a message from Evan. *This must be the vid feed he promised.* She did a silent little clap. *It's actually starting!* She accepted the comm.

"Morning, sunshine."

It'd been so long since he called her that. "Evan, I'm so excited. I'm just beside myself. Is our son waking up? Can I watch?"

"It won't be much longer."

Ugh. More waiting? "Then why did you comm?" *Oh my.* "Sorry, I didn't mean for it to sound that way."

"I understand. Well, aside from wanting to see your lovely face, I wanted to tell you about a small housekeeping item.

And I mean that literally, love. The kitchen staff wasn't able to prepare your breakfast today due to all their extra responsibilities. I'm having a little something sent up to tide you over."

"What is it?"

"Have you heard of a green smoothie?"

"Of course! Oh, Evan, that's what the celebrities drink. Super healthy. With kale and Swiss chard and . . . and stuff. You thought of everything."

"There's more. The drink has a name I think you'll like: ambrosia."

"Oh, that sounds divine."

"Right. You'll have it straightaway. Our son should be up very soon. Until then." He blew her a kiss before the screen went dark.

She went to her window, drew the shade open fully, and took in the beautiful day—

Knock, knock.

Wow, Evan wasn't kidding when he said straightaway. *It's as if they were waiting in the hall.* The door opened even before she could take the first step. "Excuse me!" It wasn't a housekeeper; two guards stood in the open doorway. *They just barged right in.* They stood shoulder to shoulder, one holding the glass of green.

"Set it there," Chelsea directed, using her most pompous tone.

"Drink it now," said the guard holding the glass.

"I'll drink it at my leisure."

"Don't make this difficult."

Chelsea remembered Evan's words: "Not until he's awake." She wanted to have her dignity restored in the worst way. She wanted to be Mrs. Evangelos Venizelos. She wanted social networks buzzing about her attire. She—

"Now."

Chelsea crossed the room. The ambrosia didn't smell half-bad. She took a sip. *Mmm.* It was green, but she tasted bananas and strawberries.

"All of it."

She stuck out her tongue and did as she was told. It was the last thing Chelsea would remember of the day.

I I 0 I I 0 I I 0

"COFFEE'S READY," CALLED CHRIS. HE, KATIE, AND AL DIDN'T DRINK COFFEE, BUT Chris had asked Sedenion how to make it. He wanted to be as helpful as possible. Mersenne had calmed down from the night before. Because no one could leave while the blue light was on, Mersenne had no choice but to be surrounded by Chris's reassuring aura, which smoothed out all Mersenne's anger. Mersenne agreed to let them stay the night even after the light had gone out late in the evening.

"It's no use," said Katie. "Too many parts are broken." She had spent the better part of the night trying to repair the gum machine. Only ten pieces of gum remained, including the one stashed under Lucky's chin. Ten pieces—about ten hours of connection with the warden, and no way to make more gum.

Chris reminded Katie that straight malted milk worked just as well. And Katie reminded *him* that it did *not* work just as well. The connection to the warden only lasted a few minutes that way. She also reminded him—because clearly he didn't respect the importance of the details, or he would've remembered himself—that the machine made the gum a special way such that the maltose and galactose sugars were released *gradually*. Chris felt bad about breaking the gum machine. Katie felt worse about losing her cool.

"And the scanner?" asked Al.

"I thought it was toast," said Katie. "It wouldn't power up. But I reseated the battery, and it booted up—good as new. Unfortunately, good as new—reseating the battery also wiped its working memory, like a factory reset. All our special programming is gone."

"We can't talk to the warden?"

"Nope. No connection to the mind-reader program either. And worse, it lost all the program modifications that enabled it to detect the Circle of Six men."

"So if they try their doppelganger trick?"

"We won't be able to tell if the person is real or an imposter."

"Can you reprogram it?"

"Not without access to Professor Richards's computer system. It has a copy of the code modifications."

"Can you get to it remotely?"

"No. Chris's house has been off the grid since the raid. Actually, all three of our houses are offline. I think the FBI made a hard cut. I don't even think Hope could get in."

"Are you saying we have to go there physically?"

"Yes. That's assuming the servers are still intact. For all we know, the FBI confiscated everything. Or worse, they destroyed the equipment."

"Professor Richards must have made a backup," said Al.

"Yes. I mean, sort of. Remember? He said there were back-ups at each data center affiliated with his research work. The Circle of Six destroyed all three data centers. Hope said there was another copy on central network storage, but TerraStore owns that storage. Hope found out the Circle of Six controls TerraStore. The copy there is essentially cheese in a mousetrap. She forbade us from accessing that backup."

Chris was glad Katie remembered the details. When the tech-nobabble reached a certain point, he usually tuned out.

Al didn't say anything at first. He started pacing. Chris had seen this many times over the years. Katie could call him Napoleon of Waterloo, or General Simpleton, or whatever, but Al really was a brilliant strategist.

Al stopped. "The gum machine . . . I assume all its parts can be 3-D printed?"

"Yes!" cried Katie. "That's what we'll do. We'll go to Chris's house, download the code—if the servers are still running—and we'll *print* the parts."

"But the house is offline," said Chris. "We won't be able to access the network to pull down the design."

"True," said Katie. "But I can do that on my percomm. The files are small. I can transfer them to the 3-D printer directly."

Melissa asked, "Shouldn't our first priority be finding your families?"

"See, Chris," said Al, "I told you she was more than just a pretty face."

"Nice try," said Melissa. "You can't vilify Chris in my eyes. He's been the perfect gentleman. Unfortunately. The more I learn about this Hope gal, the more I realize it takes a lot more than a pretty face to make the grade." She smiled at Chris, but she couldn't fully hide her disappointment.

"Melissa's right. Families first," said Katie.

"Agreed," said Al. "There's nothing wrong with our original plan. We can still nab Harrison. He may or may not know where our families are. But it's likely he does, or he can find out."

"And if we discover Professor Richards's lab is empty," said Katie, "maybe Harrison will know what happened to his equipment."

"OK then. Finding our families is the top priority. But first we need to go to Chris's house and see if Professor Richards's computers are operational so we know how much help we need from Harrison."

"Sure, but how?" asked Chris. "Hope said it was only a matter of time before the authorities placed full-time surveillance on each of our houses. FBI agents—actual people with flesh-and-blood eyeballs—are trying to capture us. All of Hope's cyber magic won't help. And they'll have guns. We'll be walking right into their hands."

"Let me think about that." Al started pacing again.

CHELSEA HANDED BACK THE EMPTY GLASS. SHE EXPECTED THE GUARDS TO LEAVE, but instead, one accessed the wall display on her bedroom wall.

Evan's face appeared again. "Chels, love. I have a surprise for you. A little change of plans. How would you like to be there, in person, when our son wakes up?"

Odd that he was talking as if they hadn't just spoken moments before. But the excitement was overwhelming. She beamed.

"All right then," he chuckled, "follow the escorts."

She frowned. "Not like this." She'd been sleeping in her workout clothes for days. "The shower? The ivory dress?"

"Yes, that's your first stop. There's plenty of time," he said. "See you soon."

She followed the escorts out of the old house and into a waiting security cart. A minute later they arrived at the side entrance of the main house, at the door to the spa. She followed the men inside, past the desk with the six towels and through the corridor, until they stopped outside the entrance to the women's showers. The guards let her pass, but once she stepped inside, both men turned away, not looking in but blocking the exit.

Around the privacy wall, she stopped as soon as she saw him—the guy, the one who'd talked to her by the exercise equipment. *Barrister.* The one who said she could call him the Bear. "These are the lady's showers, sir. Please leave at once."

He was sitting on one of the benches. He said nothing, and he didn't move.

"Chelsea." That voice. Unforgettable. A tectonic growl. Skotino stepped into sight from the shower stalls. "Evangelos explained. There's been a change of plans."

Her heart started pounding. "I get to be there when he wakes up. In person."

"*Reborn*," he corrected.

"I get to shower, and—"

"Not *before*." The word boomed against the ceramic surfaces.

Impossible. No. "No, I did everything Alexander asked of me. I've thought of nothing else." *Oh god, I smell like smear-ripened Limburger.* "What difference will—"

"You failed your son."

"What? No."

"After so many years. Here we are. Such a momentous day. And you think only of yourself."

"No, I . . ." Everything faded from her periphery. Only Skotino's face remained.

"How shameful. You promised Evangelos. You promised Alexander. You even promised me."

I did promise.

"A mother models values, not clothing. But you? Shower first, child second?"

No.

"He'll find out. He'll know you put your appearance above the most important day of his life."

"No."

"He'll know your devotion folded against the most trivial test. He'll know you reneged."

"No!"

"You reneged at the last minute, with complete disregard for *his* needs. Preoccupied with your own vanity."

No! Her own words reverberated in her mind: *Why am I making such a big deal out of it? My appearance means nothing. This day isn't about me. How selfish of me to make such an objection. After all the hard work and commitment from others, who am I to complain?* "I won't fail him. I would never." She had a new sense of dedication. She would do and give *anything* for her son. Her vision returned to normal.

Skotino glanced to Barrister. Barrister opened the locker next to him and pulled out the ivory dress on a hanger.

"Wear it," said Skotino.

"Of course," said Chelsea. She stepped forward and accepted the hanger. Neither man moved.

"If it makes you feel any better," said Barrister, "it's nothing I haven't seen before."

Taking the dress off the hanger, she saw it had a slit up the back. In the picture Evan had shown her, only the front was visible. Above the slit was a zipper. But instead of the zipper extending from the neckline and down the middle of the back, the zipper continued all the way to the slit. Stranger still, the zipper was sewn in upside down. It zipped from the bottom. With the zipper up, the dress was like a sleeveless version of the type of gown worn during a doctor's examination, completely open in the back. She opened her mouth to complain, but the words were choked off by guilt. She began to strip.

||0 ||0 ||0

"ARE YOU KIDDING ME?" ASKED MELISSA AS SHE STOOD ON THE STEPS OF THE little church. She looked back at Chris.

"No, for real," Al confirmed. "Have you ever seen a door open automatically for him?" He didn't wait for an answer. "We're in the habit of going first, so the door is already open when he walks through. But fortunately for Chris, it turns out that doors in public spaces have a manual switch, you just have to know where to look. His dad made changes to his house so he can get around."

Melissa had that look again. This time, it was like Chris had leprosy or something.

Chris shrugged.

Katie knocked again on the big wooden double door of the old church. The door didn't have a seccomm system or scanner, and never would.

Melissa continued her questions while they waited. "So when Chris walks up to a door, there's no announcement inside?"

"Nope. It's like he's invisible. The scanners don't work on him."

"Not the ones in clothing stores?"

"Nope."

"Not at the health clinic?"

"Nope."

Chris was getting annoyed. Al was acting like he was showing off his prize pony at the state fair.

"How does he get medical treatment?"

"When he was born, his doctor gave up on trying to use a scanner. He just treats him the old-fashioned way."

"I'm standing right here, you know," said Chris, more annoyed.

Melissa continued, "That's why you have to get your portable scanner reprogrammed?"

"That, and because it can also scan the warden, so we can interpret what the warden is thinking. It's crude, but helpful."

"No answer," said Katie, standing at the church door.

"What do we do now?" Chris asked Al. He wanted to add a name like Napoleon or General Simpleton. "I'm not going to stand out here for hours or days until Father Arnold shows up."

"Let's just go in and wait," said Melissa.

"It's locked," said Katie.

"No, it's not."

"Miga," said Katie incredulously, "you're halfway down the steps. How would you know?"

"Because, *miga*," Melissa replied, with her own sass, "it's a church."

Katie pushed on the door. Sure enough, it opened. "Huh. Go figure." She peered inside. "Well, we can't just go in uninvited."

"Yes, we can," said Melissa.

"That's breaking and entering . . . or just entering, if that's actually a crime. Or trespassing. Or something."

"No. It's the Lord's house. Church, synagogue, mosque, temple, monastery—pick your flavor. We're welcome. All are welcome. This place is governed by a higher set of laws."

"We could be in huge trouble if you're wrong."

"No. We'd be forgiven."

Then to Chris, Katie said, "Al's right. She's not just a pretty face."

The four youths walked down the center aisle. Lucky sniffed around.

Chris called out, "Father? Father Arnold?" Only an echo came back.

"Why don't we have Lucky track him down?"

"I don't want to use a piece of gum if we don't have to. Let's see if he shows up."

They picked a pew. Initially, Melissa and Katie hadn't seemed to hit it off. But now, Katie sat next to Melissa. Lucky sniffed around and plopped down on the cool floor.

It was quiet inside. The light coming through the stained glass was ample, but it was still dark relative to outside. Chris realized they'd been going nonstop for days. This was the first chance they had to collect their thoughts.

"Why is this priest so important?" asked Melissa.

"Well," said Katie, "over the years, we got better at communicating with the warden, but it was always a struggle. Then one day, when Chris was very connected to the warden, he remembered a conversation his mom had with Father Arnold. Chris was an infant, too young to remember. But he *did* remember, so we knew it was a suggestion from the warden to go visit Father Arnold. Sure enough, we have a chat with Father Arnold, and Chris goes into one of his trances while he merges with the warden. At one point, his mom uses the phrase *unconditional love*."

"Just like this morning?"

"Right. And *bam*, like a light switch, the warden spills out a whole bunch of words on the portable scanner. The words are clues about the Circle of Six, and hopefully how to stop them."

"And you think Father Arnold can help again?"

"It worked before. We still need to get the scanner repro-grammed, but it's a start. We're going to need all the help we can get from the warden to get our families released."

|10 |10 |10

"DON'T PATRONIZE ME, EVAN. YOU KNOW PERFECTLY WELL THE GUARDS ARE keeping their distance because I reek," said Chelsea, at the deck rail of the *Balkan Beauty*. She watched the small dinghy approach from the left. "Even you. Don't try to hide it. I see you wrinkling your nose." Chelsea lifted her arm and sniffed in a masochistic confirmation of the horrid odor, like when a family member discovers the milk has gone sour and the carton gets passed around because everyone has the uncontrollable urge to take a whiff for themselves. "I just want this day to be perfect." Fortunately, the weather was postcard perfect.

Evan stood next to her. But not too close. "The breeze is nice."

"Ha ha."

"Come on, Chels, lighten up. Our son is almost here. We'll begin the ceremony as soon as he's situated belowdecks. You'll be there in person when he wakes up—I mean, when he's reborn."

The captain yelled something in Greek. The guards and sail-ors hustled to the back of the yacht.

"What did he say?"

" 'Prepare to take on cargo.' "

"*Cargo*? Our son is *cargo*?"

The dinghy sat low in the water as it neared. Chelsea could hear the louder-than-usual engine sound as it labored. The small vessel, surrounded by a necklace of white foam, wasn't gliding atop the water but rather pushing through it.

"With the added weight of the chamber, he's too heavy for the copter. And he's too heavy to lift by hand. They'll use the cargo crane at the aft end."

The sound of the dinghy's engine dropped off. The little boat's back end bobbed and rocked as the wake caught up. Chelsea was no expert, but it looked top-heavy as it rocked to one side and then slowly returned upright, only to rock to the other side just as precariously. Sailors scrambled as the craft maneuvered toward the stern. The engines roared again, this time in reverse. There was a lot of yelling in Greek, which sounded to Chelsea like swear words. The dinghy pilot managed to reduce speed and maintain control. It took a few minutes before the crane's cable was connected to the chamber. Then Chelsea saw the shroud-covered chamber rise into the air. The crane rotated and brought it down onto a set of wheels waiting on the deck.

Chelsea moved closer, but Evan stopped her. "Not yet," he said. "The chamber is too long to fit in the passenger lift. They'll take him down in the cargo lift."

"It's almost time." That voice again. It came from behind. Chelsea turned to see Mr. Skotino, impeccably dressed as always.

Chelsea immediately touched her greasy hair and looked down. She fought the overwhelming feelings of inadequacy regarding her appearance, especially in the presence of Mr. Skotino—a man any designer of men's apparel would be thrilled to have model their clothing.

Chelsea heard the whir of copter blades above. Two quadcopters approached. One began its landing cycle while the other hovered.

"I must tell you, Chelsea," said Skotino, "this ceremony has provided me with a pleasure I hadn't anticipated. And," he added, "I'm a man who anticipates *every* pleasure."

Chelsea didn't bite.

"I'm going to have to ask Evangelos to proceed below and wait for us there."

Evan didn't hesitate. He walked past Skotino and into the cabin. He left her without even looking back.

"Don't you want to know what the pleasure is?"

"No," said Chelsea.

Ignoring her, he said, "Never before has anyone been introduced to the other six of my kind."

"Why me?"

"Because you won't remember."

"Why wouldn't I remember?"

"It doesn't matter. You won't remember that either."

The rotors of the first copter wound down as three men hopped out.

"You already know Victor Tyvold, my executive assistant."

Yes, she'd seen him a number of times. He was well dressed also, but less conservatively. He had black hair, like Skotino. He didn't look much younger, midforties maybe, but his suit was more avant-garde. She remembered the tech-savvy professionals who worked at Dr. Cornelius's research facility. Tyvold had that same high-tech, professional look. *That's one*, Chelsea counted to herself as Tyvold passed.

"And, you also know Dr. Betasten, of course."

The bald, round-faced penguin waddled past. No lab coat this time. A very plain suit. No imagination, no style, no attention to detail. It looked like he bought it off the rack. No tailoring. *That's two*.

As the third man approached, the first copter whooshed up from the helipad, and the second copter tilted forward and descended for landing.

"And this is Ken Barrister."

"The Bear," Barrister corrected as he passed with a smile and a wink.

He looked younger than the others and was dressed like he was going out on the town. Huge chest and arms, but narrow at the waist. She remembered the guys from her nightclub days, when she was dating Evan. She would surely pick Barrister out of a crowd. She smiled back at him, instinctively, but just as quickly remembered that, only an hour before, she'd been forced to strip in front of the man. *That's three.*

"One quadcopter can accommodate six passengers, but I don't allow the Circle of Six to all travel together," said Skotino. The second copter touched down. "This next set of men may not be as familiar to you."

She gasped when she saw the fourth man.

Skotino added, "Although, I could be mistaken."

It's him! From the nightclub! She remembered the incident. The beautiful black man who kissed her. She would pick him out of a crowd too, but she never saw him coming. At the time, she thought it was Evan coming to meet her at the club as a surprise. Somehow, the man had morphed into a replica of Evan. Impossible, but it was the only explanation. Had his physical form changed? Or had her perception been hijacked? She didn't know. It wasn't until the deep kiss that she'd realized it wasn't Evan and saw the man's true appearance. *It's him.*

Skotino said, "I see you've met before. This is Mark Spire."

Black leather pants. Black leather jacket. Stifling attire for a summer day. But he looked incredibly cool. Glossy black skin. Like Nigerian of the purest heritage. He slipped by without acknowledging her. No eye contact, no indication that he remembered that night at the club. Chelsea watched as he stepped into the cabin. If she hadn't known better, she would've sworn his body vanished precisely at the line of shadow, like Alice through the looking glass. *Four,* she counted.

"And this is Rick Anderson, CEO of TerraStore."

A conservatively dressed man passed her. Silver hair, cut short, flat on top, buzzed on the back and sides. Tan skin. The gray suit was refined, but she sensed the man underneath was more rugged. An unmistakable military flair. His gait had a discipline, almost a march. It made the color of his suit appear Nazi gray with a touch of SS. She noticed he was carrying a black case. *Five.*

Before she could turn to see the sixth man, Dr. Betasten called from the cabin door, "It's time. We need to start the ceremony *now*."

Skotino took Chelsea by the arm and bodily moved her into the cabin.

To be manhandled in such a fashion was humiliating. But Chelsea tolerated it. The ceremony was about to start. In just minutes she'd see her son awake. For such a short period of time, she could endure anything.

||0 ||0 ||0

"MAKE YOURSELVES COMFORTABLE AT THE TABLE HERE." FATHER ARNOLD SET down a heavy brown paper sack—which he'd carried in from the garden—on the table before stepping around the counter of the kitchenette. "I'll get us all some water. I'm so sorry for not hearing you knock. Gardening is my way of disconnecting from the world. Or maybe I should say *reconnecting* with it."

The sack looked like a ten-pound bag of flour. "What *is* this?" asked Al.

"Diatomaceous earth. It's a natural insecticide."

Al turned it to read the label. "It says *food grade* on the front."

"Help yourself." Father Arnold watched Al's confused reaction with amusement. He served them each a glass of cold water. Thanks to the church's pet-adoption events, he even had a bowl for Lucky. "You could eat it if you really wanted to. But I think you'll like these better." He set down a plate of rice cakes. The trio hadn't eaten on any regular basis for days. They'd been mooching off the hospitality of Cell Number Fourteen and Melissa's family. Chris intended to pay them back once he had access to funds without fear of disclosing his location.

Al inhaled his rice cake. Father Arnold returned with a bowl of almonds, then picked up the package of rice cakes, dumped it on a plate, and pushed it in front of Al.

After formal introductions, they told Father Arnold everything, including the name of the group of men, the Circle of Six, trying to stop the warden by killing Chris.

"Well, you're welcome to stay here as long as you need. The church basement has plenty of room. We have camping gear for retreats. And you can take turns using the shower here in the rectory."

After they found Father Arnold tending the garden, the priest hadn't taken them back to the church but rather to a small house nearby. The rectory, Melissa had explained to Chris, was the residence next to a church where one or more priests lived. It was nice inside. The furniture was the real kind, not like the pieces fabricated by a 3-D printer.

"From what you told me," continued Father Arnold, "we can't go to the authorities to get your families released. How can I help?"

"Thank you, Father. Your generosity is way more than we could ask," said Chris. "Do you remember when I came to visit with my mom and dad at the start of the summer? And you talked with my mom? And I ended up getting a bunch of words from the warden?"

"Sure. How could I forget? It was one of the most unsettling experiences of my life."

"Well," said Katie, "there's a new word. And as soon as I looked it up, I knew we had to come ask for your help. We know the warden's words are clues about the Circle of Six and how to stop them. We have to assume this new word is important."

"What's the word?"

"Nephilim."

He looked surprised. "Born from the sons of God and daughters of men."

"Forgetting something?" Chris asked Katie.

"Whoops. Hold on a sec." Katie dug into the nylon bag and tossed Chris a piece of gum. "Nine left, migo. Make it count."

Chris popped it into his mouth.

"Sorry. OK. Again, please," Katie prompted.

"Born from the—"

"Samyaza," blurted Chris, with his eyes focused on nothing in particular.

"Hold on. One word at a time, please," said Katie.

"Actually, if I remember right, the terms are related," Father Arnold interjected. Of all the angels, or so-called Sons of God, Samyaza was the leader of a group of fallen angels." He offered a small sigh. "Never thought I'd be using my divinity degree in this situation."

"Fallen?" asked Al.

"Yes. Against the wishes of God, they lusted after mortal women."

"No, not *lusted*, but rather . . ." Chris struggled with the meanings. Even with the help of the gum, the concepts were puzzlingly disconnected from the words. "Sorry, Father. I'm not saying you're wrong. It's almost as if the warden was there and has a different viewpoint and is able to add new details to what's already known."

The priest asked, "Can't you use the scanner, like before?"

"No," said Al. "We lost the connection to Professor Richards's computer."

Katie said, "Professor Richards's program uses a linguistic database to translate the warden's thoughts into words. Chris helps us interpret the meanings, but the words themselves appear on the scanner."

"Except lately, the words just fly out of my mouth. The warden must know the words, but I've never heard them before." Chris closed his eyes and tried to relax. "Let me concentrate. The fallen angels didn't *lust* after women, they just needed to . . . to . . . inflict pain." Almost an entire minute passed before Chris added, "Pharmakos."

"Interesting," said Father Arnold. "Pharmakoi were slaves or prisoners who were stoned or executed."

"Stoned," corrected Chris. "As a rudimentary form of torture. Not executed, but the prisoners usually died as a result." Chris's eyes snapped open. "The abducted women! The women who were kidnapped and never found. The ones my mom was accused of being involved with. They're pharmakoi. The place in Nevada. Remember? Those rooms—those prison cells—they were torture chambers." Chris pushed his mind deeper. "There's more, but you have to trigger it for me. What else do you know about the fallen angels?"

"Instead of describing them as fallen angels, some scholars interpret the name to mean *the violent ones*. They mated with mortal women to create offspring. This is where your new word comes in. The offspring are called Nephilim."

Chris closed his eyes. "That's not right. Not *offspring*. And the fallen angels weren't angels or gods. They were immortals who shared the same body with mortals. They didn't *mate* with humans, they *possessed* humans." Chris opened his eyes. "Like me."

"Like you?" asked Al. "What do you mean?"

"Superpowers," said Melissa, gravely.

Katie nodded but looked like she was in pain. "In ancient times, someone with Chris's powers would have been considered a god. Or Son of God, or angel, or whatever."

"When did this happen?" asked Al.

"Hard to say," said Father Arnold. "It's written in the book of Genesis."

"Genesis? You mean, like the Bible?"

"Yes. The Old Testament. The Hebrew Bible. It's the foundation of many religions. Maybe even most."

"Father," Chris continued, "you said they mated with mortal women. Just now, I used the word *possessed*. But that's not right either. Help me. Isn't there another word in the Bible that's used to mean *to mate*?"

"*Beget*?"

Chris shook his head. "No, that's not it."

"*To know?*"

"Yes!"

"I see," said Father Arnold. "Yes, there are many instances. For example, Adam *knew* his wife, Eve, and she became pregnant. Also, women who have *known* a man are no longer virgins. But it's not only the good forms of sexual activity—the evil forms too. The word *know* is even used to mean *rape* in Bible stories."

"Sexual activity? But there are meanings beyond sex, right? Broader? More meaningful? Substantial? More about the bond rather than the plumbing?"

"Yes. *To have absolute faith.* To know God is to accept God completely, blindly."

Al asked, "But if it wasn't about the plumbing, how did they have offspring? The Nephilim. Where did the Nephilim come from?"

"Some versions left the word *Nephilim* untranslated. In other versions, the word was translated as *giants*, savage giants who pillage the earth and consume humanity."

Chris squeezed his eyes. Like swinging a stick at a piñata while blindfolded, but without a friend to point him in the right direction, the meanings dangled, just out of reach. He opened his eyes. "There's something urgent the warden wants to say about the giants, but I just can't get it."

Katie buried her face in her hands. "Nephilim emergence."

"Emergence?" asked Father Arnold.

"Yes," said Chris. "That's the exact phrase that came out of my mouth. Not just *Nephilim* but *Nephilim emergence*."

Al scooted his chair closer to Katie and put his arm around her. "What happened to the Nephilim?" he asked Father Arnold.

"God wiped them out in the Great Flood."

"Flood? You mean, like Noah's ark?"

"That's right. God wiped out all who had been corrupted."

"But that's not real history," said Al. "That can't have actually happened."

"These are interpretations of translated texts. From the perspective of an English speaker, you have to seek the intent of the Hebrew or Aramaic words written during that period. While some believe the accounts to the letter, even in English, most believers acknowledge that the texts describe events of divine importance using the languages of the day. The words are holy. The meanings transcend the imperfect translation and pierce through the fog of time with perfect fidelity. It's another aspect of faith—to believe blindly. In other words, focus less on *what* you are being asked to believe, and instead focus more on the *act* of believing."

Chris mumbled, "Focus less on *who* you love, and more on the *act* of loving."

Father Arnold gave Chris a moment, and then said, "Chris, when you have some free time, let's collaborate. I've got a few homilies you could spice up. Anyway, let's get back to Samyaza. If these words are the keys to defeating the Circle of Six and free your parents, we're going to have to dig deeper." Father Arnold turned to Katie. "I don't own a percomm. May I?"

Katie seemed to shake off the dark implications of what they were learning and regained some composure. She handed it over.

He tapped at the screen. "Says here, Samyaza was the leader of fallen angels of high rank in the heavenly hierarchy. The fallen angels of high rank were also called watchers."

"Watchers," Chris repeated.

"Watchers?" asked Al.

"Yes," said Father Arnold. "*Watcher* is often used as another word for *angel*, someone watching over you."

"But, just as *to know* has an evil side, meaning *to rape*," said Chris, "*watching* has an evil side too. Watching isn't always about preventing harm. Sometimes, it's to witness harm. They like to watch. They like to watch the pharmakoi be tortured. They . . ." he stopped. "Sorry, I'm not getting any more on that."

"It goes on to say," said Father Arnold, "that the Book of Enoch lists the fallen angels who married and commenced in unnatural unions with human women and learned forbidden knowledge."

"That interpretation is too general," said Chris. "The word *knowledge* in the term *forbidden knowledge* has the same meaning as *to know*. The forbidden knowledge is—give me a second." Chris concentrated. "Time . . . future . . . prophecy . . . clarity . . . to know the future . . . to become one with time . . . to gain the opportunity to adjust one's present course through choice of actions . . . to shape one's own future . . . to have an unfair advantage . . . for the chance of reality's path doth tip."

Father Arnold said, "It goes on. Samyaza and his associates prematurely taught their human charges about arts and technologies that would otherwise eventually be discovered gradually over time by the natural human quest for knowledge about the inner workings of nature and the universe, such as weaponry, cosmetics, mirrors, sorcery, and other techniques. Samyaza and his associates had knowledge of technology before the rest of humanity."

Father Arnold glanced at Chris. Seeing no immediate reaction, he continued. "And this is from Enoch 6:305: 'The Samyaza leader said unto them, "I fear ye will not agree to do this deed, and I alone shall have to pay the penalty of a great sin." And they all answered him and said, "Let us all swear an oath, and all bind ourselves not to abandon this plan, but to do this thing." Then swear they all together and bound themselves by mutual imprecations upon it.'"

"The Circle of Six," said Chris, "by the command of their leader. They heard and obeyed. They had absolute faith. Each accepted his god completely, blindly."

CHAPTER 19

WHEN THE LIFT DOOR OPENED, CHELSEA COULD SEE THAT THE ENTIRE lower level of the yacht had been transformed. The floor, ceiling, and walls were covered with a velvety red cloth material, draped loosely, like a painter's drop cloth, with generous gathers and folds. Another peculiarity was the sconce lighting. Gone were the ship's harsh overheads. Now, along the walls, dots of radiance shed soft illumination, like candlelight.

"Come, come." She heard Dr. Betasten's voice from up ahead.

She stepped from the lift and let her eyes adjust. She saw the doctor at the end of the passageway. Standing next to a large green door, he was beckoning her like a six-year-old greeting guests at a birthday party. She proceeded, with Skotino lumbering behind her like a silk Armani golem.

"Shoes off," said Dr. Betasten.

Her shoes were more like slippers, but she understood what he meant. She started to bend down but was immediately held by Skotino's powerful hands, one on each arm.

"No, no," said Dr. Betasten. "Allow me. You don't have to do anything. You are the mother." He crouched. One hand cupped the back of her left knee with enough pressure to invite her to lift her foot, while the other hand glided down her calf, to her heel. She couldn't be sure, but she thought she heard him mumble, "Magnificent."

She noticed, then, a bowl and rag. Now, with the slipper off, Dr. Betasten gently washed her foot. She wanted to ask *why* but was overwhelmed by the bewildering gesture. He repeated the act on the opposite foot.

When the task was completed, he took his time standing up. Over the days, as her odor had become more rank, the guards, the kitchen staff, and even the housekeepers kept their distance. Not Dr. Betasten. Presently, one hand kept contact with her leg as his head rose, his face keeping close to her body, his cheek nearly rubbing against her dress. Once fully upright, he exhaled as if he had just taken in the scents of spring.

"Is Evan inside?" she asked.

"Yes," said Dr. Betasten, "Everyone is behind the green door, waiting for you." His blue eyes sparkled. "Do you like it?"

"Like what?"

"The green door." He was grinning like the six-year-old about to open presents.

"Sorry?"

"Oh, no, I'm the one who should apologize. I indulged myself. You inspire me so. You're the spitting image of Marilyn Chambers. Did you know that?"

"I have no idea what or who you're talking about."

"Unfortunate. She was a film icon in the last century. When I say *film*, I mean it in the broadest sense." Over a pursed smile, one of his eyebrows rose a fraction. "Well, we mustn't dawdle. Please, follow me . . . behind the green door."

Dr. Betasten turned and tapped several buttons on a panel next to the door. She heard a mechanical sound followed by a soft pop and hiss. The green door turned out to be more of a hatch that sunk into the room and then cantilevered to the side. Peering through, she saw the room was circular. The walls, ceiling, and floor were draped with the same burgundy material. Dr. Betasten went first and held out his hand for her. She took it, ducked, and stepped through.

Instead of the sconce lighting, six candleholders with actual burning candles were spaced evenly around the room. Below each candle was a stool. She assumed four of the stools were occupied by the men she'd just been introduced to, but it was difficult to be sure because of the flickering candlelight directly behind each man's head. Their faces were indiscernible against the glow. Shadows danced to the rhythm of the flames. In spite of meager light, one form was easy to see: her son, still lying in the chamber, under the familiar blue light. *But* . . . "Where's Evan?"

"A change of plans," said Dr. Betasten.

"What? No—" Chelsea's objection was clipped short as she was jostled from behind when Skotino's large frame came through the hatch. Then another shove as the sixth man from the copter came through.

"Seal it," ordered Skotino.

She was manhandled away from the hatch as it swung back over the opening. *Fhhhhhsht.* Then she heard a whistling sound. The pitch climbed higher and higher. Her ears popped. The sound went so high she couldn't hear it any longer. Her ears felt stuffy, like a bad head cold. She sensed the men behind her moving about. A stool was placed in front of the hatch. She stole a glance behind. The sixth man had taken the seat. His face was shrouded in its own shadow created by the candle immediately behind.

Dr. Betasten took the remaining empty seat to her left. Skotino stayed standing and forcibly moved Chelsea closer to the center.

"We can't begin without Evan. He's the father. He's—"

"Silence, bitch!" Skotino's roar made her pee. Just a little.

"He doesn't mean it like that." She recognized the whisper. Ken "the Bear" Barrister was on the stool to her right. "He means a female dog. They—"

"Silence!"

She couldn't be sure, but she thought Skotino's voice proba-bly made Barrister pee just a little too.

"Not now," said the man directly across from them, the one named Tyvold. His voice was measured but laced with frustration.

That's when she saw it. A flutter. Her son's eyes almost opened. She stepped and reached toward him, but Skotino held her tight.

"Host of my god's brother," said Skotino, "we begin."

"We hear and obey," said Tyvold.

"The fetus. Selected."

"Selected by the gods," they chanted.

"The mother of the servant is present."

"We bear witness."

"Hex-minyan."

"We Six are gathered."

The chant of the men's voices reverberated. By the draped velvet, the sound gradually dampened, until there was only silence. Chelsea waited for more. Then Skotino said, "Host of my god's brother, reveal the mikveh."

"I hear and obey," said Tyvold. He slid off his stool and stepped to the center, across from her, where a round table covered in the same burgundy cloth sat between them. He pulled the cloth to the floor. It wasn't a table at all but rather a steel column with a hatch. He pressed something along its base. *Clunk.* The hatch door rose mechanically, pivoting on a hinge, up, over, and down, coming to rest along the side of the stout column. A turquoise light shimmered from the opening. The ceiling sparkled with a pattern reminiscent of a swimming pool's surface in the sunshine. Chelsea could easily see through the opening. The blue-green light was in fact a reflection of sunlight off the ocean floor. The seawater sloshed freely. She immediately smelled the familiar saltiness.

Next Tyvold reached toward the ceiling. A thick spool of cable began to rotate, extending a line with a loop on the end. The cable dropped down through the hatchway and into the water. Once several meters were let out, it stopped. Tyvold pulled the silver chamber toward the opening until—*clink*—the head end connected with the edge of the hatchway.

Tyvold returned to his seat. Chelsea waited for the ceremony to continue, but they all remained silent. The only sound was the lapping seawater. The light from below was visible in the humid air in the shape of a cylinder or column, like a searchlight. The glow of six flickering candles surrounded the thick beam at the center.

Just as Chelsea began to wonder if they'd all become statues, she saw another eye flutter. A shrill alarm bleated from the chamber. It made her jump. The alarm stopped of its own accord. An opening appeared at the head end of the chamber. A door rolled up, like the curved door on a bread box.

"Behold," said Skotino.

"Behold," chanted the others.

She saw another flutter. But this time, his eyes opened fully.

| |0 | |0 | |0

HE WOULD LOOK BACK ON THAT DAY WITHOUT JUDGMENT. THAT DAY WAS neither good nor bad. It simply was. Unlike common humans, who, for example, had expectations of each and every Saturday—a day when arduous weekday activity transitioned to enjoyable weekend activity, and when the mundane cadence of daily life transitioned from labor to rest—that day, the day of his rebirth, carried no such expectation for him. No judgment.

He was like a squirrel in the woods. A squirrel had no concept of Friday or Saturday. No awareness of weekday versus weekend. No judgment about the virtues of work or leisure. Each day simply followed the next. And so it was for him. His new life was simply the life that followed the last. No expectation. No judgment.

Later, however, he would acknowledge the aloneness. He chose the word *aloneness* carefully. It's different from *loneliness*, which implies a time of not being alone. The day of his rebirth offered no relief from the feeling of aloneness, no respite. In his search for the meaning of his aloneness, he came to view the concept of aloneness to be tightly bound to the concept of oneness. He was unique. He was The One. Eventually he would accept the fact that he would never know a feeling of not-aloneness.

At times, he would contemplate the numeral *one*. He would ponder how the number one was created. The obvious answer was some kind of movement or growth beyond zero. But how? Surely, that growth must reach and cross the halfway point (one over two). But how? Just as surely, the growth must first reach and cross *that* halfway point (one over four). And so on.

When his mind was quiet, he would allow himself to be consumed by the thought that the tiniest departure from zero would therefore require a step quantified as one over infinity. The path from zero to one was like a pair of sheer cliffs separated by a pair of sheer cliffs separated by a pair of sheer cliffs, and so on, without end. Truly bottomless.

During these quiet times, he would become awestruck by the power required to reach the number one. The power to make one. The power to *create* one. He would conclude that going from zero to *anything* greater than zero required crossing infinity. In order to reach the number one, infinite infinities must be crossed. Therefore, he, as The One, must have been created by an infinite power.

While meditating on that power of creation, he would imagine that if the force of creation made a sound, the sound must be something like a sonic boom—a wave radiating from the point where the impossible happened, where growth crossed a distance measured as one over infinity, the point where physical existence passed from zero to one by crossing an infinity of steps, each step one-infinitieth in length. That wave would be proof of a miracle, that the underlying physical state of the universe had been altered forever. Like a sonic boom at the point where the sound barrier is broken, the wave emitted as a result of life's creation must propagate from a point where the *existence barrier* is broken.

He analogized that if the universe was created in a Big Bang, then life itself was created in a Tiny Bang—an infinitely small point where absolute nothingness became somethingness. The path traveled would be incomprehensible by the being so created—comprehensible only by the creator. The wave that emanated from the Tiny Bang would be the only evidence of the journey across an infinity of infinities. The wave itself would be a slave to time, a prisoner. Like the microwave background radiation of the Big Bang, forever traveling at light speed across the universe, so too must life's creation radiation resonate across the universe, filling it with a harmony of waves.

His feeling of aloneness—he would conclude later—was simply his perception of the wave that began its propagation at the point when he broke the existence barrier. The aloneness was the echo of his creation. The ringing would never leave him. His feeling of aloneness was confirmation of his creation.

| | O | | | O | | | O

"HE'S NOT BREATHING!" CHELSEA SCREAMED.

Although she was too far away from the chamber to see the yellow color of his eyes, she saw the urgency they conveyed. His limbs flailed against the sides of the chamber. He pounded on the glass, desperate to escape. She thought the glass might break, but the space was too cramped to get a good swing.

"He can't breathe!"

She felt Skotino's hands press down on her. As if incapable of a genuine whisper, his voice passed Chelsea's ear like the throaty warning of a predatory cat, more vibration than sound. "His first breath must wait."

Chelsea watched her son thrashing. It looked like a nature vid of a grub writhing inside a translucent chrysalis. Even though the end of the chamber was fully open, the figure inside flailed unaware. "He can't find the opening. Help him!"

"Relax. He must struggle."

As if on cue, a hand hit the top of the chamber, but the fingers landed outside. The thrashing ceased instantly. Determination replaced desperation. The fingers curled, one by one, around the edge of the chamber. Then the other hand appeared. It too gripped the edge. With a single thrust, his body vaulted out, arching backward, and into the water.

"Struggle?" screamed Chelsea, trying to understand what she was seeing.

This time, it was Dr. Betasten who spoke. "All life struggles at birth, Chelsea."

"He'll drown!" *How can they be so calm?* She tried to lean forward for a better look. Skotino held her fast.

"Shhhh." Dr. Betasten shushed her. "Children can be born underwater, Chelsea. His first breath can wait."

"What's happening to him?"

"Polychaete worms are taking residence in his tongue."

"What?"

Barrister leaned over. "I've learned not to ask a question if you don't want to hear the answer."

The swaying cable suddenly became taut. An arm rose from the water. The hand gripped the cable. The arm flexed. The head and chest breached the surface. Water streamed down across the nose and open mouth. The chest expanded, drawing in a deep breath.

"The sea," said Skotino.

"Origin of all life," chanted the men.

She heard more scuffling behind her. Skotino stepped aside. He turned her around and forced her torso down. Her chest hit the cushioned top of the stool. A different set of hands held her down. *Zzzzzzip.* Chelsea screamed as the sides of the dress fell away, exposing her naked bottom.

"The mother," said Skotino.

"Origin of all life," they chanted.

"The zah."

"He gives."

"The midras."

"She becomes."

Chelsea heard the winch moan, water cascading down, followed by splashes on the edge of the hatch. The spray sprinkled her butt cheeks.

"Oh my god," said Barrister. His voice was filled with shock and disgust.

Chelsea couldn't see anything.

"Estrus lordosis oedipus," said Skotino.

"Origin of the servant," chanted the men.

From the corner of her eye, she saw vomit splash between Barrister's feet.

She wouldn't remember what happened next. If having the ability to remember would've made the following six minutes any more bearable, she'd never know. She wouldn't remember Dr. Betasten's attempt to soothe her by saying, "It's just pain, Chelsea. All women scream and cry during childbirth."

CHAPTER 20

"LOOK, I ADMIT I HAVE NO IDEA WHAT I'M DOING," SCHOFIELD SAID finally. Eladio sat next to Schofield on the spectator benches of the parade grounds at Marine Corps Base Quantico. Schofield had invited Eladio to watch two teams of US marines play a game of Frisbee rugby, commonly known as frugbee.

"You didn't drag me out here just to tell me that," said Eladio. Schofield shook his head.

The game was into the second half, and only now was Schofield coming around to saying whatever it was he wanted to say. Eladio assumed Schofield's stalling was his idea of some kind of bonding ritual. Like in ancient Japanese culture, where two men stood in silence, their two bellies doing all the talking.

Eladio watched the game as he waited for Schofield to elaborate. In order to withstand the tug and pull of the scrum, the frugbee disc was made of a fiber composite. Hard as rock. Like playing rugby with a dinner plate. The edges weren't sharp, but nonetheless, each player wore a chain mail gauntlet lined with felt. *But no helmets.* Eladio had never tried out for frugbee. One of his high-school buddies had lost the tip of his ear. That was enough for Eladio. But he admired the marines who played it.

"I'm trying to say . . . It's about your assignment to persuade Rodriguez to help us from the outside, to understand what happened that day in the Nevada desert, and to find out what's really going on with Nolan." More stalling. "Wesson ordered me to give you whatever you need."

Aha. So, this is about chain of command and saving face. Eladio turned to him. "And now you take orders from me."

Schofield nodded. "Unofficially, of course."

"Of course."

Eladio watched an amazing play: one athlete caught the disc in midair and redirected it before landing.

"The report of Rodriguez's last mission is heavily redacted," said Eladio.

Schofield nodded.

"I need to know what happened that day in Nevada. I want to know who infiltrated TerraMed Biotech's research facility."

Schofield nodded again. "I know someone who was involved in the debriefing. I'll see what I can find out."

| 0 | 10 | 10

"HEY, NANCY, WHAT'S UP?" ANSWERED HOPE, OVER THE COMM FROM HER bedroom.

"I just got a message from the Otay Mesa point of entry."

"Yeah, I'm seeing that too," said Hope. "There's also a message from the Mexican Ministry of Economy, Border Inspections."

Nancy said, "Right. Looks like our software is being held at customs."

"Yes. From what I can tell, one of my decryption algorithms failed the border inspection."

"Your code is legal, right?"

"Oh, of course. I think they need to update their filter. It's probably—"

Hope's display lit up with a flood of pop-ups. Each was an alarm from the extensive set of autonomous programs that continuously monitored her cyber universe. "Uh, sorry, hold on a sec." The alarms were coming so fast she couldn't concentrate on any single message. "Nancy, I need to comm you back."

"It's not serious, is it?"

"No, it's a separate matter entirely. I'll contact the Mexican customs authority and get the code violation squared away. Consider it handled. Sorry, gotta go."

For the next hour, Hope scrambled to make sense of the alarms. She realized it was a massive attack, perfectly coordinated. Her personal defense network would be penetrated in a matter of hours, probably sometime the following day, and there was nothing she could do to stop it. The only reason such an attack could succeed was because the attack vectors made no attempt to hide the identity of the attacker. None. The moment her last line of defense was defeated, she would be able trace the vectors back to the attacker. The scary part was that an attacker of such sophistication would also be fully aware that they would be traced. The strategy was equivalent to a sacrifice fly in baseball.

> *PrincessLIMDIS: You see what I'm seeing?*
> *SalaciousFrog: Oh yeah. I've been watching you battle it.*
> *PrincessLIMDIS: Ever seen anything like it?*
> *SalaciousFrog: No.*
> *PrincessLIMDIS: Know of anything to stop it?*
> *SalaciousFrog: Nothing you haven't already tried.*
> *PrincessLIMDIS: Who could it be?*
> *SalaciousFrog: You'll know soon enough.*

CHAPTER 21

FROM THE BUSHES LINING THE ALLEY BEHIND CHRIS'S HOUSE, UNDER THE cover of night, Katie judged the distance she'd have to dash to get past the cop, or agent, or whoever was sitting in the pertran parked in the driveway.

"Are you sure the front of the house isn't any better?" asked Melissa.

"I'm sure," said Chris. He'd been able to surveil the entire area by using the gum and directing Lucky. "The cop watching the front is farther from the house, but there's no easy way to get inside the house from the front. The smashed garage door in the back is our best bet. It's at the bottom of the ramp, so it's harder to see."

"That's good enough for me," said Al. "Look, we don't have all night. Every minute we sit here in the bushes is another minute we could be seen. Let's move on to the next step in our plan, to get the gum machine parts printed and the code downloaded from Professor Richards's computer. Let's set up our distraction."

"I still don't understand," said Melissa. "What's a construction beacon?"

"Last week, Chris and I passed a construction site while riding our bikes. As a safety precaution, construction sites have a beacon that triggers an in-cab warning when drivers approach. It'll make a great distraction. The beacon should still work, even though the cop is parked, because the tran's dash electronics are active as long as anyone is sitting in the driver's seat. The problem is, usually the *vehicle* approaches the *beacon*, not the other way around. We need to test it first. The construction site is pretty far away, and we don't have our bikes, so Chris is going to have to fly over there and get the beacon."

Katie said, "I hope no one's looking up at the stars at three in the morning."

Chris nodded. He backed up a bit while trying to remain hidden in the bushes. He whooshed into the air. Katie, Al, and Melissa covered their eyes as the force kicked up gravel and twigs. He disappeared into the night sky.

"How exactly is Chris able to fly?" asked Melissa.

"The warden directs the air molecules around Chris to create force. Vacuum from the top and pressure from the bottom."

"It's amazing how quiet it is."

"Yeah," said Katie. "Since sound travels through air, the warden can control the noise."

"And how is it that he has more strength?"

"He doesn't."

"But when Chris smashed the helicopter, he hit it with his bare hand."

"That's how finely the warden can direct the molecules. It makes his limbs move with great speed. The air also protects his skin. The air pressure is so dense, it's like armor."

"Air against metal? How can that be enough to bend it?"

"Do you know the formula for force?"

"Of course. Mass times velocity."

Katie smiled. "Even though air doesn't have much mass, the warden makes it move fast. Very fast. That's the key. The faster it moves, the more force it creates. Theoretically, the force is unlimited, certainly enough to bend metal."

"He's always been able to do these things?"

"No. Well, looking back, sometimes he did things we couldn't explain. So I guess the warden had *some* influence when Chris was little. But once he hit puberty, that's when things really started to change."

Minutes later, Chris dropped from the sky, holding the construction beacon. The device was bright orange, matching the color of traffic cones, and about the size of a small loaf of bread. A thick plastic shell protected the electronics and battery inside.

"Now what?" asked Chris.

"Bring Lucky over here."

Al took off his belt and looped it through Lucky's collar and around the beacon. "There you go." Al gave Lucky a pat on the head when he was done. The beacon hung just below the small tube containing the spare chunk of gum. "Now you *really* look like a classic Saint Bernard, with a keg of beer and a whiskey chaser. Full bar service all the way to the peaks of the Alps." Al stood back. "OK, Chris. Have Lucky creep up on the unmarked tran in the driveway. Let's see if our distraction works."

Lucky slinked away and snaked his way over.

Glassy-eyed, Chris said, "It'll be tricky. I have to see the cop's face, but not get so close that the cop sees Lucky." After a minute, Chris said, "It worked. The cop is looking down. I can even see the red glow of the warning light reflecting off his face. I'm backing Lucky off now."

"Good," said Al. "All right, Katie. Get up close and wait. When I whistle, stay as low as you can when you slip into the garage. After you program the 3-D printer, go to Professor Richards's lab. If the equipment is still there, download the modifications that will let us detect the Circle of Six. The gum machine parts are small, so by the time you're done, they should be finished. When Lucky sees you, we'll distract the cop a third time, so you can get back out."

Katie nodded. With the scanner in hand, she stayed as low as possible. *Chris should be doing this, not me.* But she was the only one qualified to access the lab computers.

On Al's signal, indicating the cop was distracted by the warning light, she snuck past the vehicle, down the ramp, and straight into the garage, without looking back and without disturbing the yellow tape as she slid underneath.

Looks like the printer still has power. She knew the machine wasn't loud when it operated, nor were the indicator lights very bright, but she couldn't help from imagining the scene of a carousel spinning up, complete with flashing lights and carnival music, as soon as she hit START. *Tap, tap, tap.* From her percomm, she transferred the set of gum machine part specifications and then started the process. The printer's extrusion arms converged on the fabrication stage like a team of one-armed surgeons around an operating table.

While the printer did its work, she entered the house.

"That's far enough."

Oh shit. Another cop was inside, waiting in the kitchen.

"Don't even think about running." He turned on the lights. He was in plain clothes. Katie *did* think about running. Wearing a suit and dress shoes, he wasn't prepared. But she knew they would use force to stop her if she ran.

"All units," he said into his percomm, "I have a female suspect. Unit one, I'm bringing her out to you. Unit two, keep an eye out for any others." He pulled out a plastic strap. "Turn around. Hands behind your head."

She did as instructed.

"Well, well, what do we have here? A medical scanner?" He took the device and set it aside. "I'll look forward to your explanation for why you have that." He tightened the plastic strap around her wrists. Then he aimed his percomm at her, as if taking her picture. "Katie Leonard. Bingo. One down, two to go."

Once the cop led her outside, she looked for her friends without being obvious about it. The police vehicle had a steel-mesh barrier that separated the back from the front, like a cage. The cop loaded her in the back before getting into the front.

After backing out of the driveway, they approached the spot where her friends had been hiding. The cover of the bushes wasn't perfect, so they'd be easy to see. But they were no longer there.

| | 0 | | 0 | | 0

THE LIMOUSINE TILTED DRASTICALLY TO THE SIDE AS CHELSEA'S SON LEANED to get out. Barrister put his hand on the roof of the vehicle, to hold on, in anticipation of the vehicle's suspension snapping back after the kid got out.

They had dressed Chelsea's son in normal street clothes, like any other seventeen-year-old: jeans and a white T-shirt. Barrister couldn't get over how normal he looked—at least from the back. The front was a different story. Yellow eyes with rectangular slits for pupils. Barrister thought they looked like goat eyes, but during the overnight flight back from Greece, Dr. Betasten explained the pupils were more like those of an octopus, because the slits stayed horizontal regardless of the orientation of his head. Barrister wanted to ask why it even mattered but took his own advice instead: don't ask a question if you don't want to hear the answer. Sure enough, the limo rocked violently once the kid's foot left the running board.

The golf carts the Circle of Six used for transportation through the tunnels under the mountain only carried four people. At six times normal weight, the kid would probably pop the tires, so they had a forklift waiting for him.

Joining Skotino, Dr. Betasten, Tyvold, and Spire, Barrister got out of the limo and boarded one of the carts lined up in a small caravan behind the forklift. With an amber strobe flashing atop the forklift, they followed it through the network of enormous tunnels, each a hundred feet across and arched like the inside of a Quonset hut.

The caravan slowed as it approached the set of holding cells where Barrister had brought the young women, the women they called pharmakoi. He didn't want to know what they did with the girls. He assumed they shared the same fate as Veronica.

However, instead of going to the holding cells, they stopped on the opposite side of the tunnel. A metal door began to roll up, exposing an opening large enough for a tractor trailer. They followed the forklift inside. The room was the size of a gymnasium and mostly empty, except for a bunch of lab equipment in one corner, which looked similar to the setup in Greece. The forklift lowered Chelsea's son to the floor.

"That's fine, that's fine." Dr. Betasten didn't wait for the cart to stop before he hopped off and waddled to the forklift, waving an arm. His other hand gripped a black case he'd gotten from Anderson. "Leave us," he said to the forklift driver.

Behind Skotino stood Tyvold, Spire, and Barrister, watching Dr. Betasten as he fussed. It was amazing how naturally Chelsea's son moved for being so heavy. During the limo ride, Barrister had bumped against him as they rounded a turn. The kid was hard as a rock. When Barrister looked closely at his skin, he noticed a barely perceptible sheen. Not oily—more subtle, like freshly applied lotion. Aside from that, just by looking at his skin, no one would ever know it wasn't completely normal. Dr. Betasten said his skin was magnitudes harder than steel. *If Superman is the "man of steel," who could stop this kid?*

"Progress?" Skotino asked.

Tyvold glanced at his percomm. "Penetration is at sixty-six percent. By sunrise, I'll be able to predict when the last firewall will be defeated. I estimate midafternoon. Once I'm through, we'll know the exact location of whoever is blocking our searches for Chris Lumière's location. After your servant eliminates that person, nothing can stop us from finding and killing the warden's host. The warden will be forced to find another virgin and to begin growing a new host. We'll have nine months to find and kill that woman. Rinse and repeat. If successful, we'll have eliminated the warden as a threat, even without returning him to Tartaros."

"Your servant will be ready in time," Dr. Betasten called as he worked.

"He better be," said Tyvold. "Whoever is blocking my attempts to find Chris Lumière is located somewhere in South Jersey or Eastern Pennsylvania. I can't get any more precise until I'm through. The servant needs to be in the area and mobile. The moment I'm through, I'll give you the exact location. At that point, they'll see us coming. There's nothing I can do about that. They'll run. You may only have minutes to catch them before they bolt."

Squatting in front of Chelsea's son, Dr. Betasten unbuttoned the kid's jeans and pulled them down to his ankles. Then he pulled his boxers down too. *What the—?! The kid has no dick! Looks like female parts. And totally bald, too—not even a little Hitler 'stache.* Chelsea's son just stood there with some kind of tube sticking out. The tube had a yellow cylinder on the end. The whole contraption looked like one of those oxygen masks that drop from the ceiling in those airline safety vids. The kid just stood there while the doctor checked the tube by parting the nether lips with his thumb.

The vicarious sensation made Barrister grab himself. He felt mildly reassured after confirming his own organ was where it should be.

"Now," commanded Dr. Betasten.

Barrister couldn't really see, but it was obvious the kid was peeing. After a minute, Dr. Betasten opened the black case and swapped the full plastic cylinder with an empty one from the case. The doctor pulled the kid's pants back up. "Take this to Rasmussen." Dr. Betasten tossed the cylinder to Spire, who snatched it out of the air and headed out.

"Drink." Dr. Betasten handed the kid a cup of what looked like water.

Barrister shivered at the memory of the first and only other time—just hours before—he'd seen Chelsea's son open his mouth. The tongue was the length of his arm and almost as thick. The end was forked, and the two halves moved independently, like two snake tails. Then the snake tails parted at their base. That's when Barrister had thrown up, when he saw the worms writhing inside the cavity in between.

Poor Chelsea. All that crying. Dr. Betasten had kept talking to her. He'd told her the room "behind the green door" would thereafter be known as the Room of Tears. She'd just kept begging for them to stop, to let her go, and Dr. Betasten kept blabbering on. As if it wasn't goofy enough to give the room a name, he'd also said the door would thereafter be known as the Door of Tears. *Who cares what the name of the room or the door is? Poor Chelsea.* The rest of the Six had seemed to get off on it, like a bunch of sweat lodge fanatics high on mushrooms.

This time, when Chelsea's son opened his mouth to drink, no tongue came out. *Except for the fact that he has no teeth, his pie hole looks normal.*

| | 0 | | 0 | | 0

WHAT AM I GOING TO DO NOW? KATIE WONDERED IN THE BACK SEAT OF THE COP car.

The police vehicle reached the end of the alley. The cop set the destination, and the autopilot took over. He turned to face her through the wire mesh. "I don't suppose you'll tell me where your friends are. Save us both a lot of trouble?"

"Don't you have to read me my rights or something?"

"Nope. DOD jurisdiction. You don't have rights. Once—"

Tshhhhh. The entire back window exploded into a shower of tiny glass cubes. Katie's eyes closed instinctively, but she immediately felt Chris's arm come across her chest and under her armpit. When she felt herself moving, she reopened her eyes. Chris was lifting her. When or how he had cut the plastic handcuffs, she didn't know, but she was suddenly free to hold on to his forearm. She watched as, in a blur, his other arm directed her body up and through the window frame. Incredibly, he guided her head, back, hips, and knees as if riding on a cushion of air, all in a split second.

Between her feet, she watched the cop's shocked expression as Chris pulled her up and out, rocketing high above the treetops. The brake lights came on, but the vehicle was already getting smaller by the second. She realized Chris's other arm was across her stomach now, but she still held on for dear life as she watched their entire neighborhood fall away underneath. The horizon drifted down on all sides, like reaching the apex of a mountain in Montana. Roads became lines. Houses became dots with pinpoints of light from streetlamps, like strings of twinkling pearls.

"The scanner," she yelled, remembering the device was still in the police car.

"We can't risk it."

She could sense he was angling in the direction of the church. He leveled off. Katie felt weightless. The air was warm, with only a slight nighttime chill. Stars everywhere.

"I'll never doubt you again."

"I know, miga. I got your back."

Literally, she thought. She'd accused him of always thinking of himself. But Chris Lumière never stopped thinking of others. He was always there for her. That had nothing to do with the warden. She couldn't imagine a better friend.

The view was absolutely breathtaking. "I bet this never gets old."

"Nope."

They started the descent to the church.

Chris said, "I hope the gum doesn't wear off."

"What!" she gripped him even tighter.

He laughed. "One more piece gone, but you're worth it."

AFTER THE DRINK OF WATER, DR. BETASTEN TOOK OUT CONTACT LENSES AND inserted them into the kid's eyes. "Splendid." Next, he pulled a wig from a stand and adjusted it on his head. "Just until your real hair grows in. OK, the final touch." He pulled out yet another case. This one contained a set of false teeth. "Perfect fit." He stepped back for perspective. "Now smile."

Chelsea's son smiled—but only with his mouth, not with his eyes or the rest of his face. Barrister thought he looked like an Arnold Schwarzenegger–type cyborg with a painted-on smile, like the one on the face of a clown popping out of a jack-in-the-box.

"Host of my god's father," said Dr. Betasten as he turned to face Skotino, "I present to you, your servant."

"Xander," Skotino corrected. "Only Xander. From now on."

Xander. With Dr. Betasten giving names to every door and room on the yacht, Barrister had almost forgotten the names they'd rattled off for Chelsea's son. Xander was one of them.

Xander looked completely normal—no, better than normal. He was a very handsome young man. Even the wig of black hair was fairly short and in style for his age. He had his father's olive skin, or at least not as stark white as his mother's. *Skin?* Looking at him, it was impossible to tell there was anything unusual about his skin. *Amazing.* Tall and lean, he looked like he should weigh about one sixty instead of half a ton. And after spending months in that chamber, his muscles should be atrophied. But he looked fit, almost buff. Barrister had to admit he was envious. If the two of them walked into a room full of babes, Xander might get more attention.

"Yes. Xander," Dr. Betasten corrected himself. "Of course."

"How much of this"—Tyvold glanced about the medical equipment and waved his arms—"*gear* do you have to drag around with you?"

"Some."

"Better get it loaded on the plane ASAP," said Tyvold. "You, Spire, and the Bear need to be on the Philly highways when I break through."

"I have portable equipment," said Dr. Betasten. "It's already at the airport and loaded on our scramjet. But I'll need a separate vehicle once we land."

"Your cutting it close, Doctor."

"Or," said Dr. Betasten pointedly, "you're overly optimistic about when you'll break through." He recovered his composure. "Anyway, only one task remains. We need to make sure the dentures don't impair Xander's ability to use his phallus."

Xander strode out of the room, through the large door. His gait was normal. Again, no way to tell anything was out of the ordinary. Barrister knew the floor was concrete. He wondered what it would be like if Xander walked on a less supportive surface, like a wooden floor. Or for that matter, any floor that wasn't on ground level. *Could six grown men pile onto one spot in the middle of a living room and not fall through to the basement? Probably.*

Barrister followed Xander, Dr. Betasten, Skotino, and Tyvold across to the other side of the tunnel and into the pharmakos holding-cell area they called the oubliette.

"Room number six," said Tyvold. Xander continued down the corridor. Tyvold entered the secondary control room and took his usual seat. Barrister followed Skotino and Dr. Betasten into the control room. Tyvold tapped at the input panel to bring up a vid feed from room six.

Felicity, Barrister remembered. On the display screen, he saw her, the young woman he'd seduced and kidnapped only days before, bound to a chair in the middle of the room. He watched on the screen as Xander stepped inside.

"Let me go," Felicity pleaded, her voice coming through the speaker.

Barrister sensed a reaction from the men in front of him. Skotino actually grunted with satisfaction. Each man acted like he'd just tasted a decadent piece of chocolate.

They watched as Xander closed the door and stood before her.

"My father knows where I am. He can track my percomm. He's coming. You're going to be sorry." Her voice was shaking, conveying none of the confidence her words attempted. She was on the brink of tears. The patina of bravado was gone now. "What are you going to do?" she asked finally, her voice full of desperation.

"Kiss you," said Xander. Those were the first words Barrister had ever heard from Chelsea's son. He sounded normal—no, better than normal. He sounded confident, self-assured, on top of his game. Any woman would find it sexy. And not in a cheap, catcalling way.

As for Felicity, those words were completely unexpected. You could actually see her consider the thought. Under almost any other situation, she might actually consent. She didn't react. His reply didn't fit the situation. It made no sense.

Xander moved alongside her.

"No," she screamed, no longer confused about the peril.

Xander leaned down. She turned her face away. He pulled it back. Instantly, her eyes flared with elevated alarm. Barrister tried to imagine what Xander's hand would feel like against his own cheek and chin. She looked startled by the feel of his hand. She knew something was terribly wrong. Xander leaned closer. As their lips touched, she kept hers tight. But her resistance was useless. If Barrister didn't know better, he'd say it was a regular French kiss. What happened next made him look away. This time, he could only dry-heave. Trying to shut out the muffled screams, he couldn't help but notice that Skotino, Tyvold, and Dr. Betasten reacted as if masturbating, like fiends in a devilish circle jerk.

CHAPTER 22

"IT MUST HAVE BEEN THE ALCOHOL, CHELS. IT'S MY FAULT, LOVE," SAID EVAN, "IT didn't even cross my mind that you hadn't had a nip in years."

Her headache was unbelievable. "But I can watch the vid of the ceremony, yes?"

"I didn't record it."

"You said you would."

"Love, no. No, I didn't." At Chelsea's bedside inside the old house, Evan squeezed her hand. He had that queer kind of smile, like the doting husband of a woman ravaged by Alzheimer's.

Didn't he record it? Now she wasn't even sure of her recollection leading up to the ceremony. "But why *wouldn't* you?"

"Because all our family was present and accounted for. You know how private we are. The only way to guarantee precious moments of our lives aren't spewed across the global network for the entire world to see is to never record them in the first place. In our business we have a saying: loose bits sink ships. Anyway, the important thing is that the entire affair was a smashing success. And I'm glad you're as tickled as I am about our son's name."

"Xander." She repeated the name, letting it roll off her tongue. "In honor of your grandfather," she added. Even that tidbit of information came after she woke.

"Right. Pappous thought it would be too confusing to have two Alexanders. *Xander* was a perfect choice."

It is a very nice name. If only I could remember. "Keep going. Tell me what happened next."

"Well, that was the end of the formal service on the open-air deck. The podium we used for the ceremony was dismantled to make room for the reception. *Reception* is too grand a word. Just my sisters had traveled to join us. As it turned out, they were delayed and didn't arrive until late. In any case, we soldiered on. We enjoyed cocktails through the afternoon. Everyone commented on how beautiful you looked. Such a reserved dress, but you were as glamorous as always. You prattled on about how the hot, soapy shower was so heavenly." Evan smiled. "And I must say, Pappous was touched when you thanked him and confessed that his suggestion of the daily reminder about not showering made the ceremony that much more meaningful for you. It meant a lot to him."

"I said that?"

"Of course."

"What else?"

"Well, it was a spectacular day. Come to think of it, you haven't had that much sun for I don't know how long. I bet that was a contributing factor too. My fault again, Chels. I'm so sorry."

"Don't be silly. Go on."

"Actually, that's right about when you started having cramps. I've never seen you in such pain. We got you back to the main house straightaway. Dr. Betasten examined you. He confirmed you were experiencing severe menstrual cramps. That's when we realized how serious it was. Dr. Betasten gave you a sedative. After a full night's rest, here you are. How's the pain now, love?"

She touched the tender parts again. She felt like she'd ridden bareback American style for six hours straight. "Better, I guess." She'd noticed the spotting soon after waking. The medical procedure—the endometrial ablation, performed soon after she'd moved to Greece—meant she could no longer carry a child. It had also ended her periods. So seeing the blood was a shock. Was it even possible for her to have menstrual cramps?

"Wonderful. Dr. Betasten says you should be well enough to be up and around this afternoon. In the meantime, you must take it easy, dear."

"When can I see Xander?"

"Soon." The queer smile returned.

"What aren't you telling me?"

"Well, he's traveled to America."

"What! But I didn't even get to see him!"

"Of course you did."

"But I don't remember. I—" The tears came hard and fast.

"There, there. Xander must continue his education. Part of it is conducted in America. He'll return, naturally."

She wanted to ask how long, but she'd learned over the years not to trust any prediction by Evan or anyone else about when she would see her son next. "Can I go to America?"

"That's an excellent idea. How about you rest up, and then we'll see."

| | O | | | O | | | O

"THAT'S A TOTAL OF THIRTY-THREE INDIVIDUALS WHO FLED THE SAN ANTONIO data center," said Warrant Officer Kendall. Standing in front of the large display board in the Omega Force command center, Kendall gestured to advance his presentation. "Each is now a Tier 1 suspect charged with aiding and abetting a principal actor of cyberterrorism. Each was apprehended within twenty-four hours after Oscar Foxtrot secured the data center. We monitored the suspects' communications during the apprehension period, which led to two hundred fifty-four Tier 2 suspects. Of those, two hundred twenty-one have been cleared—friends, family, and the like. For the remaining suspects, we put wiretaps in place. We're tracing those contacts now."

"Drill into the Tier 1 suspects," said Eladio, standing, hands on hips. "What's the mix?" Schofield stood behind Eladio, allowing him to lead. The team of warrant officers seemed relieved to have their first lieutenant back at the reins, even if it was only when Schofield needed consultation.

"Most were minor players at the data center. However, three individuals had extensive responsibilities to maintain the center's systems. Predictably, none had direct contact with their handlers. They have no idea who they work for."

"Just in it for the money, huh?"

"Yes, sir. The funds were untraceable, as expected."

"What do we know about the data center?"

"It was a significant Hood resource. We confirmed that. It was a big chunk of computational firepower. And we pulled the plug."

"Big? Maybe," said Eladio. "But what percentage? For all we know, another data center spun up in some other part of the world even before Oscar Foxtrot's boots touched ground on that San Antonio suburb. If nothing else, though, it was a public relations win."

"Yes, sir," said Kendall. "That concludes my report."

"All right, people, back to your stations," ordered Captain Schofield, like a rooster flashing his tail. "First Lieutenant, you're with me."

Eladio followed Schofield into his adjoining office, fully going along with the display of command. Eladio wanted to know where Schofield learned his leadership style. *Hollywood?* Eladio also took notice that he hadn't been officially replaced; Schofield was still filling in.

Inside Schofield's office, the hierarchy flipped.

"I have some information," said Schofield.

"Go on."

"During Rodriguez's mission debriefing following the debacle in the Nevada desert, he reported that Fireteam Whiskey was bested by tourists."

"What?"

"A bunch of kids and a dog."

"But what about the Israeli mercenary force?"

"One man."

"What!"

"And he never fired a shot, not a lethal one anyway. He used a BSS."

"What? A blind-stun-and-snare rifle for riot suppression?"

"Exactly."

"But Rodriguez's heavy-weapons specialist—his number three—was critically injured. The marine had to have his legs cut off just to save his life. A battlefield amputation. If it hadn't been for his armor, he'd be dead."

Schofield said, "The unredacted report says it was the man's own grenade. It set off other ordnance he carried."

"Not enemy fire?"

Schofield shook his head, letting it sink in.

Incredible. Not only was the filed report redacted, but the declassified communiqué had been falsified. "Not even friendly fire?"

"Nope. And you won't believe how it happened."

| |0 | |0 | |0

HOPE HAD BEEN CALM DURING THE NIGHT AND THROUGHOUT THE MORNING, trying every bit of tradecraft she knew to find a way to stop the cyberattack. But now, with the moment of the breach imminent, she felt the walls of her bedroom pressing in on her like the walls of the Death Star's garbage smasher. She'd set up a countdown clock, showing the estimated time until her last line of defense would fall. *Three minutes.*

Over the course of the morning, the prediction had varied widely as billions of uncertainties were calculated and recalculated, jumping ahead or back by twenty or thirty minutes. Now, however, with the uncertainties all resolved and passed, the countdown clock was ticking off one estimated second for every real second.

Two minutes.

She'd coded a phalanx of artificial intelligence bots to instantly trace the attacker's identity the moment her last shield was defeated. SalaciousFrog and her other online friends were standing by, ready to investigate the results that would be neatly prioritized using artificial intelligence.

T-minus one minute.

Never in her life had she felt so powerless. No, that wasn't true. Memories, horrible memories, of the abuse she'd endured from her dad flashed into her mind. *Why am I thinking about that now?* She concluded her life in cyberspace was an escape—a place she could hide, a place she could control. Just as a person with anorexia controlled his or her diet, Hope controlled her reality by living in cyberspace.

Thirty seconds.

The violations. She cringed at the memories. The bubble she'd created by going online, the bubble that protected her from the haunting threats in her life, was now collapsing right along with her last firewall.

Ten seconds.

SalaciousFrog: Here goes.

She suddenly felt as she had as a twelve-year-old. Trying to survive the moment. The darkness of her bedroom. Afraid the door would open at any moment. The sound of his voice calling her name—half urge, half scold. The sound of the door swishing open. His ridiculous attempt to whisper. His slurred speech. The stench of booze and sweat.

Five. Four. Three.

Sweat? Chris! Somehow, the memory of Chris's delicious aroma extinguished all her fears. Her prince's pheromones were as extraordinary as her prince himself.

Zero.

"WHEN DID YOU GUYS START LEARNING KARATE?" ASKED MELISSA INSIDE THE rectory.

Katie said, "When we were about ten, I guess."

"And Bruce Cohen was your instructor the whole time?"

Katie nodded.

It was a late night. Even Lucky seemed tuckered out. He was curled up on the love seat between Katie and Melissa. Melissa petted his head while Katie stroked his furry body and belly. Dog heaven. Chris was on the couch. His eyes looked heavy.

Even though the warden's words hadn't yet revealed a specific way to stop the Circle of Six, a confrontation with the men from Nevada seemed inevitable. Because Bruce Cohen's help had been so pivotal in the battle earlier that summer, it made sense to ask him to join them now. Father Arnold had gone to tell Bruce the situation and ask him to come to the rectory. Al figured Bruce might be able to use his old military contacts, from when he was in the Israel Defense Forces, to help them find their parents. In any case, the trio could use all the help they could get.

Katie wondered how her mom, dad, and brother were getting along. She didn't think the FBI or the military, or whoever was holding them, would actually harm them. She thought about all the information that would come out in an interrogation and what the authorities would make of it. She almost giggled to herself with the thought that the feds would probably think their truth serum didn't work because the same cockamamy story would come out no matter how many times they tried. After hearing about Chris flying around and sniffing like a dog, the authorities would probably give up and find a different way to charge the families with terrorism. Initially, Katie was concerned they might come to the conclusion that her parents were some kind of super-Hoods, impervious to truth serum, and try to use even more drastic measures to force a confession. But what kind of Hood would come up with such a harebrained alibi as the story that Chris's parents would surely spill?

"It's amazing that Bruce was able to fight all those Omega Force soldiers," said Melissa.

"Marines," Katie corrected. "Bruce taught us that only service members of the army are called soldiers. Anyway, you're right— it *is* amazing. You watch the Hollywood version of the Omega Force on the pubcomm, but you never think of them as actual people. They're different in real life. Very serious. The whole thing was amazing. But Bruce said it seemed like the marines were fighting something else. And that's the only reason we were able to walk away alive that day."

"What do you mean by 'something else'?"

"He thinks they were given bad information. They seemed disorganized and unprepared. Mind you, Hope was doing her network-jamming wizardry, so they weren't able to communicate, but Bruce thinks it was more than that, like the Omega Force had been deliberately misinformed."

"Why?"

"We know the Circle of Six is hardwired into the global network. Bruce thinks the marines' command and control was infiltrated by the Circle of Six."

| |0 | |0 | |0

HOLY SHIT. HOPE COULDN'T BELIEVE THE EXTENT OF THE BREACH. HER LAST firewall wasn't just penetrated, it was annihilated.

> SalaciousFrog: *Who are these people?*
> PrincessLIMDIS: *Never mind. Stick to the plan.*
> *Concentrate on the commercial businesses.*
> SalaciousFrog: *The flight plan is commercial.*
> PrincessLIMDIS: *I got it. Move on.*

Hope pulled up the flight plan, filed only hours before: TerraHoldings private scramjet, number 5465727261, departed LAS at 11:06 a.m. local time. Arrived at PHL . . . Holy crap! Fifteen minutes ago?

That jet was sure to have carried the Circle of Six. Hope hesitated when she remembered the day in Nevada. Instinctively, she touched her left shoulder, the one the leader of the group of men had dislocated. She shook off the memory and got back on task.

The only thing in her favor was the fact that every system owned or controlled by the Circle of Six had been momentarily exposed. Her bots ripped through every node at a phenomenal rate. SalaciousFrog and her online friends had provided even more hosts for her bots. The parallel computing force might have set a world record. She imagined the batteries of solar energy stations all around the world suddenly being drained by the sheer power brought to bear on the task.

Her attackers—the Circle of Six, behind the guise of TerraHoldings, LLC—were now regenerating their defenses. Too late. Her bots had plenty of time to do their job. A merciless cyber colonoscopy. She had to trust that the AI algorithms selected the right bits to record. Like a fist up the ass and then back out with a handful of intestines, in only a fraction of a second, her cyber disembowelment was complete.

She searched through the trove of information, focusing on the records related to the flight plan. *There.* She found the ground-transportation log pulled from the Philadelphia airport's seccomm system. Two vehicles: a limousine and a utility van. Concentrating on the limo, she accessed the destination address from the vehicle's autopilot history. *Oh my god.* It was *her* address—the address of her apartment complex, everything but the apartment number.

Frantically, she fed the pertran's ID into the real-time traffic system. A map appeared on her screen. *Oh my god, oh my god.*

The limo and the van were sitting at the entrance to her apartment complex. *Right outside!*

She thought of her mom. *We have to get out of here.* But how? She needed a plan. She needed help. But first she needed time.

"Computer, lock down!"

"Panic mode acknowledged," said the voice from the sec-comm panel on the wall of her bedroom. "Security lockdown initiated. Complete. Residence secure."

She had to assume the door wouldn't keep them out, but it was something. She tapped to initiate a comm with Chris.

"Is it really you?"

"Yes. Listen. I need help. The Circle of Six is here."

"What? Where?"

"My apartment."

"Inside your apartment?"

"Hope?" called Sue from the hallway. "The panic mode is on. Are you OK?" The door swished open. Her mother stood in the doorway.

A bolt of fear coursed through Hope's body as she remembered her first confrontation with the Circle of Six. They had the ability to impersonate, to shapeshift, to look like anyone. One of the Six had masqueraded as her mom. At the time, the only thing that gave him away was a big smile and open arms offering a hug—a display of affection Sue would never tender. Standing over the threshold now was a woman who looked timid and apprehensive about disturbing Hope, worried she'd be reprimanded for interrupting Hope's important work. *It's really her.*

"Mom, we need to leave. I don't have time to explain. Stay right there, don't move." She turned back to her display. "Chris, no, they're not in the apartment. They're parked outside the complex. I think they just arrived." She was starting to panic. "Please! Help us!"

"I'll be right there. Can you get outside?"

"No. They're probably on their way up right now." She sensed herself getting hysterical. She forced herself to concentrate.

"Wait. I can tap into the feed from the security camera in the lobby. Here. I got it. I'll fork the stream to you."

She couldn't believe the scene. Toothless was on the bench, over a pool of blood. The dachshund was nowhere in sight. Two men and a teenager faced the manager's glass-and-steel enclosure. Hope recognized the black man as the one who had impersonated her mom. They were confronting the manager. She tapped for audio.

"Last chance. Tell me which apartment she's in."

"No," screamed the manager.

"I'll get it from your system anyway. Give it to me."

"No!"

She watched as the teenager smashed through the barrier with his bare hand. Glass shattered, and metal crumpled, as if hit by a pile driver.

"Give it."

"Never!" The manager was backed into the corner.

Like a Frankenstein monster, the teenager extended both arms. When he gripped the manager, it looked as if he'd grabbed putty. His fingers sunk effortlessly into the flesh.

"*Arghhhh*." The manager, gritting his teeth, pried futilely at his attacker's wrists.

The monster switched his grip as if squeezing water from a sponge. Arterial blood squirted across the enclosure, onto a pane of glass that was still intact, blocking the view of the camera.

Hope heard Sue gasp at the sight.

"Chris, did you see that?"

"Send me your address. And get to the roof," said Chris. "Get yourself and your mom to the roof. Now."

| | 0 | | 0 | | 0

THE ELEVATOR BOBBED AND LURCHED. THEN A BELL RANG OUT AS THE PANEL displayed MAX CAPACITY EXCEEDED in red flashing letters.

"Are you shitting me?" said Spire.

"We'll take the stairs." Barrister pressed the ground-floor button. Nothing happened.

"Open it," said Spire.

For a second, Barrister thought Spire was talking to him. But Xander stepped forward and pried the elevator doors apart like window curtains. The elevator was stuck six inches above ground level. Barrister hopped out and followed Spire and Xander to the stairwell. As Xander set his feet on each grimy stairstep, the grains of sand and dirt popped and snapped under his weight. When they reached the second floor, they headed for apartment 217. The hallway floor creaked and moaned.

"Keep to the sides," said Spire.

Xander walked bowlegged, avoiding the weak center.

"They're not here," said Spire into his percomm after Xander had smashed through the apartment door.

"Her defenses are back up," replied Tyvold over the comm link. "I can't access the apartment's seccomm to find out when she left. Hold on. I've got the area under satellite surveillance. Let me review the stream . . . No, they never left. Wait. They're on the roof!"

"Let's go," Spire ordered.

| | 0 | | 0 | | 0

"NOW WHAT? THERE'S NO PLACE TO HIDE," SAID HOPE, DESPERATELY. THE rooftop was completely flat except for the doorframe's triangular structure, jutting out from the surface they'd just emerged from. "The door has no lock. They can come up just as easily as we did."

"Bar the door, maybe?" suggested Sue.

Even if they managed to find a bar or piece of lumber, there was nothing on the doorframe to pin it against. Hope searched anyway. The roof was barren except for a layer of gravel. Curled corners of tar paper poked through every few feet between the white PVC plumbing tubes poking up here and there. "Even if we could, I don't think it'll stop them."

"We just need time."

Hope nodded. She circled the door structure. *Nothing.*

Sue said, "Maybe we can just hide on the opposite side of the doorway?"

"That won't—" Hope heard them coming up. There was nothing to do but try the idea. She grabbed her mom's hand, and they darted around as the metal door flew open. They crouched behind the door structure, on the angled side. There was absolutely no cover. They were completely exposed. It was like trying to hide at the foot of a ramp.

"Hey, ladies," said the big one. The men fanned out.

Hope pulled her mom back. Together they ran to the edge. Her adrenaline made her almost unable to stop. Gravel pinged off the ridge only a few inches above the roof's surface. Some of the pebbles went over the side. Hope steadied herself and peered down. No fire escape. Nothing.

"Come on, let's be friends."

Hope turned. The men moved in. The big one was the only one smiling. He moved to the right as much as he moved in, cutting off that escape path as he went. The black guy locked his gaze on Hope and shuffled left, cutting off that route. The young one—the Frankenstein freak with fresh blood on his hands and a diagonal streak of red across his T-shirt—headed straight for them. But something was odd. His steps made footprints in the gravel. No, it was more than that. The roof itself looked crushed. Before his next step, there was a loud pop. Hope felt it as much as she heard it.

The young one froze. The other two exchanged glances. "Slowly," yelled the black guy.

"Hey, why don't you impersonate my mom again?" taunted Hope, desperate for more time to think. "Then there'll be two of them. Won't that be a hoot?"

The monster took a cautious step. Rocks crunched, but the roof held.

Holding her mom's hand, Hope stepped back. Her heel bumped the ridge. She glanced back. *Three stories up. No trees, no shrubs, only parking lot.* She wondered how hurt they would get if they jumped. Would it buy them enough time? She scanned the sky.

"He's not coming," claimed the black guy.

"Who?"

"Chris."

What? How could he know? Can he read my mind? Did they have time to tap my comms while—

"He's not coming."

"I heard you the first time. And I have no idea what you're talking about."

Sue's heel hit the ridge at the edge of the roof. She stumbled and almost fell.

"Yes, you do. He's not coming because you said he should worry about the DOD."

"I never—" Her voice trailed off. *I did say that.* Like vodka-induced bed spins, the scene rotated around his face as if she were the target for a knife thrower in a circus sideshow, arms and legs splayed, strapped to a spinning board as the world tumbled end over end, round and round. Everything was spinning, except his face at the center. His eyes burrowed in.

"Chris is busy taking care of his friends. He's trying to find his parents."

No.

"He's being very careful to avoid detection. Just like you asked him."

No. In her mind's eye, she saw Chris on a street she'd never seen before, trying to hide behind a utility pole. She watched as he donned sunglasses and tiptoed—actually tiptoed, like a cartoon character—to the next utility pole.

"He's determined to please you. He's ignoring the Circle of Six, just like you asked. He's staying off the grid, just like you asked."

He is.

"Yes. He won't disappoint you again."

Hope heard a crunch of gravel. Like in a dream, the sound came from Chris's tiptoeing to the next utility pole. Chris's white T-shirt morphed into a collared shirt, then morphed again into a black leather jacket. He pulled the collar up around his jaw, like some kind of Elvis-inspired 007. With his collar up and sunglasses on, he stepped again. Crunch. He looked like an Indian in an ancient Western vid, careful not to snap a twig. Crunch.

"He's avoiding the cameras. Just like you asked."

No.

"Correction: you *told* him."

I did.

Crunch.

"You *ordered* him."

I did. He's only doing what I . . . what I ordered him to do.

Crunch.

"He told you he was sorry. You ignored him. He begged you for help. You refused. You invalidated his situation. When he needed you, you said his problem wasn't worth your effort."

I did. How could I be so callous? How could I treat him that way and expect him to help me? It's true. He's not coming.

Crunch.

| | 0 | | 0 | | 0

"IT'S OUR OWN FAULT," SAID COLONEL WESSON, SITTING AT HIS OFFICE DESK AT Quantico. "We trained you to treat the Omega Force as if they're equipment—a bastardized crossbreed of asset and ordnance."

"But they're people," said Eladio, standing across from Wesson.

"Are they? Don't answer that. First, ask yourself: are *you* a person?"

"Sir?"

Wesson used his drill instructor voice. "First Lieutenant Hector Eladio, are you a person?"

"Sir, yes, sir."

"How do you know?" He waited only a second. "Look, son, I'm not trying to beat you up. You come in here demanding to know everything about Omega Force. I'll tell you what I know. But I don't want you to just hear it, I want you to *get it*. So back to my question. Let's just go with the obvious answers. Because you were born? Because you have a mommy and a daddy? Your mommy and daddy do the wild thing, and out pops Baby Hector? Sounds reasonable. Answer me this: when you swore your oath, who swore with you?"

"My graduating class."

"Any chickens or snakes?"

"No, sir."

"Article II of the United States Constitution gives the president power, as commander in chief, to create and maintain a standing army. George Washington appointed Friedrich Wilhelm August Heinrich Ferdinand von Steuben as the first inspector general. Baron von Steuben had the miserable task of recruiting the first troops to form the Continental Army. I'm betting no one had to tell him to pick men over chickens or snakes. They took men only. By *men*, I mean not women. And those men couldn't be slaves because slaves didn't have legal rights, meaning they couldn't be sworn in. Why? Because they were owned property. Remember that point.

"Over time, society's ugly debates finally establish the rights of women and the illegality of slavery. You got your Fifteenth Amendment, your Emancipation Proclamation, your Nineteenth Amendment, et cetera, et cetera, all with phrases like 'sex, race, color, or previous condition of servitude.' Over time, the nation comes to its senses. There's always more work to be done on that subject, but it's going in the right direction.

"Later on, things get formal. They come up with this term *natural person*, which keeps chickens and snakes out of the ranks. But what about dogs, Eladio?"

"Sir, I have to admit, I have no idea where this is going."

"Hang in there. I'm sure you're familiar with the practice, in law enforcement, and in our own military, of assigning a rank to K9s. Is it an official rank?"

"No, sir."

"Correct, honorary only. Why not official?"

"A dog is not a natural person."

"Correct. Do dogs have legal rights?"

"No."

"Why not?"

"Dogs are owned property."

"Nope. In People v. Frazier, 2009, Superior Court of Sacramento County, California, the court ruled on a case in which an old lady commanded her dog to attack another old lady. The dog ends up mauling the old lady's leg down to exposed bone. Nasty. In the trial, the dog owner tries to shift criminal liability to the dog. The court, citing a previous 2007 ruling, decides that dogs don't have the 'mental state that can incur criminal liability.' Because of this legal precedent, and because of this explicit reasoning of mental state, animals are not persons under the law. But not because they're owned property. It's because they're not smart enough." He paused. "Eladio, do you think an Omega Force marine is smart?"

"Yes, sir."

"Damn right. Smarter than any normal human. So, let's fast-forward to the aftermath of Rodriguez's ill-fated Nevada mission. Court-martial gears up. The lawyers prepare their arguments. Lo and behold, Omega Force marines don't have legal rights, therefore they can't accept criminal liability. Why? Because citizens receive legal rights when they're born. But the Omega Force marines don't enter the world in the usual way. They grow out of a petri dish, so to speak. No wild thing. No bump and grind, like Mr. and Mrs. Eladio. Officially, they're the property of the US government. Remember that point about owned property? It gets worse.

"You don't even have to be a natural person to have legal rights. Entities such as corporations, which are treated under the law as if they were persons, have legal rights and can be held liable. Such entities receive their legal rights via incorporation. Think about it. Rodriguez and his team swore an oath to defend the Constitution of the United States of America against all enemies, foreign and domestic. But they were never born and never incorporated."

"That's ridiculous. They're people."

"Agreed. So incorporating them is stupid. But unfortunately, your assertion that they're people isn't clear under the law."

"Then we make it clear."

"Exactly. What's needed is legal precedence. The way it was decided for slaves, women, and dogs."

"How do you get that?"

"Somebody has to fight back. Legally. The slaves fought back and won. The suffrage ladies fought back and won. The granny with the chewed leg fought back and won. Final score: Women, one; blacks, one; dogs, zero. No dogs at the voting booth. And you'll never find a dog sitting in a courtroom, behind the table for the defendant."

"Meaning Rodriguez has to fight back. He can take an IQ test. The court will find he has the required mental state, leading to a legal precedent."

"That's just it. He didn't fight back."

"What?"

"He just walked away."

"Why?"

"You should ask him. I'm guessing it has something to do with the fact that, legally, we're treating him like a dog. Consider his other-than-honorable discharge. The discharge language was nonstandard. It reads more like a warranty transfer. Scary shit.

"When you set up surveillance on Rodriguez, your instincts were spot-on. You need to do your recon. You're smart to come here and learn everything you can. But think outside the box, Hector. Think beyond protocol, beyond procedure.

"Now get your ass back down to Tijuana. Keep your eyes open. But even more so, *feel* your way through. You're about to sail into uncharted waters, son. *Mare incognitum.* Be creative. No choice is wrong, simply untested. Go with your gut. We need Rodriguez's help. He can get inside without tipping off Nolan. Make it happen."

110 110 110

WITH THEIR HEELS AGAINST THE ROOF RIDGE, THE ADVANCING MENACE WAS nearly on top of them. Chris landed on the roof, in front of the two women, unaware he'd broken the paralyzing bewitchment aimed at Hope.

"Chris!" she cried, snapping out of the trance.

With the threat to his back, Chris reached for Hope. Too late. The Frankenstein grip seized Chris from behind like a vise. A defensive blast of air exploded from Chris's skin. Gravel and shreds of tar paper blossomed into the sky as if shot from a confetti cannon. The fingers pressed in but could not penetrate the shield of air. Hope and Sue had been knocked down but, incredibly, hadn't fallen off, steadied by an invisible hand of vacuum.

Chris broke free as he twisted to face the monster. The claws landed again, this time from the front. The resulting blast of air hit the guy with the force of a punctured steam pipe. His hair—a wig—flew off his head.

Hope screamed. Chris couldn't resist a look back. The second blast had pushed her over the edge. She was holding on by two hands with just her fingertips visible.

In a flash, Chris brought his arms around and up in a sweeping circle, breaking free yet again. This time, he took no chances. Thrusting back and away, he cartwheeled off the building. While upside down, he lifted Sue from the roof and tossed her high into the air, up and out over the edge. Airborne, he spun and rotated like an Olympic platform diver. And, like the diver about to hit the water, he snapped out of the rotation right behind Hope. *Backpack! This will be tricky.* Hope's backpack, strapped over her shoulders, made it difficult to grab her. He hadn't taken it into account. It had its own center of mass, almost like a third person to save.

Time slowed—or his mind sped up, he was never sure which—allowing him to slide his arm between Hope and her backpack like a letter opener. All the laws of physics were obeyed, yet he had infinite time to guide his hand and arm between the layers, angstrom by angstrom. Raw force alone would be deadly. If the molecules of her skin didn't have time to get out of the way, they'd be crushed. Instead, the tips of his fingers, surrounded by a cushion of air as soft as a baby's sigh, separated the surfaces without cutting. With the delicate work completed, his sense of time returned to normal. He plucked Hope, and her backpack, from the side of the building. He caught Sue in the other arm with equal dexterity and rocketed skyward.

CHAPTER 23

"WELL, I'LL BE HONEST WITH YOU. I DON'T HAVE A LOT OF candidates for the medical assistant position," said the prison administrator.

Ingrid watched him pore over her qualifications. He'd called it an interview. He was wrong about that. The meeting wasn't an interview; it was a formality. As he'd just admitted, he didn't have a lot of candidates. In fact, she was the only one.

She supposed they could simply not hire her. But the penitentiary rules were crystal clear: a pregnant inmate receives care. Period. It didn't say tomorrow, or the next day, or whenever they got around to it. There was serious legal exposure for the State of Washington.

"You have the midwife experience we're looking for," he continued. The prison administrator was the fatherly type, midfifties and roundish all over with a double chin. He tapped his screen and sat back. "You wouldn't believe the roller coaster I've been on. At first, it seemed like bad luck. But really, it's impossible luck. The medical scanner doesn't work on the inmate? How is that even possible? I was devastated."

She almost laughed at his choice of words. *Devastated?* He spoke as if he actually cared about a prisoner. In this case, a low-life convicted drug addict. The expectant mother had been incarcerated for three years and counting. No conjugal visits. In fact, no visits at all. Which meant the father had to be a guard, or a member of the prison staff, or maybe a convict from the male-only prison down the road. For all they knew, it was the guy who delivered fresh lettuce to the commissary. But the fact remained that—so far as anyone could tell—no man had had even the possibility of sexual contact.

He's not devastated. He's scared shitless, Ingrid thought.

No problem, they'd believed. The prenatal scanner would sequence the baby's DNA and identify the father. Then they'd quietly eliminate the problem. The most chilling part was that the prison authorities actually had *two* problems to eliminate: the father *and* the unborn child. *Without wary witnesses, guilty guard goes, mom mysteriously miscarries.* (She'd never claimed to be a poet.) The plan might have succeeded under normal circumstances.

But the news had gotten out that the prenatal scanner didn't function. The news created a circus. The rumor of the pregnancy had rippled through the female-only prison's population faster than a contraband pic of pubcomm sensation James Lovejoy's naked derriere. The Washington State Department of Corrections was on the warpath to identify the father. It must have been an amusing conversation when the prison warden said to the deputy attorney general, "But, but, but . . . the scanner doesn't work on her." The DAG probably chalked that up as the most fabricated, idiotic excuse *ever* to try to protect one of their own. However, it hadn't taken long for the DAG to join the choir, because the repeated attempts to get *any* scanner to work had also failed. A cover-up wasn't possible at that point because the problem was out in the open. Plan B: get the inmate's permission to draw amniotic fluid. Unfortunately, she'd refused. Now there was nothing to do but wait out the remaining six months of the pregnancy and do a DNA sequence from any easily obtainable drop of fluid, hair follicle, or skin cell.

"I searched the network for a condition that could prevent the scanner from working. Nothing. I tried every search term I could think of."

You certainly did, she thought. *I never would have found you otherwise.*

"But then, right when my string of bad luck seemed like it would never end, my search query led me to your resume. Like a miracle. Do you realize, Ms. Vunderbosh—"

"Call me Ingrid."

"Ingrid . . . that you're possibly the only healthcare professional in the world who has experience with this medical fluke?"

"Imagine the odds."

"Yeah, right?" He chuckled—it was a nervous chuckle, like a man walking off the gallows after the hangman explained he forgot to buy rope. "Yeah, a real roller coaster, let me tell you."

You just did.

"Well, I think we're done here. I'll send you the offer by the end of the day. When can you start? I mean, of course, if you accept, that is."

"Immediately."

"That's just perfect." The administrator stood.

She stood, too, and shook his hand. But then he had a troubled expression. "What is it?" she asked.

"Look, this is a rough place. It's a female-only facility, sure, but don't let that fool you. These women are just as violent as the men."

"I understand."

"I don't think you do."

"Is that so?"

"Look, I might as well say this before you accept the offer. Your appearance . . . Well, you're an attractive woman."

She tightened her gaze. "You're telling me that because your assessment of my appearance is something I should consider before I accept the offer? Or because you'd be breaking about a dozen sexual-harassment laws by waiting until I'm an employee before ogling me out loud?"

"Both," he relented. "As you probably know, those laws are breakable during the hiring process, too. I'm sure I broke half of them already. I'm taking a huge risk. Just hear me out." His voice took a fatherly tone. "You're not just attractive—you're a teenage boy's dream. Do you hear what I'm saying? Flip open a dictionary to the word *sexy* and there's your picture. No, the word *sexy* is too strong. How about *subliminally sexy*? Because it's nothing you do; it's like it's built-in." He looked embarrassed now. "I'm telling you this objectively. You must've heard this before."

"Once or twice. How do you suggest I *fix* the problem?"

"I don't know. For starters, don't wear makeup."

"I'm not wearing makeup."

He swallowed. "Well, get some clothes three sizes too big. Stop brushing your teeth. Let your nose hair grow out." He was loud now. "I don't care what you do, but—"

"Go on."

"We have a sexual predator on the loose. Your new patient claims she didn't have sex, wasn't raped, and had no contact with any man. So, he must have drugged her." The prison administrator puffed out his chest. "I won't have two rapes on my watch."

But one is OK?

"You can't trust any man. Not even me."

No problem there. "I'll be careful."

His anger, which had sprouted from the seed of embarrassment, was gone now. He appeared genuinely relieved.

Maybe this guy does care. "And don't worry, I know you're not the sexual predator."

He looked pleased but curious.

"Rapists don't care about the clothes you wear, the smell of your breath, or the length of your nose hair. I don't have to worry about you." Before turning for the door, she said, "Thanks for the compliments." She gave him a smile and a wink, knowing full well that both scored direct hits.

"BETASTEN." *BANG.* "BETASTEN." *BANG.*

Tyvold sensed the swelling fear from the pharmakos in room number one. Normally, he'd monitor Dr. Betasten's meticulous progression as he reached clarity. This time, however, Tyvold let the doctor go on his own, opting instead to monitor events occurring in the Philly suburb.

Tyvold's cyber wall was back in place. Unfortunately, so was Hope Avenir's. He had no way of knowing if the Circle of Six's information had been revealed, but he had to assume so.

Ever since the day the warden invaded their headquarters in the desert outside Las Vegas, all Tyvold worried about was the extra effort to rebuild the new headquarters here, in TerraStore's Yucca Mountain facility. He'd been steeped in frustration, but he'd judged the setback as significant but manageable.

Only now was Tyvold able to appreciate the breadth of the impact of the day Chris Lumière smashed his way into their old headquarters. The members of the Circle of Six, Tyvold included, had foolishly assumed the warden's host was the only threat. They'd completely discounted Chris Lumière's friends as any type of threat.

The girl. Hope Avenir. The one Skotino had captured and reached clarity with that day. Who would've guessed she was the mastermind behind the cyber protections? *Well, game on, bitch. I got your data, and now I'm coming for you.*

Skotino, host of his god's brother, prided himself on not underestimating any threat. However, it seemed the Circle of Six had done nothing *but* underestimate. The totality of the underestimation went way beyond Chris Lumière.

Even the dog. Manipulation by the power of Hecate was unforeseen. The dog had saved Hope Avenir. The rest of the Circle of Six thought it was no big deal, but Tyvold knew the impact on their future was astounding. *For the chance of reality's path doth tip*, he thought. Hope Avenir was a pivotal player in the warden's plan. *If only we'd killed her when we had the chance.*

How deep did the Circle of Six's underestimation go? They'd underestimated Chris Lumière, Hope Avenir, and the yellow Labrador retriever. What about the others?

The man with the special rifle was clearly a threat. He'd managed to disable half of Tyvold's surveillance equipment. The Circle hadn't taken him seriously. They'd delegated the problem to the mortal's military team. The Omega Force should have easily neutralized the guy. Instead he'd slipped through them like water through a sieve. No, more like a bowling ball through bowling pins, because none of the Omega Force marines were left standing.

Tyvold had a vivid memory of another young man in the group. Mexican. Built like a tank. Almost as big as Vega or the Bear. The other girl in their group, not Hope, steered him right into a trap. Tyvold never saw the kick from the Mexican kid that broke his ribs. If it wasn't for Barrister, Tyvold would've never gotten away.

Tyvold scoured the vid logs of the day Chris Lumière and his group had invaded their old headquarters. Half the images were blank, thanks to the man with the ink rifle. Tyvold consolidated the remaining footage and started his analysis.

The underestimation must end.

| 10 | 10 | 10

"DO WE HAVE TO FLY SO HIGH?" ASKED SUE.

"This is the first time I've flown in a populated area during the day. We're harder to see up here," said Chris. "The risky part is landing. We have to come straight down, like a rock. No guarantee we won't be spotted, but it'll reduce the chance."

"If I can get online right away," said Hope, "I can search for any reports of sightings, and quash any recorded evidence."

"Here we go," said Chris. Like a fighter pilot pushing forward on the stick, he felt the blood rush to his head as they plummeted feet first. He assumed there was a limit to the g-forces he could handle. Father Arnold's church raced up from below. As if their feet were glued to an invisible elevator, they plunged faster and faster. They became a meteor headed for the plot of land behind the church, next to the rectory. Chris's face became fat with blood. The warden was able to keep the clothes from being ripped off his body but couldn't prevent his crimson face from throbbing.

Just when he thought his head would burst, when it seemed they couldn't possibly stop in time, the force reversed, and so did the pressure. Now, blood drained from his head, pooling in his legs. The presence of the warden was strong. He felt pressure around his legs, compensating, like a fighter pilot's pressure suit, keeping him from blacking out. The intense deceleration— thrust against momentum and gravity—pressed in even harder. Chris's vision tunneled. No longer able to see clearly, he feared he'd lost control. The fear faded, however, extinguished by the awareness that he didn't have to be in control. *Have faith.*

Amazingly, the velocities of the three bodies reached zero at the exact moment Chris's feet touched ground. He started to let go of Hope and Sue, but sensed they were both unconscious. He eased them down to the ground, their bodies pale and limp. The force of the air during the landing had flattened the grass in a three-foot circle around them.

Lucky was the first one out of the rectory. Even before Chris had a chance to assess the two women, Lucky started licking their faces. The wet nose and slobbery tongue worked like smelling salts. Their natural color returned. Hope moaned. Sue, lying on her back in the flattened grass, put her hand on her forehead.

"You did it," cried Katie, sprinting from the rectory. Al, Melissa, Father Arnold, and Bruce Cohen raced behind her.

Minutes later, they were all back inside the rectory. Fortunately, both Hope and Sue recovered quickly. Introductions were made.

"That was the most frightening—and amazing—experience of my life," said Sue.

"Thanks for rescuing us, Chris," said Hope.

Chris explained how Melissa had helped them dodge the public cameras and even helped with food and shelter once they realized they couldn't go back home after the FBI raids.

"And does Melissa know?" Hope inquired. "Does she know about your . . . condition?"

"Yup," said Chris.

Hope looked relieved. "Good. We can speak freely about our plans."

Maybe Chris was wrong about Hope being jealous. Maybe she was just worried, as usual, about sharing information with the wrong people. Chris felt mildly disappointed. Sitting next to her on Father Arnold's couch, he wanted to hold her hand or put his arm around her or something. But he couldn't even get close; Lucky was all over her. Like in the masstran, his dog had hopped up on her lap even though he was way too big. Chris had initially objected, because Lucky was never allowed on the furniture at home, but Father Arnold said it was OK. Now Chris was jealous.

"Lucky sure likes you," said Melissa.

Hope nodded and kept petting.

"Yeah, I think he likes Hope more than he likes me," said Chris.

"We all do," said Al. "OK, enough kumbaya. Who was that freak with the vise grip?"

"If the other two men were part of the Circle of Six," said Katie, "that guy must be too."

"Maybe," said Al. "Anyway, how do we deal with him? Chris, what was he like?"

"He looked normal. But he felt like rock. And he was incredibly strong."

"How do we stop him?"

No one said anything. Then Bruce spoke up. "Father Arnold told me you needed my help to find your parents. Shouldn't that be first on our list?"

"You're right," said Hope. "And I can't be sitting around like this. Sorry, Lucky." She pushed Lucky to the floor. With her lap unoccupied, she grabbed her backpack and stood. "I need to make sure Chris wasn't seen. I also need to check all my defenses. The rest of you can come up with a game plan. I've got work to do. Father, is there a quiet place I can go?"

"Of course. Let me show you."

Chris watched Hope as she left the room. He could only wonder if there would be a time when he wasn't such a burden on her.

"We thought," Al suggested to Bruce, "you could talk to some of your ex-military friends."

"Like, maybe the people you arranged to move Laura, Ben, and Chris to a new home off the grid?" Katie added.

"Those people like to remain invisible," said Bruce. "We need someone who can openly confront the authorities. We need someone more powerful than the government."

"More powerful than the government?" said Al.

"Exactly," said Bruce. "Chris, do you remember me telling you about the donors who support our K9 search-and-rescue team?"

Chris had only been half listening. He was fixated on the hallway where Hope and Father Arnold had disappeared. He was wondering how much work she faced and how long it would take. He directed his full attention to the discussion. "Yes, I remember. When you arranged for us to go to Vegas, you asked to use a scramjet owned by a donor."

"That's right."

"The rich guy," said Al. "A Hillite, right?"

"You know a Hillite?" The surprised look on Melissa's face was less than pleasant.

"Yes," said Bruce. "The label gets tossed around a lot—these days, anyone with money is called a Hillite—but he's an actual Hillite. Some people consider him one of the most prominent Hillites in the world."

"When we were doing the K9 search-and-rescue training," said Chris, "two members of our team, Tony and Travis, were always joking around—except whenever you mentioned that donor."

"Yup, he's a serious character. It's why the flight plan for the trip to Vegas never saw the light of day. If anyone can help us, he can."

| |0 | |0 | |0

TYVOLD, DEEP IN HIS ANALYSIS OF CHRIS LUMIÈRE'S FRIENDS, ALMOST MISSED Dr. Betasten as he strode past the doorway of the security substation at the entrance to the oubliette under Yucca Mountain. "Hey," called Tyvold.

Dr. Betasten backed into view. The look on his face was one Tyvold had never seen before.

"What? What is it?"

The doctor's lab coat showed several spots of blood—disconcerting, in and of itself, because the Six were careful about transmission of their pharmakoi's DNA—but even more so because, of all the members of the Circle of Six, Dr. Otto Betasten was the most fastidious about protocol. Now, standing before Tyvold, he looked as if he'd lain down and rolled in the DNA. He wiped his forehead, completely unaware he was leaving a smear of fresh blood across his brow.

"Tell me," said Tyvold.

Dr. Betasten gritted his teeth.

"Now," Tyvold demanded.

"Remember your last clarity? Here—when we watched Xander on-screen?"

Tyvold nodded.

"Remember the message from the gods? About Xander drinking water?"

"Sure. We all heard it. You said it was one more message in the long series of instructions guiding our preparation for his new life. Similar to the messages about his teeth falling out and contacts for his eyes."

"Yes, but we've known about the importance of water consumption from the beginning. From the moment he was extracted from Chelsea, spanning the sixteen years of his first life, we managed his water intake. Always. From the beginning."

"Of course. You've done everything perfectly."

Dr. Betasten seemed inconsolable. "And, you saw me—today, I mean, when I administered the water during his prep, yes?" He sounded like he was on trial.

"Yes. What are you getting at?"

"I heard the message again, nearly identical, except more of a warning. But—"

"But what? If the gods have glimpsed the future, tell me. What do we need to do?"

Dr. Betasten shook his head. "We call it clarity, host of my god's uncle, but there is nothing clear about this message. It keeps repeating a warning about hydration. But without explanation."

| | 0 | | 0 | | 0

IN THE SAME TIJUANA HOTEL ROOM AS HIS LAST VISIT, ELADIO CHECKED HIS look in the mirror one last time before the walk to the nightclub. The first mistake of Eladio's previous trip had been reserving the hotel room with his real name. *What was I thinking? Rodriguez*

probably knew I was coming even before the hotel staff. This time
he used his real name again. Rodriguez would see it as a message,
like the Bat-Signal. Eladio's second mistake had been trying to
sneak around the club unseen. Tonight's plan was to show up at
the nightclub as a regular patron with no attempt to be secretive.
It sounded easy, but Eladio was more comfortable acting like a
marine than a civilian.

He'd reviewed the vids captured by his surveillance cameras
around the club to gather intel on clothing styles. The style he'd
decided to copy was simple: Jeans accented with leather—like
wearing chaps over blue jeans, except in reverse. The legs were
dark blue denim, but the crotch and the seat were black leather.
The men he'd seen on the vid wore them tight. Eladio turned
to the side. The sizing scanners used by all 3-D apparel printers
meant his pair was a perfect fit. The faux leather across his butt
looked painted on, and it had a bit of stretch to it. Even though
the style was modest by comparison, he still wasn't sure he could
pull it off. *My gluteus looks maximus.*

Turning back to the mirror, he adjusted the collar of his shirt.
It was a simple white shirt with black trim around the edge of
the collar. His sleeves were rolled up, and the top two buttons
were open. He kept his body in prime condition, and the shirt
did him justice. It, too, had some stretch, capturing the V of his
torso above his slim waist. Untucked, the tail of the shirt almost
covered his butt. His movements offered a peek underneath now
and again. That was the idea, he assumed: the sexy elements
were tantalizingly obscured, requiring sustained observation to
steal a glimpse.

Listen to yourself. He realized he was overanalyzing the situation. Big time. *I'm in a hotel room, not mission control. I'm going
to a nightclub, not the front line.* He was losing his nerve. *You look
great. Just go with it. Own it. Be yourself.* He took one last look.
Easy to say, hard to do.

Instead of taking the back way to the club, he planned to walk straight down the main drag, into the old part of Tijuana. He wouldn't be rude this time. He wouldn't imply he expected to enter Rodriguez's turf unnoticed.

It was early evening. Out the window, the sun was still up but low in the sky. Everything had an orange radiance. Thankfully, the heat of the day was mostly gone. Without a way to make contact with Rodriguez, Eladio hoped his actions would be interpreted as the jingle of a metaphorical doorbell. Rodriguez would figure out Eladio wanted to talk rather than assume he was a masochist looking for another torture session. All the cards were in Rodriguez's hands.

Eladio rode the elevator down and headed for the lobby exit.

"*Señor* Eladio," the desk clerk called.

"Me?"

"*Sí*. Your transportation is waiting."

"Transportation? I think you have me confused with someone else."

"No, *señor*. Please." The clerk snapped his fingers. Two young bellhops appeared from nowhere and guided Eladio outside. A sleek candy-apple-red convertible sat waiting. It was a luxury performance model. Eladio had only seen them in advertisements. Music throbbed from its sound system. There was also a steady purr from the "engine." All modern trans were electric, but these luxury models had dedicated subwoofers to simulate the sound and feel of an eight-cylinder power train.

A casually dressed man hopped out. "Hector Eladio?"

"Yes?"

To the two bellhops, the man made a dusting gesture with his fingertips. The bellhops scooted away, seeing their guest was in good hands. "I'm your ride."

Eladio was confused.

"You're going clubbing tonight, *sí*? To hear The Ex-Boyfriends?"

"Yes. How did you—? Never mind. Who sent you?"

"I can't tell you that. But I'm required to confirm your identity."

"OK," said Eladio tentatively.

"I was given a one-word challenge phrase along with a response word that only Hector Eladio would know."

"OK." He was still unsure.

"The challenge phrase is *Ignacio*."

Eladio almost laughed. *These guys have a wicked sense of humor.* "Is the response phrase *Mendez*?"

"Yes. And may I assume you now know who sent me?" He winked.

"Yes," Eladio admitted.

"Please. Come." The man gestured to the muscle car's rear passenger door, which glided open so smoothly it looked like the sweep of the second hand on an antique Swiss watch.

Once Eladio was seated, the door closed with the satisfying sound of a perfect union between metal and rubber. He could not imagine the engineering effort expended to get that detail just right. How could such an inconsequential detail be so unnerving? He realized how far removed he was from his own element. He wasn't just a fish out of water; he was a fish on the moon of the dwarf planet Eris.

The driver kept the tran under manual control and pulled out onto the main street as the vehicle imparted an artificial growl. The heavy bass of the music surrounded them, creating a bubble of hipness. Traffic was extremely light. The man drove casually. No, *drove* was the wrong word. He *cruised*. Leaning back, he steered one wristed. The music was at the perfect volume, with just the right amount of funk.

Thinking back to his first trip to Tijuana, he'd been an idiot. Forget about the fact that the ex-Omega Force marine would see him coming a mile away—or maybe a light-year away—in cyberspace terms. It was obvious how many mistakes he'd made. He could only laugh about it now, even after those mistakes earned him a torture session that was no laughing matter. Colonel Wesson's instructions were clear: "You have to connect with the *man*, not the marine."

Eladio was pleased to learn The Ex-Boyfriends were still the main act at the nightclub. He liked the music he'd heard during his hours of surveillance.

Eladio asked the driver in the front seat, "When do The Ex-Boyfriends go onstage?"

The driver said, "Not till late. Midnightish. After several warm-up bands. They're good too."

The street was like the Rodeo Drive of an era long extinct in the US. All the most exclusive brands had a presence here. Even though the pedestrians were some of the richest people on the planet, heads were turning toward them as if to ask, "Who's that?" Eladio suddenly realized the extravagance of having a driver. In the early 1900s, automobiles were extremely rare, and the ultrawealthy were chauffeured. By the 1950s, automobile ownership had exploded and become a symbol of middle-class wealth. Driving oneself was a symbol of independence and the personification of the American dream. But later, everyone owned an automobile, maybe even two or three. Decades after that, when electric autopiloted vehicles first came out, only the wealthy could afford them. Driving oneself—or having a human driver of any sort—became passé. Eventually, all modern pertrans were equipped with autopilot. Subsequently, the poorest of the masses were shuttled about in driverless pubtrans. Now, as was the case with fashion, the social markers had come full circle. How should the rich and powerful distinguish themselves? Only the ultrawealthy could afford to pay a worker a living wage to perform such a useless task as driving. Naturally, to achieve the maximum impact, the driving is done so all can see. No tinted windows, not even a top. The convertible was in vogue. And it explained why the driver had invited Eladio to ride in the back seat.

With so many eyes on him, Eladio became aware of his own posture. Did he look ultrawealthy? He was sure he looked more like he had a stick up his ass. He tried to get into the music, to loosen up. Instead, he felt like a mannequin in a men's clothing store, listening to the canned background music. He tried to relax, but thinking about the chola girls made him nervous. He wanted to make a good impression, even though he didn't have a chance with one. On his salary, he couldn't afford her manicure. But there's no harm in looking one's best. It'd been a long time since he'd worried about his appearance in the eyes of the opposite sex.

If his *driver* was this cool and suave, the male patrons at the club would be even smoother and more charismatic. Every stud in the joint would probably be a trust-fund baby with a luxury villa on each continent. How could he compete? He played the scene out in his mind and saw himself looking like a high-school nerd arriving at a convention of Chippendales dancers.

In any case, one big worry was out of the way. Coming back to Tijuana, Eladio had no way of knowing if Rodriguez was even in town. He'd expected he might have to spend several days making himself as conspicuous as possible. And even then, there was no guarantee he'd make contact. But none of that was a problem now. By arranging the fancy ride, Rodriguez had rolled out the red carpet. *Here I come.*

I 10 I 10 I·10

"Q? YOUR HILLITE FRIEND'S NAME IS A SINGLE LETTER?" ASKED AL, IN THE living room of Father Arnold's rectory. Throughout the evening, Al had been devising a modified plan to get the trio's families released, and secondarily to stop the Circle of Six. Hope had been working in isolation and still hadn't emerged. Chris wondered if maybe someone actually had recorded him dropping out of the sky while holding Hope and Sue earlier that day. *Will Hope be able to contain it?*

"I'm sure he has a full name, but I don't know what it is," said Bruce. "I've also seen it abbreviated as PQ, or sometimes as PQRS."

"Like the alphabet?"

"Yup. But usually just Q."

"What an odd name." Al seemed to mull it over, then asked, "And he lives in Israel?"

"Yup," said Bruce.

"That seems so far away," said Sue.

"Well, it is," Bruce agreed. "Practically the other side of the planet."

Chris felt apprehensive about leaving for a place so far away from home. But as long as his parents were missing, he had no home, not a real one anyway. He glanced at his percomm. Out loud, but mostly to himself, he said, "Today is the first day of school."

"Really?" Even Katie seemed surprised. She looked at her own percomm to prove it to herself.

Obviously still mulling, Al said, "So his name is Q. He's a Hillite who lives in Israel, inside a mountain?"

"Not just any mountain," said Bruce. "It's called Masada. It's one of the oldest fortresses in the world."

That information didn't seem to make a difference. After a moment, Al changed the subject. "What about the guy who attacked Hope on the roof of her apartment today? I have a feeling it's only a matter of time before the Circle of Six finds us. We need a plan to deal with him. Chris, tell us again what he was like."

"He was made of stone. Or felt like it, at least. I don't know. My first instinct was to just punch him in the nose. With the warden's help, I should be able to put my fist right through his head. But, from the moment he grabbed me, I sensed a warning. I knew, right away, not to even try to punch him."

"How could he move so easily if he's made of stone?"

Chris shrugged.

"Could it be that it was only the outside that was hard?" asked Katie. "Just his skin? Like a shell?"

"Sure. I guess. That fits."

"An exoskeleton," muttered Katie.

"Huh?"

"Like a bug," said Melissa. "Or a lobster."

"Exactly," said Katie.

"So, he's got built-in armor," said Al. "That's not good. If we can't penetrate—"

"Father," asked Katie, interrupting Al, "can we borrow some of your diatomaceous earth?"

"Of course. Why?"

"What are you thinking, miga?" asked Al.

"Melissa's right. He's like a bug. And you're right, too, Al. Bugs have built-in armor. But we can kill bugs with insecticides."

"Won't that hurt us too?"

"Not the natural kind."

"That's true," said Father Arnold. "That's why the bag says *food grade*. You could eat diatomaceous earth if you wanted to. Some people do."

"What is diatomaceous earth anyway?" asked Al.

"I looked it up," said Katie. "It's made from microscopic sea animals called diatoms. Generations die, and their remains fall to the ocean floor. Their skeletons don't decay but rather accumulate over billions of years. Today, thick layers of fossilized diatoms are mined from areas of land that were once occupied by ancient oceans. After the excavated material is pulverized, it looks like white powder."

"I didn't know any of that," said Father Arnold, "but I do know it's important that the diatomaceous earth be food grade, otherwise it doesn't kill bugs."

"Right. That's the key. *Food grade* means it's ground very finely," said Katie. "The slivers of diatom skeleton are so tiny they can actually penetrate the exoskeleton at the cellular level. Combined with the insect's movements, the shards wheedle their way through the armor."

"Like a knife?" asked Al.

"Not really. The holes are too tiny for blood to come out. They're so tiny that only water comes out."

"Oh no, run for your life," joked Al.

"I know, not very exciting."

"Then how does it kill bugs?"

"Paradoxically, it's the armor that creates the vulnerability," said Katie. "The ocean is the origin of all life. Water factors into everything. We all carry around our own personal puddle of seawater. Every living creature with an exoskeleton supports its shell by managing its own internal water pressure. The shell is held up by that pressure."

"So, the diatom slivers rub their way inside and let out the water?" asked Melissa.

"Yup."

"Death by dehydration?"

"Exactly."

As the planning continued, Chris just wanted to see Hope reappear from the rectory hallway. There was still no sign of her. She'd been working for hours.

1 | 0 1 | 0 1 | 0

"WHAT DID I SAY ABOUT INTERRUPTING ME DURING WORK HOURS?" SAID EVAN via vidcomm, from his Thessaloníki office to Chelsea's bedroom in the old house on the grounds of the Venizelos estate. "Chels, we've been over this. As soon as Dr. Betasten says you're better, *then* you can go to America."

"That's what I'm trying to tell you. Dr. Betasten isn't responding."

"He's very busy. I'm sure he'll reply soon."

"Evan, knowing Dr. Betasten isn't responding because he's busy with our son in America is more than I can bear. It feels like he's keeping me away on purpose."

"How's the pain, love?"

"Better. Nearly gone. A full day of rest was just what the doctor ordered—literally. I'm fine now. He must examine me, so the house staff will release me," she said. "Please, Evan."

"All right. I'll see what I can do."

The comm ended. She hadn't wanted to lie to Evan. The truth was, the pain wasn't any better. *But pain is only a symptom. A relative thing. Who cares how much it hurts? If I'm not sick, there's no reason I shouldn't be allowed to go to America.*

She remembered the days when she fantasized about having her own private physician, believing it would be the most exquisite luxury imaginable. Just the words *private physician* sounded magnificent.

Many times, she'd played out a scene in her mind. She'd visit her home village in Britain. Her motorcade would pull up to one of her ex-girlfriends' flats—as a token visit, naturally, to prove she didn't carry a grudge. Those girls had been so mean. They called her a Hillite whore once Evan took an interest in her. She'd show them. She'd roll up like a celebrity. They'd all kiss her feet. They'd hang on her every word. Chelsea had an endless string of spectacular successes all rehearsed. At some point, she'd drop the term *private physician.*

But who wants a private physician if the doctor's never in?

She also remembered why the thought of a private physician was so magical: because going to the public clinic was such a horrible experience. Just to get a checkup, you had to wait in queue for hours with mobs of people carrying every sort of communicable grossness. But now she wished she had access to a public scanner. She'd show the results to Evan, and he'd have no choice but to end her travel restriction. The staff would allow her to leave the grounds. She could go shopping with Adrienne and Triana to buy new outfits. She'd look smashing for her trip to America to see Xander.

She touched herself. The pain was still pretty bad. She wouldn't admit it to Evan, but she had lingering fears that she wasn't OK. The pain was strange because it was on the outside, nothing like any menstrual cramp she'd ever had. *If only I could get to a public scanner. What did women do before scanners and doctors?*

She crossed her room, to the vanity, opened the drawer, and took out her hand mirror. *Here goes.* She lifted her nightgown, pulled down her underwear, squatted slightly, and held the mirror so she could see for herself. *Oh my.* Even though she was no medical expert, the bruising and swelling was readily apparent. *Naming ceremony? What happened to me?*

| |0 | |0 | |0

"IT JUST SEEMS ODD, THAT'S ALL." MELISSA STOMPED ON THE PLASTIC AIR PUMP. It was almost midnight, and too late for anyone to travel. Father Arnold was right about the camping gear. There was enough for a small army. And the church basement was huge. Melissa leaned down, checked the firmness of the air mattress, and then gave it a few more stomps before closing the valve and moving to the next one. "All this talk about Mrs. Avenir—Sue—about where she's going to live and if she'll be safe or not? I just think Hope would want to be *involved* in that kind of planning."

Katie unrolled the sleeping bag over the air mattress Melissa had just inflated. "Sue's an adult; she can make her own decisions," said Katie. "I'll grant you that Sue could've expressed more concern about her daughter heading off to Israel. But Hope has always been very independent."

"Oh. Independent. Sure." Melissa started pumping again.

"What are you getting at?"

"I don't know." *Pump.* "My viewpoint's probably—" *Pump.*
"—warped." *Pump.* "It's nothing." *Pump.*

Katie touched her arm. Melissa stopped. Katie gave Melissa
her infamous out-with-it face, the one she normally reserved for
Al.

"Well, I have feelings for Chris, OK? So I probably made up a
whole bunch of stuff in my head. Expectations. You know. Chris
was giving me the 'oh, sorry, I already have a girlfriend' routine.
Which he follows with the most heartfelt blubbering of—OK,
yeah, I'm going to use the words—*unconditional love* I've ever
heard in my life. Any girl would melt. I did. He poured his heart
out. You were there. Am I wrong? And the whole time, all I
could think about was myself, about how bad I wanted someone
to love *me* like that.

"And then—finally—I get to meet the legend in the flesh,
Hope Avenir. You know, ever since I met you three, Al has been
going on and on with his 'urban candy' cracks. So I assumed
I had the edge in the hotness department. Ha! Conveniently,
nobody ever mentioned the fact that the girl's naturally gorgeous.
Like a brunette Marilyn Monroe but a bit shorter. She's quirky,
because she wears clothes a man twice her size and thrice her age
would wear. And if that's not enough, she's smart. Smart like a
fox with a quantum computer for a brain."

"Your point?"

"So I see Chris and Hope together. And zip-o. Nada. Zero.
Zilch. No kiss. Not even a hug."

"Well, like Al said, *girlfriend* is probably too strong, they
only—"

"No. I watched them both. Chris was as open as you can get.
If she's in the room, his eyes are fixed on her body. He could
eat a horse and still look hungry." Melissa stomped hard. "But
not Hope. No. Ice queen, that girl, I'm telling you. She thanked

him for saving her life, and that was it, like he wasn't even there. Gave more attention to the dog."

"Well, she's been upset with him. All of us, really. Because it causes so much work for—"

"Seriously, miga? You're gonna ride along with that line of reasoning?" *Pump, pump, pump.* "Is she *working* in that room?" Melissa yanked out the tube and pressed the valve closed. "Or is she *hiding*?"

"Look, you're probably right. I confess I don't read these situations very well. Al's better. Really good, actually."

Katie thought about suggesting they talk to Al. Al was good at assessing situations like this, but not so good at keeping his mouth shut. Katie sensed a giant hole in her own understanding of the world. Melissa was right about when Chris confessed his feelings. Any girl would melt. Katie was no exception. All she could think about was Al expressing those feelings to her. *Ice queen? Maybe I'm part of the ice-queen club, too, and I don't even know it.*

"It's more complicated than that," Katie went on. "But it's not my story to tell. Let's just say Hope had a difficult home situation. Her dad's in jail. If she has issues relating to men, who are we to judge? Besides, there's no definition of *normal* when it comes to relationships, as long as everyone is under their own free will, that is."

"You're right. Like I said, I'm too invested. The minute I saw her, I wanted them to wrap themselves around each other. Be inseparable. Need to be told to get a room and all that, so I could finally put the jealousy behind me knowing I didn't have a chance. That's why I was shocked when I didn't see any sparks between them. I started thinking: She kissed him. I kissed him. Now we're even steven. Game on, bitch. Show me what you got. But after listening to Chris pour his heart out? I don't have a chance. I never did. It's just hard, that's all. I'll get over it."

With the last mattress inflated, Melissa grabbed the sleeping bag from Katie's hand and rolled it out herself—because, Katie realized now, she'd been frozen in thought and was just standing there.

"Speaking of getting over him," said Katie, "you're right. Once we leave, once there's distance, Chris's effect on you will go away. You can go back to your normal life."

With the job finished, Melissa stood up. "All of you keep talking about his ability to persuade. You say it's a power from the warden. I'm not so sure."

"What do you mean?"

"Moving air molecules around so he can fly? Sure, that's superhuman stuff. But his persuasiveness? That's not superhuman. It's amazing, yes, but not impossible. Like—what was that guy's name?" She snapped her fingers. "This guy . . . a hundred years ago . . . same name as the concert hall in New York. Uh . . . Carmichael Hall? Car—"

"Carnegie Hall? Andrew Carnegie?"

"That's it. But not Andrew. Carnegie Hall just helps me remember. I'm talking about Dale Carnegie. That guy wrote the book on how to win friends and influence people. I mean that literally. The title of his book is *How to Win Friends and Influence People*."

Katie disagreed. "No. Even Chris says the warden is the source of his ability. He says he can feel a difference with the gum."

"Right. But I'm saying the warden's influence is more generic. I'm asking you if it's possible that the warden's true power is to help people be their best. To sharpen skills they already have. Not superhuman, but . . . *perfect human*? Or *true human*? Anyway, my point is, it includes Chris. What if Chris is naturally good at persuasion, and the warden simply helps him be his best?" She asked, "Katie, tell me, what made Chris's soliloquy so heart wrenching?"

Katie had to think for only a second. "It was completely genuine. Pure. He let himself be utterly vulnerable. Like it flowed directly from his heart."

"Yup. In fact, by definition, the intensity of Chris's ability comes from himself only—from deep inside. It's one hundred percent Chris. He channels that power from within by being his true self in the most absolute sense."

Katie asked herself out loud, "What if, while we were growing up, the warden was helping me and Al be *our* very best too?"

"Exactly."

Katie continued rhetorically, "Chris's mom and dad? His teachers? Master Cohen? Father Arnold? All the people in his life? Influenced by the warden . . . to be their very best."

"Yes. But here's where I'm going with this: once you recognize your own gifts, the door stays open," said Melissa. "When you all leave for Israel, I'm not going to let my world go back to the way it was. I have a choice."

Katie nodded.

"Could I be right?"

Katie nodded again.

"Miga, we only just met, but I have to tell you, until now I've had a pretty bleak view of the world. Since meeting Chris, it's like a light got turned on. It's even a little scary. He makes me feel like I can achieve *anything*, become *anyone*. Since hanging out with you guys, my ability to understand the social interactions around me has steadily grown. But I don't think my ability is sustained solely by Chris or the warden. I don't think it will vanish once you're gone. He gave me a seed, and I'm going to grow it. I had no idea what I wanted to be when I grew up. Now I have a sense of purpose. I can help people. Become a psychologist maybe. I have something to give. I'll always have a place for it in my brain, and I'm going to practice. The warden's influence doesn't have to be temporary. It lets us become aware of our true-human abilities, so we can nurture them. Simply stated: to develop ourselves to fulfill a purpose."

| |0 | |0 | |0

IT WAS ONE IN THE MORNING WHEN ELADIO SAW HER. FAR OFF, AT THE END of the bar on the right side, he noticed a girl watching him. He looked away, not wanting to stare, not wanting to put her off in case she was just people watching. He turned back. She was still watching him. But this time, she looked away. Very pretty. She was seated at a section of the bar that curved around to the wall. The spot was behind the station where the waitstaff picked up their orders. It wasn't easy to see past the wait station's two brass rails, but it looked like she was alone. Not a popular place to sit because the stage was in the opposite direction. A server at the wait station blocked his line of sight. The girl might have looked up again, but he couldn't see her now.

Eladio still felt tense. He knew he probably looked goofy, sitting alone, way at the end of the table. Worse, the table was huge. It could sit eight or ten people. It had a long leather couch on one side, which faced the stage, with no chairs on the other. It was the best table in the house. He had no idea why the greeter had seated him there. *I'm thinking too hard again.* He had to loosen up. *Ah, screw it.* He gulped the glass of beer nearly empty. It was his third.

Technicians, who'd been preparing since the last warm-up band, now exited the stage. Everything was ready for The Ex-Boyfriends. A drumroll started, softly at first, and then began to build. The crowd applauded. Lights went down. Mist floated across the stage and rolled off the edge, into the audience. Spotlights in the ceiling spun, focusing on preprogrammed points. People took their seats while still clapping. The drumroll continued to build. The buzz of the crowd intensified.

At the bar, with a platter of drinks in hand, the opaque waiter backed away. The girl was gone. He looked around, but she was nowhere in sight.

His own server appeared at the table. She set down *cerveza número cuatro.*

"Please, I want to pay for the beer." Eladio had to practically yell over the din. The drumroll and the crowd noise had grown even louder.

The server shook her head. "But I do have a message for you."

Eladio could hardly hear her. He leaned forward and cupped his hand to his ear.

She leaned down. Still yelling, she said, "The Ex-Boyfriends weren't always called The Ex-Boyfriends."

"No?"

"No. They used to be called *Los Cuatro Equis.*"

"The Four *X*'s?"

She nodded. The crowd roared as the band members took the stage.

I don't believe it. The four men he'd faced in the concrete hellhole took their positions on stage, behind microphones. Rodriguez, at the front, pulled a guitar off its stand and slung the strap over his head. The bassist, to his right, did the same. The keyboardist took a stool on his other side. The three were backed by the drummer, clear Plexiglas on three sides. The canned drumroll ceased. The drummer held up his sticks. He smacked them together three times and then hit the skins. The crowd went wild. The music was fantastic.

Holy shit. The Ex-Boyfriends were the other-than-honorably discharged members of Omega Force Fireteam Whiskey. *The Four X's,* Eladio repeated to himself.

He drained his glass and started into the fresh one. It was hard for him to believe his second meeting with Corporal Juan Rodriguez, USMC (OTH), could be as unforgettable as the first.

CHAPTER 24

"**H**OPE?" FATHER ARNOLD CALLED AT THE DOOR OF THE RECTORY bedroom. He had opened the door only a crack. "I don't mean to disturb you. Just seeing if you're OK."

"Thank you, Father. Everything's fine. I was able to confirm that no one saw Chris descend from the sky. Or at least, no one posted a vid. No chatter on the net. My defense systems are all locked down. Thanks for asking."

"Actually, I'm checking to see if *you* are OK."

What does it matter?

"Your friends are worried. Your mom, too, of course. But they know how important your work is. So no one has the guts to check in on you except me."

She laughed. "I'm fine."

"I admit I don't know how important your work is. I have no idea what you're doing on that screen," he said. "Let me ask a stupid question. Is it maybe time to go to bed? It's well after midnight. Don't you think sleep is a better use of your time?"

"We can't take any chances. There's too much to get done. Like the rest of the group down the hall, planning. It could take all night. We all have to do our part."

"The others finished their planning. They crashed."

"What?"

"They're exhausted. They've been going for days on end with very little sleep. They're all next door, in the church basement. Probably asleep by now."

"Chris too?"

He nodded.

Hope said nothing. Almost a minute passed.

"May I?" He opened the door another inch.

"Of course, Father. My goodness. Your generosity. I'm so grateful."

He came in and sat on the edge of the bed across from her.

"We're the ones imposing on you," she added. "By the way, what is this room?"

"The rectory has three bedrooms. But it's only me here. Clergy often move around within the diocese. Over the years, visiting priests have stayed here for a few weeks at a time before moving on."

The room was simple. A bed, a nightstand, a dresser, a closet, and a small desk and chair. She wasn't at the desk because, best of all, there was wall-to-wall carpeting; she preferred sitting cross-legged on the floor. So much nicer than linoleum. She thought about the apartment. They could never go back.

The stress of the last several weeks had taken its toll. Sleep was the wisest option at the moment. She felt suddenly depleted. But underneath, there was another feeling, one she'd experienced before, a feeling that was gradually surrounding her.

"What is it?" he asked.

"Nothing."

"They laid out a sleeping bag for you. But, if you'd feel more comfortable, you're welcome to sleep here of course."

The feeling. Why was she fighting it? She'd been pushing it away—same with the nagging fatigue.

"It's Chris, isn't it?" he asked. "I know the two of you have history. I know about your father. You don't have to sleep in the same room with Chris. Or anyone, for that matter. You can stay here. The door has a lock."

"No, it's not that." *But it is. Sort of. Not exactly.* "You don't understand. It's Chris, yes. But not what you're thinking."

"Would you explain it to me? It might help."

"He has an influence on people," she said. "This summer, after my dad was arrested and while my mom was getting treated, I stayed with the Richardses."

"And?"

"And I became a different person."

"A bad person?"

"No, I guess not. Just different, that's all."

"A better person?"

"No."

"How can you be sure?"

"It was uncomfortable. And I feel it happening again. Now. And, well, I guess I'm afraid. Now that I think about it, I know one thing for certain: he makes your fears go away. No, wait, that's not right. He makes you *face* your fears."

"That doesn't sound bad."

"I know. It's like getting into a pool. You have to get over the shock of the cold water and then you're fine. It's so strange. I have an awareness that at this very moment of my life—right now—there's a fork in the road. If I go to the church basement and lay next to that boy, my life will change forever. Just being near him will influence my choices. It feels like the right choice, but it also feels like the harder one. I'm afraid I don't have it in me. I don't know what you call it. Stamina? Constitution?" She shook her head. "Sorry, I'm not making any sense."

"Oh, trust me, you are. My love for God and my commitment to the church started long before I was ordained. I faced a lot of fear along the way. But it was mostly fear of the unknown. When people take the low, easy road, they take it alone. When you take the high, hard road, people will help you."

"How can you be sure?"

"Because that's the difference between the two routes. The high road is harder because it involves helping others along the journey. But it's also the reason you'll experience more joy."

Joy? Maybe it's time I allow myself to have some joy. Hope folded the screen and stashed it in her backpack. She stood and slung it over her shoulder. "Thank you, Father. I won't be needing this room. I'm going over to the church basement."

Outside, Father Arnold's garden seemed magical under a cloudless sky full of stars. With so much lush, dense foliage all around, the air felt heavy with nature.

Near the middle of the garden was a bird fountain next to a decorative stone bench. She sat for a moment. Under the stars, she felt the familiar sensation of smallness that an enormous starry sky can bring. Father Arnold was right. She'd taken the low road her entire life. She'd suppressed the feelings of compassion for others. Ben and Laura weren't just being detained; they were being taken to a place where the level of interrogation would be extreme. Same for Al's parents and Katie's family. She could help them. She wanted to help. She let the feeling come. Her face wrinkled involuntarily as the wave of tension crested. She wiped away tears. It wasn't a full-on cry, but she felt better. A lot better. She couldn't remember the last time she cried. Her resistance to crying seemed ridiculous now. She felt so much better. *Crying isn't a weakness. It's medicine, the built-in kind.*

Inside the church, she found her friends in the corner of the basement. She used her percomm for light but kept it against her body so only the slightest glow shined the way. She heard breathing. She didn't know if they were all asleep, but it sounded that way. Just as Father Arnold had predicted, there was an empty sleeping bag next to Chris.

She tiptoed between the bodies, making sure not to make any noise. Given the depth of slumber around her, she probably could have turned the light on and stomped right in without waking anyone. Kneeling on the empty sleeping bag, she let a tad more light fall on Chris. He was out cold—mouth open, his chest expanding and falling rhythmically. This was better than looking at his picture on her percomm.

She remembered the kiss in the masstran. She would tell him in the morning that she changed her mind—that she was no longer saying no. Watching him now, his open mouth was especially inviting. She thought, fleetingly, that she could kiss him good night.

One arm was out, across his chest. She tilted the light so it illuminated his hand. *His hands.* She estimated the number of fantasies about Chris she'd enjoyed over the years. Probably more than a thousand. Nearly all of them involved his hands.

I won't fight it anymore. The decision was made. She took the fork in the road, the one heading in the right direction. Chris needed to find his parents. She would help him. They would all help the warden find and stop the Circle of Six. It was the high, hard road.

She lay down herself. With years of tension cracked open and raw, she too fell fast asleep.

|10 |10 |10

LIKE A PAINTER WORKING HIS WAY OUT OF A ROOM, BARRISTER SWEPT THE beam of blue light back and forth across every inch of the apartment lobby, backing up toward the exit as he fanned. The blue light from the portable lamp, Spire had explained, used a technology similar to the light in Xander's chamber. It destroyed DNA left on surfaces.

Barrister swept the rays across the shattered remains of the manager's office. He made sure no DNA evidence remained on the manager's body, nor that of the old man on the bench. The lamp was easy to use, but being thorough took time. The device had a display screen connected to a specially designed scanner that showed an augmented-reality view of the area. If a concentration of the Circle's DNA was detected, it showed up on the screen as a glowing film. He simply shined the light until the glowing blob shrunk down to nothing. At one point, he had to flip over the old man's body so the light could reach the contaminated underside.

He had to sweep the air, too, because his own body was throwing off skin cells full of DNA even as he worked. Fortunately, Xander didn't throw off any skin cells. Spire said all his waste ended up in his pee.

Finally reaching the lobby exit, Barrister removed the temporary sign he'd posted, informing residents the door was out of order and to use a side entrance. He swept the remaining surfaces and backed out of the lobby completely. In the black of night, his percomm buzzed. He fumbled to answer it while juggling the lamp.

"Don't forget to take down the sign," said Tyvold over the comm.

"I got the sign. Worry about yourself. Did you clear the seccomm logs?"

"Yes, but your fat head is still in plain view of the outside cameras. Get your ass in the tran so I can delete the rest of it."

"I'll be right there." As he put his percomm away, he saw two bluish eyes in the shrubs next to the door. Because of the darkness, it was impossible to see what it was. He leaned closer. "That's where you ran off to."

The little dachshund was trembling violently. Oddly, Barrister sensed its fear. It was a simple matter to rule out temperature as the cause because it was a mild night. No. Very faintly, he could sense the fear.

"Sorry about your owner, little guy. I can't take you with me. You're on your own now. You best stay where you are till we're gone," said Barrister. "Stay," he commanded, in his best authoritative voice.

After a few strides, he reached the limo. The utility van where Dr. Betasten was tending to Xander was parked behind the limo.

Barrister climbed into the limo's front passenger seat. "Done," he announced to Spire, in the driver's seat.

Tyvold's voice came over the tran's speaker. "Well, goodie for you."

"Let's go after them."

Spire said, "Tyvold doesn't know where Lumière and the rest of them are."

Barrister thought he was the only one to whom Spire directed his contempt, but there was an unmistakable edge in his voice toward Tyvold. "What? I was in there all that time, and you don't have the location?"

"Yet," Tyvold qualified.

"You commed me six times while I was in there, asking why it was taking so long."

"Just shut up," said Tyvold.

"What the hell."

"Just shut up," said Spire.

| | 0 | | 0 | | 0

"MOVE OVER," SAID RODRIGUEZ.

After three hours of playing without a single break, The Ex-Boyfriends had brought the house down. The four men in front of him paired off, two on each side. Eladio scooted to the center to make room.

Normally, he'd feel trapped, especially after the torture session. But instead, he felt like he was meeting his childhood baseball heroes. The performance had been amazing. Incredible. Eladio wanted to shake Rodriguez's hand. Or hug him. But Eladio wasn't the only one. The table was surrounded by fans equally as excited.

Fifteen minutes passed, and the band members still hadn't been able to sit down. They seemed to know everyone. Even though none of the patrons acknowledged Eladio—they acted as if he was invisible—he could hardly get over the fact that he was going to meet the band members too. It was obvious now that the table was special, reserved for the stars of the night and their guests.

As the glad-handing wound down, Eladio glimpsed the girl. She was at a different place along the bar. She had an amused look on her face. Eladio guessed she'd known, all along, the significance of the table where he'd been seated. He got the impression she was enjoying watching him figure it out. He couldn't help but notice she was still unaccompanied.

The mob of fans finally trickled to an end, and the four band members slid across the leather, boxing him in, with Rodriguez on his right. They pushed up against him on both sides. *These men got physical as a profession and had no problem being physical if needed.*

"Don't overanalyze."

"What?"

"The situation. You're overanalyzing it. You do that."

Eladio opened his mouth to protest but couldn't argue.

The server set down five shot glasses, poured tequila—a brand Eladio had never seen before—and left the bottle on the table. They raised their shot glasses. Eladio followed the lead.

"You make the toast," said Rodriguez. "And don't think too hard."

"To *Los Cuatro Equis*," said Eladio.

"*Los Cuatro Equis*," they repeated.

Eladio tipped it back. Very smooth. His glass hadn't even hit the table when the guy to his left started refilling glasses, except Eladio's.

"We metabolize it faster," explained Rodriguez. "You. Just relax. We'll get to talking. Don't worry. But first, we have a little problem."

What have I done now? Eladio wished he hadn't done the handful of beers or the shot.

"That girl. The one you've been eyeing. Don't deny it."
Rodriguez tilted his head toward the bar. There was no question
who he was referring to. "You need to understand. That girl is
my sister."

The four men roared with laughter when they saw Eladio's
face. The slap on his back came down hard. He couldn't help but
laugh too.

"Priceless," said the guy on his left. "Fucking priceless." He
poured Eladio another shot.

"You're messing with me." Then he added, "I should say, *still*
messing with me."

"That's right. You overanalyze. It's your nature. We mess
with people. That's our nature. You're lucky to be alive. But I'm
sure you know that." Rodriguez knocked back his second shot.
"Well, I guess introductions are in order. I don't need to tell you
real names since they don't matter, and you've read our dossiers
anyway." He thumbed in the direction of the guy next to him.
"He's my eyes."

Eladio knew the slang for the four fireteam positions: head,
eyes, fist, and hack. Rodriguez, as fireteam leader, was designated
the call sign Number One, also known as the head. The man
being introduced, Number Two, was the sniper, his eyes. The
man was slender and the tallest of the bunch. Bass guitar player.
With his blond hair and blue eyes, he stood out compared to the
predominantly Mexican crowd.

Eladio nodded.

"Next to you is my fist."

Number Three was the heavy-weapons expert. A barrel of
a man. Drummer. He looked Latino, with his brown skin and
black hair. He seemed to be growing out his hair and beard—
both were bushy and wild, untrimmed across his neck and
cheeks. His beard had grown longer since Eladio saw him during
the torture session. This was the man who'd been in the room

the entire time, entirely silent. This was the man whose legs were blown off during their final mission. Though, just by looking at him, Eladio couldn't tell he'd even been injured. *Prosthetics? Probably. Or can they regrow body parts for the Omega Force?*

"Nice to meet ya. No hard feelings about the other day, I hope. You showed up uninvited. We don't like that."

"Sorry about that."

"I know. I made sure." He grinned.

"And this is my hack."

Number Four was also Latino, and the smallest of the team. Clean-shaven. Keyboard player. He was the cyber-infiltration expert. The hacker.

"Nice to meet you on more civilized terms," he said.

Eladio nodded.

"Now," said Rodriguez, "I know the old man sent you down here. He's the only reason you're still alive. What's so important that you need to talk to four OTH marines outside of regular channels?"

Eladio hesitated. He wanted to confide in these men, but he'd assumed they'd talk somewhere more secure.

"You can talk here," said Rodriguez.

"The entire building is wave traced," added Number Four, the hack. "The sound waves of our voices are cancelled three feet from the table. The vectors of every photon and the vibrations of every air molecule are calculated in real time relative to every device, retina, and eardrum in the place. No way to record audio or video without me knowing. I even know the duration of eyeballs focusing on us. If there's a lip-reader in the crowd, I'll know it."

Impressive.

"By the way, I had to pull the background on your secret admirer over there. She's been glancing at you all night. Three times since we sat down. Everything checks out though. She's innocent. Well, by the looks of her, she's dressed to kill, but you know what I mean. Don't worry, Valentino, I'll get her number for you."

"Nolan says our systems have been compromised," Eladio explained.

"Nolan. *Humph*. He's your problem right there."

"Right. Wesson doesn't trust him. And even if he did, we can't trust the data he's working from."

"And?"

"And Wesson believes your Nevada mission is related. If you help us find the connection, it could lead to the disclosure of facts that would clear your names."

"You're not here on a goodwill mission. What's the objective?"

"Wesson believes the Omega Force program has been compromised at the highest level, including the nascent Nu Force. We have to find out. But we can't use regular channels."

"And you want us to investigate?"

"Yup. If Omega Force command has been compromised, we can't go after them with regular marines. I know firsthand—" Eladio emptied his second shot "—how that turns out."

Rodriguez nodded. "Enough talk for tonight, OK, Hector? Just relax. For Christ's sake, just relax."

CHAPTER 25

HAIR DRIPPING, KATIE STEPPED OUT OF THE RECTORY BATHROOM. "YOUR turn," she said to Al, who was waiting outside. "Hold on," she said, stopping short. She sniffed. "Food?" She realized how hungry she was.

"Yup," said Al. "During the eternity you were in the shower, Bruce's friends from the K9 search-and-rescue team, Tony and Travis, brought a van we can use to go to the airport. They also brought three dozen eggs and a sack of potatoes." Al pushed her out of the way and shut the bathroom door.

Chris, Hope, and Sue were at the rectory's kitchenette table. Chris and Hope were talking, and Sue was listening politely but looked like a third wheel. Lucky was underneath the table. Chris probably told him to lie down so he wasn't in the way. But his dog was intently watching the kitchen floor for any fumbles. The fragrance of breakfast was almost overpowering.

Katie saw Melissa on the couch and joined her. "Did you leave any work for me?"

"Nope," said Melissa. "The church basement is all picked up. Nothing to do but wait while they get breakfast on."

Katie tousled her wet hair. She'd slept like a rock. Hope had been there when they woke, so she'd apparently joined them at some point during the night. Katie wanted to ask her if anyone saw Chris flying, but Hope had been hovering around Chris from the moment they all got up. *Something changed. Or maybe Hope truly did finish her work and was finally able to break away.*

Melissa said, "Tony and Travis are fun to watch. Bruce and Father Arnold too. If I was twenty years older, I'd try to get one of them to marry me. They could have their own cooking show on the pubcomm. They could call it *Four Cookin' Bachelors*."

Katie nodded, and then said, "She's smiling."

"Who?"

"Hope."

"So?"

"It's been a long time since I've seen her smile. They seem to be getting along. Don't you think?"

"Yes," agreed Melissa. "She seems to be warming up."

"Come to think of it," said Katie, "I haven't seen Hope in front of her screen since we've been up. Have you?"

"No. Ever since we finished in the basement, she's been talking to Chris nonstop."

"It was sweet of you to invite Sue to stay with you."

"Yeah. Father Arnold is so welcoming. But staying here with him, even for a few days, until she can find something more permanent seemed a little awkward. I guess that's what she's decided to do anyway."

"Really?"

"Yeah. Hope explained it while you were in the shower. She said the Circle of Six will hunt her mom down because the attack on the roof is evidence it's been Hope shielding us from their cyber searching. The Circle of Six know if they can get to Sue, they can get to Hope. Because her network was penetrated, they know all about Sue now. Hope said it will be safer here because the church property doesn't have any networked electronics. No seccomm system, no scanners, nothing."

Sue had been the first to say she wasn't up to it. No one disagreed. There was no telling what challenges were ahead. Just the rooftop rescue from the apartment complex was more than Sue could handle.

Melissa continued, "If Sue stays with me, I'll get mixed up in it. At this point, I'm free to go. I don't want to be another person Hope has to hide."

The plan to kidnap Harrison had been abandoned in favor of going to Israel to meet the powerful Hillite Bruce said was even more powerful than the government. The place in Israel promised relative safety while they tried to free their parents and figure out a way to deal with the Circle of Six.

| |0 | |0 | |0

"I'M SORRY. I JUST CAN'T." CHELSEA STAYED BENT OVER AND SPIT ON THE DUSTY road the two women used for cardio exercise. Adrienne didn't say a word. Without looking up, Chelsea could tell her sister-in-law was nearly at the boiling point. "I guess I'm not ready. It's too soon," Chelsea grumbled convincingly.

"You should have waited for the doctor's approval," Adrienne scolded. "I never should have agreed to go for a run with you."

"I know. You're right. I see that now. I was wrong." Chelsea had begged Adrienne to go on the run. That was step one. Now Chelsea complained with gusto. Adrienne's frustration was primed to explode. "You go on ahead. I'll be fine. I'm going back to the old house, to rest." Chelsea held her breath, waiting to see if Adrienne took the bait.

Seconds ticked by. Finally, Adrienne said, "I'm required to escort you. You cannot be out alone."

Chelsea was ready for that. "What do you mean? We're as close to the house as we are when we normally finish our run." Which was true. Chelsea had made sure they only reached the top of the hill, the spot where they usually finished, where Adrienne ran off to start her real workout. It was the perfect spot for Chelsea to begin her act about being unable to continue. *Time to light the fuse.* "Maybe it's just a stomachache," Chelsea whimpered. "Maybe it's something more serious.

Maybe you should comm Triana and ask her? Have you ever had—"

"Enough! Enough with your whining." Adrienne tapped her wearable. *Beep.* "I leave you." She glided down the hill like a lioness.

Chelsea kept one hand on her stomach and one eye on Adrienne. She waited until her sister-in-law was well out of sight. Then she turned away from the estate and trudged off into the dry brush. Soon she'd reach the old orchard. On the other side of that was the village where the workers who supported the estate lived. She'd stay clear of it, skirt around, and eventually reach the road that led to town. *I wish I could remember the name of the town.* Seventeen years ago, when Evan had proposed marriage, he took her to the local bank to show her the magnificent family ring. *My ring.* But she'd only gone that once. The town was small, but it seemed to have every modern convenience. She had no idea if there was a public scanner, but she had to assume the town would have one. *I have to find out what happened to me during the naming ceremony.*

110 110 110

WITHOUT WARNING, THE LIMO LURCHED FROM THE CURB OF THE SUBURBAN Philly street, not far from Hope's apartment complex. Barrister glanced to the side mirror and saw the van containing Dr. Betasten and Xander also peel out and follow.

"I found them," said Tyvold over the speaker. "Holy Family Church. In Gladwyne, Pennsylvania."

The autopilot braked just enough to careen around the corner, blowing right through the stop sign. Barrister was happy he wasn't in the same vehicle with Xander; he'd probably get crushed. Behind them, the van skidded around the corner, too, as if the two vehicles were connected by a chain.

"Took you long enough," said Spire.

"Many calculations are involved. You don't understand."

"And I don't care," said Spire. "How many are inside the church?"

"I'm not sure."

"You found them but you're not sure how many?" The sarcasm was thick.

The tran accelerated toward the freeway entrance. Barrister glanced again to the side mirror as the van reached the ramp behind them. The van's suspension bottomed out, and sparks flew from the back.

"I'm working with probabilities here, OK?"

"Oh great, another one of your statistical goose chases."

"Step right up if you can do better. The probability streams lead to the church, but the church itself is an abyss. The probabilities get sucked up like a black hole."

The limo merged into the morning traffic, immediately entered the VIP lane, and accelerated to a speed far beyond the legal limit. The two vehicles looked like Indy 500 race cars, one drafting behind the other with only inches between.

No one had explained to Barrister why they had to kill Chris Lumière. He didn't really care. *Don't ask if you don't want to know.* It would all be over soon. Surround the church. Kill them all. Done.

110 110 110

DURING BREAKFAST PREP, CHRIS HAD BEEN A SPECTATOR. NOW, WITH everyone but Al finished eating, roles were reversed. Chris washed dishes while Hope dried. Sue was clearing the few remaining places. Katie cleaned the kitchen while Melissa put the clean dishes away.

"OK, let's go through it one more time," said Al, speaking with his mouth full.

Father Arnold said, "How about someone else reviews? If Al doesn't finish eating, you'll be here all day."

Sue waited to clear Al's plate, since he'd just taken his third serving. Chris nearly forgot how much food his friend could put away.

"Good point," said Bruce. "Keep shoveling, Al. I'll summarize. Father Arnold and Sue will stay here, at the rectory. Melissa will go home. Tony and Travis will drop the rest of us off at the airport." Bruce looked at Sue. "My boys will take care of everything, Sue. They'll check in on you once a week. If your plans change, please keep them apprised."

Chris knew they could trust Tony and Travis. He remembered the trip to Calexico earlier that summer, where he and Lucky searched for mock survivors in buildings of compromised integrity. One structure collapsed under Chris's feet. It was his first real connection with the warden. Chris learned later that Travis had been the first to reach him after Lucky led his team to the site of the cave-in. Tony had coordinated the landing of the medevac copter. Both men had served with Bruce in the Israeli special forces. They were American Jews who had gone to serve in the Israeli military to earn their citizenship. They'd ended up continuing their military careers together. In addition to keeping an eye on Sue, they would manage Bruce's martial arts studio until all this got sorted out.

Travis said, "Anything you need, you let us know."

Sue nodded. She seemed embarrassed for all the fuss, but also appreciative.

"Philly to Tel Aviv is about three hours by scramjet," continued Bruce. "As a precaution, we won't follow the flight plan. It could be double that before we land in Israel. During the flight, we'll finally have secure communications."

"Hey," said Hope playfully, pretending to be offended.

"No slight implied, Hope. It's just that we'll be on a network Q controls, is all."

"I know. Just kidding."

Just kidding? Chris couldn't get over the transformation. Similar to the weeks she'd stayed with them that summer, Hope was coming out of her shell. At the time, she'd said the calming effect happened after spending time in close proximity to him. But the feeling was always tainted by the constant stress of managing her network. *Is the burden gone? Or is she just able to deal with it now?*

She smiled at him. As if she always smiled. As if she always joked. As if she always talked about secure communications with levity.

"Once we can communicate more readily, we'll find out if Q's made any progress in finding your parents."

Are they OK? Chris wondered what information the authorities had gotten out of his parents. And what they'd make of it. He thought about the Fuenteses, the Leonards, and especially Teeter. Harrison would have hell to pay if they didn't receive adequate care.

"Under Q's protections, we'll have a base of operations, and we can find out more about TerraHoldings, LLC, and the Circle of Six."

"We need to get some more malted milk powder, so we can talk to the warden," said Al, after swallowing.

"And repair the gum machine," said Katie. "We only have six pieces left."

"Six plus one," corrected Al. "Lucky's sacrificing his chances with the babes by wearing that thing under his chin."

"Do they have 3-D printers in Israel?" asked Chris.

"Of course," said Bruce.

Hope's percomm lit up and vibrated. She had placed it on the counter, so she could keep an eye on it while she dried dishes. She glanced down. Chris couldn't help but look too.

SalaciousFrog: You're still under attack. Defenses holding.

Chris managed to look away before Hope's head came up. She smiled, handed the dry plate to Melissa, and took the next one from the stack.

Curiosity got the best of him. "Anything important?"

"Just my online friends helping me keep everything locked down."

"All good?"

"All good," she confirmed.

Al lifted his plate and shoveled the last bite of scrambled eggs and home fries into his mouth. Sue took his plate.

"This is the last one," said Chris, taking it from Sue and dunking it into hot, soapy water. "Just a few more minutes, and breakfast is history."

"Great. OK, people, say your good-byes. Let's saddle up," said Al. "To the van. To the airport. And off to the Promised Land."

Father Arnold quoted, "Genesis 12:1: 'Leave your country, your people, and your father's household, and go to the land I will show you.' "

| |0 | |0 | |0

ONLY MINUTES HAD PASSED SINCE HOPE AND THE OTHERS LEFT THE RECTORY for the airport.

"Sue, I'll be in the church if you need me," said Father Arnold. The priest was wearing his black pants and black shirt with the distinctive collar, but no coat.

Sue nodded.

Once he was gone, the rectory seemed especially quiet. No pubcomm, no seccomm. She realized she'd never been in a building without electronics imbedded in every wall and under every surface. The lack of background noise, a noise she apparently never consciously heard, was disturbing. The only sound was a hum from the kitchen. She stepped to the counter. The lone sound was the refrigerator, an old-fashioned type.

In the silvered surface of a pot lid drying in the dish rack, she saw her own reflection. Although the image was stretched and warped like the mirrors in a carnival fun house, her weariness was apparent without distortion.

She heard a soft *thunk*, then a rattle like a distant cowbell, followed by a wheezing sound that dissipated to nothing. Even the refrigerator's compressor had cycled off. Now it was *really* quiet. And it was because of the eerie silence that she jumped when the door opened.

Sue said, "I thought you went to the church."

"I did." The priest's sleeves were rolled up. He looked like he'd been working. But how? Barely a minute had passed. Father Arnold could hardly have walked to the church and back.

"Forget something?"

The priest just stared at her. And then said, "Where's your husband?"

"What?"

"Hope told me everything."

Sue looked down. Her greatest fear. The reason she was reluctant to stay with the priest. He would want to talk. He would do what priests do. He would try to counsel her. He probably couldn't help it. She knew it would happen. Maybe she even wanted it to happen. But so soon?

She kept her eyes on the drying pots and pans. He approached her from behind. She couldn't bear to look at him.

"Seventy times seven," he said.

"I don't know what that means."

"That's how many times you're forgiven. It represents God's forgiveness," he said. "It must be a terrible burden on you." He put his hands on her shoulders.

What? It felt strange. She was unable to move.

His fingers squeezed gently, and his thumbs circled in a massaging motion, entirely inappropriate. "How many times did you let him have her?"

What? She couldn't move. She looked in the reflection. His hands were black!

"Yes, seventy times seven. 490. That's all you get. The verbal abuse. The physical abuse. The rape. How many? More than 490? No doubt. Your god gave up on you a long time ago. He has his limits. His love is conditional. Your god only helps those who help themselves. You didn't help yourself. And you certainly didn't protect your daughter." The hands stopped massaging. "Now. Tell me. Where are they?"

110 110 110

THEY'D DROPPED SPIRE OFF RIGHT IN FRONT OF THE CHURCH. BARRISTER HAD protested. The shiny black luxury vehicle sitting at the curb of the street in the modest Philly neighborhood looked like a dollop of caviar on a slab of Spam. *So much for surprise.* Spire didn't care. He'd darted from the limo, appearing as a shadow at high noon.

Barrister waited. In the rearview mirror, he kept an eye on the van with Xander and Dr. Betasten inside.

"Get in the back," said Spire as soon as the limo door opened. Barrister hadn't even seen him come out of the church. He had the girl's mom with him. "Sit there," he said to her.

Barrister hopped out of the passenger seat and moved to the back, with the woman.

"Keep her quiet and still," ordered Spire. "We missed them," he said to Tyvold, over the comm link. "But I've got the bitch's mom as a bargaining chip. We had a little chat. They're going to Israel. Tel Aviv. We need to get to the airport. Now."

The limo bolted from the curb, with the van right behind.

"On it," said Tyvold. "That narrows it down. Only two flights a day. The first one is currently over the Atlantic Ocean. Therefore, it must be the other one. It departs in ninety minutes. That's not enough time to cancel the flight without leaving a trace."

"You have to delay them."

"Yes. I know just the thing."

| |0 | |0´ | |0

"I'VE NEVER SEEN ANYTHING LIKE IT," SAID TONY.

The road to the passenger terminal of PHL was jammed with hundreds of pubtrans. The line of autonomous taxis stretched out to the highway. The terminal looked like an ant hill under siege by an enemy colony. The pubtrans moved inches at a time under coordinated computer control, reacting to gridlock, jerking in waves, like streams of bottles moving in staccato fashion through a factory on intersecting conveyer belts.

"Fortunately, we have the VIP credentials from Q," said Travis. "Thank goodness. Can you imagine if we were caught in that? We'd miss our flight for sure." With Tony and Travis up front, Chris sat with Hope, behind them. Travis added, "The traffic jam looks recent. The airport police only just arrived."

From the window, Chris saw pubtran vehicles snarled around the departure and arrival levels. Even on the VIP lane, traffic had slowed while navigation computers recalculated routes to avoid the mess. Creeping along in the precession of luxury vehicles, Tony's old white panel van was a funny sight.

Tony said, "Nothing to do but ride it out."

"Did you bring your BSS?" asked Al. He, Katie, and Bruce were in the back of the van. Al was referring to the blind-stun-and-snare rifle.

"Yup."

Chris felt comforted. The BSS turned out to be a deciding factor in the Nevada battle against the Omega Force.

"What about the wireless transceiver?" asked Al. Al and Bruce continued a lively debate about what equipment was needed to ultimately confront the Circle of Six if, yet again, the group of men were protected by the Omega Force.

Chris tuned them out. "Tony?" asked Chris, keeping his voice down. "This Hillite guy we're going to see—what do you know about him?"

"Nothing," said Tony unconvincingly.

"You always get serious whenever someone mentions Q. Why? I mean, if you don't even know anything about him . . ."

"Simply the fact that he's a Hillite, I guess. And because he's supposed to be a powerful one."

"What is a Hillite?"

"I don't want to talk about it. Bruce wouldn't like it."

"Bruce is busy arguing with Al. Tell me."

Before answering, Tony looked at Travis and got a reluctant nod. "Well, I only know rumors," he said. "Imagine a person with that much wealth. You ask me how much? I have no idea, but more than you can spend in a thousand lifetimes, I'm sure. So Hillites have to be gluttonous, right?" Keeping his voice low, he continued, "One of the Hillites has a nickname: Jabba the Hillite. People say he's grotesquely fat and controls a global network of cronies."

"Does Q control a global network of cronies?"

"I hope not."

Chris considered this. He trusted Bruce. The Hillite they were going to see had to be good. He just had to be. "Why do they call themselves Hillites? Where does the word *Hillite* come from?"

"It's sort of a religion. Hillites claim if you practice the religion, you can have anything you want. There's a book, like their Bible, written over a hundred years ago by a guy named Napoleon Hill. I've never read the book, but apparently it explains how anyone can get anything they want."

| | 0 | | 0 | | 0

SPIRE REAPPEARED AT THE JETWAY SERVICE DOOR OF GATE B15 OF PHILADELPHIA International Airport. From the limo parked on the tarmac, Barrister watched Spire slip down the gangway and trot back.

"They're not on the flight," said Spire even before the vehicle door closed behind him.

"Are you sure?" asked Tyvold, over the comm link.

"Are *you* sure that this is the only flight to Israel?"

"Yes."

"Well, then how do you explain the fact that they're not on the plane?"

Tyvold said, "Maybe my delay tactic worked too well. Maybe they're still stuck in pubtran gridlock?"

"No, the flight's full."

"Maybe the airline filled the seats?"

"Why don't you stop with all the maybes and look at the fucking data, Mr. Tech Guru."

"All right, all right. Hold on."

While they waited, Dr. Betasten's image popped up on a comm link from the van behind the limo. "What are you people doing up there?" Over Dr. Betasten's shoulder, Barrister could see Xander at the back of the van. He had his own special chair next to medical equipment. No expression on his face. Dr. Betasten, on the other hand, looked frantic.

"The usual, Doctor," said Spire, "Tyvold lost them again."

"Just shut up for a minute," said Tyvold. "You're right. There were no last-minute substitutions on that flight."

"I already told you that."

"There are no other commercial flights."

"Check *all* flights."

"I checked *all* flights. No commercial or charter flights are going to Israel. Maybe they're going somewhere else first? Or maybe the mom lied to you."

"No way."

"I'm telling you, there are no— Hold on."

"What?"

"There's one charter flight with *no* flight plan."

"That's impossible."

"Exactly."

Barrister was thrown back against the seat as the limo took off. On the screen, he watched Dr. Betasten fall to the floor as the van behind them also shot forward. The vehicles looked like two railcars behind an invisible rocket-powered locomotive.

"I got it," said Tyvold. "Prepping for takeoff. Runway 27-R. Gotcha now!"

| | 0 | | 0 | | 0

"THAT ISN'T THE SAME PLANE WE TOOK TO LAS VEGAS," SAID HOPE, SITTING next to Chris in the white panel van's middle row of seats.

"No, you're right," said Bruce. There was concern in his voice, too.

Tony hopped out, went to the back of the van, opened the trunk compartment, and started unloading.

"Is it even a scramjet?" asked Al.

"I think so," said Bruce, still unsure. He got out too. Chris followed Bruce, and Hope followed Chris.

A woman appeared at the open door of the plane. She was dressed in a neat uniform: light-blue short-sleeved shirt and navy-blue slacks. Her hair was up in a tight bun. The lapels of her shirt showed four stripes. "*Shalom*," she called. "You must be Bruce Cohen?" She trotted nimbly down the steps.

"Yes," Bruce called back. "*Shalom*." He stepped away from their group and met her at the bottom of the ladder. They started a conversation.

The plane they'd taken to Vegas was small, Hope recalled, with room for about twelve people. But no pilot. This one was huge, the size of a regular airliner, or bigger even. The Vegas flight had been her first, and she hadn't seen many planes up close. It was difficult to get a sense of perspective having seen them only in ads on the pubcomm.

Tony shut the van door and came up behind them. "Yeah, it's a scramjet, all right. You can tell by the engines. See there?" He pointed. "And the shape of the wings."

The woman in uniform turned and went back up the steps. Hope couldn't help but notice she pressed something just inside the aircraft's doorway as she entered. *A button?*

Bruce rejoined. "Yes, it's a different plane," he confirmed. "But it's all part of the plan. We even have a pilot. She said Q thought we'd appreciate the amenities. This plane is a flying hotel. There's a shower, full kitchen, and bedrooms. And, if you can believe it, a 3-D apparel printer."

"Wow," said Katie. "Can it print parts for the gum machine?"

"I don't think so. Clothing only." Seeing her frustration, he added, "Don't worry. We'll get your parts printed as soon as we can. Or we'll just buy a new gum machine. I'm sure Q can keep the transaction private. Don't worry."

Hope glanced down at her own clothes. She considered the idea of a change. It was only a few months before that she'd stayed at Chris's house. Laura had taken her shopping. She remembered Chris's reaction when he saw the new clothes. "Katie?" asked Hope. "Would you help me choose an outfit?"

"Of course!" Katie lit up. "It'll be girls' night out, miga."

"Bruce." Everyone turned. The pilot was at the hatch again. "Is your entire team here? Any stragglers?"

Bruce shook his head. "This is it."

"In that case, please get everyone aboard immediately." The tone of her voice indicated there would be no debate.

"Is there a problem?"

"Unidentified vehicles approaching. If they're not friendlies, then they're not friendly. We need to be in the air. Now." She returned to the cockpit. Again, Hope noticed the pilot touch something as she passed. Not a second later, the aircraft started making all kinds of noise. The engines started to spin up while flaps went up and down.

Everyone, including Lucky, bade good-bye to Tony and Travis and then climbed aboard.

Inside, everyone was still standing when the plane started to roll. Chris took Hope's hand and pulled her to a seat on a circular couch. Katie, Al, and Bruce joined them.

"There are no seat belts," said Katie.

"No," said Bruce. "I think this plane is one hundred percent luxury."

The cabin was decorated like an exquisite lounge of the ritziest and most modern type of hotel. The furnishings looked more lavish than Hope had ever seen in her life, either in person or on the pubcomm. Except for the oval windows, it was hard to tell they were in a plane. The effect was less like a plane and more like a luxury cruise ship.

Chris was looking out the window as they taxied. With his hand in hers, she actually felt excited. She would help her friends find their families. She would be with Chris forever. She'd never again have to worry about her appearance because Chris would defend her virtue. She could wear attractive styles. She knew her body could turn men on. For once in her life she wanted to turn a man on. One man in particular. One incredibly special man.

She brought her other hand over. He looked at her, smiled, and then looked out again. Thinking about the arrangements, her mind started to race. She wanted to sleep with him. During all the nights at the Richardses' house, she'd had her own room. In the church basement, the night before, Chris had already been fast asleep. She was thrilled by the thought of them finally being together, truly together for the first time. She caressed Chris's hand. She had plans for his hands.

The aircraft swung out onto the runway. When it accelerated for takeoff, Hope was surprised at how quiet and smooth it was, nothing like the sound and vibration she'd experienced before.

"Uh-oh," said Chris, pressing his nose to the window.

"What?" said Bruce.

Even as the plane rolled faster and faster down the runway, they struggled to get a view outside. Hope saw it now too. A black stretch limousine and a utility van had pulled onto the tarmac, too, and were now gaining on the plane.

"Who is it?" asked Chris

"Who cares," said Al. "Go, baby, go."

The two pursuing vehicles began to fall behind. The nose of the plane rose, and the aircraft lifted off effortlessly, as if it had power to spare.

110 110 110

RACING AT ONE HUNDRED TWENTY MILES PER HOUR DOWN THE RUNWAY, THE limo chased the plane, followed closely by the van. They caught up and started to pull up alongside. But it was short-lived. The plane continued to accelerate. The front tire left the runway.

"I got the tail number," said Spire. "486F7065."

"Good, that'll help," said Tyvold. "In fact, it might be our only way to track it. Skotino sent you a message. You're to go to our private hangar and board our scramjet. There's a chance we can get to Israel before them."

Spire watched the jet's wheels retract as it made a gentle bank to the right, heading east. The limo slowed to a less conspicuous speed. "What do you mean *a chance*? More probability bullshit?"

"Yes, but—now it's more than that."

Even over the comm link, Barrister could sense Tyvold was doing massive multitasking.

"If we can't communicate, our bargaining chip is useless," said Spire.

Barrister looked at Sue Avenir. It made him think of the puppies. The mom looked trapped and scared. Like the spikes were about to pass through the air holes of her cage, she had no idea what was in store for her.

"No time to argue. Go. Every minute counts."

CHAPTER 26

"**Y**OU DIDN'T TAKE MY ADVICE," SAID THE PRISON ADMINISTRATOR, IN HIS office.

"I did," said Ingrid. "You can't grow nose hair overnight."

Actually, she hadn't taken her new boss's advice. She could've arrived, on her first day of work, disguised as a seventy-year-old man, and he wouldn't have even recognized her. Going the other direction, if the regulations allowed, she could've worn a candy striper's uniform with some impractical shoes and looked like she'd just stepped out of a centerfold. He would've had to adjust his fly in ten seconds flat.

When Ingrid first planned her investigation into reports of a pregnant woman in the female-only prison, she'd naturally considered using a disguise and a pseudonym. But TerraMed Biotech already knew her face and her name. They were sophisticated enough to see through a disguise and a fake name. Far more important was keeping a watch on her employment data associated with the Washington State Department of Corrections. Whoever took a peek was surely a threat.

The prescribed uniform for her new career was similar to a paramedic's: black boots, black nylon trousers with plenty of pockets on the sides, and a conservative black short-sleeved, button-down shirt. All the med techs working at the prison complex, both men and women, wore the same type of uniform. But she let her genetically engineered assets do their thing. The trousers were strategically fitted, as was the tailoring of the shirt.

All these steps were intentional, part of her tradecraft. Her appearance created something of a cognitive disruption field. Even straight women became preoccupied with a threatening yet subconscious sense of competition at the mere sight of her. She wore a stethoscope, draped around her neck, resting across her chest—but it wasn't the stethoscope that people noticed, especially from the front. She wore an equipment belt, with a portable medical scanner clipped at the hip—but it wasn't the scanner that people noticed, especially from behind.

Presently, her new boss, the prison administrator, was adjusting his fly.

Twenty seconds. That's just about right. Ingrid was always amazed at how men thought no one noticed. They tried to make it look like they were tucking in their shirt or pulling up their pants. The thumb goes down far enough to hook the underpants, followed by a little hop.

"Well, you've been warned," he said. "Head over to C Block. Ask for Dr. Ferrara. You'll be assisting him. He's going to want to know everything you learned on how to care for a pregnant woman with a baby that's invisible to the prenatal scanner."

| | 0 | | 0 | | 0

FINDING THE SMALL GREEK TOWN WAS EASY. THE HARD PART WAS WALKING. Walking made the pain worse. It felt like feminine itch all the way down her thighs. Plus, she really had to pee.

Initially, Chelsea was surprised at how much she remembered from the trip to the bank after so many years. But the surprise faded as she also remembered the town had few prominent landmarks. Every street looked the same. A river split the town down the middle. It wasn't a huge river but looked deep enough to have to wade across. The central bridge—made of stone, with a pronounced arch—was maybe thirty meters side to side and barely wide enough for two lanes. But there was no traffic. Not many people either. *Thank goodness.* She adjusted things below her waist as discreetly as possible but knew it probably looked like some obscene gesture.

Shops and storefronts faced the river on both sides. Fortunately, everything was well marked. It only took a few minutes to find the clinic. All public clinics around the world had a sign with a purple cross. Carrying only her water bottle, she walked bowleggedly inside. It was completely empty. No need to wait in queue or—

Oh my god.

Only then did she remember—along with the implication—that she didn't own a percomm. *How could I be so stupid?* She had no way to get the scan results. One's percomm worked like a pass. That was the 'per' in *percomm*—meaning personal. The machine wouldn't even acknowledge her without one. *Ugh!*

The itch was unbearable. She had an overwhelming desire to find a stick and dig in. Looking to her left, she saw another familiar symbol: the stick figure with a skirt. *First, I'll visit the loo. While on the pot, I'll devise a plan.*

The washroom was empty. She dashed to an open stall, shut the door, and relieved herself. She unfurled a handful of tissue from the roll, pressed, and scraped. *Ahhh.* It was that satisfying kind of pain, like scratching a mosquito bite until it bled. She imagined her expression looked like one of those women applying ointment in the hemorrhoid adverts. She didn't care. With more paper, she dug and dragged.

Feeling relieved—in so many ways—she stood, pulled up her athletic shorts, and turned. *What is that?* She'd been in such a rush to sit, she hadn't noticed a half dozen disgusting little worms in the toilet bowl. Each was a few centimeters long and not much thicker than a strand of hair. Before she could get a closer look, the automatic flush whooshed everything away. *Dear god!* She couldn't get out of the clinic fast enough.

Again, she asked herself, *What did people do before scanners? Hospital!* Having never broken a limb or even been terribly ill, she'd had no reason to go to one in her lifetime. *A big white building, right? It can't be hard to find.* She could ask someone— but, no, she needed to avoid that if possible. She looked up at the purple cross above the clinic entrance. She tried to think of the universal symbol for *hospital*. She was sure it was blue. Either a cross or the letter *H*.

There has to be a hospital here, somewhere. She looked both ways down the street. Nothing in sight. *Time to explore.*

I I O I I O I I O

"THE BAD NEWS IS WE WON'T HAVE COMMUNICATIONS DURING THE FLIGHT AS we originally hoped," said Bruce, returning from the cockpit. "We can't risk it. Whoever tried to crash our bon voyage party knows way too much. The good news is we're traveling at Mach three along a deliberately convoluted flight path. We'll be hard to track. That means we'll also be in the air twice as long as the required three hours. It'll be night, local time, when we land in Tel Aviv."

When they'd boarded, Hope noticed her percomm had been knocked off the global network. She thought it had something to do with the button the pilot was pressing at the door hatch. She'd taken a close look when she'd entered the plane. If it was a button, it wasn't like any type she'd seen before. It looked like a rectangular tin box about the size of her thumb. It had a symbol on it that looked like a rounded letter *W*. It didn't look like part of the plane, but more like somebody just glued it there.

Without a network connection, there was no way for her to check the status of her defenses. She'd have to trust her AI bots, SalaciousFrog, and her other online friends. The only network available was from the plane itself. Hope guessed it was a hospitality link. Since she was confident in the safety measures of her percomm, she succumbed to fascination and gave it permission to connect to the plane's local network.

Bruce was barely reseated following his visit to the cockpit when the pilot's face appeared on multiple display screens around the cabin. "Well, you people must be serious."

"What do you mean?" asked Bruce.

"We just reached international airspace, and look who showed up."

They all looked out at a fighter jet.

"There're two," said the pilot. "One on each side. Israeli Air Force. Our escort."

"Wow," said Al. "That is the most badass plane I've ever seen. Look at the missiles."

"Yeah, missiles." The pilot chuckled. "Believe me, the most impressive weapon on that aircraft is the pilot. Defense aircraft are remotely controlled or fully autonomous. Not these."

"Can't be hacked," said Hope.

"That's right. I've been working for Q for over a decade, and I've never seen *this* before. And that's not all. Instead of landing at TLV, I've been instructed to land at Nevatim Airbase."

"Why?" asked Bruce.

"That's what I'd like to ask you. However, my final instructions are to not ask you any questions. After our narrow escape from the two vehicles during takeoff, I can only assume Q is taking no chances." She shook her head. "Well, there's only one thing for me to say. Enjoy your flight." The screen returned to its idle state, showing the plane's location and other flight data.

"Well," said Katie, "you heard the lady. Enjoy your flight. I don't need to be told twice. You boys stay here and do whatever boys do." She took Hope by the hand. "We're going to get gussied up."

Katie pulled so hard, Hope felt as if her other shoulder would dislocate. But Katie's excitement was contagious. Hope surprised herself with a giggle and immediately had a fleeting thought that it might have been her first.

Hand in hand, they stepped through the narrow passageway heading aft. On the right was a series of doors. On the other side was a grand meeting room behind a wall of glass. Hope was thankful Katie slowed down because they both had to take in the sight.

The opulence was incredible. Even from watching programs on the pubcomm while growing up, Hope had never seen a room so exquisitely furnished. She couldn't guess what material the table was made of, nor the dozen chairs surrounding it. Along the walls, warm illumination highlighted art niches, each displaying a sculpture, plant, or other artifact. The combination of colors was expertly coordinated using a pallet of earth tones: chocolaty browns and mossy greens accented by toasted yellows and dusty pinks. Hope knew that interior design required skill. Whoever decorated the meeting room—indeed, the entire interior of the aircraft—must have had doctorates in interior design, architecture, and art history.

Continuing along, the passageway opened to an enormous great room. The ceiling, floor, and walls all converged, becoming one enormous cylinder, maximizing every inch of space within the aircraft's body. Hope knew commercial aircraft had a cargo level under the passenger area. But here, the great room utilized the entire volume of the fuselage. Somehow, the plane looked even bigger from the inside; the room was huge.

A curved staircase led down to a floor that wasn't flat. Instead, the path split into trails leading through rolling hills of couches nestled between the curving paths—each a different shape, each accommodating three to eight people, and each surrounding a small table. A few of the paths went quite high on the sides, so some of the gathering spaces were also high. Here, too, the earth tones created an inviting and nature-inspired atmosphere.

It resembled a majestic river valley with huddle spaces sprinkled along the mountains on both sides. It was easy to envision impeccably dressed elitists discussing world events in hush tones over cocktails.

"Wow," said Katie. She'd paused halfway down the stairs. "When we boarded, I thought that first room was ritzy. But this is unbelievable."

A chandelier, not currently lit, dominated the high ceiling. Surrounding it, long, thin poles reached down to just above each table, providing a sophisticated glow. In fact, the lighting alone was incredible. A smoldering radiance glimmered from underneath the tables, from beneath the couches, and along the snaking paths. The paths converged on the other side of the great room, at the base of a matching staircase leading up to yet another passageway similar to the one they had just come from.

"No kidding. What do you think it cost?"

Katie turned, her expression serious now. "Twelve senators sleeping, eleven banks foreclosing, ten sharks a-loaning, nine Ponzis scheming, eight lawyers a-lying, seven addicts addicting, six businesses a-bribing, five prostitution rings, four sweatshops, three bribed judges, two inside traders, and a child in a porn gallery."

"You really think so?"

"I don't know, miga. I'm just so blown away by all the Hillite talk. I don't know what to believe. Is it possible to legally earn this kind of wealth? I guess, deep inside, I hoped it was all rumor. But look at this place. And it's not even his house; it's his plane. And apparently he has a fleet of them. Holy cow."

Hope nodded. "Is it OK to make new clothes? Or would that be like a vegan trying on leather shoes?"

Katie's excitement returned. "Nah. I can't stop thinking about my mom, dad, and brother. Any distraction is welcome." She grinned. "What the heck. Time to do something for ourselves, girlfriend. I've worn the subsidized clothing my entire life. I'm not going to miss this opportunity." She turned back. "The 3-D apparel printer has to be farther down. Let's go."

The opposite passage led to a galley. *Galley* was an understatement because it looked more professional than any kitchen she'd seen on any cooking program. An executive chef from a Michelin-acclaimed restaurant would be right at home. Continuing on, the passage led to what looked like sleeping quarters.

Hope pulled Katie's hand to get her to stop. "Let's not go any farther. I feel like we're invading someone's privacy."

"OK. What do you suggest? Should we go back and ask the pilot where the printer is?"

Hope smiled. "If Al were here, what would he do?"

Katie shook her head. "You lost me."

"Occam's razor."

"Huh?"

"Remember? The solution to a problem is usually the obvious one." In a raised voice, she said, "Computer, where's the 3-D printer?"

"Pardon. Don't you mean *virtas*?" came a female voice from no discernable direction.

Hope laughed.

Katie seemed confused and somewhat alarmed.

Hope squeezed her hand to let her know it was OK. Then said, "My apologies, virtas. What's your name?"

"My name is Gladys. Pleasure to make to your acquaintance, Hope Avenir and Katie Leonard."

Katie smiled now, understanding that the plane's AI was far more sophisticated than a regular seccomm system.

The voice continued, "The fitting booth and apparel fabrication system are located thirty meters forward." Gladys sounded completely natural, not nearly as robotic as the seccomm at home. Then Hope's percomm vibrated. On the display, it showed a map of the plane's interior with a highlighted path.

"Nice," said Katie. "I guess we wandered a bit too far, huh?" She giggled. Then mischievously added, "Oops."

The highlighted path led them back to one of the doors across from the glass wall and meeting room. Sure enough, there was a sign next to the door. They'd been so distracted, they'd walked right past. Before stepping inside, Katie called up to Al, Chris, and Bruce, "Hey, boys. There's a kitchen back there. Why don't you rustle up some grub while we get stylin'?"

"I vote for chips and salsa," added Hope, surprised at her own sassiness.

The arrangement inside the room looked very similar to the system in the boutique that Laura had taken Hope to earlier that summer. On the right was the printer itself. On the left was the scanner booth that allowed the computer to make a perfect fit. And straight ahead was the kiosk to select fashions from the database.

Katie turned to Hope. "You know what Melissa said about you?"

"I'm sure I don't care."

"No, seriously. She's totally jazz. And don't worry; Chris never strayed."

"But she tried. Melissa baited him. I know she did. I could see it in her eyes."

"Sure. But give her a break. We're talking about Chris. You know, Melissa wasn't the first to take a fancy, and she won't be the last. Remember 'the Queen' from high school? Dawn Perkins? Even she couldn't resist him. If you're going to be part of Chris's life, you'd better get used to it."

"You're right." Katie's choice of words, 'part of Chris's life,' was thrilling. More than ever, Hope wanted to be in his life. Forever. No running away like before. The feeling of complete and utter commitment brought her peace somehow, like passing a point of no return. "OK. I give. What did Miss City Slicker say about me?"

"She said you look like Marilyn Monroe with brown hair."

"That's nice."

"Except . . ."

"Except what!"

"Except your clothes look like you got them from a man twice your size and three times your age."

Hope steamed up, but she knew Katie was just upping the ante.

Katie seemed to enjoy getting her riled up, or maybe sensed she needed sufficient motivation to follow through without getting cold feet.

"So. Ready to make a change?" Katie asked.

A change. Her life had been *nothing but* change lately. Katie was right. She'd always tried to hide herself from the world—to be invisible. It was time to show off her true self and face the world with confidence. "OK," agreed Hope. "But not too sexy. Not too revealing. Not too body conscious."

"OK. Pretty and attractive, but not screaming it."

Hope nodded and smiled.

"Show cleavage, but cover the nipples."

"Ha!" Hope laughed out loud. Again, another first. She could trust Katie. And she realized now what a good friend Katie had become. She also had a new appreciation for what a good friend she had always been to Chris. And Al.

"Are you planning a treat for Al?"

Katie's reaction was one of shock, as if she'd just been outed, as if her feelings for Al were state secrets. Then her expression relaxed. She smiled a pirate's smile. "Oh yeah. I think I need to make up for lost time." She interlaced her fingers, extended her arms with palms out, and cracked her knuckles. "Let's get started, miga."

"I DON'T CARE IF YOU HAVE TO DROP XANDER OUT THE HATCH MIDFLIGHT, RIGHT on top of their fucking aircraft; I want them dead," said Skotino from the secondary security station under Yucca Mountain. Over Tyvold's shoulder, Skotino watched the vidcomm view of the private hangar at PHL as Dr. Betasten and Ken Barrister transferred Xander's equipment out of the utility van and into the scramjet. Spire was "supervising," as usual.

"I pulled the specs on their aircraft," said Tyvold. "It's a luxury liner. A Spruce Goose III. A big, fat, flying pig. You'll have a speed advantage. You can get to Israel first."

After hearing Tyvold over the comm link, Spire spoke up. "If you can't track them, who cares?"

Normally, Tyvold would object. But at the console facing the vid feed, he simply glanced back to Skotino, standing behind him.

"Well?" pressured Skotino.

"I told you," said Tyvold. "There's someone else in play. It's not just Hope Avenir's people. A completely independent force is also blocking me."

"You're outnumbered," said Spire.

Tyvold continued, "Fortunately, this other force isn't as sophisticated. I just need more time."

In unison, Skotino and Spire said, "We don't have more time."

Tyvold said nothing.

"That's it? That's all you got?" said Spire.

"Use the radar," said Tyvold finally.

"Seriously? That's like finding a needle in a box of needles. All the blips look alike."

"Only one blip is headed to Israel. It can work."

On the vid screen, Dr. Betasten waddled from van to jet with no particular urgency. Barrister had tried to help carry equipment, but the doctor insisted on moving certain pieces himself.

"Faster," Skotino boomed. Dr. Betasten started to scurry like a field mouse. "By the gods, if that plane manages to land, you will all fester in dextral hell. Get in the air. Now!"

Like a sonar ping, the sound of Skotino's voice reflected off the six holding cells of the oubliette and returned as a wave of fear. One of the pharmakoi was especially receptive. Skotino closed his eyes, absorbing the sensation. Like a siren song, it beckoned him. *Forget the radar. My god knows the future.*

Tyvold read his mind. "Room number four," he said. "Patricia."

I I O I I O I I O

"BECAUSE CHRIS AND AL HAVE SUDDENLY GONE MUTE, I'LL SPEAK UP. YOU BOTH look very nice," said Bruce, admiring Katie and Hope, who had just returned from the apparel printing booth of the aircraft.

That's not the half of it, thought Hope. *We look awesome.* Katie had done an amazing job. Hope had decided on an outfit not unlike the one Laura bought her: a turquoise skort and a white spaghetti-strap top.

Katie had gone with an actual miniskirt in baby blue and a pink tube top that complemented her tall and lean build. Because her breasts were of average size, the tube top was alluring but not skanky. She had that boyish kind of physique that would allow her to wear a shirt unbuttoned all the way down to her navel and not worry about parts falling out. Boys always said that more than a handful was a waste; Katie was a generous handful with nothing wasted. *And* they defied gravity. In fact, everything about Katie was firm and hard. Her ripped abs made her midriff look fabulous under the tube top. *Years of karate really pays off*, she thought. The miniskirt hugged her modest hips, with plenty of stretch, looking almost like another tube top.

Hope, on the other hand, had been wishing for breast-reduction surgery every Christmas. The changes started around the age of twelve and were completely out of control by fourteen. Many nights she'd lain awake, thinking how her life would have been different if her chest wasn't so conspicuous. She wasn't fat by any means, but everything had a smoothness and a jiggle. When she moved, parts of her body lagged behind, caught up, and then bobbled in place until everything settled back. Her breasts defied gravity, too, but that was only because of youth. In a matter of years, she'd be tossing them over her shoulder like the rifle of a Continental soldier.

The 3-D printer's design catalog had every bra style known to man. She selected a full-coverage model. It looked like a miniature straightjacket but did the job perfectly. Katie, however, was au naturel under the tube top.

"Too bad all the seats are taken," Hope teased. She turned to Katie. "I guess you'll have to sit on Al's lap." Both girls cracked up when they saw Al's expression.

The boys had found some food, even tortilla chips and salsa. Next to that was an assortment of cheeses and sliced meats and a basket of bread. And—believe it or not—soda pop.

"Did you leave any for us?" asked Katie. She sat next to Al.

Hope sat next to Chris. The food was picked over, but there was still plenty left. Hope had seen soda pop advertisements but had never tasted it. "Cola?" she asked Chris.

It took him a second to register that she was talking to him. He didn't say anything. He just opened the bottle and poured it into a glass for her. It was a real glass, not plastic. She picked it up and watched the foam dissipate. She brought it to her mouth and let the spray of popping bubbles tickle her lips. She took a sip. *Mmm.* She glanced to him. He was staring with his mouth open.

"Your turn," said Katie to the men. "How about a tuxedo for each of you?"

"My clothes are fine," said Al. "How about we stay right here?"

"Yeah," said Chris flatly. "Besides, the scanner won't work on me."

"*Suit* yourselves," said Katie. "Ha! Get it?"

Neither Chris nor Al laughed, nor even smiled. It wasn't that funny, but the crack should have rated a groan at least. Hope started to wonder when they would recover. She decided to indulge herself and just look into his azure eyes. She glanced to his lips, the way she had on the masstran, confident he knew what she was thinking. Then his expression seemed to clear.

"What is it?" she asked.

Only to her, he said, "I have something I want to say."

"Go on."

He looked toward Al and Katie, who were chatting. Bruce was tapping at the display screen, preoccupied, or maybe he was just trying to ignore the sexual energy in the room.

"Later," said Chris. "Later."

CHAPTER 27

"IN RETROSPECT, WE MADE MISTAKES," SAID RODRIGUEZ. "WE ASSUMED the band of youths and the dog were a distraction."

At eight in the morning, the club was deserted except for a small staff preparing food for that night. The kitchen staff had fixed breakfast for Eladio and the four OTH marines. Huevos rancheros, the most authentic Eladio had ever tasted.

"You were expecting the traitorous MI8 agent who murdered Dr. Cornelius?" Eladio asked.

"Yes. We weren't about to be fooled by her. But she never surfaced. And the band of youths turned out to be unpredictable," said Rodriguez, "Yes, we made mistakes. But if I had to do it over again, with perfect hindsight, I'm not sure what I'd do differently."

"Why were they unpredictable? Unconventional methods?" asked Eladio. "The BSS? The dog?"

"Fuckin' dog," said the fist.

"Correct," said Rodriguez. "But also because of one of the youths: Male. Caucasian. Tall. Slender. Brown hair."

"How so?"

"He could fly."

So it's really true. Eladio nodded. "Schofield said as much. It's hard to believe."

"Believe it. And not just fly; he could zig and zag in midair. I swear, he could be three feet in front of me, I could unload an entire magazine, and he'd dodge every bullet."

"Really."

"With all the advantages of genetic engineering and my superhuman reaction time, it might as well have been you fighting him that day. No offense."

"None taken," said Eladio. He mulled it over. "What does your gut tell you?"

"The curious thing is that they had every opportunity to kill us but didn't."

"Blew my fuckin' legs off," said the fist.

"Yeah. But you were lobbing mortar rounds on them. And, well, knowing you, 'pretty please' wasn't going to get you to stop."

The fist shrugged in a "damn straight" sort of way.

Eladio asked, "Can you rule out the rogue agent?"

"No," said the hack. "Nothing should be ruled out. Our communications were jammed. That's expected when dealing with Hoods, but the attackers had knowledge of our internal systems. Command and control was compromised. We don't know by whom. Therefore, the agent may have been involved even if we didn't see her."

Eladio said, "The information in the report was heavily redacted. What do you know about the agent?"

"Her name is Ingrid Vunderbosh," said Rodriguez. "British MI8. Her primary mission was to protect the Nu Force prototype. And secondarily, to protect Dr. Cornelius."

"She murdered him."

"So the story goes. There was never any reason to doubt Omega Force command."

"But you have doubts now?"

Rodriguez nodded.

| | 0 | | 0 | | 0

INGRID CROSSED FROM THE PRISON ADMINISTRATION BUILDING OVER TO C
Block to meet again with Dr. Ferrara. She'd received some

initial training on the prison's systems, and it was finally time to examine her new patient for the first time. As far as Dr. Ferrara knew, her job was to assist in the pregnant inmate's treatment. Ingrid needed to be careful not to let on that her real goal was to find a connection to TerraMed Biotech.

As she crossed the grounds, she noted every security feature of the prison. It was a recent design. The entire complex was walled, of course, but each detention block was also surrounded by a razor wire fence with a single gate. Like the compartments of a ship with bulkheads that could be sealed to prevent one punctured compartment from flooding the rest, an uprising in one block could be contained, preventing a spread to the others. C Block housed the women who had some kind of medical issue.

At the gate to C Block, Ingrid passed through the security scanner with the knowledge that the scan resolved to credentials showing her true name. It was a risk, using her true name, but she needed to determine if TerraMed Biotech had any connection to the pregnant inmate. The name Ingrid Vunderbosh was the same name she'd used under the employment of TerraMed, when she'd cared for Chelsea Venizelos. If, in fact, TerraMed Biotech was involved, she had to assume the name Ingrid Vunderbosh would force a reaction. That reaction would tip her off, serving as an early warning signal.

Once inside C block, Ingrid was directed to the infirmary. She found Dr. Ferrara. Until that moment, she'd only been briefly introduced to him.

Dr. Ferrara tapped at the tablet cradled at his elbow. "Says here you have experience with the condition."

"Well, I've never been pregnant myself."

"I was referring to the scan errors."

"I know."

He eyed her. Then he lowered the tablet to his side and turned his attention to the expanse of glass on the wall next to him. He made a hand gesture. The room lighting dimmed. Gray liquid crystals in the wall of glass vanished, revealing an adjacent room. A woman wearing a gown was sitting on the examination table. She was slumped forward, with her pale face partially shrouded behind long strands of straight brown hair.

"Two-way glass," he said. "She can't see us."

"Yes, I know how two-way glass works."

He eyed her again. "Are we going to have trouble working together?"

"That's up to you."

"I want to be perfectly clear. I'm in charge."

She eyed him back.

"Well?"

"Well what? You didn't ask me a question. You said you're in charge. Fine. Take charge."

His stare lingered as he brought the tablet back up to the crook of his elbow. *Tap, tap, swipe.* "Female. Caucasian. First name, M-e-t-i-s—pronounced 'May-teece.' Prefers nickname, May. Last name, Lincoln. Twenty-one years old. Born August 14, 2036, in Bellevue, Washington. Single. Never married. Extensive rap sheet. Drug possession, mostly. The rest is loitering, panhandling, and resisting arrest. That last one earned her a long stay here." He tapped. "Transmitting her record to you now."

Ingrid pulled the industrial-sized percomm–medical scanner unit from her belt and followed along.

"Medical history is unremarkable. Current complaints are consistent with long-term drug use. Veratetracyclean—street name Black Radish. Parafennalbuteral—street name Lip Lock, or known out East as a Wet Wilma. There's also evidence of early gateway variants, including the typical hemp derivatives and opioids." He looked up. "Questions before we begin?"

"Nothing vaped?"

"No, all ingested or hypodermic."

"What's her state of addiction now? Any impact of the drugs on the fetus?"

"She's been locked up here for more than two years, and therefore clean at the time of conception. Of course, there's no way to know about any long-term effects."

Ingrid looked at him. "Who got her pregnant?"

He raised his eyebrow. "We told you. We don't know."

"You know the environment. You know the people here. Guess. Who got her pregnant?"

He frowned. The asshole-in-charge attitude softened. He seemed to reconnect with his medical training, like the rusty Hippocratic oath creaking into motion. "I don't know," he said. "I really don't know."

| | 0 | | 0 | | 0

CHELSEA LAY ON HER BACK. THE CLINIC LIGHTS REMINDED HER OF THE ONES IN the examination room she had visited during her pregnancy with Xander.

After she explored the town, it wasn't the hospital symbol she'd found but rather the one with the winged staff with two snakes twisted around it. Oddly, when she first arrived at the doctor's office, the place was empty. She tracked down an English-speaking passerby, who explained there was a sign on the door, written in Greek, that said the doctor would be back at six o'clock. Apparently, the doctor held working hours throughout the day and evening, separated by a long break. Enduring the wait, she hoped he wouldn't return drunk after enjoying a three-martini lunch, or groggy after the Greek version of a siesta. He arrived a few minutes before six. He seemed nice enough.

"All right, lets ease off your undergarment."

It would have been faster if you'd told me to get naked before hopping up here, she thought. It was getting late. Evan and the estate goons hadn't tracked her down yet, but a search party could show up any second. *Hurry up.*

With latex-covered fingers, he tugged on the waistband of her underpants while she rocked her hips. "Now, let's see what we have here . . ."

How about you just tell me what's wrong.

"Hmm. Yes. Significant bruising . . ."

I already told you that. Frustrated, she strained her neck for a better view. His balding head was visible between her thighs. He reached back for something. She was alarmed by the size of the instrument he brought forward. It looked similar to a pair of tweezers but bigger, more like tongs. "What are you going to do with that?"

He didn't answer. She felt the instrument touch. Then she watched as he carefully lifted it. Chelsea screamed. A worm— just like the ones she'd seen in the toilet that afternoon—was writhing and twisting between the tips of the oversized tweezers.

"Bloody hell! What is that?" She sat fully upright. *Dear god, there's more!* She heaved, but nothing substantial came up, just the sourness that had once been the sip of water he'd given her minutes before.

He offered her a towel and a pan, but when she threw her leg over the side, to get down, he dropped both items. He caught her before the pan clanged to the floor. Holding her shoulders, he asked, "Do you trust me?"

"What? It doesn't matter. I have to—"

He shook her, gently but firmly. "Do you trust me?"

She went with her instincts. "Yes."

"I must give you a sedative, so I can—"

"What sedative?" she demanded.

"Diazepam. You may know it as Valium. You won't be unconscious, but you won't care either."

She knew the drug. What he was saying sounded true. She nodded.

"You have to relax so I can help you." He reached back to the counter behind and tore open a paper package containing a syringe. He opened a glass door on the cabinet above the counter, selected a small vial, and inserted the needle. Thumb on the plunger, he pressed, forcing out the unwanted air. Then, holding the plunger like a cigarette, he pulled, filling the syringe. Once the needle was free, he flicked the tube with his finger. He eyeballed the tube's graduation as a stream of fluid squirted into the air. He turned and swabbed alcohol on the inside of her elbow. "Do you trust me?" he repeated.

She nodded again.

"I'll discover what is happening here. One thing is for certain: the helminths must be removed." He inserted the needle into her vein and pushed.

110 110 110

DURING THE TRIP TO AND FROM LAS VEGAS, EARLIER THAT SUMMER, HOPE had noted the distinct shudder when the smaller scramjet transitioned out of supersonic flight mode. Now, she watched the air speed displayed in the luxury airliner's cabin—Mach 1.12, 1.06, 1.03, 0.99—and she felt no shudder at all. No sonic boom. Either the larger plane had the ability to prevent the sonic boom entirely or was somehow able to insulate the cabin from the boom's effect.

During the entire trip across the Atlantic, the two military escort jets never left their side. The planes had been difficult to see in the darkness, except for the faint glow of the cockpit's instrumentation under the canopy. Up ahead, in the distance, Hope saw two parallel rows of lights. She assumed it was their landing strip because the plane banked smoothly and lined up with the gap between.

Incredibly, the fighters followed them all the way down, one on each side. It reminded Hope of history vids she'd seen, from nearly a hundred years ago, of the space shuttle *Columbia* flanked by chase planes as it landed on the desert floor. Only when the scramjet's landing gear touched down did the escort jets pull up and away.

"Welcome to Nevatim Airbase," said the pilot. "If you look out the right side of the aircraft, you'll see your greeting party."

In the darkness, it looked like a cluster of lights by a hangar. The plane turned off the runway and taxied toward the hangar. As they approached, Hope saw there were three vehicles waiting: two jeeps and what looked like a turretless tank with four giant wheels on each side. Both jeeps were full of soldiers. One had a machine gun mounted on its top.

"Wow. Cool," said Al.

"An Eitan Mark III armored personnel carrier," said Bruce, "escorted by two Plasan Sand Cats."

"Nothing but the best for you, apparently," said the pilot, emerging from the cockpit. "Better hustle."

Outside, one of the soldiers pushed a gantry ladder to the side of the plane. The pilot opened the hatch. The sounds from outside flooded the cabin—not just the sounds of a military airport, but regular sounds too. The difference was startling. Hope decided her hearing had acclimated to the artificially quiet environment inside the plane.

"Let me give you a hand." Chris helped Bruce with his gear, including the BSS. Al carried the sack of diatomaceous earth. Katie carried the nylon bag containing her busted-up gum machine and the few remaining pieces of gum.

With her backpack over one shoulder, Hope was the last one out. She paused at the hatchway. It was a beautiful night. No clouds. All stars. The night air was very warm. And even with the tarmac so many feet below, she felt the residual heat from the sun-baked asphalt radiating up. She turned to the pilot. "What is that button?" Hope pointed to the thing on the inside of the hatchway.

"It's not a button."

"What is it?"

The pilot shrugged. "A reminder."

"Of what?"

"Of who you are."

It sounded like a riddle. "I don't think I would forget who I am."

"Of who you are, relative to the universe."

"Oh."

"You don't have to press it. Just a touch is enough."

"But why?"

"Respect. But I know that's not the answer you're looking for. I guess the simplest answer is: for good luck."

"Can *I* touch it?"

"Of course."

Hope did. And then said, "*Shalom.*"

The pilot smiled. "*Shalom aleichem.*"

When Hope reached the ground, everyone else was already inside the eight-wheeled vehicle. She'd barely sat down in the armored personnel carrier when the female soldier outside slid the heavy door shut. The convoy of three began to roll. One of the jeeps—the one with the big gun on top—led the way, with the other taking up the rear, behind the APC.

Hope knew electric motors of modern trans didn't make much sound, yet she got the impression that these military vehicles didn't make any sound at all. Even the sound of the tires on the road seemed to be cancelled out somehow.

She was about to ask *Who are these people?* when Chris put his index finger to his lips.

The soldier driving the vehicle rotated his seat to face the inside. He pointed to the headset he was wearing and then pointed to the ceiling. Bruce was the first to understand. He detached the headset above him and donned it. Everyone else followed. Following Bruce's example, Hope adjusted the mic in front of her mouth. As soon as her hands were free, she held Chris's hand again. Lucky was seated on the floor, pressed between their legs, like a book between bookends. Lucky forced his nose under their hands.

"Please limit all conversation to only that which is absolutely necessary. Please nod if you understand." Everyone acknowledged. "We are taking you to Masada. ETA, forty-five minutes. I'll have more information once we arrive." He swiveled around to face forward once again.

| | 0 | | 0 | | 0

EYES BLINKING, SKOTINO RETURNED TO CONSCIOUSNESS AND TO THE PRESENT moment inside room number four of the oubliette. The knife was still in his hand—the knife with a double-edged, serrated blade and a hilt decorated with a circle of six golden dots with one larger dot in the center. He wiped the blood from its blade, using Patricia's bare thigh, and sheathed it. He tossed the latex gloves, stood, and glanced at his percomm. It had been one of the longest clarity communions he could remember.

Patricia, unconscious now, was an amazing pharmakos. She had a hard defiance that protected a terrified vulnerability. *It was meant to be. My god, who once ruled over twelve, now over six, has revealed the future. For the chance of reality's path doth tip.*

For such a long clarity event, incredibly, only one word had crossed the threshold from the future to the present: *Masada.*

Chapter 28

"**W**E'RE NOW INSIDE THE CONFINES OF THE NATIONAL PARK," SAID the APC driver. "The Israel Defense Forces, along with UNESCO, control this area. You may speak freely now." He rotated his chair again to face them. "Sergeant Major Cohen, I understand you've been here before?"

"Sergeant major?" repeated Al. "Whoa."

"Retired," Bruce clarified. "Yes, I was here once before."

"Very good. You can give your team a complete history lesson later, to satisfy their curiosities. I'm not a tour guide. Bottom line: Masada is a fortress—always has been, always will be. Public visitations ended years ago, once the terrorist attacks became too frequent. But the cable car system still remains, and it's still the only way up or down. We'll arrive in a few minutes." He looked directly at Bruce. "Once we stop, please lead your team past the old visitor center and to the terminal station, and board the waiting cable car. An aide will greet you at the top." Then he added, in a softer voice, "Your modesty is admirable, Sergeant Major, but I'll simply remind you that your service to the IDF is for life."

Bruce nodded.

The driver didn't ask if they had any questions; he just swiveled back.

Like ghosts floating across a graveyard at night in complete silence, the three vehicles glided along the access road, until coming to a stop in front of the old visitor center. Once the door was open, Bruce, Chris, Hope, Al, and Katie all stepped out with their belongings. Lucky took a leak on one of the eight tires.

"Sorry," said Chris to the soldier who had opened the door.

Hope wasn't sure if the soldier didn't speak English, but it was the driver who responded from inside the vehicle. "Better here than in the cable car. Now get going. And watch your step: there are no lights along the path."

The vehicles had dropped them off at a circular drive in front of the visitor center. The building's windows were boarded up, but Hope could easily imagine a day when school busses and touring coaches lined the curb, surrounded by rivers of tourists and throngs of schoolchildren running to and fro. Chris took Hope's hand. The group followed the path around the right side of the center to the cable car station behind.

Al glanced back to the two groups of soldiers—men and women—as they filed back into the jeeps. He elbowed Chris. "I'm telling you, there's nothing sexier than a woman in combat uniform toting an assault rifle."

"Oh, please," said Katie.

"No, it's true," said Bruce. "Try a search sometime. Tourists post more pics of female soldiers on street corners than any other single sight in Israel. The fascination is probably helped by the fact that mandatory service age is from eighteen to twenty."

Rounding the side of the visitor center, Al looked up and asked, "Is that it? Masada?"

In front of them was a huge mountain, but flat on top, like a mesa. Hope estimated it had to be a thousand feet high. She began to understand why Masada was considered a fortress. There simply was no way up.

"What are those spire things on top?"

In the backdrop of the night sky, Hope could barely make out what Al was referring to. It looked like a series of poles, thicker at the bottom, sticking high into the air, narrowing to a point. There was no rhyme or reason to the angles. It reminded her of that science experiment in high school, the one where touching the conductor full of static electricity made all the hair on your head stand up. The mountain resembled a prickly pinecone, or maybe a spiny sea anemone.

"It's a defense against helicopters or drones or anything else that gets too close," said Bruce. "It'll all be easier to see in the morning. Let's go. I don't know about you guys, but I'm exhausted."

Hope didn't want to sound weak, so she was glad when Bruce said it first, but she was tired too. The APC ride had been so quiet she'd caught herself nodding off a few times.

There were two sides to the terminal station, one for each cable car, each on a separate set of cables. The area was fairly quiet, except for the noticeable hum of the electric motor inside the terminal building, where the cables wrapped around a huge flywheel.

Hope followed as they all piled into the cable car, which was built for crowds of tourists. Thirty people could fit comfortably, double that if crammed in.

The controls looked easy to operate: an industrial-sized green button to start the cycle and a red one under a clear plastic protective lid—an emergency stop. Bruce pressed his palm on the green button. The car began its gentle ascent. If the Hillite named Q was willing to help them free their families and provide a safe place from which to track down the Circle of Six, they would soon find out.

"You all need to read about this place," said Bruce. "It's the site where some of the most epic standoffs in all of human history occurred."

"Q lives here?" asked Katie.

"Yup."

"Isn't that like living in Fort Knox?"

"Maybe even better. It was also a palace for Herod the Great. He fashioned it into a luxury vacation spot, complete with a Roman-style heated public bath. You gotta see the view from the lower terrace. Incredible. It makes you feel like standing with your arms up to the heavens and yelling, 'I am the ruler of all that the light touches,' like some Mayan king."

"Herod the Great? Wow," said Katie. "Q took such a historically significant home as his own? Isn't living in Masada sacrilegious or something?"

"Yeah. Seriously," agreed Al. "Like living at Graceland. Isn't Masada a national treasure?"

"Well, because a Hillite lives here, it justifies the use of government funds to protect it. Or, I should say, Hillites pay the government for protection. As a result, the archeological site gets protection too. A win-win," said Bruce. "By the way, I could be wrong, but I think a Hillite owns and lives at Graceland. It's sad, but governments around the globe no longer have the budget to protect and maintain such treasures. To a terrorist, each is a dream target."

After rising above the height of the visitor center, it was easier to see the surrounding area. Beautiful, but desolate. "I thought the area would be built up more," said Hope. "There's nothing but rock, desert, and that little lake over there."

"The national park is enormous. The Israeli government has preserved the site quite well, I think. There isn't even an army presence inside the park, only at the gates. You're right, it's extremely barren. It's one of the reasons Masada is such a fortress. The armies that laid siege here were forced to endure very harsh conditions, with no source of potable water. That's not a lake over there; it's the Dead Sea. It used to be bigger. A lot bigger."

"No water?" said Al. "Then a siege would be easy. You just surround the mountain until your enemy gets thirsty."

"Yes. One would think," said Bruce with uncharacteristic mystery in his voice. Hope had no idea he was such a history buff. Or maybe he was just reconnecting with his Jewish heritage. "There are legends," he continued. "Some have been verified. Most have not. Even the verified accounts could be described as miracles."

Halfway up, the other car passed them, going in the opposite direction. It was like looking into a mirror in reverse, except that the other car was empty. No one said a word for the remaining minutes to the top. Hope felt the nagging sleepiness gnaw at her. She wondered how her mom was getting along. She couldn't imagine what it must be like for Chris, Katie, and Al to not know what happened to their families. *Mr. Q, the Hillite, better have some answers, or this is going to be one colossal waste of time.*

The cable car bobbed at the top as the heavy cable passed over wheels connected to support beams held up by massive steel girders. The platform at the top didn't go all the way to the plateau but rather just below it. The matrices of girders affixed at 45-degree angles to one another, looking like a skyscraper under construction, formed polygons of raw stability. The girders were secured to the side of the mountain at steel pads built into the rock. The bolts were the size of Hope's thigh.

The platform attached to an excavated ledge with a walkway, just below the mountain's brow. The walkway had rock on three sides and was open on its face. To the right was a modern door, built into the rock. To the left, a stairway made of huge timber planks, like railroad ties, led to the top. Straight ahead was another modern door with a young man, maybe midtwenties, waiting in front of it. "*Shalom*," he said.

"*Shalom*," Bruce replied.

The rest of their group was slow on the draw, including Hope. Maybe it was because they were tired, or maybe because they lacked confidence with the exotic greeting. The delayed response came out as a mishmash of mumbles.

"I'm Jewlz, Q's aide-de-camp." He wore a one-piece short-sleeved getup, like a tunic. It gathered at the waist with what resembled a length of rope, instead of a belt. Sandals completed the ensemble. Hope couldn't decide if it was a local style or some kind of goofy period dress. The materials were modern, so the outfit wasn't trying to be a costume from two thousand years ago. He held his hands close and high, like a chipmunk nibbling a sunflower seed. Facing Bruce, he asked, "And you are?"

"Bruce Cohen."

Jewlz shook Bruce's hand, holding it briefly as he looked directly at him and repeated, "Bruce Cohen." Chris was next. Jewlz greeted him the same way, repeating his name, as if committing it to memory. When it was Hope's turn, she couldn't decide if the behavior was creepy or warm. Maybe it was similar to the Japanese custom: they bow, then touch percomms, and always take a moment to actually read—and appreciate—the credentials of the other person before conversing. A sign of respect. On the other hand, what Jewlz was doing could all be an act.

Finally, Jewlz turned to Lucky, who was sniffing around. Jewlz simply extended his palm, raised his eyebrows, and waited.

"His name is Lucky," said Chris, realizing that even his dog was included in the ritual.

Jewlz repeated, "Lucky."

"Where are your manners?" Chris said to Lucky, snapping his fingers. Lucky froze, with eyes on his master. To Jewlz, Chris said, "Please, call him to you by saying his name." Jewlz did, and Lucky went right to him. "Now," continued Chris, "with your right hand, make a fist, as if you're holding a treat." Chris demonstrated. "He knows you don't have a treat. You're not tricking him. It's just how he learned as a puppy. That's right. Now say, 'Sit.'"

"Sit."

Lucky did. Jewlz was enthralled.

"At this point, it's customary to bring the back of your hand to his nose so he can sniff you. He will remember your unique scent for the rest of his life. Next, drop your hand a little lower, open it, and say, 'Shake.'"

As Jewlz shook the paw, he repeated, "Lucky."

"Finally, you can give him a pat on the head, as praise, to let him know he did a good job."

With the ritual finished, Jewlz stood straight, with a childlike smile. "Enchanting." His hands returned to chipmunk position. "Welcome, all. Please, follow me." The center door opened with a swish.

Bruce followed without hesitation.

Al didn't move right away. He turned to the rest of them with a questioning look. Chris shrugged and nodded. So they followed.

The inside was modern but stark. Smooth floor. Bare walls. The ceiling offered illumination but from no particular source, as if the entire surface was glowing. Obviously, this area was a relatively recent addition, not part of the archeological site. They followed Jewlz down a short set of stairs. After several turns, they arrived at a hall with a series of doors along one side.

"Six bedchambers," said Jewlz. "One for each of you. Even your canine companion."

"Bedrooms? Hold on," said Chris. "I thought we were going to meet Q?"

"In the morning," said Jewlz.

"But we—"

Bruce put his hand on Chris's shoulder. The grim look on his face suggested they needed to be patient.

Al quipped, "When in the palace of Herod the Great, do as the Romans do."

"Ah, I see you have a poet in your group," said Jewlz.

"Lucky won't need a room," said Chris. "He can stay with me."

Hope squeezed Chris's hand. *Me too*, she thought.

"As you wish. You'll find food, drink, and lavatory facilities inside. The local time is now three o'clock. A chime will sound at six. I will be waiting for you here at half past." Jewlz turned and vanished behind the corner.

"Three hours from now," said Chris. "I guess that's almost right away. I didn't realize how late it was."

"I'm eager, too," said Katie, "but if I can just close my eyes for a few hours, I think I'll be in better shape to talk to Q."

Al agreed.

Bruce was already on his way to the first room. "Nighty night," he said, just before the door swished closed behind him.

As the group proceeded down the hall, one by one, they peeled off. First Katie. Then Al.

At the next door, Hope turned to Chris. "I want to stay with you."

He smiled. She followed him inside. Lucky sniffed around.

The room was extremely modern, like a suite in the most luxurious hotel she could imagine. Looking at the bed, Hope thought, *King-sized. Why am I not surprised?*

Chris casually explored the room, checking things out.

She put her backpack down and walked over to check out the bathroom. A generous sink area, a separate toilet room, a walk-in shower, and a separate tub—one of the big kind, like a hot tub. Gorgeous marble everywhere.

Chris was just looking at her. He was standing next to a small refrigerator under a countertop, with cupboards above.

"Hungry?" she asked.

"You have no idea," he said. "But first . . . Remember on the plane? I wanted to tell you something."

She nodded.

He sat on the bed and held out his hand.

She took it and sat next to him.

A splashing noise came from the bathroom as Lucky lapped water from the toilet bowl.

"So romantic," Hope said playfully.

"I know." Chris laughed. "Actually, it's perfect ambiance, because I have no idea what I'm doing. In fact, worse—I don't even know what I don't know."

"So?"

"So we go slow," he said.

"OK."

He paused. "That's all I got."

"Really? That's what you wanted to tell me on the plane?"

"Oh. Right. OK. Hmm. How do I say this?"

"You're killing me," she said. "Look, Chris Lumière, I'm no expert, but let me give you lesson number one on dealing with women: It's your thoughts and feelings that get us hot and bothered. Tell me, you big tease. Tell me what you're thinking."

"I . . . It's embarrassing."

"That's the best kind. Go! You're killing me."

"I mean, it's not just embarrassing . . . Maybe *shameful* is a better word."

"Go on."

He leaned back. "This." He put his hands up. Without touching her, he shifted his hands like a mime, as if she were a campfire and he was warming his hands, or like he was sensing the aura of a shimmering idol. "All this."

She looked at herself. "What?"

"You're incredible. You're gorgeous. Not just when you walked out with Katie today. Not just the outfit, which is smokin' hot, by the way. You—"

She kissed him. It was a long, deep kiss. It was the unfinished chapter of the kiss on the masstran. She released him. "And?"

He squirmed.

"Just say it."

"I want to touch you."

"What part of me?"

"All of you," he said. "Give me a break. I haven't thought that far ahead."

"Bullshit."

"OK, fine. You're right. But real life is not the same as imagination. I'm trying to convert feelings—no, *longings*—into words. I don't want to be a perv."

"Impossible."

"No, you said it yourself: girls are all about thoughts and feelings. I'd gamble you don't have doubts about mine, and I'm happy to share my feelings with you all day long. But there's more."

"You're right. I misspoke. The flesh matters to women too. I guess it's a matter of priorities. No, that's still wrong. It's a matter of order. Yes, that's it. Your instinct to go slow is perfect. Everything will come together at the right time."

He smiled and relaxed.

"Give me your hand," she said. She held it with both of hers and caressed it.

"What are you looking at?"

"Nothing in particular." Eventually, she looked up. "I'll tell you what, I'll get cleaned up, and when I come out, it'll be your turn in the bathroom. When you come out, I'll be under the covers, undressed. Then you can get under and take off *your* clothes."

He nodded.

"Or you can come out naked."

"No, no." He laughed. "I like your plan."

She dashed back to the bath area. It was fully stocked. For one person, anyway. She called out to him. "Only one toothbrush."

As she washed her face, she wondered if he could sense her many fantasies about his incredible hands—if that was why he'd gestured touching her all over. *No*, she decided, *every boy wants to touch. Thank goodness he doesn't know what a turn-on his hands are.*

After brushing her teeth, she set the toothbrush down, stepped back from the sink, and assessed her body in the mirror. After having endured catcalls her entire postpubescent life, she was surprised by her feelings—a subtle fear of inadequacy. She decided it must be because of how much she cared for him. She never doubted the sex appeal of her physical endowments, or her ability to get a man fired up. Yet, now, there was so much at stake. *What if he doesn't like what he touches? Am I being absurd? Is it even possible for guys to dislike touching skin where the sun never shines?* The gravity of the moment made it all that much more thrilling. *This is it*, she thought. She had dreamed about this moment countless times, played it out in countless variations. *This is it.*

She found Chris stretched out on the bed, fast asleep. Mouth open. Not snoring but breathing heavily. She walked to the bedside and watched him for a minute. She lifted the covers and slipped in next to him. Nothing. He didn't even stir.

She thought about waking him. *No.* She decided to leave the lights on and just lie next to him. His hands. His lips. Even with his mouth open, his lips were tantalizing, in a French kiss sort of way. If only she could see his blue eyes, under his eyelids.

The fog of sleep came quickly. *Just as well*, she thought. *It can wait. Another time.*

CHAPTER 29

IN THE MORNING, JEWLZ ESCORTED THEM TO A SPOT OUTSIDE ON THE LEDGE across from the cable car platform. With no greeting at all, Q got straight to business, but the Hillite had his own idea about which of his Masada fortress visitors he would be meeting with. He pointed to Hope and Chris. "Her. And him. Only."

"What? Wait," said Al. "*All* our families are being held without due process, not just his."

"Frankly, Mr. Fuentes, I'm not interested in the fate of your loved ones. If I can help them, I will, but I have other priorities."

From the moment they had stepped outside to meet Q, he seemed full of hostility, as if he was angry with them. Hope remembered when Chris and Bruce talked earlier that summer about the mysterious Hillite and his generous funding of the K9 search-and-rescue team. From that description, she would never have expected such hostility.

Q was short for a man, about her height. But she suspected it was from age. He might have been six feet at one time, but he had that compressed look that old people get. He looked about seventy years old. Or he could've been fifty and spent his life under the blistering sun in this sand-blasted land. Or maybe a hundred years old and had the benefit of plastic surgery. His complexion was light brown, and he spoke with an accent. Hope assumed he was Israeli, but considering the surroundings, it was a challenge to entertain any other possibility. He was bald, except for a translucent crown of white stubble. He resembled a Jewish Gandhi without the mustache.

Hope was thankful for the few hours of sleep. It'd given her the strength to deal with Q. Even the food was awesome. She didn't know what half of it was, but everything had been delicious. So many things made with fresh vegetables or fresh fruits—all from the mini kitchen in the bedroom. The bread was even warm. She didn't know how they did it.

The morning heat was intense. Hope wondered how hot it might become by midafternoon. She realized the tunic was probably more function than fashion. Like Jewlz, Q also wore a tunic and sandals. However, Q's tunic had more embellishments, but not garishly so. He wore spectacles. During her lifetime, Hope had seen very few people with corrective lenses. Eyeglasses were something you only saw in period vids on the pubcomm.

"Why didn't you just say that in the first place?" said Katie. "We would have stayed home, saved ourselves a lot of trouble."

"The situation is different now," said Q.

"How?" asked Katie.

"That's what I'm going to tell Ms. Avenir."

Al said, "We all need to hear."

Q said nothing. Apparently the absence of even the remotest possibility meant no response was warranted.

Chris asked, "Why me?"

For the first time, the hostility started to ease. Q looked at Bruce and then back to Chris. "When my friend Bruce contacted me weeks ago, asking for permission to use one of my private planes, I was certainly surprised to learn you had stumbled on a group of Hoods abducting young women. I was even more surprised that you planned to rescue them. But I couldn't think of anyone better than Bruce to help you. He told me about you, Mr. Lumière. To be honest, I'm not sure *why you*. I just sense it." Q looked at each of them in turn.

"You all know Chris best. I dare any of you to tell me I should ignore my instincts."

Katie shook her head.

Al acquiesced.

Bruce asked, "How long will you be?"

"Three hours. No more."

Bruce nodded. "We are here at your invitation. We need to plead our case to win your support. We'll do as you ask. Q, let me just say, I was humbled, just now, when you called me your friend. As your friend, I implore you—please hurry. There's so much more to explain. It's not just the warrantlessly detained families. There's much more. There's great danger. Danger driven by great evil. I don't know how much time we have before it finds us."

Al asked, "What should *we* do? Just wait here?"

"We need to be ready," said Bruce. "I'm going to get the BSS from my room. Want to join me?"

"Sure," said Al reluctantly, but Hope detected excitement in his voice.

"Katie?"

"Nah. I'll take Lucky for a walk. He hasn't done his morning business yet," she said. "I should probably take the cable car down. I'm sure you don't want a dog squatting on your ancient artifacts."

"No, stay up here," said Q. "The area below is not guarded. There are suitable places on the plateau above. Jewlz will accompany you."

Chris pulled a wad of plastic bags from his pocket and handed one to Katie.

"And remember," said Al, "don't watch him. It makes him blush."

"Very funny," said Katie. "Come on, Lucky." She followed Jewlz up the steps.

Bruce turned and headed for the center door, with Al following.

Q said, to Hope and Chris, "This way. Follow me."

Hope followed Q and Chris to the far door, which turned out to be an elevator. The inside was air-conditioned. Hope was relieved because she'd gotten overheated during just the few minutes outside.

"Down," said Q.

"I'm sorry. Unable to comply." Hope recognized the voice from the plane. It was Gladys, the AI virtual assistant. "I'm detecting weight in the elevator car that is unaccounted for. After subtracting your weight and that of Ms. Hope Avenir, I can only assume there is an undetected passenger present."

Q glanced at Chris.

"Did Bruce also tell you about my, uh, condition?" asked Chris.

Q nodded. "Gladys, override."

"Override sequence initiated. Redundant authentications will be required."

"Begin," said Q.

"Please present the key you *have*."

Q made a fist with his right hand. Hope saw a ring, a fairly large ring, like a high school or college ring. He touched it to the elevator panel.

"Accepted. Please present the key you *know*."

"Phineas Quimby. Authorization code 1 16 1866."

Quimby? thought Hope. *Does Q stand for Quimby? Does he trust us enough to hear his true name?*

"Accepted. Please present the key you *are*."

Q leaned to the panel, where a red light appeared. He let it shine into his right eye.

"Authentication accepted. Override authorized."

The elevator descended.

Chris took Hope's hand. She was pleased. After the chime had woken them up that morning, he'd been a little miffed she hadn't roused him for their tryst. He was probably embarrassed and disappointed. And maybe he felt responsible for her disappointment—disappointment she couldn't completely suppress.

Hope realized the elevator ride was taking longer than expected.

Chris was the first to speak up. "How far down are we going?"

"The mountain is three hundred meters high. We are going another three hundred meters below that. In total, about two hundred stories."

The door opened to a hallway not unlike the ones above—featureless, but much larger. Hope judged it to be about thirty feet across and thirty feet high. The square tunnel extended into darkness. As they stepped from the elevator, the light seemed to follow them, illuminating the area where they walked but not much beyond that. The effect created the sensation that the tunnel was infinitely long.

They reached a door on the right marked *641*A. Next to the door was a rectangular observation window. Q gestured. Soft lighting came up in the area beyond the glass. It was a room with black walls, a black ceiling, and a black floor, and filled with rows of glossy black pillars, each about two meters high.

"When you arrived, did you notice the body of water nearby?"

"Yes," said Chris. "Bruce told us it's the Dead Sea."

"It is. We are near the spot where archeologists discovered some of the oldest surviving documents of mankind: the Dead Sea Scrolls. The documents form the foundation of many religions. Do you know why the scrolls were there?"

"No," said Chris.

Hope shook her head.

"Well, you're not alone. No one knows for sure. But all historians agree on one point: the scrolls were hidden to preserve the religious manuscripts beyond an event of mass anarchy. Whoever hid the information had a sense of a growing and impending destabilization of human civilization. And they were right. The lawlessness and destruction that followed nearly wiped the information from the face of the earth. The scrolls include core texts of the Hebrew Bible. For example, the teachings Moses received from God, essentially God's law." Q turned to them. "Decades ago, I sensed a similar destabilization of our modern world. I'm now convinced the integrity of our institutions is weakening every day. So I created this place to store the entire digital record of humanity. I call it Echo."

"What? That's impossible," said Hope.

"Why impossible?"

"You don't have access to data stored by others."

"True. But what if—instead of trying to access data stored by others—I simply recorded the transmission of the data passing across the global network that initially created it? In so doing, I could re-create a copy of the stored data."

"Fine, but all the transmissions are encrypted. You can't read them."

Q looked at her with a penetrating stare. "I know very little about you, Ms. Avenir, but I do know that encrypted communications never got in *your* way."

"You brought me here to decrypt data for you?"

"No. I'm just pointing out that I can record data without processing it. And someone like you could decrypt it, if so motivated."

"OK, I'll grant you that. But recording *everything* is still impossible."

"Why?"

"Civilization generates too much data."

"How much?"

"I don't—"

"Twelve thousand exabytes per year," said Q, "give or take a few bytes. The world's population has been declining for decades. And the continually declining birthrate means the amount of data generated will be even less in the future. That estimate includes everything—every video communication, every financial transaction, every conversation overheard by every seccomm system on the planet, with all duplicates included. If one million people streamed the latest viral episode of whatever cinematic piece of goat dung happens to be popular at the moment, then all one million transmissions are recorded here."

"My point exactly. It's too much data."

"Why?"

"The required storage technology doesn't exist. It would be enormous."

"Really? Ms. Avenir, how much do you weigh?"

"Excuse me?"

"I'm asking you how much you weigh. You don't need to be exact. If you're vain, feel free to lie."

"One hundred thirty pounds."

"One gram of DNA can store two hundred fifteen petabytes uncompressed. Using 3-D holographic compression, a gram can hold three hundred exabytes. Let's see . . ." His eyes looked up as he tapped his chin and began mumbling. "One hundred thirty pounds converted to grams . . . times one billion gigabytes . . . carry the one—"

Hope giggled. She glanced at Chris, but he wasn't getting the humor.

Q brought his gaze back down and winked at her. "Anyway, the DNA contained in the volume of the average human body can store twenty-three million exabytes. You, Ms. Avenir, can store about two thousand years of recorded data all by yourself—literally, two millennia."

Hope looked through the glass. "That's DNA in there?"

"Yes. Actually, a more complex arrangement of RNA, but basically, yes. My experts predict it will remain stable for sixty thousand years. No power required. The temperature of the surrounding rock, this far underground, remains consistent."

"What about speed? How can you encode the molecules fast enough?"

"Passive quantum lithography."

"3-D printing? You're 3-D printing DNA?"

"Not quite. The molecules are already in place. The process simply organizes them."

"What do you mean by *passive*? I'm not familiar with that technique."

"That's the key to the speed. The data doesn't have to be processed in order to be written. The data stream writes itself," said Q. "Consider Thomas Edison's gramophone. The sound vibrations went directly onto the rotating drum of tinfoil, essentially freezing the sound in real time, preserving it, with the ability to be reproduced at any time in the future. The gramophone analogy is the inspiration behind the name I selected for this underground repository beneath one of the greatest fortresses of all time: Echo. This"—he extended his arm in a sweeping gesture and turned—"is a high-fidelity recording of the cacophony of digital vibrations representing all of human knowledge—frozen, preserved, able to be reproduced and decrypted at any time."

"How do you read the data?"

"A scanner. Essentially, we use a medical scanner to report the exact positions of the molecules. Except . . ."

"Except what?"

"Except, we are unable read *your* data, Ms. Avenir. It isn't merely that your data can't be decrypted. It's as if your data doesn't exist at all. Using the gramophone analogy, your data doesn't vibrate. Its only evidence comes from the data surrounding it. Do you know what my team of experts has nicknamed the data that you generate?"

Hope shook her head.

"Dark data. Just as dark matter can only be detected by measuring how the surrounding regular matter is affected, your data can only be detected by its effect on the surrounding data. You, Hope Avenir, are a digital black hole, detectable only by your digital event horizon."

| | 0 | | 0 | | 0

"AND OVER HERE," SAID JEWLZ, "IS WHERE THE ROMANS BUILT A MASSIVE earthen ramp. The Jewish rebels were fully protected, so the Romans had no choice but to get their siege engines closer." Looking out from the edge of the mountaintop fortress, opposite the visitor center below, Jewlz pointed to an enormous wedge of earth rising toward the fortress. It looked like a freeway on-ramp from the time of Fred Flintstone.

"Amazing," said Katie. Maybe the APC driver wasn't a very good tour guide, but Jewlz certainly was. "Did it work?"

"Yes, eventually."

"We were wondering why a simple blockage never worked. How did the fortress dwellers get fresh water?"

"A complex system of cisterns captured rainwater. I'll show you." He motioned Katie back to the edge facing the visitor center, over the upper cable car terminal. She followed him under the crisscrossing antihelicopter spires.

"See? Along the ridge, there." He pointed to a spot not far from where the cables connected to the mountain. "And also—" He stopped midsentence and was looking toward the visitor center.

Katie saw it too. Two vehicles had pulled up. A limousine and a utility van behind it. "Who's that?" asked Katie.

"I don't know. But they are not permitted to be here."

She watched as two men got out of the limo and two men got out of the van.

Jewlz said, "Come with me."

She followed him back down the lumber staircase to the ledge. The four men had reached the lower terminal and were inside the cable car. Katie asked, "Can they get up here?"

"No. Only people approved by the virtas can operate the controls," said Jewlz. "Gladys," he called out, "identify visitors."

"No visitors detected."

"How can that be? I can plainly see—"

"Jewlz!" Katie screamed. "We have a serious problem! We cannot let those men up here."

"As I said, there is no way—"

One of the men, a young man in shorts and a white T-shirt, had climbed the access ladder in the cable car, opened the roof hatch, and was now climbing the support arm leading to the cable—the same cable that reached all the way to the top.

"Gladys," said Jewlz, "notify Q of the situation."

"Acknowledged. Notification sent."

"Gladys," said Katie, "connect me with Bruce Cohen."

"Connected."

Immediately, Katie heard both Bruce and Al. They were laughing it up about something.

"Al! Bruce!"

The laughter stopped. "What?"

"They're here. The Circle of Six is here. One of them, the monster with the vicelike grip that Chris described, is climbing the cable. Bring the BSS. Bring the gum. Bring the diatomaceous earth. And get out here!"

110 110 110

"NO, YOU MUSTN'T LEAVE JUST YET," SAID Q. "THERE IS MORE YOU MUST SEE."

"Later!" said Chris. "We have to get back up." Hope and Chris were already in the elevator. They held the door for Q, who was shuffling as fast as he could.

"We are safe here," said Q. "There's no need to worry." The doors closed. "Up."

"We are *not* safe," said Chris. "Listen, we trust you. But you have to trust us. What defenses do you have?"

"None. The Israeli military provides all our protection."

"Alert them. Tell them to come. Tell them we need help."

"Very well. Gladys, I declare an emergency. Intruders. Notify the authorities."

"Acknowledged. Notification sent."

Q said, "It may take time for them to respond. This has never happened before. They may suspect a malfunction."

"You have to comm them personally. Please. You—"

Even before the elevator doors fully opened, the sound of Lucky's urgent barking prepared them for the panicked scene unfolding. The monster who had squeezed the life out of Hope's apartment manager had Al, Katie, Jewlz, and Bruce backed up against the rock wall. From behind, Lucky was barking at his feet. The guy was taking swipes at him, but Lucky stayed out of reach.

Bruce had apparently unloaded the BSS on the menace. Epoxy-coated carbon fiber snare strips were stuck to the guy's legs, chest, and arms. There was a trail of strips from the platform leading to where he now advanced on their cornered friends. At one point, the guy must have pulled a strip from his chest, and ripped away his T-shirt along with it, because the torn shirt, still entwined in strips, lay on the ground halfway from the platform.

"Chris! Here! Catch!" cried Katie. She whipped the nylon bag. It was a perfect throw.

Incredibly, the monster snatched it out of the air, effortlessly, and tossed it over the mountain's edge. The shock on Katie's face was unbearable. Then an apparent epiphany. She yelled, "Lucky has one." She pointed to her throat.

Suddenly, the menace seemed to completely lose interest in Al, Katie, and Bruce. He turned and zeroed in on Chris.

Al took advantage of the moment. With both hands overhead, as if throwing a soccer ball from the sideline, he threw the paper sack of diatomaceous earth. The sack exploded in a cloud of white dust across the guy's back. Uncaring or unaffected, he kept moving—and at an alarming speed, Hope noticed. Unlike the creaky, gravel-covered surface of her apartment roof, the guy had no trouble gaining traction here. Still ignoring the group behind him, the monster closed in on Chris, Hope, and Q. Lucky barked while backing up, but it made no difference.

Hope remembered the security mumbo jumbo with the elevator. It would take forever. They were trapped.

Even before the cloud of diatomaceous dust had fully cleared, and while there was still room to get by, Chris took Hope by the hand, pulled her to the platform, and into the empty car. Chris whistled for his dog. Lucky stopped barking and raced around even as Hope slapped down on the green button. The car swung away from the platform. Lucky leapt across the widening gap to where Chris held the door open.

The shirtless teen climbed from the platform, up into the labyrinth of girders. As the car glided away, they watched him scale the industrial-sized jungle gym and then leap onto the moving cable. The car bobbed as the cable took the weight. Hand over hand, he closed in on them.

"This isn't any better," said Hope. "He'll reach us before we reach the bottom."

"I know. But I only need a few seconds," said Chris. "We have to stop him here and now or he'll get us all eventually."

The guy came even faster by allowing himself to free-fall between each swing. The rhythmic force sent waves across the cable that grew in amplitude with each grab. The car rocked so violently that Hope and Chris had to hold on to avoid being thrown to the floor. She wondered if the support arm might break. Fortunately, the waves made it hard for the guy to grab the cable, and he was forced to slow down.

"How are you going to stop him?"

"I'll fly over there. I can knock him off. We can stop the cable car and go back up. Be ready to press the red button."

"You don't have any gum."

"I had Lucky carry a piece, just in case." Chris bent down. "Come here, pal."

Lucky had trouble moving. He had all four legs splayed out to steady himself as the car rolled from side to side. His nails were fully extended as he tried to get traction on the smooth floor. With the scratching sound of dog nails against the slick man-made surface, he scrambled toward Chris, nearly crashing into him.

Chris got hold of the plastic cylinder attached at Lucky's collar and worked to get the lid open.

Hope turned back to check the monster's progress. "Whatever you do, don't let him get a hold of you."

"I won't," said Chris from behind. "If I can't knock him off, I'll come back for you and Lucky, and I'll fly you away. We'll find some other way to stop him. I may have no choice but to rip the cables off the mountain."

The slope of the descent became less vertical as they neared the bottom. The freak was close enough now for her to see his bare chest and the white powder across his shoulders.

"Hurry up."

"I am."

Lucky barked.

"What's wrong?"

"Nothing."

"What are you waiting for?" She turned.

Chris was halfway up the maintenance ladder.

"Chew the gum already."

"I will." He climbed the few rungs and opened the hatch above.

Lucky barked.

She looked out the window. Hand over hand, the monster kept coming. Several strips clung to his body at odd angles, making him look like he'd just rolled out of a haystack.

Lucky barked again.

Chris hadn't appeared yet. *Did he fly straight up? Where is he?*

Lucky barked three times.

"Not now," Hope yelled, turning. She froze when she saw Lucky pawing at the edge where the door met the floor. "Oh my god." *The gum? Chris doesn't have the gum?* She turned back and pressed her face against the glass to look up. Chris had climbed the support arm and was now making his way toward the monster, also hand over hand.

"Oh my god, no. Chris, no!"

Lucky barked again.

She lunged toward the spot where Lucky was pawing but was knocked to the floor. On hands and knees, she crawled. She peered into the narrow gap where Lucky was scratching. There was a bright-blue morsel down in the door's track. It had fallen down under the roller wheel. She reached, but the space was too tight, and only her fingers made it through. Frantically, she forced her hand as hard as she could. The metal edges sliced into her skin at the knuckles. No good. The gum was still out of reach by a good six inches.

"Chris!" She ran back to the glass. "Chris!" *Why is he doing this? He doesn't have to do this.* "Stop! Don't!"

She watched as the two figures clashed. The monster reached for a hold on Chris. Chris kicked at the arm the guy was hanging by. No good. Chris swung back, and then kicked again with all his momentum. Nothing. Chris avoided the free hand swiping at him. With another tremendous heave, Chris kicked yet again. This time, in a surprising move, the guy grabbed Chris's kicking leg *with the hand that had been holding on to the cable*. Chris couldn't possibly hold all the weight. Both of them tumbled.

"No!" As if in a dream, she watched their bodies fall silently. At such a height, she had to press her face against the glass to keep them in sight as they dropped. She saw them hit. "No!"

Their bodies were small. The car was still bobbing, but she peered through the glare of the glass for any movement, any sign of life. Eventually—she wasn't sure exactly how many seconds had passed—she felt the car slow as it approached the bottom platform. She had to pull herself away from the sight of the two bodies. Turning, she saw her mom at the platform, held at gunpoint by the lumberjack-sized man, the one who'd cornered her on the apartment rooftop.

Hope's desperate need to know if Chris had survived was suddenly sidelined by the sight of her mom with the gun to her head—a sight that forced Hope to recall her own experience of being held at gunpoint by the Circle of Six.

You can't fool me, thought Hope. She'd seen the trick before. It wasn't really her mom. It was the black man who was able to change himself to look like Sue Avenir.

Lucky barked when the cable car door opened.

"Step out," said the big man.

She wasn't fooled. She went for the green button by the door.

"It's really me."

The sound of her mom's voice forced her to stop and look.

"Bullshit," said Hope, fighting the paralysis.

"They came to the church. Father Arnold is dead." The words grabbed Hope like a tractor beam.

"No."

The big man said, "How else would we know that information? We've been chasing you. From the church, to the Philadelphia airport, to here. Somehow, you managed to stay one step ahead. But now it's over. Do exactly as I say, or your mom dies." In a strangely conversational voice, he added, "How could you leave your mom completely unprotected?"

Even though the cable car was no longer bobbing, everything in her field of view began to twist and fold.

"I didn't," said Hope. *But I did*, she realized. *Tony or Travis should have stayed with Mom. How could I be so stupid?*

"Come out of the cable car," said the man. "Come help your mother. Be a good daughter."

Like a sleepwalker, she obeyed.

"Keep going," said the man, once Hope reached them. He followed behind her while still holding Sue. "Ignore the dog."

Lucky? Was Lucky barking? She heard the barking. Or did she? She tried to cling to the sound, the sound that wasn't there. Or was it? The barking was like the blare of an alarm clock trying to penetrate the fog of a catatonic slumber.

"Drop the weapon." The unknown voice had broken the spell. Two IDF soldiers held a position near the corner of the visitor center, rifles aimed.

Hope glanced behind her and saw, plainly now, that it *was* the black man in disguise. *I knew it!* But now there was no way to get back to the cable car.

One of the two soldiers motioned for her to come forward. He kept his finger on the trigger and his aim on the two men behind her. With Lucky at her side, she ran.

"Drop the weapon," repeated the soldier as she passed.

She didn't stop or wait to see what happened, she just kept running. At the circle drive, she saw the IDF APC, along with the two jeeps, each with a group of soldiers.

The APC driver beckoned her. "We came as fast as we could," he said. "Who are—"

Two shots rang out. *Oh god.* Hope realized the Circle of Six had discovered some festering guilt in the soldiers' pasts and used it to paralyze them, to bind them in a tangle of second-guessing and self-recrimination. It had worked on her just moments before, when they'd accused her of being a bad daughter, and earlier, on the rooftop of her apartment building, when they'd accused her of ignoring Chris's pleas for her help with freeing his parents. The two soldiers were surely dead.

At the sound of the gunfire, the other soldiers—the ones next to the jeeps—crouched down and scanned for the shooter. One of the groups of soldiers didn't have time to find cover before automatic rifle fire ripped through their ranks. The two Circle of Six men emerged from the side of the visitor center, firing the weapons they'd taken from the two executed soldiers. The group of soldiers fell to the ground, each of them dead or dying. Bullets continued to ricochet off their vehicle.

The second group of soldiers managed to take cover behind their jeep and returned fire.

"Over here," yelled the APC driver.

Hope and Lucky dashed to join the driver behind the heavily armored vehicle.

The remaining group of soldiers had the two Circle of Six men pinned down behind the wall of the visitor center. One soldier manned the machine gun atop the jeep. He cocked it and began firing controlled bursts. He yelled, to the driver, "Get the civilian out of here. Call for backup."

The driver hadn't even had time to react when all attention turned to a figure rising from the boulders at the foot of the mountain, coming straight for them. The gunner swiveled the machine gun, took aim, and fired. Bullets pounded the monster, making a sound Hope never would have expected—not like hitting flesh, but not like hitting metal either. Incredibly, the bullets had no effect, except that his denim shorts exploded into puffs of fabric. Freakishly, the guy had some kind of tube at his crotch. Connected to the tube was a yellow box, and it, too, exploded under the hail of bullets. The machine gun bursts continued, but the threat kept advancing. Brass casings rained down from the machine gun at the same rate the blunted bullets rained down at the monster's plodding feet. The guy was bald now, after the wig had been blasted off.

The soldiers behind the jeep, in self-defense, ceased covering fire on the Circle of Six men and instead fired at the bald and naked form advancing upon them.

The monster reached the soldiers, grabbed the jeep, and flipped it as if it were a toy. Horribly, the machine gunner was crushed underneath. The remaining soldiers backed away. One wasn't so lucky. There was a momentary scream accompanied by a spray of blood. The soldier's comrades tried to free their friend. Hope couldn't watch. One by one, the soldiers popped like so many zits.

"Get inside," yelled the APC driver. "We'll be safe. I'll comm for help." He had his sidearm out and fired three shots at the freak now headed their way.

Hope couldn't trust even the safety of the APC. She glanced in the direction of the mountain, where the monster had emerged, and searched for any sign of Chris. Nothing. She turned and ran.

"No!" the driver pleaded.

From behind, she heard three more shots, and then the sound of the APC's door slamming shut.

She ran. With Lucky at her side, she ran as fast as she could. She resisted the temptation to look back and just kept running. But before long, she tired. Finally, she decided it didn't matter if she looked back. In the distance, she saw the APC was on fire, and . . . *the naked, bald freak was charging after her!*

Drenched in sweat, she found new strength and started running again. She scanned the horizon ahead for anything or anyone to help her. To the right, about a half mile away and parallel to the road, was a berm. The berm had a chain-link fence with barbed wire on top—apparently the border of the national park. To the left was a desolate expanse once occupied, according to Q, by the Dead Sea. She had no choice but to keep running straight. The view of the road ahead was distorted by thermal waves rising from the asphalt. It was no use. The heat was unbearable. She simply couldn't run anymore. She looked back.

At first, she didn't see the guy. Then, through the shimmering waves, she saw him get up. He was way back there. He stumbled and fell. He got up again, staggered, and dropped to his knees.

She didn't wait to find out why. She pressed on. *This road must lead to a gate. There'll be more soldiers there, right?* Unfortunately, the paved road ultimately transitioned into a dirt road. She followed it. Gradually, the parallel gaps in the brush narrowed, becoming lost in uniformity, until any remaining trace of the road finally vanished into featureless sand and dry shrubs. She saw why. The strip of the ancient shore she'd been following had narrowed to a place where the berm rose to high cliffs at the end of the seabed. The barbed-wire fence curved from the right and up the wall of rock ahead. She had no choice but to walk on the dry seabed.

The ground was crusted with salt. Lucky yelped. She went to him. The points of the crystals were incredibly sharp and had found their way into the delicate skin between his toes. Lucky began to search for paths with the least amount of salt.

Behind her, she heard the distant sound of a helicopter. Judging by its proximity to the column of smoke, she figured it must be above the visitor center. It circled. She waved. But it was too far away. The helicopter began to spin as if it was being held by its tail. It looked out of control, or as if it lost power. The rotors slowed to where she could actually see them turning. It went down faster than it should have for a normal landing, but not so fast that it would crash. With too much terrain in the way, she couldn't see it actually hit. Again, her instincts told her the soldiers weren't in control of the situation. She continued on as fast as she could.

"ARE YOU READY TO BEGIN?" ASKED Q. ONE OF THE ROOMS WITHIN MASADA had been prepared for the small ceremony.

Katie pulled herself together and nodded. Al and Bruce nodded too.

As stern as Q had been initially, he was extremely compassionate about their loss. The three of them, in shock, couldn't think pragmatically. Q had taken care of everything. It was he who'd encouraged them to have the ceremony, to try to find closure, to start the process.

It had taken the IDF the rest of the day to secure the national park. They had taken advantage of the cooler hours overnight to retrieve Chris's body. Bruce had volunteered to identify it. Katie knew—looking down now—that inside the military body bag in front of her, Chris's body was crushed and disfigured. She was thankful for the bag because she didn't want to have such a horrific image haunting her for the rest of her life.

The rest of my life? she asked herself. *That could end tomorrow. We could all be dead tomorrow. Just like Chris.*

She cried again, causing Q to wait before starting the ceremony. Al held her tight. Al had cried when the body was brought up, but he wasn't crying now. She was thankful for that, too, because when he cried, she felt like she would never stop. Crying—it was as contagious as yawning and as irrepressible as hiccupping. She didn't know how he was able to stay strong.

No one had heard from Hope. The IDF had found her percomm, smashed, in the middle of the dry seabed. A barely detectable trail of dog blood continued away from that spot until it ended abruptly without a trace. The Circle of Six men and their vehicles had disappeared along with the bald and naked monster. *Did Hope get away?*

Katie's sobs lessened.

Q started the ceremony. "Dearly beloved, we are gathered here . . ."

Katie wasn't really listening. Chris's death simply didn't seem possible. She expected the zipper to open and Chris to roll out like his old self, smiling and joking with them.

Her attention returned when she heard the music and realized Q had stopped talking. She recognized the tune. "On Eagle's Wings." *Oh my god, Chris!* The tears came again. *Who wrote this godforsaken song? It's torture!* She felt like it would rip her heart out.

It was too much. She cried out, "Chris, it was *my* fault." She lunged, breaking away from Al. Reaching the table, she put both hands on the bag. "I never should've tried to throw the gum. It was all my fault. I'm an idiot. I—" Her voice was choked off by more tears. She buried her face in her hands. Al came to her side, wrapping her under his arm once again.

"No," said Al.

"No," repeated Bruce. "It's not your fault. No way. We all did what we could. You mustn't blame yourself."

The music continued to play, twisting her heart like a towel wrung dry.

When the song finally ended, Q said, "I now invite you to say a few words."

Al and Bruce looked at her. She shook her head. "I already said what I needed to say."

Bruce looked at Al.

Al cleared his throat. "I have no memory of a life without him. He was more than a friend. He was more than a brother. I looked up to him. And I was humbled because he looked up to me." He squeezed Katie's shoulder. "I remember one time: The three of us were at my house. We were getting a little out of hand. My dad yelled at us. I yelled back with some wise-crack. My dad said, 'Don't be a smartass.' And Chris yelled back,

'Better than a dumbass.'" Al chuckled, and Katie couldn't help but laugh too.

Somber again, Al said, "Chris, you always had my back. And I followed you everywhere. Maybe that's why it seemed like we were always going in circles."

The word hung over them like a storm cloud. *Circle of Six*, thought Katie. *Those fuckers.*

Al continued, "I don't know anyone who gave more of themselves than you. You never asked for the warden's presence. You never wanted to be a hero, or anyone's savior. You only wanted to love others and to help everyone." His chin started to quiver. "I miss you, buddy."

She could feel Al's entire body tremble.

He wiped his face. "I love you, man. I—"

Convulsive sobs cut off the words. Al buckled over and bawled onto his crossed forearms, with his friend's lifeless body underneath.

It was Katie's turn to be strong. *I loved you too, Chris. We all did.* She held Al. A duo now, a trio no more.

ACKNOWLEDGEMENTS

I AM GRATEFUL, BEYOND WHAT I CAN EXPRESS HERE, TO THOSE WHO HELPED make *Evil Alive* a success. First, I would like to thank my editors, starting with my developmental editor, Scott Alexander Jones, whose relentless criticism always managed to motivate as well as teach. I thank my copy editor, Wendy Weckwerth, who provided a second set of eyes with an unfailingly fresh perspective. And thanks go to my proofreader, Kris Kobe, who reminded me that proofreading is an art just as much as writing—yet the proofreader must also master the *science* of proofreading to a degree worthy of rocketry, an aspiration he truly exemplifies.

Second, I'd like to thank my sister, Holly O'Brien, for being my test reader, who invested weeks of effort, providing significant feedback across multiple drafts. I also want to thank Holly as well as my brother, Brian Hunkins, for logistical assistance at author appearances around the country.

Third, I'd like to thank my remaining test readers: Patrick Nowicki, Matt Geurink, Charlie Roberts, Marshall Simpson, Jim Kehoe, Jonathan DenHartog, Jeffrey Hill, Maryjo Peirson, Bill Protzmann, Stan Hunkins, Casey Nordendale, Jen Hunkins, Laurie Graves, Marlys Widmark, and Jim Hunkins.

And of course, this book would not be possible without my team of professionals. From Beaver's Pond Press: Alicia Ester, Hanna Kjeldbjerg, and Lily Coyle. Athena Currier, who did the cover design as well as the internal design. From Eight Moon (formerly Peter Hill Design): Megan Junius. And from New Counsel, PLC: Harold Slawik and John Roberts.